NEXT TO THE GODS

A WORLD BUILDING SCIENCE FICTION SERIES

Dear Jennifer & Craig

I hope you enjoy the Journey as much as I did in helping with [illegible]

Karl

NEXT TO THE GODS

When Gods Walk Among Us

BOOK OF THE PAST

RAOUL PETER MONGILARDI

EDITED BY: JOHN R. DOUGLAS

Printed in the United States of America

ISBN–13: 978–1477559475

DEDICATION

This novel is dedicated to Robert Edborg for the past, present and future, and to John R. Douglas, my editor, for his keen understanding that a wild muse dances around virtue.

CONTENTS

1. Sphereworlds 1
2. No Stars for Auros 17
3. The Smoke Ponds 30
4. In the Presence of the Arhahn 43
5. Music in the Sphere 51
6. On the Mountain of Beginnings 65
7. The Song in Winds 74
8. By Will of Annevnos 90
9. Where Dreams Sleep 102
10. Auruaii 109
11. The Spherewar 125
12. Metamorphoses 136
13. Planetfall 150
14. Goddess of the Moons 175
15. Varrick, the Hammer 196
16. The Lord of Dragons 217
17. A New World 228
18. Stellar Seas 236
19. Colonial Court 254
20. A Promise to Coexist 271
21. The Reach of Mankind 285

Authors Note

The mother of necessity commanded a few liberties be taken, not the least of which is the concept of the Sphere itself. From a comparative astronomical perspective, there is no known example of such a solid gargantuan object in space. In order to situate the Aurocearian Sphereworld relatively close to Earth, I considered the vast superstars such as the "Pistol Star," 25,000 light years closer to our Galactic core and the "Eta Carinae" star, a mere 7,500 light years away. However, for story purposes, I chose to place the Sphereworlds in the "Pleiades," replacing the star, "Alcoyne," to make it easier to be seen from Earth.

I am most grateful to Bill Stiegerwald of the Goddard Space Flight Center for his help in estimating the radius of the Dyson Sphere (the Aurocearian Sphere) and to his colleagues, Christopher Wanjek, Mark Hess, and Phil West of the Johnson Space Flight Center, for steering me to the good gentlemen at Goddard.

Thanks also to Amy C. Fredericks and Mike Lowenstein at the Jet Propulsion Laboratory (JPL) in Pasadena, for suggesting the candidate stars. The Aurocearian mastery of science is dependent upon control of molecular motion, which in the Aurocearian "high science," provides clean, virtually limitless and perpetual energy. It seemed a logical progression that beings capable of harnessing such energy would also employ highly efficient macro "Constructorbots" and micro technology systems for replication, repair and assembly.

Regarding the relatively short time span needed to travel and communicate to and between Earth from Aurocearia and other cosmic locations, moving beings around the cosmos quickly is a conceit as old as the genre itself. However, in considering how to facilitate rapid travel and inter-galactic transmissions, I decided to use Dark Matter as a means to augment real-time communications. Regarding the names of the Oscileans (dragons), they are named for divisions of a pipe organ.

Homini porta caeli

The gate of heaven given to man

Sphereworlds

Constructing the sphere shell had been a titanic struggle, challenging Aurocearian mastery of unified fields of energy. An effort doomed to fail without the tireless help of Constructorbots but at last, the final gargantuan segment of the sphere circumference was ready for assembly.

Despite his supra-evolved vision, Moniah Talsaiyr could not visually encompass the billion-mile radius of the Sphere. For months, his ship had flown over the outer surface, making what could only be a cursory inspection of an object dwarfing even the largest stars in the known universe.

Everything appeared nominal from his vantage in the void ship, as Moniah surveyed the toil of four thousand years. He nodded to Admiral Sey and turned to look through a portal the size of a small moon on the surface of the shell.

"One gate to eternity," Moniah said, referring to the inner radius of the portal that now served as the only access to the Sphereworlds of Aurocearia.

The ship thrust its bow into the threshold of the portal and Moniah turned away, his weary mind and body queasy with the view as he nervously wiped a bead of sweat from his upper lip while examining a hologram image from a distant drone, in which the Brobdingnagian sphere dominated fluorescing gasses in the center of the Suum Nebula. From the perspective of the drone, the Sphereworlds appeared as a silver star, surrounded by the crimson plasma of the nebula while interspersed throughout the scene, glimmering pinpoints of infant stars flickered silently.

Moniah's heart leapt with joy to return home. He gazed within the sphere portal, at the centermost Triune star illuminating a planet of blue seas, clouds and brown colored landmasses. The hub of worlds, visibly larger than its neighbors, the home world of Auros Prime emerged as a luminous crescent of azure blue behind the iridescent green of the Water moon, Ves.

The crew of Moniah's ship fell silent, enraptured by an exquisite and dazzling display of eleven worlds and moons of varying size, surrounding Auros Prime. Controlled by unseen gravitational forces, like slaves to a master, the planets were held in precise orbits in a non-heliocentric solar system with Auros Prime in the center. The beloved home world with its water-moon Ves was now at equal distance between its three Triune stars that in turn governed the smaller planets and moons in the periphery of the system.

Captivated, Moniah lingered in his weariness, spellbound by the vista of his worlds, which were all distinctly different despite their commonality of life-sustaining atmospheres. Here, the planet Detate revolved so that its northern hemisphere rotated into shadowy dusk while the stormy clouds of its closest neighbor, Simatos, flared with the finger strokes of lightning. In the outer empyrean, the planet Braxos emerged into light, its southern ocean sparkling in the kiss of dawn.

Exhausted and oblivious to the muted voices of other Aurocearians and sounds in the command bridge, Moniah considered how long he had lived to see this day of worlds within worlds. It seemed implausible the sacred project would at last be finished and the Sphereworlds would soon be a whole and seamless realization.

With only the subdued pulsing of the ship engines resisting impossible forces of gravity as it struggled to enter the sphere portal, no hint was visible to Moniah from his quiescent vantage of the immortal entities, creatures and would be gods—vying for supremacy on those beautiful worlds. Unconsciously, Moniah moved closer to the viewing blister dome.

"You are a titan Annevnos," Moniah whispered in salute to the Engineer whose design he surveyed.

Suddenly, Moniah cringed in pain as the familiar flash of memory overtook him again. He touched his brow with trembling fingers, resisting the blaring images and sounds that for some inexplicable reason tormented him with frequent intensity. As the numbing pain subsided, Moniah became aware of the voice of his friend.

"My lord, Arhahnis is requesting communication with you," Admiral Sey said.

Moniah turned slowly, offering a pale smile of reassurance to the Admiral, and then directed his attention to a metal cone rising up from the floor. He waved a hand over the glowing cone.

An image came to life, floating over cone in glowing umbra, depicting his brother, Arhahnis, in perfect detail, smiling back at Moniah.

The golden pupils of his purple eyes were like stars in darkened skies, studying the First Lord quizzically.

"Brother, have you experienced any anomalies?" Arhahnis said with the familiar soothing tone of his mellifluous voice.

"The Sphere exerts a tremendous gravitational field on the ship. However, our new engines are able to deflect these forces," Moniah said in a gravelly voice, touching a cold sweat on his lip. *Had it only been two days without sleep?*

Arhahnis angled his face to one side causing his long mane of golden red hair to shine while he listened to the council of someone Moniah could not see, and then he faced Moniah again.

"You make superb progress. My brother, in this new world, we have no stars for Auros," Arhahnis said. There was a poignant regret in his tone.

"Time and space is the mind of God," Moniah replied.

"True spoken. Kaylon will give you coordinates to the rendezvous. I await. A moment! Someone begs your attention," Arhahnis said and the hologram image clicked to a different view and the welcoming smile of Lirea. Her soft green brown eyes twinkled as she touched delicate fingers to the nape of her neck.

"My love," Moniah said.

"Meliphor and I have decided to attend. Are you pleased?"

"Both you and the empress honor myself and the Arhahn. I salute your bravery my love," Moniah replied.

Lirea blew a kiss. Sparkles of iridescence wafted from her fingers and the hologram darkened. Moniah turned to signal Admiral Sey who had stepped back to allow privacy for the royal communication.

"Admiral…" Moniah began.

"Yes my lord, I hurry us to Ves," Admiral Sey interjected.

"Initiate containment Admiral. This brief stopover is a secure operation." Admiral Sey paused to light an Ol pipe.

"A partnership with the powerful is never safe," he chuckled, patting Moniah on the shoulder.

"Saeonar, I need you," Moniah announced.

An Auran wearing a distinctive long robe emerged from among the now busy crew. He wore a waist sash and a long holster on his right thigh. As he passed the helm station, a lovely Aurie followed him with her sparkling eyes but the Wizan Saeonar took little notice.

"There's time enough for love aboard ship," Moniah teased. Saeonar spread his cloak with hands on his hips and flexed his jaw.

"There is precious little time in following you, my lord," Saeonar replied.

"I promise greater ease in the future. Dispense with titles," said Moniah and Saeonar fixed Moniah with a determined expression.

"In two thousand years your step has only quickened and aboard ship I shall address you in title, as is my habit," Saeonar said and turned his attention to the enormity of the portal. The ship was now crossing into the outer rim, the curvature of which passed beyond the field of view in two mammoth arcs, ten thousand miles to the starboard and port.

Stepping out of earshot of the other crew, Moniah spoke quietly. "Arhahnis is aboard the Quattral vessel. Lirea and Meliphor are with him." Saeonar rolled his tongue across the inside of his cheek and turned to the blister dome.

"My lord, I don't like it. The Arhahn himself on a ship with Annevnos," Saeonar said, locking eyes with Moniah, he added, "with Meliphor and Lirea attending!"

"Meliphor is very wise; she stands with Arhahnis to project confidence. This devotion has inspired my Lirea to join them," Moniah said, but uncertainty danced in his eyes.

"It is through Annevnos we suffer and see what he and his Quattral have wrought. In their design we are prisoner," Saeonar hissed.

"No, my friend, Aurankind rejoices in our endeavor. So, be fulfilled," Moniah said and cuffed Saeonar on the shoulder. Saeonar attempted a reassuring smile. Moniah turned around to look up at the flight bridge.

"Admiral, my friend awaits below," he said.

The bow of the void ship was now within inner sphere space and the subdued rumblings aboard ship caused by its constant battle with the outer sphere shell's immense gravity lessened their vibration. Moniah felt his stomach relax as the voices of the crew lost their strain and edge.

While the void ship crossed from outer to inner sphere space, Saeonar studied the finer resolution of the sphere shell material of the outer edge of the portal. Seen edge on, the material was burnished silver dotted with what appeared to be tiny cones, although, in reality, each of the igniter cones was hundreds of miles in diameter.

A fleet of Constructorbots emerged from one of the many control stations.

"Look, constructor drones," Moniah said, pointing.

"More robots."

"Servants of the Sphereshell, my friend. They will fly over the inner and outer circumferences, making repairs, checking the outer shell igniters," Moniah said while Saeonar groaned suspiciously.

The Constructorbots appeared in their millions as a vast swarm of tiny spheres, emerging in wave after wave from their automated bases to fly to designated areas of the inner and outer shell. In the dark clarity of space, one could detect their Saen lasers, effecting repairs and sealing imperfections.

Within the Sphereworlds, planets, moons, other space vessels and the glow of white light from the Triune stars reflected in the large, magical eyes of Moniah.

Dawn swept across the green watery surface of the moon Ves, while the constant twilight of inner sphere space bathed the northern continent of its neighbor, Auros Prime, in shifting hues of light, alternating with darkness at play in brilliant aurora, reflected from the nearest Triune star.

A compressed version of its earlier state, like its two counterparts, the star gave off sufficient light and energy to sustain life while permitting the sphere shell to accrete residual heat through the sphere's outer shell igniters.

The pain returned and Moniah winced while grabbing a rail before him. His real time vision clouded and another of the persistent memories overtook him, back--back three- thousand years to the day the sphere shell was created…

* * *

Moniah held Lirea close, a cold wind buffeted her satin robes, her hand felt chilled in his. Nearby, atop the palace temple dome, an Oscilean, sensing the tensions of the Aurocearians around him swept up its wings and unleashed a seismographic roar punctuated with fire and smoke. Saeonar comforted the beast, waving to Moniah who smiled in return though his lips quivered with concern.

Below the palace acropolis, it seemed every citizen of Auros Prime was gathered in the city, their attention transfixed on the sky. A brilliant flare of light erupted in the west, beyond the Smoke Ponds region, when the Prenadrone device that would forever alter their world- lifted from the planet to race at hypersonic speed into the purple blue atmosphere, leaving a thin wispy trail of smoke like a needle threading silk, as the only visible trace of the Prenadrone's path.

In a heart stopping instant, cries of fear and wonder arose as the sky darkened and the day chilled when the Prenadrone detonated, causing the star's outer surface to separate and race away from the core structure, reducing the mass of the star. Now it would be divided to form the three smaller "Triune" stars. This process would help ensure the longevity of the stars—a critical concern for stars destined to be enclosed within a sphere. Within minutes, the detached outer radiance of the star expanded forming the billion-mile sphere of light and plasma around the home world planetary system. Master designer Annevnos Sehtba and the Quattral Engineers succeeded in forming the sphere shell by encircling the home worlds in a glow of ionized matter that would become the foundation of the solid sphere.

It was in that hour the music changed. Oscileans sang a mournful paean, lamenting the translucent sphere of golden light that blotted out the firmament and would eventually divide Aurocearia from heaven, engineer from artist, priest from poet and strike at the heart of cosmic purpose.

The voice of Saeonar came to Moniah as if through a tunnel, dispelling the vision and pain through a fog until he became aware of his body again, his sweating hands gripping the view port rail with sweat running down his brow and his robe clinging to him like a second skin. Gathering his wits, emerging from the dream trance, Moniah said nothing to Saeonar and stared directly ahead. Beyond the blister dome, the moon Ves loomed in seas of a thousand shades of green murky depths and carousing softer currents.

"We are at landfall with Ves, my lord," Saeonar said, he added, "Should I accompany you?" Other sounds of the crew fused into his present reality, Moniah licked his lips forcing back a feeling of nausea and turned to face Saeonar.

Moniah forced himself to smile. It would not do to allow anyone, even his trusted Wizan brother, to learn of his strange illness. He would speak to the Taen doctors later. For now, time needed his every focus.

"No my friend, remain here but keep a sharp eye," Moniah said. Again, he took hold of himself and mopped his brow, avoiding the scrutiny of Admiral Sey who had noticed a faltering in the normally resolute bearing of the First Lord.

"Yaw to port, cavitation roll at fifty degrees," the Aurie with the sweet smile announced, bowing to Moniah as he approached Admiral Sey.

"Correct and stabilize," Admiral Sey said before leaning toward Moniah.

"You are my eyes," Moniah said and strode from the bridge.

* * *

Moniah's shuttle dropped from the underbelly of the void ship to plunge toward the watery surface of Ves. Intended primarily for inspecting the mother ship, the shuttle's design allowed for only one passenger within a pod of transparent material attached to a molecular drive engine and stabilizer planes in the aft section for use in atmospheric flight.

The shuttle plunged into the surface waters of Ves. Its concentric ring of stabilizer planes rotated to the top of the pod, driving the ship deeper into the sea. Moniah adjusted interior lighting and activated a holographic display panel. Outside the pod shuttle, schools of iridescent fish tacked and cavorted to avoid the intruding vessel.

Moniah leaned forward, surrounded by cool green gloom, scanning the view before he was transported into one of the miracles of Aurocearia for, as the shuttle descended, the sea became lighter, as if he were, by descending, actually entering into shallower waters. Herein lay the miracle of the planet Ves for that was precisely what was happening.

The heavier, more dense waters of Ves lay near its surface while deeper currents gradually gave way to water levels infused with greater amounts of oxygen and hydrogen so that the farther one descended the more breathable the atmosphere became. In fact, the seabed was surrounded in a thick super-charged bubble of hot gasses fed by the core of the moon. These gases, mostly comprised of hydrogen, continually bubbled up to the heavier currents. The result was that in certain areas, even hundreds of feet below the surface waters, an atmosphere existed capable of sustaining non-aquatic life forms.

A small blip appeared in a section of the display screen and Moniah adjusted his descent to veer to port, disturbing the repose of a floating Watermin.

For a moment Moniah was hypnotized into a state of peace and relaxation he had not experienced in memory as the murkier waters gave way to lower levels, first pale green, then Jade, then blue-green, until he flew into a vast expanse of rolling crags and valleys aglow with phosphorescent coral and moss.

Flowering plants bedded on small islands with roots trailing the water, drifted and bobbed past Moniah's field of view. The islands appeared to barely sustain the weight of vines and cumbersome sponge-like plants. Each island glowed in a display of vibrant coral-hued colors, their flowers extending tendrils to taste the passing currents.

High above, in the denser currents, giant whalefish ambled through sparkling clouds of plankton. As the giants disturbed the higher currents, eddies dripped down into the more oxygen-rich levels, creating swift moving rivers that floated through the atmosphere, seeking ponds and lakebeds in which to settle.

When the riverbeds became full, they would bubble up, defying gravity, raining bioluminescent creatures upward again in tides rich with extravagant color.

A dreadful need to sleep tempted Moniah. He immediately powered up the shuttle cabin air vents to blow cooler air at a higher volume. The shuttle angled toward a series of hills and deep fissures where kelp forests swayed in undulating groups, towering hundreds of feet above the seabed.

The shuttle pod came to rest in the hollow between two large rocks. A river tide ran through at that moment and spun the shuttle fully around.

"Atmosphere and barometric pressure suitable. Gravity, two-three-eight. Moisture content at seventy percent," The shuttle computer announced.

Moniah released the seat strap and touched a section of the clear plexiform material next to him. A door section opened and he stepped gingerly out of the shuttle onto soft mossy ground.

Immediately, he was assailed by an almost overpoweringly complex aroma of sand, damp sodden ground, salt and a strange fruity scent akin to a field of flowers. Such an onslaught to his olfactory senses might have induced nausea in his already sensitive state but instead Moniah breathed in the pristine drafts. He felt refreshed from the stale atmosphere of the cool metallic "ship's air" he had endured of late.

The lower regions of Ves presented a bizarre symphony of distant echoing whale song, wind, water sloshing, beeps and chirps. A Watermin flew down toward him trailing wispy currents of heavier water. The creature, equal parts bird and fish, settled on his shoulder to extend its long moth-like tongue to flick at the embroidery of Ol leaf pattern on the shoulders of his robe.

The Watermin was a baby, the size of a small bird, with multicolored wings atop an iridescent green and blue body. Its fish head sported trailing whiskers under the chin and larger whiskers at either side of its mouth.

"I suggest it is better for you to come closer to the rocks," the familiar but disembodied voice of Medean said. Moniah turned slowly to face the rocks. The Watermin cooed but remained on his shoulder. Medean emerged from the tall kelp, his flowing green robe perfect camouflage.

"I have found a friend or rather it has found me," Moniah said.

Medean stepped completely out of the kelp, his gold pupils, aglow in luminous green and purple eyes, radiated his familiar wit and vast intelligence. The Auran friends embraced but Moniah coughed and then seized Medean tightly by the shoulders in panic.

"I--I cannot breathe."

Medean reached quickly into a pocket and pressed a small brown clod of what felt like dirt into Moniah's palm while Moniah gasped for breath.

"Relax, breathe slowly. Good," Medean said. He added, "Here, eat this." More relaxed, Moniah relinquished his powerful grip and examined the clod of dirt.

"For love sake, why?"

"The feeling of suffocation you experience is normal here. This compound will act quickly to readjust your lungs and more urgently it prevents a fungus from taking root," Medean replied. Moniah chewed the brown clod pausing to turn and view the distance.

"Making me eat this…you deserve my opinion of the taste," Moniah said.

Medean smiled at the Watermin, which was still fascinated by the inviting but inedible embroidery on Moniah's billowing robe.

"The min must wonder what manner of plant you are," Medean said.

"Weary," Moniah chuckled. He added, "We are safer in the kelp?"

"You were standing in a tidal stream and the incessant singing of the Throns could attract attention we've taken pains to avoid," Medean said.

"Are you certain the Quattral cannot eavesdrop?"

"To my knowledge they have always avoided Ves but your concern about their motivations is valid. I am haunted by my own visions and memories," Medean said reaching out to pet the Watermin. As much as Moniah loved Medean, it was always disconcerting to realize that in his presence one's personal experiences were subject to Medean's powers of intuition. Like many Greenrobes of the Mysterium, Medean could feel future events as well as perceive, through emotion, the thoughts of those near to him.

"If we can regain the old way, rejoin the purpose of the councils and temples…" Moniah began, but Medean's expression softened to a patient frustration. Moniah wanted to hear Medean assure him, but in his heart, he knew the society Aurocearians had created was polarized and no longer a cohesive cooperative.

True, most Aurans and Auries were peaceful beings, intent upon the nurturing of Art, science, and exploration, but a lack of cultural diversity challenged their awesome intellectual powers and divided their will.

The titan priests, Arhahnis and Ammanmus had corralled the society into a rigid system of intricate guilds, cults of pride, wherein Aurocearians, by wearing mantles, displayed their talents and expertise. The custom proved an effective means to foster discipline in the social polity but stifled spontaneity.

"We are forever beyond the garden, Moniah. When Arhahnis convened the Awclotan councils, he ratified the plan for creation of the sphere. I, too was swept along in the belief the sphere project would determine who would control the high science," Medean said as he reached out to stroke a curious fish. He glanced at Moniah who sighed with resignation. Medean added, "But we have divided the realm. The Quattral perceive the union of the triumvirate temples as a direct threat to their freedom."

"We can rectify this-"

"No, now hear me, for *here* is the crux. Your Talsaiyr dynasty is the royal apex of the governing bodies, thanks to Arhahnis and Ammanmus. This power structure is something Annevnos and the Quattral cannot trust, for in doing so they must relinquish their very purpose in submitting to Arhahnis," Medean said.

"Annevnos could seize control of the sphere."

"And now you see," Medean sighed. He smiled and added, "This air does you good. It was a good choice to meet here."

"Yet the efforts of so many to create the sphere, surely this is its very protection," Moniah said with a futile attempt to wipe water from his eyes.

"Greater damage to the Suum than expected occurred when the star was detonated to form the sphere shell. You and Admiral Sey should have revealed this fact before the Fleets married the Quattral in the sphere project. Now, Arhahnis realizes this violation of the Gods' precinct has occurred and he must wonder to what degree this endangers our future," Medean said.

"We created the sphere to enhance the Suum, to…protect it," Moniah said. He added, "I grow weary of reexamining our intent."

"We created the sphere to sustain the life enhancing properties of the Suum, Moniah. There is no escaping our motives." Finally delivered of his thoughts, Medean paused to study Moniah with pity. The handsome First Lord was sallow of cheek, his skin pale and his multiple pupils fairly quivered with stress, his long black locks of hair floated about broad but hunched shoulders. Medean added, "You are truly weary my brother."

Moniah checked his wrist chronometer.

"I must go up to the Quattral platform," he said.

A buzzing sound unlike anything heard even in the strange undersea world stilled the peaceful chirps and bleeps of the lower life forms around them. The Watermin rolled up its tongue, beat its wings, chirped and took flight.

A river stream descended from the higher currents a few miles away and from it a swarm of silvery objects broke free, circled, then formed a long V pattern like a waterspout, digging its way through the currents to take aim on the spot where the two Auran's stood.

"Not as alone as we hoped," Medean said and, seeing the confusion on Moniah's face, tugged him toward the shuttle.

"Come with me," Moniah yelled over the increased buzzing.

"No. I will see you on Auros Prime," Medean said and shoved Moniah into the pilot seat. With leaden arms, delirious and nearly in shock, Moniah activated the shuttle engines and the craft lifted off just as the swarm arrived. On closer inspection, they were fearsome creatures, each about a foot long, part bioform part artificial insectoid, whose wings beat in a rapid blur.

Moniah watched helplessly as they swarmed over Medean but the mystic emitted an energy field that sizzled the water-air around him like seltzer as he strode into the kelp. The insectoids seemed confused, darting here and there, crashing into each other.

A deep blue water stream descended from on high, it rushed through the tall kelp then rebounded to rise almost vertically again and as Moniah's shuttle lifted, he saw Medean rising between two giant Whalefish. Medean held fast to the creatures' side flukes as they careened into the upward stream. The Whalefish ejected large oxygen bubbles that clung to their bodies, providing Medean with breathable air while he was carried away.

In the wake of the tidal stream, some of the insectoids became entangled in the kelp or smashed on the rocks while others whirled about aimlessly as the moss ground opened to reveal large crustaceans that methodically gobbled up the machine invaders. Moniah breathed a deep sigh and settled back in his seat. Too exhausted to think, his powerful body numb with every move, Moniah toggled the autopilot return and drifted into unconsciousness, lulled by the sway of the shuttle as it sped ever higher, into deeper waters.

* * *

Admiral Sey bolted forward in his command seat the instant Moniah's shuttle broke free of the surface, startling the crew.

"Capture and secure."

Saeonar, whose eyes had never left the surface waters of the moon while Moniah was out of contact beneath the seas, hurried to a scanning screen depicting the interior of the pod shuttle. Noting the nominal life signs, the Wizan offered a prayer of thanks.

"Status?" Admiral Sey said, turning to Saeonar.

"Lord Moniah is asleep."

* * *

Anger and resentment surged through Moniah at having missed so many adventures in exploration of his native worlds, his humbling experience on Ves the most recent and telling example. What a catastrophe his life seemed. *Let me count the ways*, he grumbled, trying to open the Star Chamber doors.

He was a poor excuse for a Wizan and could barely understand the songs of Oscileans—a primary responsibility of his high rank. No, it was more than that; it was a gift he had forsaken to put all his power into machines and, speaking of machines *what was wrong with the damn door?*

Were his very limbs in rebellion?

Could he not even manage a door? There was no time for this physical paralysis; Arhahnis was waiting on the Quattral ship but then...*why was he, Moniah, on Auros Prime?* Was he losing his mind, the painful memory flashbacks taking more of a toll than he suspected?

In the blink of an eye, Moniah found himself seated at the Daid table with Medean, Arhahnis, Ammanmus and the famed scientist, Tius. Moniah reached for a decanter of Oprasia wine but paused fearing his disjointedness and the wine could send him into oblivion. Still, his thirst overcame reticence and he reached for the wine but again his reluctant arms failed him.

A myriad of holograms appeared over the hover table surface, images of all the inner sphere planets and moons, around which a transparent model of the sphere shell glowed with an annoying pulse of gold light. *Turn that off!* Moniah thought, *it's silver, the sphere shell surface is silver and this gold is biting my eyes.* No one paid him any attention.

Why are we here? Must we reexamine everything? Saeonar is the better Wizan; he should be here not I.

Tius stood and spread his arms wide tracing the pattern of the sphere shell.

"It shall nurture the Suum nebula, in this Annevnos proves his brilliant design."

"Burning the Suum, how does this nurture?" Arhahnis' voice said from the other side of the table, but Moniah could not see him for the many glowing representations of planets blocking his view. He was reliving history again! Moniah realized in torment, aware he might be in a dream state, a fact that only served to augment his anger.

Am I forbidden any peace, even in sleep?

"The sphere fire shall transmute power back into the nebula by infusing the Suum with enhanced electromagnetic energy," Tius replied, retaking his chair.

"The sphere is a natural defense against rogue planetoids. For example, consider the odds of an asteroid--or meteor--achieving trajectory into the portal. Even if it succeeded in finding such a direct path—the portal Saen weapons would obliterate the intruder before the object passed into the inner realm," The Taen priest Ammanmus, said.

Moniah tried to lift his arms but thwarted again his soul cried out for mercy. *What a hapless creature I have become. Is all that I am evaporating into a cloud of madness?* Moniah cursed himself and even worse, he could feel his connection to the Wizan Mysterium, the essence of his heart and mind, slipping into some unknown realm of weakness.

It was as though where once the powers of the Mysterium had constituted his reality and destiny—now he felt it increasingly difficult to discern reality from a dream trance. Was he truly losing his mind, becoming two beings cohabitating the same form?

Moniah felt that he would soon expire if he could not slake his thirst. He prayed for guidance from the Gods while entreating them to end the chatter of his brethren. With a supreme effort, he reached again for the Oprasia decanter. Success! It was a small but potent victory over his shattered state. As he lifted the decanter to parched lips, the sweet nectar rolled into his mouth…

* * *

Moniah awoke with a start. Choking, he batted a decanter away from his lips and wiped away a splash of water dribbling down his chin. As the fog of sleep dissipated the strong friendly face of Saeonar leaned over him.

"You cried out for wine but water was nearest at hand. Let me fetch the Taen physician," Saeonar said, turning toward an intercom. Moniah coughed, sat up and rubbed sleep from his eyes.

"Do not summon a Taen. How long have I been unconscious?"

"The best part of the day but, never fear, I informed Arhahnis you were…delayed," Saeonar said, gently pushing Moniah back to a reclined position.

But there was no time for further indulgence of his physical need for rest. Moniah's eyes flashed at Saeonar, who stepped back shaking his head in resignation as the First Lord sat up and stood up reluctantly, leaving behind the siren call of Admiral Sey's luxurious bed.

"What is our position?" Moniah said, brushing a long strand of black hair from his face.

"At station keeping with the Quattral platform," replied Saeonar.

"Excellent. Prepare for disembarkation."

* * *

Saeonar and Moniah strapped into the pilot and copilot seats of the void ship's largest shuttle. Saeonar quickly worked preflight controls then tapped the molecular ignition sequencer and the two Aurans were pressed back in their seats as the shuttle launched from the void ship.

Moniah activated an aft viewer to study the void ship's long clamshell-shaped bridge area. The ship pivoted to present a side view of its graceful hull, which tapered in the aft section into the molecular engine array.

"No apparent damage of any note, Admiral, other than minor compression signatures from micro meteors along the port hull," Moniah said into a speaker plate, bidding farewell to what had been his shipboard home for many months.

Looking out the forward view, Moniah studied the Quattral platform where his beloved and his brothers awaited. True to the engineer's taste for simple design, the ship was an enormous dome resting in a rectangular concave superstructure. It hovered in close proximity to the one remaining open segment of the sphere shell construction. Beyond the open section, distant stars flickered through the purple gasses of the Suum nebula.

It occurred to Moniah that the longer he remained in inner sphere space, the effect was not as though one moved through an enclosed area, but rather as if one had *passed into* another, darker solar system. Arhahnis had seized the pith of their new fate and there were no stars for Auros. The planets of inner sphere space appeared as vibrant bodies set against a starless background yet warm white light from the Triune stars imbued the enclosed solar systems with beauteous aurora that gained in intensity in the inner realms nearest the largest of the three stars.

Though the spectacular vista was not new to Moniah, it had been months since he had last traveled within inner sphere space. While he gazed at the astronomical wonders before him, his heart took courage and he realized the quaking of his spirit was probably due to simple fatigue combined with a case of space sickness. Feeling emboldened, Moniah steeled himself for his encounter with Annevnos.

As the shuttle approached the platform ship, Saeonar confirmed docking coordinates then lowered the speaker volume to reduce a confusing overplay of voices from the Quattral platform. Moniah leaned forward in his seat to scrutinize the jagged edges of the final open section of the Sphere shell where thousands of macro Constructorbots surrounded a mammoth plate of sphere shell material, gently urging it toward the gaping maw of heaven. The shuttle made its final approach to the Quattral platform where a small sliver of light appeared.

"We are locked into the docking beacon," Saeonar said leaning back to wipe his hands over his face. A warning klaxon stunned him into rigid attention as a crackling voice announced from the speaker, "Shuttle, prepare for outer shell ignition."

Moniah and Saeonar exchanged nervous expressions, each aware those across nearly a billion miles of the sphere shell's exterior curvature, fiery eggs of light were springing to life within the cone igniters. The fires soon danced into full corona flame, transforming the Sphereworlds into the lord of stars.

Beyond the open section of the sphere shell, the inferno fires raging on the sphere's outer surface obliterated visible light from space.

"How can this procedure be safe?" Saeonar asked, his eyes and attention refocused to the docking bay. In silent fury Moniah reached behind him into a receptacle to retrieve a broad, intricately designed object consisting of two equal-sized pieces of polished metal. He placed the two metal objects onto the shoulders of his robe and fastened them in place with a connecting clasp. By wearing his mantle, Moniah the Auran became, for all to see, Moniah Talsaiyr, First Lord.

"*There* you are," Saeonar chuckled.

Moniah, tight lipped, stared straight ahead while ruminating. He accepted the fact that Annevnos was indeed a titan of technology but it smacked of supreme hubris to ignite the sphere shell while so many members of the royal house— *his* family—were aboard the Quattral platform in close proximity to the open section.

For hundreds of years Moniah and Annevnos had been at quiet odds, the supreme technocrat Annevnos resistant to the authority of the Wizan First Lord and his void fleet, but they had also been a tandem force in overseeing the creation of the Sphere. Where one supervised fabulous automated equipage, the other rallied Aurans and Auries to the cause, unifying them into a collective army of scientists.

Moniah was well aware that sphere ignition was a highly controlled process but there was no pressing need to effect a demonstration. Like the inferno on the outer surface of the Sphere itself, the First Lord sensed a deep ember in his soul, rekindling his old fire.

Exhaustion had propelled him into melancholia, damaging his ability to practice his Wizan skills and making him susceptible to the will of others. No more. In their infinite wisdom and compassion, the Gods designed each Wizan with a talent befitting his temperament. Saeonar, for example, possessed the high skills of manipulating electro magnetism allowing him to summon great powers.

He would never be tempted to use those powers against a fellow being in anger or for cruel intentions and where Saeonar was concerned, it was a fitting gift to bestow upon his great and loving heart.

Moniah's gifts were in the language of the Oscileans and their wondrous music. If the Gods deemed that he would not be endowed with mastery of the Spectrum, like Saeonar and others, if he was to remain a living balance able to utilize charisma to unify purpose and heal discord, so be it, but there was no sacred edict commanding him to submit to the tyranny of others.

No Stars for Auros

"It is the curse of Aurocearians to be born unlike other creatures that come to mortal life as young and grow whole experiencing pleasure and pain. For us, the children of Diasentue, birth severs eternal bliss and the memory of Heaven is erased upon first breath. This, my brothers and sisters, is why life cannot compare to the dream memory of our origins and why it is that those of us who are furious of this reality—renounce mortality and seek only to be reunited with the Godsrealm."

-Arhahnis Talsaiyr

When the shuttle settled into the Quattral platform hangar, Moniah stood quickly and moved to the air hatch, Saeonar at his side. They did not speak each sensing tension in the other. Moniah watched Saeonar adjust the strap to his Coracle-diant holster, setting its length against his right thigh, concealed beneath his outer robe.

Once outside the shuttle, no one greeted them in the capacious hangar. Saeonar pointed to a circular elevator platform near the firewall.

"Strange," Saeonar said, jerking his head to the left and right to survey their surroundings before he activated the elevator disc. The device rose up quickly and only the cool dry odorless air flowing over them dispelled a vague nausea Moniah experienced from the sudden motion.

Moniah closed his eyes to breathe deeply. He would soon be in the Presence and he needed to project strength and calm during this, his last but most arduous and delicate task of Sphere construction. He could hear Saeonar at his side, quietly muttering the incantation of tranquility. A gentle feeling of relief poured through Moniah and his heart swelled in pride for love of his dear and trusted allay. Where would he be without Saeonar?

When he opened his eyes again, the elevator slowed to come to rest in the upper command bridge within the opaque sphere. The large room consisted of dozens of control stations, configured as hologram interactive hubs overseen by members of the Quattral and Imperium guilds. The command bridge itself afforded an excellent position to survey the frenetic endeavors of the scientists, whose muted but urgent voices competed with the low throb of machine noise to create an atmosphere charged with expectation.

Moniah had not laid eyes on Annevnos for at least a year but he was fairly certain the Prime Engineer was standing in the nearest of one of four supervisory operational hubs, his head suffused and engulphed in multiple holograms.

Then, out of a dream and so out of place as to make him laugh aloud, there was Lirea hurrying toward Moniah, her motion elegant, a gossamer gown swirling about her luscious frame. She paused before him. Her eyes glowed openly with the very sight of him.

"Your color is ruddy from space flight and you have lost weight, my love, but your shoulders are still broad and strong," Lirea said, running a finger over his shoulder mantle and down to smooth her palm over the sheen of his waist-length, midnight tresses. Moniah held her fast in the silver speckled pupils of his magical eyes—where he knew she found love—drinking her in.

He cupped Lirea's face with his hands and her arms went round his neck as they kissed.

"You will have to take me with you on future trips to the void. This separation does not do our love justice," Lirea whispered.

"I am done with the void, your arms are all the mystery I require," Moniah replied as quietly, touching his lips to her forehead. Saeonar made a sound in his throat. Lirea took Moniah's arm and they stepped off the elevator platform. Saeonar unobtrusively surveyed the large control room. The sight of so many Quattral Engineers assembled in one place, effectively outnumbering the royal party, made him quake.

"There is Annevnos, my lord," Saeonar said, tilting his head.

"I see him," Moniah muttered distractedly, his hand entwining with Lirea's. Moniah expelled his passion in a patient breath while Annevnos ignored the arrival of the First Lord. Moniah leaned to Lirea and kissed her brow before turning his attention to the floating golden and Whitestone thrones where Arhahnis and Meliphor waited.

The First Lord made no announcement of his presence, thereby ignoring Annevnos in kind. Saeonar paused a few feet from the Arhahn's presence and genuflected. Meliphor dipped her head in response. Arhahnis smiled at Saeonar and then leveled his riveting, magnificent eyes upon Moniah.

"Rise Saeonar. And so, brother, history finds us at another crossing," Arhahnis said.

Moniah squeezed Lirea's hand and stepped closer to the throne, bowing from the neck.

"At your will, my Arhahn."

Arhahnis laughed and, taking Meliphor by the hand, they stood for the official greeting. The emperor Arhahn and his consort presented an elegant couple, robed in Taen blue with green Ol leaf embroidery. Meliphor wore her firestone mantle but the shoulders of Arhahnis were bare. In an instant Moniah saw the sly wisdom of his brother, for in not wearing his mantle, the Arhahn was the only Aurocearian in sight defying tradition and thus standing alone.

Arhahnis nodded in the direction of two holograms at either side of the throne. The displays deactivated while Himself and Meliphor stepped down from the floating thrones, which silently came to rest on the deck.

A tall blond Auran approached. His head surrounded in headsets into which he spoke rapidly, but, seeing Moniah, he tugged the wireless headsets away and announced, "The First Lord," with a stentorian voice.

Saeonar beamed with satisfaction, taking note that instantly all those preoccupied souls at their duty stations turned to view the throne area, forcing Annevnos to do the same.

"My right arm is rejoined to me," Arhahnis said, placing one hand on Moniah's head. Moniah sank to one knee, bowed his head again, and then stood in one fluid motion. Meliphor embraced Moniah, she kissed his cheek, and satin waves of her ashen hair brushed his hand. Her scent of fine incense, soft, clean and rich, washed over him. But she drew back in trepidation while Moniah gazed into her glimmering blue eyes. A tremor of her lower lip in that instant, betrayed her faltering courage.

Moniah held her arms firmly but gently for a beat, his eyes locked with hers, imparting reassurance until her beautiful aquiline features regained their outward composure. Then he stepped back and clasped arms warmly with the blond Auran.

"Kaylon, bless you good friend," Moniah said.

"What kept you?"

"Space sickness," said Moniah, with a wink.

"And look who comes now," Saeonar interjected. Moniah frowned at Saeonar and turned to face Annevnos.

"You have done well, lord Moniah. We monitored your ship's gravity deflection fields. Excellent work," said Annevnos. He added a minimal salutation to the emperor, "Arhahn."

"It was a task but we managed," Moniah said.

Looking into the face of Annevnos was a disconcerting experience. Black eyes and gold pupils stared into the onlooker with heartless determination. His pale expression set in a mane of long white hair was devoid of the ability to smile in any natural manner other than in quick spasms, presenting the effect of impatient boredom interrupted occasionally by manic joy. Annevnos lifted his chin while his pupils flashed, creating a riveting visage.

"Now we make an end to our long work on the Sphereshell. Are you ready to assist?" Annevnos said, indicating a control island of instruments with a wave of his hand.

Moniah stepped closer to Annevnos where he paused and met the ferocious eyes dead on without cringing. He was tempted to mention the insectoids he had encountered on Ves but immediately thought better of it. For one thing, the very fact he was safely aboard negated the attempt to thwart him and he had no intention of giving Annevnos the satisfaction of knowing whether or not Medean was harmed or, for that matter, if the mystic had escaped. Moniah felt a pulse probe at him and realized, as he had long suspected, that Annevnos was an adept in the art of Mesmer.

However, tipping his hand would only empower Annevnos. The First Lord held his stance for an uncomfortable moment. His very silence returned the challenge. Annevnos blinked and turned away to stride toward a master control island. Moniah and Kaylon followed him to banks of holographic controls where Moniah and Annevnos could oversee the entire area of operations.

Muted overlapping voices floated up to them. Annevnos punched a control and the vast bubble surrounding the command center shifted from opaque to transparent and clear in the blink of an eye, flooding the huge room with an unobstructed panorama of the planets of inner sphere space and the last open section of the Sphereshell. Annevnos inserted a remote communication link into one ear.

"Inter-relational operations monitor your plasmic and hyperbolic orientation sequencers," Annevnos said, scanning a hologram. Nearby, Kaylon stepped into the hub of another control island.

"Sphere plate being moved to final astrogation coordinates," he said, glancing at Moniah. With delicate motions of his hands, Moniah focused hologram images on the open section. Here, he warned Admiral Sey to stand off. There, he moved the Quattral platform further away from the event.

Moniah stared out of the bubble, where millions of Constructorbots maneuvered a continent-sized metallic plate, slowly edging it toward the open section of the sphere shell. Each of the macro-Constructorbots was fitted with beacon lights, creating a sea of flashing white that showed each robot's precise trajectory as they beat a silent, hypnotic tattoo while the sphere plate rotated, starlight reflecting from its silver sheen. Soon it would be fitted into place and blot out the only remaining sight to outer space aside from the portal. Annevnos turned to Arhahnis.

"When this plate is secured, we will need to effect an adjustment to the orbital plot of the moon, Ves. Only then will all planets be properly aligned," Annevnos said, turning away to redirect his attention to the vast sphere plate while it settled ever closer into the maw of heaven. Meliphor moved closer to Arhahnis, her hand sought out his. He glanced at her, his wondrous eyes watering.

"We have made darkness of our skies," Arhahnis whispered.

There was no sound, no final cosmic thunder to announce the final fitting of the last sphere plate, only a last fleeting glimpse of the pink gas of the Suum nebula along the edges of the plate before an unending black dominated the heavens of the inner Sphereworlds planets.

Millions of lasers from the Constructorbots appeared as fiery rivers where plate material was joined to the greater sphere. During the procedure, the nearest planet, Detate, acted as a natural shield from the closest star but now it passed through its perigee and careened away, causing the Triune star to infuse the command bridge with glaring light.

"Activate dome filters," Moniah grunted to Kaylon and the star glare softened as bubble filters darkened the room. Murmurs of relief abounded as a view of the planets appeared in finer resolution, comforting in their assurance of home and safety.

"Macro and micro system actuators online," Kaylon purred and all eyes shifted to an overhead holoscreen image of the water moon, Ves. Moniah leaned forward, studying a screen intently.

"Prepare particle flow for astrogation correction," he said, glancing at one of the screens near Annevnos. On the huge deck below, a hundred scientists abandoned control stations to hurry to similar hubs. Moniah's face appeared before Kaylon.

"Magnify Ves to fifty times current power," his image commanded with intensity and another image of the water moon increased dramatically. In the magnified image, thousands of shiny drones could now be seen clearly, orbiting Ves. Moniah glanced at Saeonar whose eyes reflected a quiet state of panic. The Wizan's right hand rested near his side, ready to draw forth his Coracle-diant wand from its concealed holster.

"Particle flow established," The Quattral Auran, Seratt, announced. On the magnified image, drones emitted a series of intense red beams, which joined in the moon's atmosphere to create a glowing magnetosphere of energy.

"Initiate directional vectors," Annevnos said, without trace of emotion compared to the other anxious tones surrounding him. The Quattral platform ship projected Saen molecular lasers of green light that conjoined with the artificial magnetosphere generated by the geostationary drones and slowly, imperceptibly at first, the moon began to move from its previous orbital path. A trembling occurred in the Quattral ship.

"Report," Kaylon blurted before Moniah could form the word.

"Behavioral analyzers detect polar variance frequency." The nervous voice of a scientist answered from the main control floor.

"Project," Annevnos demanded and another large hologram activated, depicting some of the neighboring planets with a grid to the right of the image, showing the remaining eleven worlds and among them Ves, glowing red, hurtling toward the ship. Mesmerized, everyone froze in place, glued to the sight of the juggernaut Ves, careening toward the ship.

Meliphor grasped hold of Lirea's hand, pulling her close while Saeonar swallowed his apprehension and moved closer to Arhahnis. The Arhahn stared ahead, remote and quiet as though his will alone could prevent catastrophe.

"Bring teleologic convergent sequencers into multi-phase at six thousand gravities," Annevnos said, his eyes glued to a parabolic projection of the moon trajectory. Ves was slowing in its slingshot though it still bore down on them with an unstoppable momentum.

"Divergent and dynamic dimension qualifiers nominal," Moniah said.

"Omni-orientation transfield matrix suspension fully operational," Kaylon said to Moniah.

"My heart is a drum," Meliphor whispered to Lirea, her eyes fixed on the water moon. Suddenly, interior gravity relaxed. A klaxon sounded and voices buzzed in confusion. Moniah spun around and hurried to pull Lirea to his side with a free hand, reaching for the control station with his other. Saeonar locked his feet under one of the thrones and held onto both the Arhahn and Meliphor with his hands.

Kaylon, cool and calm in nearly any circumstance, took advantage of the lessened gravity to float up a few feet to a screen angled the wrong way and bopped it with a free hand, readjusting its focus.

"Project molecular braking beam now, disengage all systems on my command," Annevnos thundered over the confusion. His hands held him in place while his hair floated like seaweed. Throughout the decks, a sideshow of capes, mantles, electro-styluses, papers and bottles drifted in the air.

Aurans and Auries reached for footholds or held on to their stations to resist the upward push of reduced gravity as Ves hurtled toward them. Fortunately, the moon was slowing continuously. Moniah felt a pang of palpable fear from Saeonar even though he was not facing him. He turned to see the Wizan reach for his Coracle-diant and, drawing it from his thigh holster, created a force shield of electromagnetic sonic and light energy around himself, Arhahnis and Meliphor. Within the translucent dome, gravity returned and Arhahnis, Meliphor and Saeonar studied the others from the safety of pulsing golden light.

But, something was wrong; Saeonar was still emitting great fear. Before Moniah could communicate with him, Lirea—her eyes closed—in harmony with Saeonar, interceded.

"Do nothing, Saeonar," her telepathic voice said, ringing in Moniah's ears. It was then Moniah heard the beautiful music, as though his Wizan senses were suddenly augmented by the loss of gravity. Or was it simply Ves, singing in the sphere? One look at Annevnos told Moniah that he, too, was experiencing the music of the spheres and, for an instant, Moniah and Annevnos' minds were linked, each feeling a spectrum of music and energy remembered from the immortal realm. Their hearts afire, Moniah and Annevnos luxuriated in the energy, which transmitted the subtle exquisite allure of cosmic structure.

"Now," Annevnos announced as echoing thunder, severing the telepathic link. Outside the ship platform, the geostationary drones deactivated. Ves slowed, and then appeared to simply halt its movement relative to the ship.

The ship klaxon silenced. Inside the control station dome, all the floating detritus fell to the decks in a gentle rain of clicks and bangs. Silence descended with the return of normal gravity. Everyone's eyes were glued on Ves with apprehension but the water moon floated gracefully, orbiting between Simatos and Auros Prime.

The heart pause of adrenalin gave way to spontaneous deafening cheers. Everyone on the lower deck converged to praise Annevnos and Moniah. In a single beat, emotions swayed from fear to a din of joy and triumph. Annevnos remained implacable while the First Lord raised his hands in acknowledgement. The elation subsided when Annevnos and Moniah turned to face Arhahnis.

Within the force shield, Saeonar turned completely around to check the perimeter and only then returned his Coracle-diant to his holster. The protective bubble shield Saeonar had created blinked and dissipated into a fine mist of golden sparkles from which the Arhahn stepped forth.

"It is finished, Arhahnis," Annevnos said.

"Half our lives in this task, Annevnos."

"A moment in time for the future," Annevnos replied, allowing himself a fleeting trace of warmth in his tone before he stepped down from the control station.

"My lord, with your permission I will fix the date of Sphere shell completion as 08.5000.02," Kaylon said, defining the month year and day.

"So be it," Annevnos said and directed his attention to his aide, Seratt.

"We have lost the stars," Meliphor interjected, gazing at the spectacle of planets.

"Moniah will bring you the stars, Empress," Annevnos said, drawing her attention to his black eyes. She quelled a shiver. The statement struck deeply into Moniah but he gave no outward sign of his discomfort. On the surface, Annevnos might have simply alluded to Moniah's role as First Lord of the void fleet but there was something much more significant in the Engineer's words, a meaning, an inflection, Moniah could sense after having experienced the strange mental link with Annevnos.

"We return to Auros Prime. Will you join us there?" Arhahnis said as a formality.

"I remain to monitor the sphere plate adjustment," Annevnos muttered while Saeonar and Kaylon secured a guarded exit from the control deck. The delicate truce between the Quattral and the royal Talsaiyr and their scientists was at an end.

Arhahnis and Meliphor took seat in their ornate thrones, activating the anti-gravity propulsion units and the devices lifted from the deck. The thrones emitted a quiet hum while conveying the Arhahn and his consort down a flight of stairs to the main control deck. Moniah took Lirea by the arm to follow the thrones with Kaylon at the lead and ever-cautious Saeonar bringing up the rear. Without another word, the Imperial family and their entourage took leave amidst bowed heads.

As Blermetal doors closed behind the royal party, Seratt, the lieutenant of Annevnos, hurried to his master's side. Annevnos stared at the closing doors.

"And so we bid farewell to the emperor, our usurping priest Arhahnis and, we must not forget clever Meliphor and her dull-witted companion, Lirea." Seratt chuckled. Annevnos was waxing his sharper edge.

"How easy it would have been to break Arhahnis in my hands. In his presence I am reminded how I detest him, a minion of lesser entities who has brought us to exile beyond the pure realm. Yet, patience is the virtue I must, for the present, master," Annevnos said, turning away from the door to survey the control decks.

"Did you note how Moniah Talsaiyr challenged you?" Seratt asked, moving to catch Annevnos'expression.

"As usual, Seratt. However, I found Saeonar the more transparent, scrutinizing me with contempt. What to do with a religion holding sway over a third of the populace? I wonder if Moniah has become their leader?"

"I doubt it, although it cannot be denied Moniah is chiefly responsible for bringing the Arhahn to power," said Seratt.

"Do not make a title of his name in *my* presence,"

"Forgive me, lord Annevnos. We have little to fear of the Wizan. What have they wrought? Nothing."

"Your ego is a danger, Seratt. The Wizan and their flying beasts manipulate considerable power. They are blessed from the origin days in this way. Never forget Wizans are a proven and substantive threat. Moniah and his Talsaiyr dynasty shall not relent until they control every facet of our society. Already, they have the Taen priest, two high Wizans, and do not forget Lirea—dull to be sure, but she *is* a Wizene adept. I suspect Arhahnis will now seek to join Kaylon to the Talsaiyr dynasty retinue."

"Surely not Kaylon, he is a powerful and independent mind."

"His power is one with the Talsaiyr and, with the sphere complete, Kaylon will feel vulnerable, his standing in the mantle guilds…uncertain."

"Then we should strike, now," Seratt said, daring to grab Annevnos by the arm. The Prime Engineer had merely to look upon the offending hand for Seratt to pull it away as if he had touched fire.

"Seeking immediate gratification, Seratt, is your weakness. Such a tactic would foster rebellion. We would fail."

"The Arhahn has but few ships, and the Wizan cannot attack without forswearing their creed. The time is now!"

"You will learn patience," Annevnos said leveling his black eyes upon Seratt, who instantly regretted his words as Annevnos' golden pupils flashed, emitting a filmy essence that washed over Seratt's head and dug into his eyes. Seratt felt his mouth gape and as the Mesmer plasma invaded his being, he faltered to his haunches. From somewhere through the numbing of his mind and the distant sensation of his body, Seratt could feel the iron grip of Annevnos, holding his arm.

Seratt moaned as the Mesmer wave dug deeper and still the golden pupils bored into his soul.

"Yes…lord," Seratt heard his voice croak.

Abruptly, Annevnos turned away and Seratt fell to his knees and coughed, wiping sweat from his brow while touching one hand to the floor to prevent himself from collapsing completely. Haltingly, Seratt rose to his feet.

"Do you love me, Seratt?"

"With all my will and heart, my lord."

"Then hear me well. I am your only salvation to unmake the mortal coil," Annevnos said and Seratt lowered his face, a tear ran down his cheek.

"My lord, I have never known a memory of the immortal realm."

"My curse and *our triumph* lie in the fact I have never for an instant, forgotten it," Annevnos said before draping himself in a Skren cape and striding toward a quiet gathering of Quattral elite, awaiting his counsel.

* * *

With the grace of a bird, the Imperial shuttle flew away from the Quattral platform, activating sonic protector arrays to jam Quattral spy apparatus. Within the comfort of the shuttle, Moniah fumbled nervously with a floatdroid offering tea and refreshments.

"Here. Let me," Lirea said, pouring tea and choosing fruit and Talmis bread to arrange a plate for Moniah who craned his head to one side to look up the aisle. The thrones of Arhahnis and Meliphor occupied the center of the shuttle cabin, blocking his view to the flight deck.

"Moniah! Let Saeonar and Kaylon fly the ship," Lirea said.

Moniah relented, patted her hand and leaned back, resting his head on her shoulder and looked out of the large port window to his right. The shuttle trembled while entering the blue-silver skies and white clouds of Auros Prime. A storm raged somewhere to the western region but the shuttle's vector into the atmosphere held for clear skies over the capital, Rentu-Treaur.

The ancient twin cities occupied two plateaus with the ceremonial center, Rentu, slightly higher, containing the enormous palace acropolis of Sumae-Thumaen that, set back from its gardens and temples, overlooked a waterfall of lush sweep, tumbling through a narrow vine-trellised ravine.

The twin city, Treaur, sprawled across its acropolis and down gradually descending slopes of gardens gleaming with spires, intricate mosaic-covered domes and the cloud kissing reach of the mammoth Council Hall. To the north of the Council Hall, two-mile-high towers surveyed a placid sea, its pale blue breakers rolling serenely toward the curving shoreline reflecting golden sunlight.

Dominating the entire region, arising from fertile grassy mists, the sacred mountain soared so high above clouds that a constant arc of snow issued a crescent of glittering white crystals from its summit into cold blue sky. The dramatic effect of the immense mountain was all the more pronounced due to the fact that it stood apart from any chain. It was a view that always brought comfort to Moniah's jaded and weary heart.

When the shuttle angled toward the palace acropolis, a wing of Oscileans with Wizan riders came into view. The wings of the flying Oscileans undulated in slow majestic rhythms of leathered tapestries of color while their robed riders waved to the shuttle that descended to land within the marble tiered walls of Sumae-Thumaen palace where an honor guard of Wizans awaited.

* * *

The High Taen priest, Ammanmus, blew warm air into his hands. He sniffed the cold air and inclined his head to the Palace Chamberlain, Alaysi, who was busy inspecting the shuttle as it settled gently down.

"It is difficult to fathom why Himself did not wear his mantle for the Quattral operation," Ammanmus said.

"The tradition of the mantle is largely *your* invention Ammanmus. I caution you to husband raising this issue with Arhahnis," Alaysi replied, nodding to Saeonar, who he could see waving from the pilot blister. Ammanmus frowned at Alaysi, who returned the look with his own wry and amused expression, a touch of rose from the cold on his cheek, his brown eyes wide with a harmless challenge generated by the twinkling fireflies of his silver-gold pupils.

"It is a good custom," Ammanmus blurted.

"Agh! Not now."

"How else may Aurankind take the measure of one another? For example, in a thousand years I have forgotten you are a poet but your mantle reminds me you possess this talent," Ammanmus said, tapping a design of stones on Alaysi's shoulder mantle. Alaysi arched an eyebrow.

"I was not aware it has been that long since I composed anything of note."

Saeonar bounded from the shuttle to a roar of greetings from his fellow Wizans while the Oscilean beasts rumbled a chorus of song and grunts. Moniah emerged, breathed deeply, and, smiling, took hold of Lirea's hand. When Arhahnis and Meliphor came into view on their thrones, a loud whooshing sound swept through the air as the Oscileans raised their wings and the Wizans sank to bowed knee. Meliphor smiled.

"Delightful. Such a warm welcome after the exhausting tension of the void," she said, while Arhahnis took Moniah by the arm.

"Have the Oscileans refrain from salute fires until we are within. I have felt close enough to danger of late." Moniah chuckled and simply smiled at Arhahnis who led Meliphor and the high priest Ammanmus to enter the portico and pass through the tall inlaid brass doors of the palace. Inside the threshold, Arhahnis turned around to address the honor guard.

"Wizans all, we thank you," he said. Saeonar bowed. Alaysi waited while Moniah turned to Lirea and they walked arm in arm into the Wizan circle. Saeonar withdrew his Coracle-diant, raising it high and the other Wizan guards followed suit, their Coracle-diants issuing beams of warm orange light into the air, startling birds overhead.

The Oscilean beasts lifted their heads to the sky and, as one, issued flames from their mouths, creating a circle of fire around Moniah and Lirea who laughed with abandon while Moniah embraced her as their hair commingled in floating updrafts and their laughter competed with the roaring flames. Lirea placed her lips a breath from Moniah's.

"Home again," she sighed. Moniah pulled her close and looked about into the large friendly faces of the Oscileans, whose Wizan masters-chanting drowned in the music of the fire. With puffs and grunts, the creatures ceased their firestorm.

Alaysi clapped his hands and petted the flank of a giant Oscilean as he strode into the circle.

"Haolae, Alaysi, but where is Kaylon?" Moniah said, clasping arms with the Chamberlain.

"I fear he slipped away, Wisdom."

"Pity. I'll see to it later. Make rooms ready for Saeonar. He is aching bones as am I," Moniah said, stroking the face of Saeonar's Oscilean while Lirea, ever the diplomat, thanked the Wizans for their salute. The creature rumbled a sweet song in response to the touch of Moniah. The smooth short hair on her long jaw was velvet to the touch and her large, friendly eyes twinkled beneath expressive wiry eyebrows that twitched to deflect gnats.

"You are a sweet creature, Montre," Moniah sang to the Oscilean. He added, "Where is my Prestant?"

"He pined for you in the Maulin trees...dozing...he flies to you now," she sang in a purr of musical phrases.

Moniah kissed her nose. Montre was a beautiful Oscilean with green and brown hair along her ten-foot long neck, graduating into alternating iridescent patterns of hair and scales along the torso and then tapering into smaller scales and hair down the length of the long tail. Two retractable wings, leathery and supple, of green, brown, blue and deep burgundy, were located just behind the neck on her mighty shoulders. The wings stretched thirty feet into the air to preen while Moniah scratched the sensitive place behind the ears where Oscileans so loved to be touched. The creature stomped one of its clawed forepaws, its body quivering with delight. Saeonar whispered a dismissal to the guard then rubbed his hands together.

"I will go to the Dome temple," he said, but Lirea put one arm round his waist.

"Come within, Saeonar. Rest and be comforted," she said, buffing his blushing cheek.

"Well...I am dehydrated from the void," Saeonar relented, but Moniah knew he was actually referring to the drain on his system from using his powers aboard the Quattral platform where he had protected the Arhahn and Meliphor with the energy bubble.

Alaysi hurried into the palace ahead of Moniah, Lirea and Saeonar, issuing orders to floatdroids. Saeonar turned once, sang an order to his Oscilean and Moniah bid his brother and sister Wizans farewell. The tall brass doors closed, refracting the purple of twilight onto the giant Oscilean, Montre, who moaned a quiet song of regret. She stared at the doors for a long moment then turned fully around, swept her tail about her rump and back legs and lowered her torso slowly to settle with a thud onto the marble courtyard.

An Iln Kite bird circled overhead, its delicate song teasing Montre to fly and play but the Oscilean simply lifted her long face up and grunted a short spasm of gray smoke followed by a long rumbling groan of resignation.

The Iln Kite chortled a response and spread its white wings to soar over the palace domes and spires, catching the evening drafts, while high above, the planetscapes of Ves, Simatos and Detate filled the heavens.

The Smoke Ponds

Moniah adjusted the saddle seat straps, climbed the three stirrups, slung his right leg over and settled into the seat. Lirea patted Prestant on the neck then climbed up the stirrups to the helping hand of Moniah while Prestant used the tip of his long dexterous tail to nudge Lirea gently on the back.

"Your scent is true again…gone is…the smell of machines," Prestant sang.

Moniah chuckled as he and Lirea locked the saddle seat shoulder straps into place. He turned to smile at Lirea.

"It warms my heart to fly with Prestant again," she said.

"To the smoke ponds," Moniah sang in the language of the Oscileans and with one powerful lunge of his great wings, the Oscilean was airborne. The air was cold and Moniah lit glow orbs handing one to Lirea who placed the warming orb beneath her robe.

Below them, through the broad strokes of Prestant's wings, a view of the palace acropolis gave way through morning fog to the sapphire rush of the waterfall whose cold clear mists they could smell before the Oscilean angled to the west and the Mountain of Beginnings. They flew over the Cerian forest at the base of the Mountain, taking a wide turn where the air was rich with winter sage and the piney scent of Maulin trees.

To one side, Triune sunlight reflected from the long glass smear of minerals covering the north face of the mountainside. Lirea leaned forward to wrap her arms around Moniah's waist.

"What a pleasure this is beloved," she cried over the rushing air. Moniah turned his face to kiss her then lowered his goggles to protect his eyes from the biting chill. Ahead lay dense forests interspersed with geysers and beyond, in the fertile moss covered rolling hills at the western slopes of the Mountain—gentle purple mists arose from the giant fern glens of the Smoke Ponds.

Had it been years since he visited the place of his birth? How many years? Time was fast becoming a blur to Moniah, a year or two hundred years, what difference did it make to beings who lived century after century in virile youth. An Iln Kite swooped close, trying in vain to keep pace with Prestant. Moniah considered the infinite variety of animals, Iln Kites nesting eggs, Watermins, Thronspinners—all the wondrous beings who lived and died in cycles while the Oscileans and Aurocearians remained untouched by the aging process, free of infirmity.

So accustomed were Aurocearians to their longevity that it took a conscious moment of reflection to take notice of the natural life cycles of other beings. In fact, the ecobiologist guild seldom studied the phenomena anymore, preferring to scrutinize macro systems of the Sphereworlds planets.

Moniah remembered dwelling in the tall reeds near the hills surrounding the smoke ponds.

It was on those moss laden hills that Wizan and Wizene first sang to the Oscileans and the creatures revealed their names, "Perfect", "Augmented", "Halfstep" and others whose songs were now scattered over Auros Prime. Where Lirea first embraced Moniah, descending through smoke mists in glowing flower petals as large as she that unfolded as she floated down into his arms.

For the first time in months Moniah remembered his past without the pain he had felt always when he tried to relive events and sensing his mood, Lirea hugged him tighter. Visiting the Smoke Ponds was a sacred release for Aurankind, a time for rapture and celebration and Moniah was certain his Tajaen or family, the Talsaiyr, would soon join them but for now, he needed to arrive in private with Lirea to take advantage of the setting for his trance.

He knew Lirea would resist when she learned he planned to enter deep trance but would relent when she realized the urgency of his quest. It was time to face the music of truth, to dispel the fog of memory in the mists of the ponds and see the past.

Prestant upbeat his wings to slow their descent onto a gentle rise deep within the fern glen. Lirea unstrapped herself from the saddle and dismounted the Oscilean with fluid grace. She turned round, hugging her arms over her chest and breathed deeply but before Moniah could speak, Medean emerged from the mists.

Though she was happy to see the mystic, Lirea's alert eyes swung back to Moniah even as she embraced Medean.

"We missed you on the Quattral platform Medean but how good it is to see you again, Haolae," she said.

"Haolae Aswarie Lirea, I was detained with a trip to Tem-Onj. My lord, you have accomplished amazing feats. I trust you are more rested than the last time we met?" Medean said, petting Prestant, who nudged the mystic's chest with his long snout. Moniah clasped arms with Medean, helping him pull the cumbersome saddle seat from Prestant's back.

"Ammanmus took charge of me at the palace with help from Lirea. I was no match for them and was put to bed."

"You collapsed my love," Lirea said.

"Ammanmus is a fine physician," said Medean.

"Remember how it was here…before mantles. While you two consort I am taking the water," Lirea said pulling off her robe. Moniah and Medean watched her step gently to part a fern, moving a reed flower with the tip of her toe, her delicate ivory body aglow against the verdant green. A Thronspinner buzzed toward her, singing playfully, and she tapped the bumbling creature lightly with her index finger, releasing a spray of fine Wizene golden mist into the air to the delight of the Thronspinner, which followed her down to a nearby pond.

The soft burbling sound of the Smoke Ponds issuing their warm smoky mists and the lark call of the Throns was the only sound as Lirea stepped into the water, creating ripples of green phosphorescent light to radiate away from her body.

"You will enter a powerful state of dream memory if you begin a fugue trance with me. Are you certain it is required?" Medean said, locking eyes with Moniah.

"I must *see* Medean. Had you been on the Quattral platform with us you might have experienced the longing I felt from Annevnos. It was…ferocious, a sensation barely masked by his rapture in the music."

Medean turned away, his thoughts clearly troubled as he watched Lirea invite Prestant toward the Smoke Pond. In the water the giant Oscilean was even more graceful than in flight. As he glided through mists toward a fruit tree on the far side, his deep reverberating song rippled the water.

Medean shook off complacency, spinning to face Moniah.

"Then before the fetes begin, we must," he said.

Moniah called for Lirea who hurried toward him laughing as she waved aside a small swarm of Thronspinners toying for her attention. She scooped up her robe and swept it around her.

"There is the look of strange work about you," she said moving closer to Moniah, her smile fading as she examined his resolute expression. Moniah took her by the hands. Her eyes darted to Medean beseechingly but he could only support Moniah.

"I need you to augment the Mesmer with Medean," Moniah said quietly. Lirea pulled her hands back, fire flashed from her eyes.

"No! I am not a mesmaun, Medean…"

"Aswarie Lirea, you are Wizene and though I share your concern Moniah must be empowered," Medean said stepping closer to Lirea. She backed away.

"At this moment I am not Lady Lirea but I am a Wizan who is set against this with all my being. What are we about? Mesmer was forbidden by Arhahnis a thousand years ago. Oh, I see it in your eyes, if our enemies employ it then we must. Yes? One thing, my clever lords…Where are these enemies? Who are they—the Quattral?"

Moniah tried to quiet her but Lirea's fury was not spent, she turned to call for Prestant.

"Bring the Oscilean, perhaps he can sing reason to you that I fail to impart," she said, waving for Prestant's attention but Moniah seized her hand and turned her gently to face him.

"Everything we are is about to change."

"Arhahnis has consolidated power—let him continue with his vision; there is no need for you to suffer the risk of Mesmer." Moniah ran his hands over his face and clenched his fists.

"We must anticipate Annevnos to be certain what his true motivations are," Moniah said looking around. The day was moving on and soon the revelers would arrive. Lirea looked at Medean.

"Gentle green robe what makes you headstrong males so determined to undo what remains of peace," She said, placing one hand on his cheek.

"Do you remember the first time you encountered Annevnos Sehtba, my lady?" Medean asked. Lirea glanced at Moniah, the gentle mink line of her brow furrowed.

"He came out of the woodwinds and sands…" she added, "He was alone—it was ages ago." She caught an electric glance between Moniah and Medean.

"He was contained rage Lirea, *remember*?" said Moniah, pacing.

"And?" Medean stilled Moniah and held Lirea's gaze in his knowing eyes.

"Why would an Auran emerge from Birthfire in rage, my lady?" he added, "was it not the bliss of our days, and were we not as playful as young creatures? Do we not return here for the sake of that remembered joy?"

Lirea stared at Medean. She was seeing back to the odd days when the Arhahn first encountered Annevnos. There had been a shift in the rapturous plenum they had all first known and though those days were lost to eons, she had lived them and, in the back corners of her memory, something lurked and now peeked forth.

She led Moniah by the hand and they walked through the reeds deeper into the Smoke Pond glens until they reached a broad soft patch of fire moss. Lirea turned to Moniah and Medean moved to position himself beside Moniah.

"There is deeper unknown meaning in Annevnos," she said. Moniah kissed her hands and closed his eyes. Lirea took two slow measured breaths and placed her hands on Moniah's head. As he knelt Medean placed one hand on Moniah's lower back and another on his forehead. There was a loud crunching sound as Prestant rumbled into the clearing, crushing a bush. The giant Oscilean stared at Moniah and sniffed the air.

The Mesmer wave washed through Moniah gently at first, rolling over his will, drowning his conscious thoughts. With the power of Medean adding to Lirea's abilities, the wave soon overwhelmed any sense of here and now and Moniah lost touch with his physical being in a way he had not known since giving himself over to Wizan.

There was no sudden onslaught of pain or the creep of nausea he had known during his memories aboard ship, instead, he seemed to linger for a short time—who knew how long—in a state of remove from the present. Where and when was also unclear but he felt a distinct presence as though the Gods were near. It was the same joyous state he had first known and he wept, for it was true he could not penetrate the veil of mortality to recall his soul's journey in the Godsrealm. Arhahnis was right.

In his unconscious state, Moniah shot his right hand into the air pointing to heaven and electrical plasma burst from his fingertips sending an arc of current crackling into the branches of a Maulin tree.

Prestant swung his long neck into a pond and sucked up water then stood to his full height to eject the water onto the burning leaves and the fire was extinguished, leaving only gray embers raining down. The giant Prestant grew very still, slowly lowering his head until his face was very near to Moniah. Now, Wizene, mystic and Oscilean guided Moniah to the places he needed to see…

Moniah was dimly aware that by being at the Smoke Ponds his ancient memories of them were enhanced dramatically but as soon as his conscious mind formed these thoughts, the Mesmer wave overtook him and the mists parted to reveal the past. There were the Oscileans forming from turbulent clouds to fly down and join their entranced Wizan familiars as though the Arhahn had called them from heaven in an act of supreme giving.

He could see himself scooping up water to wash his face while Prestant and Second Tone sang to him, "Gratify self…we shall not sing…call us in love," the creatures warned him--then he was standing at the top of the carbon crater looking into a molten caldera. Around him Auran's and Aurie's gathered around the rim of the caldera while the Oscileans circled overhead shooting streams of hot blue smoke from their nostrils into the boiling pit.

And there he was with Saeonar, gathering chunks of molten blue-tinged silver that bubbled up from the Oscilean smoke. They fished out the silver globules and while it was still malleable, Aurie's used their eyes to shine forth narrow, powerful beams of light while the Auran's toiled to create the first delicate wands, which they called Coracle-diants, the hands of the Gods.

Now he saw Lirea flying along the ferns, she and Meliphor and there too Iskanye—chasing silk birds, collecting their wing-tossed threads to fashion robes but, as quickly, he was arm in arm with Lirea and with a gentle step, her hand in his, they took flight.

Moniah could feel the wind in his hair. He called to Lirea but she did not reply, her gossamer wings beat rapidly, bearing them away from the Smoke Ponds toward the summit of the Mountain. His feet settled onto hard gravelly sand and when he looked about Lirea was gone. He gazed toward the Smoke Ponds and saw that no living creature could be detected. Overhead, the sky was filled with the pink-tinted stain of the Suum nebula. Only Ves, and the airless moon Icrass, adorned a strangely primeval sky.

Fear seized his heart as he realized he was a witness to pre-history and Moniah scrambled around the high pass and stumbled to the north face trail where he grasped a boulder while his chest heaved for breath. There was no city, no palace acropolis, only the mighty roar of the waterfall racing down the ravine between the plateaus.

The voices of Medean and Lirea sounded a chorus in his mind.

"As it was…"

The mighty Triune star was suddenly eclipsed. A cool deep dark settled over the Mountain summit and the sky became so clear that Moniah was a part of it. In the pitch darkness he saw the Suum Nebula erupt into being, poured from a brilliant vortex that pained the eye to behold. Time raced by, he could see subatomic particles collide while around Auros Prime plasma of fire red, gold, orange, green and towering storms shot through with lightning, encircled the planet.

Now it was day. The ocean beyond the Mountain sent columns of water vapor miles into the air and on the summit he saw what no Aurocearian had ever beheld, *the birth of Arhahnis.* A spinning orb aglow in gold and red burned down from the sky generating a high singing pitch. It hovered near the summit, very close to Moniah. As it cooled, the Birthfire orb pulsed radial kinetic energy that crackled the sand, fusing it on impact.

As Moniah watched, the design of the Gods executed mortal life devoid of a protracted evolution for the orb became translucent, and within it white steam and particles formed bones, red gasses tissue and blue inky smears became blood vessels, muscles, flesh from coalescing pools of pink and then the orb sang out a thunder and shattered, releasing the two legged form within.

Moniah felt his cheeks run with tears as he watched Arhahnis stumble to the dirt, his powerful body and dense molecular structure impervious to the abrasive atmosphere. He heard his brother's name, Arhahnis, *incarnation of dreams.*

Moniah yearned to help but his form was itself a dream visiting the past and he could only look on lovingly while Arhahnis pushed himself up from the dirt, his muscles quivering, his long red and black hair billowing in the rain and sand-swept tempest of that ancient cauldron of life.

"Now it comes. See it Moniah," Medean's voice called through a tunnel of music, wind and rain. On the summit, Arhahnis gazed over Auros Prime. His large almond-shaped eyes magnificent pools of blue-purple in which the sparkling incandescent golden pupils floated like stars and in those first mortal eyes a flash of something Moniah had never seen, emotion so powerful, so filled with fear and love and then anger, no not anger, fury.

As he watched, too stunned to breathe, Moniah saw Arhahnis lift his arms toward the heavens and issue a thundering lament of such force that the very sands shuddered under his feet. Above Arhahnis a shimmering golden vortex swirled over the summit and Arhahnis beseeched it with sounds not to be heard again.

No words could have been adequate to describe the sonic caterwaul Arhahnis emitted and Moniah's heart quaked for he knew it was the cry of mortal renunciation.

Arhahnis threw up his arms toward the swirling window to the

Godsrealm but the hypnotic vortex dissipated. Arhahnis roared again, shattering rocks. Hissing plasma shot from his eyes and hands, forming a burning seed trailing an arc of brilliant red light into the air. As the arc lost its velocity it fell back toward land.

"Looooook," Lirea's voice sounded within Moniah.

And now Moniah found his astral projection self, standing in the hot sands and shade of the Woodwinds to the east of the Smoke Ponds. He watched as the burning seed Arhahnis created, trailing effervescent smoke, careened overhead and then plummeted to the ground with sufficient force to cause a thunderclap of sound. The impact of the seed threw hot sand into the air—he could feel it on his face and could actually smell the ozone of sand fused to glass.

The constant breeze under the canopy of the Woodwinds dispersed the smoke quickly and Moniah hovered closer, even closer, to the blackened crater where, suddenly, a Birthfire orb rose up. The orb song was uneven and disharmonious fluctuating between high frequencies that screamed in Moniah's ears and low thrumming modulations.

The Birthfire orb looked to be about twenty feet in diameter, the same dimension as that from which Arhahnis had been born but the surface of this orb was covered in a black, oily substance.

Moniah was transfixed as the surface cleared and he could see dark purple pools form a brain around which white gas created bones and, as the blood vessels, organs, tissue, muscles and skin completed the Auran form—Moniah felt his skin raise with gooseflesh for when the Birthfire orb cracked and disintegrated into sandy winds, Annevnos was born.

The Auran destined to become the great engineer faltered in his waking moments of life but did not fall. He looked at his hands, felt his arms and chest and then the black eyes grew fire in their gold pupils and he whirled round to face the Mountain.

Moniah followed Annevnos' gaze to the summit where he could feel—even at this distance—a titanic outpouring of love from Arhahnis who he knew was at the center of the swirling matrix of light energy that cascaded from the summit to flood the planet with rains of bio matter.

As Moniah watched through eyes swollen with tears, remembering what he had not been alive to witness first hand, seeds fell from heaven and plants sprang from the dirt. Birds, Thronspinners, WaterMins and insects struggled from the ground while plants twisted up out of the dirt.

It was an ecstatic sight but Annevnos simply stared at the summit with rigid focus and though there was no articulation of speech from Annevnos, Moniah could feel his thoughts, *why was Arhahnis transforming*

Aurankind into this form?

At last it was clear, Annevnos was enraged because with each moment Arhahnis continued to create life, he was imprisoning Aurankind deeper into a mold from which they could never escape. A mold of mortal life further and further removed from heaven. Arhahnis had created Annevnos in a moment of renunciation of mortality and now, himself beyond that pain, the Arhahn was unaware of the existence of his polar twin.

Annevnos seemed to shrink in resignation while from the sky thousands of Birthfire orbs dripped down from heaven, containing Moniah and everyone he knew. Annevnos slumped to the ground to stare into the sand with uncaring eyes while small miracles of new life crawled up from the steaming ground around him.

It was a lethargy Moniah knew Annevnos would soon shatter when he regained his sole and driving need to return to the Godsrealm but how? What modus would he employ and would he destroy Aurocearia to do it? Moniah convulsed as the trance evaporated in a numbing shock wave through his nervous system. The pain began to recede taking embers of the vision with it. His last dream memory glimpse of the forlorn engineer was to see him weep and from his tears the ground near Annevnos trembled as Mantis ants sprang up from the sand to fly around him.

* * *

Moniah awoke with a start and found himself flat on his back on the fire moss. Lirea breathed a sigh of relief and hugged him. She placed a decanter to his lips while Medean stood and steadied himself against a tree.

A gust of hot fruit-scented breath flooded over Moniah and he saw the giant face of Prestant loom over him. Moniah tried to sit up but Prestant grumbled and Lirea cradled his head in her lap.

"Be still."

"I am well," Moniah insisted as much to comfort Prestant, as to reassure Lirea. He added, sipping water, "You were there."

Lirea looked about nervously and Medean returned to crouch beside the First Lord. A trickle of blue-silver blood dripped from his nose onto Moniah. Lirea tore a patch from her sleeve and Medean took it to wipe his nose, then patted sweat from his forehead.

"You were alone, my lord," said Medean.

"But I heard you," Moniah said looking up at Lirea, who leaned down to kiss his forehead. He smiled at her then sat up and studied

Medean, whose expression was distant and weary. The sound of wing beats could be heard at some remove, growing closer. Medean stood and stepped back to gaze into the sky.

"Twenty Oscileans or more. Saeonar and a Wizan wing but I do not see the others."

Moniah stood with help from Lirea and Prestant who gently grasped Moniah by the neck of his robe to help pull him to his feet.

"Arhahnis will ride the wing. He never travels here by ship," Moniah said, reaching behind him to pet Prestant's snout.

"You must promise me you will never attempt Mesmer again for I shall not participate," Lirea insisted, locking eyes with Moniah and turning to stare at Medean. Moniah wondered if Medean had seen some part of the vision. The swoosh and flap of many Oscilean wing beats was upon them, conjoined by a chorus of happy voices. Trumpets sounded from the Wizan Maetie, the Arhahn's personal honor guard, and the sky darkened with passing shadows. There was Saeonar, Alaysi, Ammanmus and Iskanye and then Arhahnis and Meliphor riding "First Tone" whose silver thread saddle glistened in what was now a sunny day.

The entourage landed in a series of thumps and thuds and the Oscileans brayed and chortled with each other impatient for their Wizan masters to remove the saddle seats.

Prestant sang and cavorted about, happy to have the company of others of his kind, including the rare breed of miniature Oscileans, one of which flew to Arhahnis. The small creature cooed in the arms of his creator. Born of giant sires and hatched from the same-sized eggs, they were identical to the giant in every way including the ability to spit fire and sing the magic language.

Some of the Maetie unpacked plectrums and began strumming music to merge with the twittering of birds and Oscilean song and everyone paused while insects, Thronspinners and other creatures flew around Arhahnis.

Moniah never tired of the amazing sight for whenever Arhahnis traveled into the countryside he was greeted by animals and insects, gravitating to the origin of their being. Thronspinners scattered gossamer over his head, Iln Kites strutted and sang, Mantis-ants buzzed around him and birds, electrified by his presence, sang and dashed here and there filling the air with joy. Throughout it all, Arhahnis remained oblivious, laughing as he tickled the miniature Oscilean.

When he looked about, it was as if Arhahnis sent an unconscious message and the excited creatures slowly gave way, abating their frolic to disperse into the wilds. He set the miniature Oscilean gently down and strode toward Moniah while Meliphor, Iskanye and Lirea encircled a floatdroid laden with refreshments.

"You have been a worry to me, brother," Arhahnis said and Moniah felt the powerful gaze of the Arhahn peering into his innermost being.

"I am sorry to know this."

"I love the Smoke Ponds as do you—is it not best to relinquish some degree of care and strife after all our struggles to enjoy this place?"

Moniah caught sight of Lirea sipping Soffa. From her body language, he could tell she was trying to ignore the queries of Ammanmus and Iskanye while Saeonar watched intently as he strummed his plectrum.

"I came here to find a means to end strife," said Moniah impatiently. "At least in part." Arhahnis tilted his head to one side, his golden pupils flashing like stars. Without turning to see, he knew what was happening and reached up to pluck a flower from an Ol vine.

"You are naïve to imagine you will conceal your thoughts from the minds of others. Lirea is transparent to those who love her and you have asked a great price of her, Moniah."

"I do not force my Aswarie, she acts of her own accord."

"But there *is* great force in your love Moniah, a force that in itself compels others to undertake matters against their nature. Today, you witnessed—through the love of others—what you were not meant to behold. You have broken my edict to invoke Mesmer and now Aurans beyond these precincts have felt your meddling in myth."

Moniah felt his stomach churn; his face tightened in anger. Arhahnis parted a dangling Ol vine to step through the bramble where he could survey the next glen. A warm breeze billowed his robe and golden-red hair.

"Would you have us live in the safety of myth?" Moniah said as he followed.

"Myth is the truth that survives and as such it is my will, my design," Arhahnis said, turning to study Moniah as his words sunk in. The First Lord was thunderstruck.

How could he have so gravely miscalculated his loyalty to Arhahnis? His mind spun while the Arhahn walked to the top of a rise to gaze up at the planet Detate, hanging so low in the horizon that the soft bronze of its desert continent seemed about to fall upon them.

To the east, the moon Ves temporarily softened the shimmering daylight as it crossed the lower edge of the star. Moniah suppressed a chill and moved closer to Arhahnis whose gaze remained transfixed to the sky while he spoke.

"All our artists, poets, musicians, priests, the scientists—all could have lived here on Auros Prime. Why did we foster ourselves on those worlds as well?"

"Our millions. All those minds so close to one another," Moniah said and Arhahnis wheeled to face him.

"Out of your own lips Moniah. The Oscileans have comfort with each other. Other creatures are best in love nesting close to their own kind. But Aurankind, well, our blood does not mingle in the communion of birth, we are not one but many manifestations of the Gods."

"Yes, in brotherhood," Moniah protested "in choosing our familial bond our society is sweeter for it."

Arhahnis stepped closer to Moniah and as he did the surrounding sounds of leaves in the wind, the insects and birds and the merrymaking of the camp muted as if withdrawn to a distance.

"You force my hand in matters I have labored over in a delicate manner. I only hope time will prevail for our needs."

Moniah offered no response and Arhahnis strode down the path to Meliphor who hurried to clasp him round the waist, leading him to Alaysi who had set a fine table under the sway of branches. Moniah stared at the happy throng and then ambled into Far Clearing glen where he lay beneath Ol vines to gaze up at the wondrous sky. He must have dozed for he awoke to the soft touch of Lirea stroking his hair.

"There you are," she said leaning back to regard him quietly. Moniah took her hand in his.

"I am at pains to know when I am awake or dreaming."

"With all you have done, you deserve the rest and I'm happy to see you at ease. Come," she said, standing, pulling him by the hand. Moniah started to apologize for having put her through the ordeal of Mesmer but thought better of it as she led him through a thick tunnel of Blumbleberries.

Laughter abounded around them, intermingled with the lyrical sound of Meliphor singing and music played on plectrums and winds. They came to a small pond and Lirea threw off her garments to enter bubbling mineral waters. Moniah abandoned his cares and disrobed to join Lirea in the warm undulating currents.

Nearby laughter threatened their privacy and Moniah put a finger to his lips.

"Shhh," he said while he clambered out of the pond to the top of the gold sand crest where he carefully parted reeds to peek into the next glen. Lirea joined him and they watched Saeonar dangling from the feet of his

Oscilean, Montre, while below Iskanye and even somber Ammanmus tugged at his feet.

In the next pond, Arhahnis cupped his hands and filled them with water to anoint Meliphor. As he dripped the water onto her ashen hair, a cocoon of soft warm light glowed to life around them. Beyond the next rise Alaysi came into view, swinging as if in slow motion on a long vine from which, as the vine reached its zenith, he dove into the deep pond.

Reality was strange, sad, a putty-like substance compared to the nirvana of the Smoke Ponds' sacred mysteries and Moniah was thrilled to be free from time and care as he and Lirea crept back into their mineral spring to embrace.

Nearby, Alaysi swam up from the depths and broke the surface to find Medean standing waist high near the shore taking in the scent of flowers. Alaysi paused as Medean turned and it seemed he had never beheld such beauty for the mystic pulsed with an ardent glow, his frame still moist. A Thronspinner warbled delicately and Medean reached out to Alaysi.

"You are beautiful Medean."

"Are you ready to help me?"

"Say what you will."

In the Presence of the Arhan

Alaysi mounted the Oscilean "Unda Maris" before the others broke camp at the Smoke Ponds. He settled into the saddle seat while the Wizan, Lanis, sang to his beast,

"Convey Lord Alaysi to the Dome temple…I will join you there."

"Thank you for your help Maetie Lanis," Alaysi said, leaning down to Medean who waited until Lanis stepped away before speaking.

"You will ride with the moonshine Alaysi, let Unda Maris fly with speed as Lanis has instructed him. Matters require your utmost speed."

Alaysi winked, and strapped in.

"Lord Alaysi, you'll soon need these," Lanis said, tossing a pair of goggles to Alaysi. He caught them to place around his neck while the others stepped far enough away to avoid the outstretched wings of Unda Maris. The giant crouched and with a single upstroke of his mighty wings lunged into the air.

* * *

It was early evening when Arhahnis and his retinue were safely again ensconced in the capricious expanse of Sumae-Thumaen palace. Spring had come and twilight expanded to a slow sunset rendering the evening sky with planetscapes while the scent of flowers and vines covering the trellised marble and silver balustrades, wafted in a gentle breeze around him. He paused to study the distant behemoth of the Mountain of Beginnings.

The cloudless evening afforded a clear vista and he could plainly see refractions of light from the glass-like fissure that ran ten thousand feet up the north face, from the edge of the tree line to the summit. Essentially an enormous mineral deposit known as the "mountain eye" by some and "the glass smear" by others, the fissure was roughly triangular and seemed larger than the last time Arhahnis had looked at it.

Perhaps some minor quake had revealed a greater portion of the reflective material. By concentrating focus of his supra-evolved eyes, Arhahnis could almost see the place where he had come into mortal being and where now a single flame burned.

The lower edge of the glass smear plunged in vertical jagged veins for thousands of feet down vanishing points on the nearly perpendicular slope. Arhahnis turned away abruptly and stepped inside his Solarium. His court musician was sipping tea at the console of the Sieuwan, a large musical instrument of five keyboard manuals, organ pipes, tone spheres and graduated vertical strings reaching as high as forty feet to the barrel vaulted ceiling. Noticing the Arhahn, the Musemaun set down his cup and waited while the emperor took seat in a single chair in the center of the room.

"Play me something to attune my soul, Musemaun," Arhahnis said and then closed his eyes and placed his hands on his knees. The music began with a quiet flowing legato augmented by a persistent rhythmic pulse in the bass.

As the piece progressed, Arhahnis' breathing matched the bass and his body began to emit a nimbus of light in time with the music. Soon, musician, instrument and listener were as one and in the spirit of music were oblivious to the gentle but persistent chime of a servant floatdroid.

Meliphor opened one of the doors and peeked into the music room just as the piece ended. She stepped aside allowing an Auran wearing a brass and jadestone mantle to enter. He paused immediately with his mouth slightly agape, watching the Arhahn's body send off a final series of light pulses as the music echoed away to silence. Arhahnis turned his head slowly to regard the Auran who sank to one knee with his arms outstretched.

"You may go now Musemaun, I thank you," Arhahnis said as he stood. He added, "Rise Tius."

Meliphor led the musician out and closed the doors behind her. Tius approached the presence, who offered him a glass of Oprasia wine that he accepted with a slight bow.

"I missed lord Alaysi, his wit is always a pleasure to encounter," said Tius.

"My brother has duties elsewhere. I trust we shall soon call you brother," Arhahnis said taking seat and indicating the chair in which he had just meditated. Tius hesitated then sat down cautiously but before he could reply the trumpeting call of an Oscilean filled the air. Arhahnis followed by Tius went out to the terrace where Tius pointed at a shadow, circling overhead.

"Moniah arrives," said Arhahnis as the Oscilean swooped down to the terrace where despite frantic upbeats of his wings to retard his momentum the giant air creature landed his tonnage with a thud that cracked the marble floor. Unaccustomed to frequent close proximity to the creatures, Tius backed away to stand within the safety of the doorway as Moniah dismounted. Prestant groaned an apology then taking note his mishap was of little consequence to the Aurans, proceeded to concentrate his attention on a large vase of honey sprouts, which he gobbled up while the Aurans greeted one another.

"So, good Tius, tell us," Arhahnis said removing a green clump of Ol vine from a pouch he wore on his velvet sash. He placed the vine into a silver pipe and leaned toward a floatdroid. A round lid popped up on the machine's top from which a flame flickered to life, which Arhahnis used to light his pipe.

Daunted by the presence of the First Lord, Tius addressed Arhahnis in formal title.

"Infinite, our agents stand ready in the Colomeran cavern."

Moniah could not contain his relief and clapped his hands then rubbed them together; this was the best possible outcome. So much of the preliminary plan had hinged on the ability of the powerful Tius to use his alliances for the success with the coup.

Lirea had seen it clearly after all, while Moniah lived in space preoccupied with the Sphere construction, Arhahnis and Tius consolidated political power within the Governing council and that body, with high mantles of governors on every world within the Sphere—overwhelmed the stalemate influences of the Taen, Greenrobe and Wizan temple hierarchy to overwhelm the Quattral.

If the Talsaiyr dynasty and its government could guarantee control over the Colomeran machine, the fate of Aurocearia would not rest in the hands of Annevnos.

"Is all in readiness?" Arhahnis enquired.

"We await Kaylon," said Moniah smiling at Tius who seemed unable to contain his agitation and who was equally surprised at the taciturn manner the Arhahn and First Lord displayed on the eve of a crisis.

* * *

Kaylon checked the onboard chronometer display on the cabin wall and cracked his knuckles as he looked out of a side port window. The Satar ship was angling down to descend through evening clouds. By his estimate, he should arrive at the palace on schedule.

A chime sounded. Kaylon frowned. He was the only passenger on a secret flight and Moniah had expressly forbidden any communications.

"Yes," he barked.

"Prime Annevnos on secure channel, lord Kaylon," The voice of the pilot announced. Kaylon hesitated but it was clear Annevnos knew where he was. Kaylon swiveled his seat to face an egg shaped floatdroid.

"Transmit the signal," he said and a hologram of the face of Annevnos appeared over the top of the droid.

"Am I disturbing you lord Kaylon?" the normally mellifluous—some accused—mesmeric voice of Annevnos said, although the effect was drained of its commanding tone in transmission.

"Not at all, Prime Engineer."

Annevnos' eyes sparkled and he seemed to stare into the soul of Kaylon while searching his face.

"My adjutant Seratt shall meet you at the Colomeran facility."

"This will be a great service to us, lord Annevnos."

Annevnos smiled with the rapid joyless twitch for which he was known.

"I wonder, will you be attending the annual pilgrimage of Arhahnis to his mountain?" Annevnos asked and it seemed the image of his face grew larger, stifling the atmosphere of the ship's cabin. Kaylon shifted uncomfortably in his seat.

"I have, forgive me; I am a bit airsick of a sudden. Strange."

"It shall pass. You have spent many months in space and the descent into planetary atmosphere is no doubt affecting you. You were saying?"

"I am not decided if I will attend."

"With so much to consider, why I wonder, does Arhahnis deem it necessary to heed the call of priests and their inventions of tradition. Is he not the high Taen and if so is the pilgrimage not his own device?"

Kaylon tapped a hand to his chest then coughed and missed the spasm of a smile Annevnos let slip. While wiping his brow, he caught sight of a flicker of real fear in the engineer's eyes.

"Will you attend, Annevnos?"

It was as if the air in the cabin cleared of a frightful presence, Kaylon could even feel the pulse of the quiet engines again, his engines, Moniah's engines. Annevnos tilted his head back.

"Priests do not summon me," he said and the hologram glowed so that Kaylon had to squint—but he could not look away.

"There is no God but destiny in the Suum. The life force is the Godsrealm from whence we originated. It is ours, yours and mine."

Kaylon tore his attention away from the hologram. He straightened his powerful form and squared his shoulders, then smiled.

"Interesting. In one thought, you mention destiny and the purpose of life. It seems to me, these are very much the concerns of priests of Taen and the Wizans of the Mysterium though apparently, you deny their substance."

"Well, then I say Godspeed."

The hologram faded and Kaylon pushed himself to his feet to stretch and pace the cabin. He ignored the pilots warning they were about to land and gathered his things to stand by the side hatchway, anxious to escape the claustrophobic atmosphere of the Satar shuttle he now sensed was contaminated.

* * *

"Ammanmus remains the key, if he will stay his course and support the councils," Moniah said to Tius who watched in fascination as Arhahnis, oblivious to any sense of formality, shed his robe and stepped into the waters to float on his back in the reflecting pool.

"Kaylon informs me Annevnos has shown great interest in the fortress on Icrass," Arhahnis said softly but Moniah spun at his words to stare at him.

"We should have kept the Orb here," Moniah said.

"Impossible. It is too powerful," Tius interjected.

"Destroy it then."

Arhahnis lit his Ol pipe, his tone level and final.

"We cannot destroy that which we do not understand." The floatdroid chimed. Moniah and Arhahnis broke their gaze.

"Who?" Arhahnis demanded.

"Kaylon Olashi," A voice announced. Moniah set his wine glass down quickly and sprung to his feet.

"At last."

"Admit him," The Arhahn commanded and stepped out of the reflecting pool, as he swept his great robe about him, Kaylon entered the Solarium to find Moniah all smiles, striding toward him with open arms, framed from behind in the sparkling glow of sunset.

"We were discussing the Orb of Icrass," Moniah said embracing Kaylon who, noticing Arhahnis, bowed his head and began to genuflect.

"Rise, Lord Kaylon, there is too much to be about for ceremony. Come close to us here by the terrace. What news?"

"Infinite, I doubt whether we will prevail much longer in keeping Annevnos and his close Mantles from satisfying their curiosity and visiting the Orb," said Kaylon, accepting a glass of wine but politely nodding away the Ol pipe.

"Even with the Wizan guard and Ammanmus' most trusted Taens keeping it secure?" Tius said.

"All of this will fall to irrelevance after today. Annevnos will be determined to regain control of the Colomeran. Then, we will address the Orb matter," Arhahnis said and he paused to add quietly, "after the Mountain, after..."

"Give me leave to remove it to safety now," Moniah pressed and Arhahnis wheeled to confront him.

"I have given you my thoughts." That was that. Moniah looked to Kaylon.

"Will Annevnos join us at the Colomeran?"

Kaylon chewed his lip. Tius stared at him with a blank look. Arhahnis waited expectantly while gazing out to the sunset.

"He contacted me aboard the shuttle."

"Unexpected."

"Go on Kaylon," Arhahnis said, transfixed by the Triune's fading rays.

"My impression from his words is he will not join us."

Silence. Tius heaved a sigh and stared at the Ol pipes. He reached for one, paused, then snatched it up and lit it, inhaling deeply.

"Excellent, we shall have to act as a blur of energy while others are asleep in the purpose of the Gods," Arhahnis said glancing at Tius.

"On the strength of our will, Arhahnis," Kaylon said and Arhahnis turned slowly to smile at Kaylon with great satisfaction. Kaylon withdrew thin black reeds from a pocket in his robe.

"Kamis root?" Moniah made a face and waved his hand.

"Each to his own tastes, Moniah," Arhahnis chuckled, accepting a piece of the root.

Moniah checked his chronometer, "The time is come," he said and Kaylon joined him on the terrace where Moniah approached Prestant. The Oscilean lowered its long head to meet the eyes of the First Lord. Forty-eight feet from nose to tail; Prestant folded back his colorful wings and lumbered to Moniah, shoving his long thorny whiskered nose into Moniah's stomach repeatedly. Moniah rubbed the beast's ears and Prestant whimpered a comical sound to emanate from such an impressive creature.

"Now my son of winds, sing me to Saeonar," Moniah said, scratching Prestant's four-foot jaw. The Oscilean emitted a beautiful melody to which Moniah replied, "Hear me Saeonar, and let no wings fly until we are within the Colomeran compound."

Prestant angled his head away and sang out a low sonic pulse and seconds later he looked at Moniah and opened his mouth. To the amazement of Tius the voice of Saeonar issued from the Oscilean,

"We fly with the mooooons."

Bored, Arhahnis turned to Kaylon who was also captivated by witnessing one of the most secret mysteries of the Wizan Mysterium.

"Come safely back to us Kaylon," said Tius and Arhahnis blessed Moniah and Kaylon by touching their brows with his fingers. Prestant's large eyes, the size of small melons, rolled upward as Moniah stroked the soft patches behind his ears.

"We are ready when you are my friend," Moniah said as he climbed the stirrups. The normally confident and handsome face of Kaylon showed a nervous strain as he mounted to sit behind Moniah. They fixed on the shoulder straps. Arhahnis stepped back and waved.

"Eveet!" Moniah commanded and Prestant took wing. Cool air flowed over them while the steady wing strokes made a rhythmic rush of churning air around their faces. Kaylon moaned as Prestant turned sharply to one side, pointing a wing straight down to bank to the south. Night had come and Moniah scanned the sky for errant shuttles.

"Sey promised, agh, to enforce the sky law," Kaylon said, his voice atremble. Moniah nodded glancing over both his shoulders but there was no sign of ships. Arhahnis had long insisted that no void vessels be permitted within the atmosphere of Auros Prime and the edict had quickly been passed into law by a population who, despite their comfort with vast machines, were not comfortable with ships as large as islands, floating overhead—especially when those ships were prototypes.

Moniah pointed to what appeared to be a very bright star. He could tell it was Admiral Sey's void ship, hovering high over the city to reinforce the safety of the skies. A gust of wind buffeted Prestant, whose wings tipped first right, then left and Moniah, startled, jumped, as Kaylon instinctively threw his arms around Moniah's waist.

"Easy Prestant, quiet now," Moniah said bending forward to pet Prestant's neck--but the Oscilean shook his head as if trying to throw off an annoyance and sang out in complaint.

"Is he well?" Kaylon cried out.

"Something in the Quattral compound is making his ears ring."

Moniah reached into a saddlebag and withdrew two large sponge earplugs. As Kaylon swallowed in fear, Moniah undid his shoulder straps and stood up while leaning forward. Prestant arched his neck back and turned his head as far around as possible while Moniah put the earplugs in. The creature nodded emphatically, signaling he was relieved of the pain but it wasn't until Moniah was safely seated and strapped in that Kaylon heaved a sigh of his own.

"We land," Moniah said shortly there after; pointing below to a series of metal concentric arches situated in the southernmost corner of the city, well beyond the twin acropolii. Before the largest arch a forecourt was illuminated on four sides by inverted pyramids with their bases facing up, glowing brightly. The arches formed a graduated pattern that descended to vanish below ground where miles below, lay the heart of the Sphereworlds.

Prestant lost altitude, gliding down in a series of four turns. At the last instant, he snapped his wings back and up and they were on the ground. Kaylon took his bearings. From the air, the arches appeared small but now the maw of the forecourt arch towered hundreds of feet into the dark night.

Music in the Sphere

As Moniah and Kaylon dismounted, thick Blermetal doors opened in the large arch and a single Auran approached.

"Seratt," Moniah said with the slightest nod of his head.

The Prime Engineer's adjutant wore his official mantle of brass plates emblazoned with a sphere, three stars and the written symbol of the Quattral guild. Seratt stopped abruptly when Prestant grumbled a shuddering warning. Moniah patted the beast's neck.

"Wait near the trees," he sang. Seratt smiled as he recognized Kaylon.

"Haolae lord Moniah, lord Kaylon. The Prime Annevnos has matters to attend to that demand his presence elsewhere," Seratt said, scanning Moniah. He appeared relieved and confused that Moniah was not wearing a Coracle-diant. Moniah suppressed a smile. He seldom wore the Wizan wand and on this occasion, he was certain it was best he had not.

"A simple inspection hardly demands Annevnos' attention," Moniah said and Seratt beamed a smile that was at once condescending and insincere.

He led them into the arches and just as they stepped within the threshold, Moniah turned around and sneezed as signal to Prestant. When the doors closed leaving Prestant alone in the dark forecourt, he sniffed the air and sang out a low tone that wavered into a treble register, then he sat down to stare at the doors.

* * *

Fifty miles away at the top of the Wizan foothills, Saeonar paced the upper inside ring of the Dome temple. He sipped warm tea and paused to glance at his Oscilean, Montre, who lay in one of the many open niches. Laughter and song drew him to the inner gallery where he looked down into the great round chamber to see Alaysi and a host of Wizans gathered around the central glow orb. Saeonar smiled and was about to enjoy another sip of his Ol tea when Montre sang out.

"Moniah and Kaylon…step within…the place of noise." The Oscilean song told them what was happening. Saeonar kissed Montre and hurried to the balustrade.

"Brothers and sisters take wing," he cried and the lower chamber became a sea of movement as Alaysi and the Wizans sprang to action. Saddle seats were slung over mounts and Coracle-diants fixed to holsters. A parade of Oscileans lumbered up the broad walkways at either side to join Saeonar and Montre. In short order, Alaysi and Saeonar were airborne, leading a wing of three hundred into the night.

"Silent wing beats in the night—enough to make the spirits fright," Alaysi called out to Saeonar from his Oscilean. Saeonar leaned on his reins so that Montre flew within thirty feet of Alaysi's mount. The two Oscileans synchronized their wing beats so as not to collide.

"That is bad poetry Alaysi," Saeonar called out over the whoosh and flap of six hundred wings.

"Agh! What do you know of couplets?"

* * *

Inside the facility, other Quattral Aurans murmured at sight of Moniah but kept their distance. Moniah noticed that among the majority of steely faces a few actually smiled as he passed by, some bowed their heads! They proceeded through a tall sparsely furnished chamber where the only comfort was a soft golden light emanating from striated glass fixtures on the ceiling, lending the otherwise barren space a feeling of warmth.

On the far side of the chamber, two glow orbs set atop thirty- foot torchieres flanked tall thin Blermetal doors of midnight black.

"The Prime's elevator. Follow please," Seratt said and the doors opened quickly and silently to reveal a smaller room with dark red marble walls and a black polished floor. Set into the black was a perfect circle of gray metal flooring. Although smaller in scale, the room could hardly be described as intimate or comfortable. A deep rhythmic sound emanated from the floor. Seratt walked to the center of the round plate and touched something attached to his waist sash. A thin brass rod extended from the center of the seamless floor circle plate. Moniah and Kaylon moved onto the plate to stand near Seratt.

Seratt touched a series of buttons on the rod's tip and a brief flash of blue tinted light appeared around them.

"Dampening field," Kaylon said and Seratt nodded but without any warning he touched another button and the round floor circle suddenly dropped away. Stomachs rising they descended rapidly. For an instant Moniah felt his ear canals fill with pressure but the dampening field took hold and all sensation of movement was quickly suppressed. They plunged in a hollow tube cut through the rock, strata of stone sped by around them at a dizzying pace. Looking up, Moniah could see the light from the room above, retreating rapidly to a mere speck.

Even at their rate of descent it would take some time to reach the Colomeran cavern and Moniah collected his thoughts. They were about to enter the epicenter from which magnetic energy radiated to collecting stations in the Sphereshell. The Colomeran was the heart of Aurocearia, controlling planetary orbits by emanating vacuum energy to ensure the inner worlds would not collide.

By this means, all the inner Sphere planets were made slaves to Auros Prime, which lay at the center of the Sphereworlds. The dilemma was that for a thousand years the Ecobiosynthesis guild led by Tius, had gradually lost control of the Colomeran apparatus as the Quattral gained control of the Sphere shell project.

Moniah could now see why he had forced the Arhahn's hand for if they failed to correct the situation tonight...he noticed Seratt was studying him and although Aurocearians had experienced a loss of telepathic powers since the garden time—save for Wizans—Moniah decided to distract Seratt.

"You have improved the dampening field, Seratt."

Lights spaced at hundred foot intervals in the elevator shaft illuminated their progress into a cool darkness with pulses of soft white light. Kaylon took a cautious step toward the edge of the platform. He reached out and touched the blue light surrounding them and his fingers sparked against the invisible shield.

As expected, Seratt took the bait and anxious to demonstrate Quattral superiority he moved confidently to the edge; only a few feet beyond his reach hewn rock face sped by and up. He lunged at the open air with both fists and a crackling sound erupted from the force of his fists against the shield, which for a second flashed a blue dome of light around the platform.

"Indeed we have, lord Moniah."

There was a growing feeling of heat as the elevator plunged deeper into Auros Prime. Seratt made adjustments on the controls and the temperature cooled.

In another instant, the strata of rock surrounding the platform disappeared and the platform descended in a breath-taking moment into the vast Colomeran cavern. Despite having visited the Colomeran before, Kaylon unconsciously stepped back toward the center of the platform, hypnotized by the interior vista six miles below the surface.

The subterranean cavern stretched into an unfathomable distance in all directions around them and the elevator platform slowed its descent to hover just below the circular elevator shaft opening. They peered over the edge. Two miles below a sea of apparently ant-sized Aurans moved about between four titanic quadrangles from which mile-high Tesla coils filled the air with arcs of controlled current aimed toward the enormous geodesic sphere of the Colomeran itself.

Echoing sounds of machines and a steady murmur of voices wafted up to their birds-eye vantage while Constructorbots hummed by like streams of giant pearls far below, ferrying equipment to a thousand locations. The Colomeran sphere was larger than Moniah remembered, at least a mile in radius; it floated between the pylon towers like an imprisoned star.

Even with the many sources of artificial light, it took some minutes for Moniah to refocus his eyes. His silver pupils finally adjusted, glowing brighter in the thinly lit gloom. Moniah looked at Kaylon, whose pupils appeared as fireflies dancing in his orbs. He pointed to the geodesic dome.

"The directional resonator is floating now."

"Indeed my lord, fully operational," Seratt interjected, stepping closer to Moniah. Kaylon overcame his fear of heights to move a little closer to the platform edge than he would ordinarily feel was appropriate. Between the ride on Prestant and the death defying elevator trip, Kaylon appeared to be struggling for courage to battle his fear. He looked over the edge of the platform to peer down at the Colomeran and removed a small scanner from a waist pouch and aimed it at fourteen hovering discs that spun around the geodesic sphere. The discs maintained equal distances from themselves and the Colomeran.

"This is a fine refinement of the representation of the planets and triune stars," Kaylon said turning to Seratt.

"As you know, each of the actual planets contains a sphere half the volume of the Colomeran resonator below us. Therefore, control of planetary orbits is now maintained by those units, interlinked with this master."

Kaylon keyed a control on the scanner to signal operatives below and slipped it back into its pouch.

"They have refined vacuum frequency," said Moniah and Kaylon shook his head in wonder.

"A perfect application of this form of energy."

"The former instability is a thing of the past. We now tune the frequency and graviton variant by sound and particle beams directed from stations throughout the complex," Seratt said, moving to the other side of the platform where he peered into the distance with a set of binoculars. A beep sounded from something on his waist sash and he pulled it away then spun to stare at Moniah with open hatred but, lightning quick, Kaylon seized the device from Seratt, crushing it with one hand.

Below them, the steady pulse of sounds accelerated with voices raised in confusion.

"If you will permit me to borrow those," Kaylon said taking the binoculars from a bemused and stunned Seratt and handing them to Moniah who moved to the edge of the platform to peer below. Kaylon took hold of Seratt by the shoulder and easily moved him away from the force shield control rod.

Through the twin lenses Moniah saw Aurans flood into the cavern. Their sheer numbers stunned the Quattral who turned about and looked at each other as they moved away from control stations.

"Now Saeonar," Moniah whispered.

* * *

Outside the facility, Prestant sang out to his fellow Oscileans and stirred up dirt as he danced about while overhead the sky beat with the thunder of the Wizan wing and a chorus of song filled the night air.

A warning klaxon wailed from the forecourt arch and the Blermetal doors began to close.

"Now, now, mustn't shut the turn of time," Alaysi said covering his ears while the assembled Oscileans let loose a barrage of thundering sonic pulses at the doors. In the dust and foggy chilled air one could actually see the sonic waves converge on the doors, forestalling their closing.

But the creatures had to cease their aural assault to allow the Wizans to storm the arch, and as they ran headlong at the entrance the sound dissipated and the doors began to close again, reducing by steadily increasing inches the golden prize of light within. Saeonar unsheathed his Coracle-diant and took aim at the doors while his cohorts followed suit. In a second, three hundred currents— of electromagnetic light and sound—converged against the doors.

The entrance exploded in sound and color, arcs of electricity flew about and the air fell heavy with smoke and ozone but when Alaysi waved dust from his face, shifting this way and that in his saddle-seat, he saw that one of the doors had melted away and the Wizans were hurrying inside.

Alaysi sighed and looked about. Three hundred Oscileans stared at him with blinking caution.

"Shall I give you my poem of Ves?" he asked of the creatures.

* * *

Kaylon overrode the elevator control and the disc quickly sank two miles to hover a few hundred feet over the facility. Seratt gasped and crouched to the floor of the platform as the cavern above them came to life with dozens of other disc elevators bearing Wizan invaders, their Coracle-diants glowing like torches under a sea of blue light shield umbrellas.

A platform hummed close to them on which Moniah could see Saeonar. A quick glance below showed that the Ecobiosynthesis guild was in control while Quattral Aurans appeared too stunned for retaliation. Because open revolt was a new form of behavior for Aurankind, Moniah had gained a distinct psychological advantage but securing control of the Colomeran operations remained an urgent priority for the coup to succeed.

"Saeonar, assist the eco guild in the north quadrant. You there! Lanis? Land your team near the pylon and lock out the sonic amplifier," Moniah said pointing to his targets, his eyes beaming through the muted hazy light of the cavern.

Elevator platforms landed throughout the facility and in a matter of minutes light shields from Coracle-diants could be seen forming around key control centers. Moniah paced the platform taking reports and issuing orders and soon enough it was apparent the plan to control the single most important nerve center of Aurocearia was a success.

Their success was due in part to the sheer audacity and speed of the Wizan attack but also because any act of sabotage by Quattral operatives could easily have resulted in catastrophe for the Sphereworlds system. A little less than three hours into the operation the situation had stabilized. Moniah was triumphant. The Quattral were now the minority staffing the Colomeran device.

Throughout his defeat, Seratt stood quietly with arms folded before him staring at the operations center he had lost. When at last he felt the iridescent sparkle of Moniah's eye light on his face, he merely looked up and sighed.

"By command of the Arhahn, the Colomeran will from henceforth be monitored and controlled by the Governing council and Wizan representatives," Moniah said handing the binoculars to Seratt.

"An inspection, my lord?" said Seratt.

"To correct an oversight."

Kaylon released the control of the elevator platform to Seratt.

"We are finished here," he said, locking eyes with Seratt, who depressed a button.

"Up," Seratt said and the platform began to rise swiftly.

* * *

In rooms located near the top of the mile-high dwelling pylon where Annevnos lived, Seratt lifted himself from the floor and rubbed his jaw. An angry welt in the shape of a fist stung his cheek. Annevnos followed him with his terrible eyes as the adjutant arose unsteadily to his feet.

"Moniah has acted swiftly and with brilliance and you, Seratt, have placed my heart in darkness."

"If you had been there my Prime but do not despair, ours is the superior cause." Annevnos turned away to walk slowly toward the long curving window where he gazed at the distant Woodwinds desert of his birthplace.

"Cause? What do you know of my cause?"

"Forgive me lord, I cannot hear you clearly."

"Make ready for the council. I want to see your plans well in advance. Do you understand me?" Annevnos said, enunciating each word, one hand on his worried brow.

"Clearly, lord Annevnos."

"Oh, I dearly pray you do, Seratt."

Seratt waited for a moment but the Prime said nothing more and after rubbing his brow stared into the distance. Hundreds of feet below the level of his chambers in the pylon, clouds floated by spitting lightning and the day fell into gloom. Seratt bowed despite the fact that the Prime was facing away from him and quietly took his leave with a new, determined stride.

* * *

The temple of Surrant Wonder together with the council hall and palace of Sumae-Thumaen formed the crown jewels of Aurocearian architecture. Each building a distinct expression of design, the intricacies of the palace complex with its cupolas, gardens, spires and domes dominated its acropolis in a seemingly random plan while the huge council hall effected a more solid appearance, comprised of a wide base that tapered into a long nave towering a quarter-mile into the sky.

Adjacent to the council hall, the temple of Surrant, built by the Taen order, was a fluid wave of stone at the base with wing-like twin towers that soared five hundred feet above a wide mosaic plaza. Arhahnis

Talsaiyr and his chief priest, Ammanmus, had long ago created the order of Taen, which soon became the state religion of most Aurocearians.

Chiefly comprised of physicians, philosophers and a respected guild of biologists, the practitioners of "Taen" sought to define the most ardent desire of Aurocearians for connection to the mysterious Godsrealm from which they knew Arhahnis, acting as catalyst for the Gods, had brought them into mortal being.

This belief was a crucial psychological element for the fact remained that no Auran or Aurie could remember anything before the time they descended from the sky to form in the Birthfire orbs.

As the time of the garden faded, Arhahnis the first incarnate Aurocearian, sought out Moniah, Medean and Ammanmus, who were among the first beings. Soon after, Aurocearians developed into an organized society and it became clear Aurans and Auries possessed highly individual personalities despite their common lineage. The mystic "Greenrobes" of whom Medean was the spiritual head, avowed a less structured and ecumenical philosophy that allowed free expression of their unique mental abilities while the Wizan, with their powers over natural forces and special communion with Oscileans, formed a secretive "Mysterium" rite.

Arhahnis sensed the greater populace of many millions remained in need of a tangible means to worship and recognize the Gods. Especially when mortal life seemed without end for there was no aging, illness or death and as the society increased in its complexities of fantastic scientific and artistic achievement, Aurocearians sought to identify their pantheon of Gods through the most noble and loving attributes of their selves.

The genius of Arhahnis lay in his delineation of those attributes, which he, Ammanmus and Moniah identified as the sacred forty manifestations of the Gods, the supreme spectrum that included the Mysterium and mystic temple branches. In this way, the umbrella of Taen consolidated religion and the power of Arhahnis as the absolute pinnacle of the temple hierarchy with Ammanmus as the right arm of ecclesiastical authority.

Under the weight of the temples, the pyramid of Aurocearian political apparatus descended first through the Governing council, comprised of mantles chosen to govern regions and supreme governors responsible for each of the twenty habitable planets within the Sphereworlds.

Under the Governing council all the other guilds of scientists, engineers and artists fanned out to form the collective society with one new guild—the void fleet—unaccounted for in the scheme of power. Moniah was quickly rectifying this as he, Kaylon and the Grand Admiral, Evstenos Sey, perfected their vessels and staffed the prototypes with those loyal to the Imperial or "Awclotan government" but the Quattral also contained masters of shipbuilding and there was no law to restrict the operation of ships to any one guild of mantles.

Now that Moniah had seized the Colomeran facility matters grew more uncertain and so, reflecting upon this history, Ammanmus entered the expanse of Surrant-Wonder. He walked up the long nave, eyes fixed to a golden altar wall where forty spheres glowed in fabulous carven detail around a central starburst representing the ultimate manifestation of the unifying godhead, Diasentue. A statue of the incarnation of the Voice Entity, Necontis, represented in the form of an Auran, towered thirty feet before him, its arms raised with one palm out-turned, in which a single orb of light pulsed down the length of the nave.

"Alaysi told me you would be here, where are your thoughts my darling one?" Iskanye said as she stepped up to the altar dais. Ammanmus shook off his thoughts and turned to face his beloved. Iskanye wore her long blue veil, accenting the soft silver tresses of her hair. Her brown-blue eyes danced with gold pupils and her full lips parted in a smile as her brow creased with concern. Ammanmus cupped her heart-shaped face in his hands.

"We should be at the palace for the avowal of Kaylon," Iskanye added while she adjusted a fold of Ammanmus' robe but Ammanmus pursed his lips and turned again to face the altar wall which darkened into a deep luster as clouds from the gathering storm outside diminished the light pouring in through clerestory windows high overhead.

"The Talsaiyr dynasty grows like a sponge in a basin, absorbing mantles. This is not what I intended," Ammanmus said, moving closer to the altar wall to light incense. Iskanye hesitated then followed him.

"You are an architect of this reality. Why are you opposed to Arhahnis inviting great minds to become Talsaiyr. We did." She added, "It would be a different matter if there was coercion." Ammanmus gazed up at the forty orbs then leaned forward to kiss the feet of the statue of Necontis.

"Iskanye, there is, for who refuses to become Talsaiyr? Arhahnis has not communed with the entity in some years and I fear his obsession to consolidate power in our house will anger the councils and sow distrust."

"Is this why you humiliate us by refusing to attend the avowal of our new brother?"

Ammanmus locked eyes with his consort. Iskanye had proven to be a personality as powerful as his own and her love for Moniah was a further concern. Ammanmus loved her deeply and he knew her devotion to him was true but…

"If you feel embarrassed—attend."

Iskanye bent forward over the brazier to light incense. Ammanmus looked at her, remembering the first time he had seen her near the base of the Mountain. How he had scrambled toward her Birthfire orb entreating it with his arms, begging to be rejoined with the spirit within that all his heart yearned for from a memory of life in heaven he could no longer recall. She floated down from the petals of her Birthfire orb and held him close, then crouched to touch his feet, which were dripping blue-silver blood from the stones and sand. With a single warm touch, she had healed him.

Now, alone in the vast temple, he saw his high priestess in a new light for it was clear she believed Arhahnis and Moniah were all but infallible in their plans to dominate civilization.

"If you will not attend then nor shall I," Iskanye said touching her fingers to her lips in the sign she was preparing to pray. Ammanmus snapped his robe behind him and strode away. When his footsteps echoed into the far reaches and she heard the distant boom of the bronze doors closing behind him, she stepped back and opened her arms wide, gazing up at the altar wall.

A murmur of thunder resounded from on high and the sound of rain echoed in the silence of the empty temple.

"Great Necontis, voice entity of Diasentue whose manifestations I entreat, hear my cry," she said lowering the veil from her head.

"I call upon the manifestations of Taen, of compassion, understanding, love for all creatures, nurturing, caring, beneficence, knowledge, patience, humility, peace, generosity, kindness, wisdom, healing, nature, order, faith, discipline, diversity and gentleness."

Now she paused and lifted the veil to cover her head again.

"As a priestess and friend of the Wizan and Wizene, I invoke the Mysterium of the mystery of creation, wisdom in character, command over the elements, the gifts of mystery of music, light, magnetism, water, sound, flight, the vision trance, strength in anger, matter, energy, of the seen and invisible, of the heard and silent, communion with the soul and mastery of desire."

She opened a large coffer and removed a single piece of green cloth, which she draped over the feet of the statue. Having invoked the manifestations of Taen and the Mysterium rites, she stepped out of her shoes as a symbol of the tranquil mystic Greenrobes and knelt to touch her face against the cloth.

"I invoke the power of clear sight, of vision and the peace of meditation. Through all these incarnations of the immortal realm I ask each to augment the First Lord, my brother Moniah Talsaiyr and his Wizene, Lirea Talsaiyr. Help them in the tasks and sacrifices that lie ahead."

Her office complete, Iskanye stood and replaced the green cloth in the coffer. She tossed a final handful of incense on the brazier and with bowed head, retreated from the altar without turning her back upon the incantation she had offered.

* * *

Daylight broke through the storm clouds and poured through the tall amber windows of Sumae-Thumaen, filling the throne hall of the floating stones. A golden slab holding a shoulder mantle, hovered on a floatdroid before an enormous white marble throne worked with carved flower blossoms, Ol leaves, graceful Iln-kite birds and filigree. Marble Oscilean heads on the throne arms gazed serenely to either side, as if spellbound by the colorful floating stones shaped as spheres and rectangles, lining the walls.

Alaysi entered with just enough time to ensure all was in readiness before Arhahnis followed. The Arhahn, robed in midnight blue, his shoulders covered in silver embroidery to affect a severe contrast to the ivory hue of the throne, took his seat of power. Anxious to get on with it, Arhahnis waved impatiently to Alaysi who pressed a button on his waist sash and two doors opened at the formal entrance between the floating stones. Moniah, Saeonar, Meliphor, Lirea and Kaylon entered the throne hall and bowed from the waist then confidently strode toward the throne dais.

Moniah turned his attention to Kaylon and Saeonar.

"Without each of you we could not enjoy the successes which have matched our wits with those of the Quattral."

Kaylon and Saeonar bowed their heads in thanks. Moniah lifted the shoulder mantle from the slab. He approached Kaylon.

"Kaylon, your brother Saeonar has refused to become Talsaiyr in order to maintain an objective peace between the Wizan and Taen temples. However, we ask you, as one voice, to divest yourself of your Tajaen name Olashi, and this day become Talsaiyr."

Kaylon looked to Saeonar. "Brother this honor is welcome to my heart. I shall never renounce the bonds we made when the house of Olashi was born."

Saeonar clasped arms with Kaylon, "A new destiny awaits you brother, go forth into the royal house with my blessing and my humble pride."

Now Kaylon removed a small shoulder mantle, handing it to Saeonar. Arhahnis rose to his feet, as he descended the dais toward the others, Kaylon sank to bent knee. Moniah lifted the mantle from the float droid and handed it to Arhahnis.

"Kaylon, welcome and now become, Talsaiyr." Arhahnis set the brass and polished stone mantle onto Kaylon's shoulders.

Moniah, Saeonar, Meliphor and Lirea chanted the greeting softly, "Haolae, Haolae."

Kaylon stood to face the blue purple eyes and golden pupils of Arhahnis who touched certain carved images on Kaylon's new mantle.

"Here we inscribed your sign as a master of the Ecobiosynthesis guild and here as master of the void fleet guild. On this shoulder you wear the triple orbs of House Talsaiyr and finally at request of the First Lord, is the symbol of Seal Bearer to the First Lord, Moniah."

Arhahnis stepped back. He took Kaylon by the arms and, in a rare demonstration of affection, kissed Kaylon on both cheeks whispering,

"Haolae, brother."

Arhahnis returned to his throne. Meliphor, Lirea, Moniah, Saeonar and Alaysi set their hands on Kaylon's mantle offering a private greeting.

"Such a handsome and brilliant brother in our midst brightens our lives."

"As Seal Bearer to my beloved I am now at ease for his safety, welcome."

"*My* right arm."

"I remain your brother in spirit, always."

"There are rooms awaiting you brother, come within."

And so it was done, the royal house could now announce yet another family member, a member whose power and abilities had passed the test of time and were well known. No one mentioned the absence of Ammanmus or Iskanye. Arhahnis abbreviated the ceremony to draw attention away from this awkward fact.

Even Moniah, who shared Ammanmus' political worries concerning a dynasty rife with nepotism, was caught up in the moment of heady triumph. In two day's time he had led the Wizan coup at the Colomeran and now, at last, the avowal of a powerful and trusted allay into the inner circle was a reality. For the avowal of Kaylon as Talsaiyr was something Moniah had wanted to occur for centuries.

"Tomorrow, Moniah and I shall journey to the mountain place," said Arhahnis.

It was time for the Arhahn's annual pilgrimage to the sacred mountain so the announcement was not a surprise. In fact, Moniah had fretted over security concerns so close on the heels of the coup but Arhahnis had the look in his eyes and that strange quality of light about him, which always foretold his impending connection to the Gods.

"We will accompany you," Meliphor interjected but Arhahnis wagged a finger.

"No. Kaylon, remain here with Meliphor and Lirea. In our absence, you will command the palace safety." Kaylon bowed as Meliphor and Lirea exchanged worried glances.

"Talsaiyr by less than the stroke of the clock and already Kaylon is put to task," Alaysi said.

While the others surrounded Kaylon, leading him to a reception chamber, Moniah lagged behind. Exultant feelings were eroding to a sense of a nameless, creeping paranoia threatening to crowd out his brief triumph. The floating stones settled to the floor, their low thrumming sound fading to silence as Arhahnis left the throne hall. Without the presence of the Arhahn, the stones' energy became dormant and it was this vacuum Moniah felt welling within him as well.

Lirea turned at the doors to look at Moniah but then proceeded to join the others.

In five thousand years, Arhahnis had communicated with the Voice Entity Necontis several times but recently his sacred encounters had become more infrequent. Most troubling of all, it seemed to Moniah this removal from the immortal powers coincided exactly with Arhahnis' sense of infallible direction.

Moniah shook himself from his thoughts at the touch of Lirea.

"It is a beautiful thing my love but you are no stranger to its charms," she said, a bemused smile at play on her lips.

Moniah chuckled despite his pensive mood. He had been staring at the throne, more concerned with its master than riveted by its inherent artistic masterwork.

"Have I lost *more* time," he said cocking one eyebrow.

"Only a few moments. Listen, Saeonar and the Musemaun are making beautiful music and Arhahnis is even laughing. I have not seen him so relaxed in a great while."

Lirea took Moniah's arm.

"Come and enjoy, what troubles you today of all days. You have longed to bring Kaylon to our house."

"Arhahnis has my thoughts," Moniah whispered. Lirea pursed her lips and pecked Moniah's cheek.

"But even he is at ease today."

"Yes, I know. My concern is for his greater self, Lirea. When he calls to the outer realm, rivers run, thunder claps and souls quake."

On the Mountain of Beginnings

A warm wind blew across the open upper deck of the royal air barge. Arhahnis paced the foredeck, arms folded behind him, while Moniah scanned the Wizan escort ahead of them with binoculars. The sky undulated in a sea of brown, blue, red and green wing beats. Saeonar, flying Moniah's Oscilean, Prestant, flew as the vanguard of the Wizan formation. He waved at Moniah who returned the gesture with a broad salute.

Ahead lay the sacred mountain, dominating the forward view, its glass eye soaring into clouds and refracting brilliant almost painful daylight so that Moniah covered his brow with one hand against the glare. Arhahnis pointed to a large gathering of Aurans far below in blue Taen robes, walking toward a fertile area of rolling hills at the southern base of the mountain.

"There is our errant Ammanmus," Arhahnis called out over the steady wind. Moniah folded his arms across his chest, repressing his dissatisfaction that Arhahnis allowed such a disproportionate number of priests to attend the pilgrimage in which all were welcome. With lines of loyalty being drawn between the culture at large, the Quattral and the Governing council, it seemed a poor decision to transform the event into a function of the state religion.

The barge banked to the right and retracted its solar molecular wings to descend onto a rolling moor of verdant grass and wild flowers.

Arhahnis disembarked to be met by Ammanmus, while Saeonar watched the Wizans set up a perimeter, Moniah scanned the crowds. There were a few Greenrobes intermingling with the crush of priests but between the mob surrounding Arhahnis with applause and the Oscileans braying for food there was too much confusion to see if Medean was among the mystics. Moniah slapped his hands absently on the barge's guardrail and strode down the gangway, frowning because Medean was absent in the sea of robes.

Arhahnis raised his hands to grasp a hand here and there, or wave to someone else outside the moving hubbub. While Moniah stood back to allow the Arhahn his praise songs, he synthesized the government in a thought, Arhahnis and Annevnos perceived with all their senses, frequencies and precisions of molecular and electro-magnetic energies denied to other Aurocearians. This was why the Taen temple and Quattral guild were created, as virtually polar opposites. Arhahnis seized the minds and hearts of Aurocearia, dominating overall cultural purpose while Annevnos soared to control the high ground of vast technocratic power.

The two beings both created and stood outside of history, opposites in intent for the future of Auros. There was no denying Arhahnis as the father of Aurocearia but what was Annevnos? The song of an Iln-kite bird interrupted Moniah's musing.

The long graceful bird flew over the mob.

"My Lord!" Saeonar called out over the crowds and Moniah caught sight of the Wizan nudging his way through the press while, near the forest edge, Oscileans were at last free to nibble the rich grasses and take drink from mountain-fed springs. Saeonar removed his flight gloves and strode toward Moniah. He surveyed the gathering Taen priests.

"This is a different matter for security than expected. Too many damn strangers," Saeonar said.

Moniah patted Saeonar on the shoulder.

"We're among friends." Saeonar chewed his lower lip, chapped from wind.

"Did *you* expect this gathering?" Moniah raised his hands slightly then dropped them to his sides.

"Can we be certain they are all friends?"

Moniah simply shook his head and touched a finger to his lips. Arhahnis and the High Priest Ammanmus, made their way to a small altar under a Melot tree.

"There will be no sleep for our camp tonight," Moniah instructed.

Overhead, the planet Simatos and the water moon Ves eclipsed the more distant planets of Ceria and Anceria.

A cooler breeze stiffened the air and the Triune star near Auros Prime began to set over the far-away Wizan regions where purple, rain-laden clouds billowed upward while twilight approached from the realms blocked from view by the mountain.

Arhahnis lifted his hands and looked up into the unseen heights of the mountain. Ammanmus dribbled incense into a brazier and waited for Arhahnis to end his prayer. Nearby, a small multitude made camps of tents.

Free of his brief office, Arhahnis lit an Ol pipe, accepting a cup of hot Soffa from a Wizan who bowed and withdrew to a more discreet distance. Moniah signaled he would approach the presence but Arhahnis held up his hand and Moniah halted himself and Saeonar, who smiled perfunctorily at passers by.

"I revealed the intent of your journey to other priests. It seemed we should be with you," Ammanmus said, lighting his own Ol pipe.

"I see," Arhahnis said wistfully, his gaze fixed to the evening sky where five planetscapes pulled the eye to vanishing distances of vivid crescents and glowing orbs.

"The task of assembly kept you from the avowal of Kaylon?"

Ammanmus lowered his face then lifted his chin.

"I regret that decision."

Arhahnis tapped his Ol pipe against his palm.

"Let it be a lesson, brother, for in the enormity of the sphere shell, within the millions of square miles of facilities around the portal there are but a handful of Moniah and Kaylon's void guilders serving in such desolate surroundings. Otherwise, that vast resource is populated by Quattral and machines," Arhahnis said, watching Moniah bundle his cloak about him.

Ammanmus waited a beat until Arhahnis turned to him,

"Infinite, the machines are set to task, they have no loyalty and the Quattral have the same limitations of population as do we. *There* is the balance."

Inviting lights blazed from the windows of the royal shuttle.

"Come to the barge to dine," Arhahnis said, squeezing Ammanmus by the shoulder.

"I will be pleased to see Moniah and Saeonar," Ammanmus agreed.

* * *

Some distance away but sufficiently within the confines of the tents not to arouse suspicion, an Auran wearing the mantle of a historian, settled into his tent nestled under the wide branches of an ancient Melot tree. He closed a flap, entrapping a Thronspinner drawn by the light and sneered at the ridiculous, primitive surroundings.

Still, he had to admit to an emphatic feeling of respect for Arhahnis, for the Talsaiyr emperor was adept in reminding everyone of his origins through these nostalgic pilgrimages.

The confused Thronspinner bumbled against the Auran who swatted it against the tent fabric. He then retrieved a small pulsing red bead from his robes and swallowed the device, counting quietly with mute lips while consulting a chronometer, waiting for the signal to take effect.

Within his mind, the Auran spy heard the voice of Annevnos calling his name. Initially the voice seemed to come from a distance,

"Cieyos, Cieyos, do you receive me?" Annevnos asked within his mind.

"I do my lord," Cieyos thought spoke.

"Report."

"I am within the camp near the mountain. The convergence has been referred to as the Canticle of Arhahnis."

"How cryptic."

"I concur, empty poetry."

"Do you sense the purpose?"

"Not as yet. As anticipated, the Wizan surround Arhahnis. However, the Taen Ammanmus is here as well." Silence. Outside the tent, Cieyos heard muted conversations and the occasional moan or grumble of an Oscilean.

"Arhahnis indulges his time in empty fancies. The canticle of Arhahnis indeed, what nonsense." Cieyos pressed fingers to his temples in reaction to the anger directed into his mind.

"Yes, my lord," His own mind responded begging for release.

"Remain and observe," Annevnos said at last and then the sensation of invasion faded and Cieyos carefully settled down to sleep. His hands were clammy and his brow covered in sweat. He paused at the sound of a low rumble and saw the outline of an Oscilean in the moonlight just outside his tent. The beast snorted then moved on.

* * *

In the purpling of predawn Arhahnis, Moniah and Saeonar quietly took leave of the royal barge. While dew still covered the grass, they joined Ammanmus at the base of the mountain. Moniah's spirits lifted for there too was Medean under a Spallow vine, warming his hands over an incense brazier. The Aurans proceeded up a path shrouded in heavy mist, Thronspinners flitting about them.

"Listen to the Throns sing," Saeonar said to which Ammanmus nodded in the direction of Arhahnis.

"Haolae, Medean," Moniah enthused clasping arms with the mystic who bowed to Arhahnis.

"We are pleased to see you Medean," The Arhahn said but then cast his eyes to the mountain path and meandered to a private remove from the others.

"Did you hear the Auries song last night?" Medean asked Moniah.

Ammanmus signaled Saeonar who excused himself to council with the priest while Arhahnis remained silent and remote.

"I was fast asleep when the prayer songs were offered," Moniah replied. Arhahnis lifted his arms and stretched then nodded to Ammanmus.

"I am with you," Medean said to Moniah and then joined

Ammanmus and Saeonar who posted themselves as guards from a vantage affording them a view of the greater area of the sleeping multitudes. Without speaking Arhahnis and Moniah continued up the mountain path, following its curving ascent beyond the mists into a crystalline morning light.

Before mid-day they reached a stone bridge leading across a howling abyss even Moniah avoided peering into. Another turn led them to the next ascent trail that wound its way past veins of jagged marble and still higher past wind hewn volcanic rock. The arduous process left little energy for conversation and the brothers proceeded in silence, stopping only once to eat sparingly of Kor fruit, bread and energy rich fire pearls.

By late afternoon, beyond aching legs and challenged hearts, the color of the sky became a dark blue and the wind gusted cold with scents of fresh water and the pungent aroma of plants not found below.

High above, the ultimate summit of the mountain was lost to fast moving clouds in a deep blue heaven. Their destination emerged around a long bend where a lesser summit afforded a stunning view of the capital, Rentu-Treaur.

A small, oxidized torch set in a brass base blazed forth, marking the place where the first Aurocearians had come to life. Even if he had still the breath to speak, Moniah's heart was now to deep in memory to try. Exhausted, his emotions laid bare by the mountain, he could only gape between chilled breaths as his eyes set upon familiar patches of rocks and dirt burned into colors of mineral rich veins and hardened sand, fused to glass.

Moniah paused to stare at the place of Arhahnis. His chest heaved and he drank deeply from a water vessel, wiping sweat from his eyes. He poured water over his sweat-laden head and gasped as the frigid water ran over his flesh. Arhahnis moved toward a large area of amethyst, minerals and scorched rock.

"There I came to breath. See, it is unchanged. As familiar to me as a dream of the night before and yet as distant."

Moniah could only nod agreement he studied Arhahnis but could not fathom his mood. In the past, Arhahnis never allowed anyone to follow him this far.

Arhahnis walked closer to a jagged peak where far below the palace acropolis caught waning daylight, glittering from its spires.

Moniah removed himself to the place where the path met the lesser summit where he settled with a groan on a flat rock near the torch. The torch flame danced in windy gusts beating out pulses of slim heat and the First Lord unrolled his cloak tucking it around his shoulders. His eyes fixed on Arhahnis who knelt in the dirt in a flurry of gusting robes and fiery mane.

As Arhahnis prayed, Moniah felt his mind slip into regret. He feared for Aurocearia as it plunged toward a future controlled by technology. The governing codes, so meticulously worked out in order to maintain discipline and honor so that priests, engineers and artists could peaceably coexist was now coming undone. Little by little, every day, and it sickened his heart.

Arhahnis stood but faltered, He turned about as if blind.

Moniah leapt to his feet, his attention riveted to Arhahnis who was obviously disoriented in trance but something told Moniah to remain at distance, as if in response to his concern Arhahnis thrust one hand out to his side and back, in signal that Moniah should not approach him.

A strange wind of constant pressure overtook the summit. Moniah shoved his hands near the torch to warm them and stepped away from its glare for the sky grew very dark even richer than the normally deep blue and clouds were sweeping across the summit making it difficult to keep Arhahnis in his field of view.

A musical sound was in the wind gaining intensity in progressive chromatic chords that reverberated from the surrounding rock and the air was so cold Moniah could see his breath. A comet of spinning light of white and gold descended from on high. The comet stopped abruptly to hover over the summit. It seemed to spin rapidly and music more beautiful than Moniah had ever heard filled the day that had become as night.

The comet issued a beam of snow-laden light and plasma that bathed Arhahnis who sank to his knees. As he watched spellbound, Moniah saw a brilliant orb of gold coalesce from the comet. Moniah stood frozen in place, mouth agape as the orb sank lower to hover directly over Arhahnis.

Smaller orbs of blue and gold plasma radiated like satellites from the larger body. Twilight was lost and darkness grew with each passing moment. The comet was now the only source of light, reducing the torch to pallor by its presence. Arhahnis looked up at the comet and Moniah could tell by his stance the emperor was calm and had regained his sense of place.

In an instant, a face of silvery incandescent light formed in the center of the gold orb, which like a pulsar, reverberated sonic energy in a steady rhythm. The manifestation appeared so quickly Moniah back stepped, stumbling against a boulder. The First Lord regained his footing to stare awestruck at the face of an Auran whose expression of terrible wisdom pulsed within waves of silver vapor.

The face hovered closer to Arhahnis who shielded his eyes from the glare.

"Necontis," Arhahnis said, his voice crackling.

"Again you heed my entreaty, Arhahnis," The voice emanating from the Necontis entity flooded Arhahnis and Moniah with kinetic energy. Overcome, Moniah felt his cheeks run with tears, his lips trembled as the musical voice infused him with the power of unbridled love.

"The weight of intrigue between Aurans brings your heart to sadness Arhahnis," Necontis boomed.

"Our worlds are changed voice entity, I fear for the future," Arhahnis cried, instinctively standing to move toward the warmth of the voice and light.

"Aurans and Auries labor in love but you do not increase as the creatures you dreamt to life. What portends for mortal time," Necontis said, gazing at Arhahnis with what appeared to be an expression of compassion, its eyes, pools of radiant color.

Arhahnis spread out his hands. Moniah subdued a sob of conflicting emotions watching his brother commune with the immortal entity, full of pride and love for Arhahnis' bravery while his own heart remained fearful of what Necontis would yet impart.

The voice entity energy surrounded Arhahnis.

"Hear me, Arhahnis. The godhead bestows Aurocearians mortal life unbounded by time. Diasentue will not suffer a seed to grow that fails to nurture. You are bound by peace to pursue knowledge for the purpose of sustaining other life forms that it has pleased Diasentue to create."

Moniah leaned forward his every facet of being, like Arhahnis, intent upon the words of the voice entity and the musical ecstasy it generated. The entity flashed a brilliant series of outwardly radiating light rays that suffused the atmosphere.

The entity Necontis continued,

"Search the stars for a successor to knowledge Diasentue has blessed you to possess and convey all that is Auros, to the peoples of the void."

Moniah felt the words as much as his ears heard them. Arhahnis lifted his face daring to confront the glowing image of Necontis.

"Guide me," he begged and the music of the comet vortex, irresistible in its beauty, transformed into a gentler chorus. It was the sound of patience and longing.

"Those you chose as successors shall be as one with you. For Auran and Aurie, male and female, only what future you create foretells the destiny of Aurocearia. I give you a prophecy Arhahnis, hear me, when in the future the gods summon Aurocearia, the power that will transform Auros will be unseen, inevitable and inexorable."

Despite the overwhelming supernatural event, Moniah suddenly thought of the Orb Necontis had given Arhahnis during the garden time and which was now hidden at great effort on the outer moon, Icrass. He yearned to question the entity for he was certain the Orb was a key to coming events but his voice had turned to dry parchment, and merely quaked in his mouth. While the question trembled on his lips, the face in the vortex dispersed into random light waves as suddenly as it had appeared in a thunderclap and comet was gone as if it had never been present.

Arhahnis toppled slowly forward to lay face down in the dirt. Moniah stumbled to his feet, only then aware he had been on his knees. He raced to Arhahnis, helping him to sit upright.

* * *

When Cieyos discovered Arhahnis and Moniah were gone, he joined the other pilgrims of the tent camp, trudging to the base of the mountain path to find the priest Ammanmus, the Wizan lackey Saeonar and Medean in resolute posture, and their stern expressions enough to discourage the curious.

For the rest of the day Cieyos milled about the camp, careful to pretend he was preoccupied with meditation. When conversation was unavoidable, Cieyos was careful to keep his responses obtuse. Inwardly, he was a mess of emotions. Fear, fear of the wrath of Annevnos was the true preoccupation of his mind.

When night fell and the pilgrims began to chant, Cieyos resigned himself to sit on a patch of moss. Then he saw the pulsing light, following the astonished cries of the pilgrims who gazed as one at the lower summit.

A long deadened sense of a time and place he had denied for thousands of years called out to Cieyos and for a moment he yearned to join in the chants and songs that welled up from the pilgrims. But the yearning passed leaving the sole desire to prove himself to Annevnos, whom he believed could cure the ache of his mortal heart.

* * *

At the palace, Lirea hurried into the chamber of Meliphor who wept in the arms of Alaysi. The chamberlain was at a loss to console the empress and Lirea swept Meliphor into her embrace. Alaysi stood up and fumbled over a server floatdroid.

"You have heard the voice," Meliphor croaked through tears. Lirea looked to Alaysi who was trying to pour tea though his nervous hands put more on the floor than in her cup.

"I heard only a music and a cold wind awakened me," said Lirea taking the cup to steady it to Meliphor's lips. From somewhere outside, Oscileans cried a lament and there followed a determined knock at the doors. Alaysi hurried to open them to find Kaylon with three Wizans in tow.

"What goes on here lord, I mean, brother," Kaylon demanded leaning his face around to peer into the imperial chamber.

"The empress has called for Lirea but what happens outside I do not know."

Kaylon flexed his jaw and turned to the Wizans.

"Endeavor to silence those caterwauling beasts if you please." The Wizans withdrew and Kaylon tugged Alaysi into the darkened hall. Through the distance, one could hear songs and laments as though unseen forces awakened creatures normally dormant in the gloom.

"The city is alive. I am told the priestess Iskanye is making her office at the temple. Did you see the mountain?" Kaylon said bobbing his head in the direction of the terrace gardens and the mountain beyond.

"I have never known the like Kaylon, never," Alaysi whispered.

Kaylon glanced in the direction of the gardens.

"If you need me…" He said. Alaysi patted his arm and Kaylon took his leave. Alaysi watched the tall golden haired Auran stride away making orders plain as he retreated into the palace.

"Pride has come to our halls and never was its face so strong, its step so sure, its heart more beautiful," Alaysi said.

The Song in Winds

"For the animal shall not be measured by man. In a world older and more complete than ours, they move finished and complete, gifted with extensions of the senses we have lost or never attained, living by voices we shall never hear. They are not brethren, they are not underlings; they are other nations, caught with ourselves in the net of life and time, fellow prisoners of the splendor and travail of the earth."

-Henry Beston, *The Outermost House*, 1928

Prestant soared over the Aurocearian megalopolis of Rentu-Treaur, uplifting his wings, braking his descent speed, making a loud snapping sound like a sail unfurled in a strong wind. Five hundred feet below him, Montre roared a musical phrase guiding Prestant down the wind and through clouds, toward the high peak of the Council Hall.

Prestant angled his long neck downward and caught sight of Montre, perched atop the nave roofline of the Council Hall. With a thump, his huge claws digging into marble, Prestant landed next to Montre and licked her face. The creatures gazed across the nocturnal cityscape and saw other Oscileans gathered on rooftops. Montre snorted and looked up to stare at the water moon Ves, revolving one hemisphere of its surface into twilight, displaying subtleties of shadow and light in green and blue oceans teaming with life.

"Saeonar sings…in new songs…out in the void black," Montre sang to Prestant who angled his huge head back, snorting in a lungful of cool air.

"Moniah was in the metal beast…with Saeonar. Great power…making the air…turned as in the past days…of garden time…when first metals forged," Prestant sang.

"Augmented and Harmonic sing of storm winds," Montre sang, flexing her wings. Prestant shivered, dislodging a small piece of stone, which Montre seized before it tumbled from the building. The Oscilean crushed the stone to powder in her fore claw.

"At sunsweep I sing with Major, Diminished, Minor, Perfect and Tonic—of hatchlings," Prestant grumbled. Montre folded back her wings, blinking, as a light flurry of snow tickled her long eyelashes, "By sundark you and I will sing of today to Octave and Wholestep."

* * *

Designed for speed and stealth, the Dartship broke free of the relentless gravity of Auros Prime in the middle of the darkest night cycle. The Silvery black ship reflected scans without showing any evidence of its own existence and moved so quickly as to seem a quivering wave to the naked eye. The ship increased its velocity to supra-drive for a tenth-of-a-second burn, passing through the vast Sphereworlds portal as a blur of darkened light.

An automatic station tracer scan located in one of the portal's sentry posts sought out the ship but by the time it locked onto the Dartship's slippery exterior, it had passed into the outer void.

Moniah patted Saeonar's shoulder.

"Well done, but did we break a sound barrier leaving Auros?" Saeonar made a final trajectory adjustment on the green glowing controls, unstrapping himself from the pilot seat and sighed.

"Unavoidable, I'm afraid."

"We ask for everything and are fortunate to receive some measure of our need," Moniah chuckled. They moved back to the main cabin where cloaks, rations and two weapons were secured to the soft seats, despite the ship's inertial dampeners.

Saeonar lifted two molecular pistols from a strong box. What were obviously now weapons had been adapted from construction laser repair guns by Kaylon. Saeonar and Moniah locked eyes in the dread of reality, knowing instinctively they were poised upon action and consequence.

"Our landing coordinate fixes us directly outside the fortress entrance." Moniah listened intently, watching Saeonar check the safety and activation sequencers of the guns. He lifted one of the weapons, turning it over in his hands to gauge its weight and balance.

"I have good news," Moniah said, unscrewing the lid from a thermos. Saeonar peered at the flight bridge to check the autopilot and view. All was well. On one side, he saw the glowing pink of the Suum Nebula and on the other, the massive silver black curve of the outer sphere shell. The Dartship was now flying between two realities, the Sphereshell and space.

"I have ears for good news. This mission gives one pause," said Saeonar, as he checked two oxygen masks.

"Grand Ambassador Danis succeeded," Moniah said. He added, "The Obervatore fleet controls the Awclotan Council—with the help of

Tius, of course—and we are now very much alone in the void." Saeonar rubbed his hands together,

"Danis Resto! There's an Auran who should be adopted into house Talsaiyr. The Observatore fleet will put back-bone in our rear flank." Moniah sipped from his thermos as he mulled over Saeonar's observations. It was true, the powerful Auran lord Danis and his equally formidable allay Tius, were perfect candidates to round out the power core Arhahnis was making of the royal family.

Moniah stretched his legs, "Arhahnis is quick to act when certain of his purpose. We could return and find Danis and Tius are already become Talsaiyr." Saeonar threw up his hands,

"Ammanmus will scream for mercy. As you longed for Kaylon to become a royal, Arhahnis has coveted Tius."

"Very true. Why didn't you become Talsaiyr, Saeonar? Tell me the fullness of your reasoning."

Saeonar blushed. He was forever shy of demonstrative behavior.

"In my garden is a tree the priests assure me is easily three thousand years old. Kaylon is that tree and he will never bend or waver from his determination to serve house Talsaiyr. I am a reed. I must bend with the Wizan wind. I am loyal to you, Moniah, but know this…for my path *I* must choose what steps to take."

Moniah set his thermos down and stared past Saeonar out of a side portal to watch the seemingly unending curvature of the Sphereshell race by.

"At least for the present the Quattral cannot fly without our knowing it," he said, voicing an errant thought and Saeonar nodded, clearing his throat while reaching for a decanter, obviously relieved they were switching gears to focus on the immediate challenge. Saeonar glanced at the flight board. Moniah met his eyes and knew that Saeonar was considering asking Moniah what had occurred on the mountain with Arhahnis but Moniah's preoccupied expression and the delicacy of their covert mission quelled his instinct.

"Icrass," Moniah said with lamentation in his voice that caused Saeonar to shudder. Long before completion of the Sphere shell, Arhahnis had used Constructorbots and Saen plasma to move Icrass outside of the Sphereworlds and there it remained, orbiting the outer Sphere.

Everything about Icrass infuriated Moniah, from the immense energy required to maintain the moon with its airtight fortress temple in a protected orbit outside the Sphere shell, to say nothing of the efforts needed to maintain Icrass' energy deflectors, lest it be reduced to ash during outer Sphere shell ignitions.

"The damned moon is a curse and an invitation," Moniah hissed but Saeonar had moved to the pilot seats in the front of the craft and didn't hear his comment.

Arhahnis had allowed it to be known that he was authorizing an inspection of Icrass for scientific experimentation but Moniah knew Annevnos was well aware that Arhahnis lavished attention on the moon for hidden reasons. The damn Orb! If the orb did not exist, there would be no Icrass.

"Velocity, four thousand clicks per second. The ship is a marvel, Moniah."

Moniah joined Saeonar in the small pilot's cabin to enjoy the view out the forward window where he watched the impossible arc of the Sphere shell roll toward a dirty speck, Icrass.

"Excellent work, Saeonar."

"Thanks to Kaylon. He plotted the moon's trajectory. After that it was a simple enough matter to synchronize our departure with the orbit of Icrass as it nears its perigee by the portal."

"If we are betrayed and the sphere ignites before we reach Icrass—our concern in these matters will be in the hands of the gods," Moniah said, to which Saeonar grunted his assent.

Once in orbit, the Dartship soared into a valley of ugly gray crags while moving toward a single massive Blermetal doorway built into the side of a mountain range.

"Land us by the door, the Taen will tractor us in. No need to trudge about in these…" Moniah decided, casting a space suit aside. Outside the craft, moon dust rose up as the Dartship settled to a landing. Moniah keyed in a sequence on the control panel and almost immediately, the huge Blermetal doors opened. A warmth and hum surrounded the Dartship while it was pulled inside the doors.

"Like being consumed," Saeonar whispered.

Inside the mountain, Blermetal doors closed with a rumble, sealing the ship within. A rush of air filled the cavern from rusted, louvered vents overhead and another set of heavy oxidized doors with a six-foot span opened before them. Moniah and Saeonar squinted through gray dust to confirm the presence of two Auran priests.

"Pressure and atmosphere nominal," Saeonar confirmed, before opening the ship airlock. A peculiar frozen, acrid smell invaded the main cabin. Moniah and Saeonar strapped the molecular pistols to their robe sashes, and prepared to step outside the ship. Saeonar paused to sheath his Coracle-diant before donning an outer robe. Moniah frowned at him but nodded. They emerged into the dirt and sand laden no man's land of the airlock. The oxidized doors screamed in torment and then quieted as they swung back to reveal a misty chamber, from which Taen priests approached them and bowed.

"Haolae, lord Moniah, Wizan Saeonar. Please enter," the first priest said, standing aside to invite them within. He had to jump aside when they bounded past him to escape the pressure doors closing behind them with a grinding, followed by an echoing thud.

Moniah scanned his surroundings. For the most part the fortress temple interior resembled most Taen structures, except, of course, for the dirt. The fortress showed every moment of its ancient age. Unlike buildings on Auros Prime, the Icrass fortress was anything but pristine. Its marble floors were soiled and cracked, once finely carved stone walls held pockets of mould and murals whose brilliant color on the barrel-vaulted ceiling were faded and dank. It was clear the hostile environment exacted a terrible price on the structure.

The senior Taen took the liberty of clasping Moniah by the forearm, at which Saeonar frowned and grunted.

"I' am Provost Taen and this is my adjutant," the priest explained, confused by Saeonar's obvious displeasure with such familiarity. The priests were so accustomed to the code of secrecy they did not offer their names.

"I present Wizan Saeonar Olashi," Moniah said guardedly and the priests bowed slightly to Saeonar. A figure strode toward them in the dimly lit chamber.

"Litos!" Saeonar called out as the figure came closer. Moniah was relieved to recognize their fellow Wizan but taken aback by the drawn and sultry appearance of the Auran who made no secret of his being pleased to see his cohorts. Moniah noticed a cloud of apprehension flash in the expression of the Provost Taen. Was he disturbed by the presence of Litos?

"Wisdom, my lord Moniah, I understood you were to arrive tomorrow but I learned differently," Litos said, eyes flashing at the Provost Taen. Moniah contained his impatience, his senses acute and enervated by the very fact of being within the Icrass fortress. Moniah turned to the Provost's aide,

"Why would my friend be misinformed? He is in the service of myself and the Arhahn." The Taen aide reacted strangely at the mention of Arhahnis' name, kissing the fingertips of his right hand and tapping his chest.

"The First Lord's mission was not known to me," the aide replied.

"I see you know too little," Moniah said. He added, "Provost?"

The Provost appeared genuinely tired but the withering look Moniah fixed upon him was relentless.

"It is foolhardy for us to transmit detailed information."

"And *you* obfuscate," snapped Moniah, who jerked his head at Saeonar and Litos. The three Wizans stepped away from the priests. "How many Templars are you?" Moniah asked Litos.

"We are still fifty, my lord."

"Lord Moniah, something has transpired in the Orb chamber. The Taen are unwilling to reveal what it was but I fear we must go there at once," Litos leaned very close to Moniah, "they act as if they worship Arhahnis." Moniah glanced at Saeonar who, with his back to the priests, mimed the finger kissing action near his chest.

"Have you been to the Orb chamber?"

"We are not allowed in the upper chambers."

Moniah's eyes blazed. No wonder Arhahnis had chastised him at the Smoke Ponds but Moniah was livid to think that Taen machinations rather than his own efforts were the seed of the Arhahn's anger.

"That will change," Moniah muttered and he wheeled to face the priests. "Wizan Litos will accompany us to the Orb. You will conduct us, Provost, now." Saeonar winked to the other Wizan Templars, the elite soldiers, who watched at a distance. The Provost Taen hesitated.

"The Arhahn has commanded that only Taen have access to the Orb receptacle."

"Now Provost," Moniah thundered and the Provost turned without another word to lead them to a wide circular staircase upon which they carefully climbed on slippery mould to arrive at an upper floor.

"Do you smell that?" Moniah asked of Saeonar.

"It permeated the fortress when the…event took place," said Litos, taking his bearings in the unfamiliar surroundings.

"Ozone," Saeonar chimed in, tapping his nose with his knuckle.

At the top of the stairs, they entered a long hallway lined on either side with small shrines representing the forty manifestations of the Godhead, Diasentue, illuminated by small glow orbs.

There were twenty shrines on each wall with illustrations of the creeds of the Taen and Wizan temples. At the corridor's end they reached an octagonal outer chamber adorned with walls of golden bas-relief panels depicting visitations of Necontis to Arhahnis during the garden time. Against one wall, a shrine held a large golden statue of Necontis.

The Provost touched the feet of the statue and it silently rose straight up revealing another round inner chamber. Moniah stepped inside and stopped short, perplexed to discover statues of the Talsaiyr, including himself—all with hands upheld, their palms turned outward, facing toward a large bronze coffer.

A quavering sound starting as a low hum and oscillating to higher registers emanated from the coffer. Moniah stepped closer to inspect the coffer but Saeonar stayed him, grabbing his sleeve.

"What?"

"I detect very unstable electromagnetic energy. Quite powerful, I tell you I cannot be near it," Saeonar said, backing off.

"The Orb?" Moniah asked, pointing to the coffer.

"Yes, Wisdom." This was new. The Provost used Moniah's Wizan salutation.

"What has happened here?" Saeonar demanded. The Provost led them out of the room where, Moniah noticed the hair on his nape settled to a more relaxed state.

The Provost looked at Moniah, Saeonar and Litos and then heaved a sigh.

"There are Taen brothers who have formed a cult. You must understand this is intended to honor the Arhahn as a sacred entity," he explained, clearly happy to divest himself of the hidden, until now, truth of the situation. Saeonar made a clucking sound and Moniah stared in disgust at the Provost, who reached up and touched the statues feet, which lowered again to conceal the coffer chamber.

"These brothers are known to each other as, Taen Arhahns. One of them opened the coffer and beheld the Orb," Saeonar leaned toward the Provost.

"Taen Arhahns?"

Litos put his hands on his hips.

"I have heard this whispered."

"What in the god's name," Moniah raged. He spun to face the Provost.

"If these misguided priests believe Arhahnis is sacred why did they disobey his will?"

"My lord, see the priest who opened the coffer," the Provost responded wearily.

"He is *alive*?" Saeonar interjected, incredulously.

The Provost merely nodded and led them to a nondescript door and a softly lit room where an Auran lay in a bed. While Moniah, Saeonar and Litos held back, the Provost approached the bed where the Taen Arhahn was asleep. His hands were heavily bandaged and a terrible burn mark scarred his face.

"Atep, the First Lord has come," the Provost said quietly. Moniah stepped gingerly forward.

"Taen Atep, I am Moniah Talsaiyr. Tell me what happened to you." Moniah restrained an impulse to wince when sightless white eyes opened to confront him.

"The future, Wisdom Moniah," Atep croaked. He coughed and added, "What it must be to have the Greenrobe sight…a terrible burden."

Saeonar lifted a glass of water to Atep's lips. He sipped it while holding the glass with trembling fingers.

"The future?" Moniah said gently.

"The Oscileans understand, do they not sing of the storm?" Atep replied reaching up to touch two fingers to Moniah's arm.

"Nothing will prevent the changing, nothing…"

Moniah glanced at Saeonar and Litos, who returned his gaze with apprehension. A soft wavering hum emanated from them. Litos pulled back his outer cloak to see his Coracle-diant pulsing with a muted phosphorescent orange glow.

"Look," he whispered.

Saeonar threw a fold of his cloak over his shoulder and withdrew his Coracle-diant from its holster. The Wizan wand glowed with the same strange light. Atep closed his eyes and trembled. Moniah motioned toward the door and he, Litos and Saeonar stepped out of the room.

Atep's eyes flashed open and he grasped the Provost by the arm.

"You must rest, Atep."

"Tell Lord Moniah, his purpose succ…ssor." With that, Atep drifted off to sleep. The Provost withdrew to the hall to join the others.

Moniah motioned for Litos and Saeonar to cover their Coracle-diants. "Litos, I want you to keep this as quiet as a smoke pond," he said, adding, "if anyone should venture near Sine-Togan, you are to destroy the Orb."

"Understood, Wisdom," Litos muttered.

Overhearing the instruction, the Provost stepped into their midst.

"Wisdom, you are beyond your purview to command this. Sine-Togan is a temple…"

Moniah's eyes silenced the Priest.

"Provost, you are a failure and while you claim to disavow these Taen Arhahns, I am not convinced you are not one of them. You are relieved of command. Litos, you are in command."

The Provost let his gaze drop to the floor.

"Shall I then return with you to Auros Prime?" Moniah looked at Saeonar whose eyes darted to Litos.

"No. Remain here. I will announce to the priests my decision that Wizan Litos commands the fortress. Try to undo some of the damage you have wrought and nurse your fallen priest."

* * *

Alaysi strolled in the gardens of Sumae-Thumaen palace, pacing. Triune daylight waned.

"I am here," a familiar voice said amidst the evening song of Windwhistlers and Alaysi smiled, seeing Medean standing in a thicket of flowers.

"You have done well Alaysi. The Colomeran coup succeeded in large part due to your speedy action with the Wizans. Are you well? There are circles of care under your eyes."

Alaysi pulled back to stare into the green-purple eyes of Medean whose gold pupils throbbed in loving warmth.

"Nights in this palace burn late. Admiral Sey visited me. He promises with Kaylon now a Talsaiyr, the loyalty of the greater fleet rests with Moniah," Alaysi said while leading them to a bench.

"What of the Auries?"

"Meliphor is recovered; she was distraught during the Arhahns pilgrimage. Iskanye and Lirea have gone to the Dome temple to meet with Templars. If they succeed in securing their oath to Moniah…"

"They will turn the councils firmly to Arhahnis. And never was this coalition more needed," Medean said, removing his Ol pipe kit from his robe. He filled the pipe slowly.

"Do you know Moniah is returning from the outer darkness?" Alaysi looked at him blankly then his eyes lit and his lips parted with a sardonic smile. "That speck which should for our hearts desire be made to ash by virtue of the Sphere's fire," he added.

Medean set one hand on the knee of Alaysi.

"You will be happy to know Ves is purged of the insectoids that attacked Moniah and I."

Alaysi leaned forward clasping his hands and refused the Ol pipe Medean offered.

"What did you learn of them?"

"Little I'm sorry to say. Most were destroyed by native species much as our bodies devour invasive bacteria. However, what few pieces we could find were quickly dissolving into smaller particles of nano-machines. Eventually, these pieces evaporated before they could be completely analyzed."

"Only the eco guild—who would never create such things—and the Quattral are capable of this," Alaysi said tapping his clenched fists to his lips, jerking his head toward the sky.

"Why has Moniah gone to Icrass? He hates the place."

Medean leaned back to rest his head against a tree, pulled a draught of smoke from the pipe and struck its ash out.

"Moniah is acting on command of Arhahnis on matters I am not free to divulge. Suffice to say there is concern for the safety of the Orb." Alaysi slapped his knees and stood. He paced and then threw up his hands.

"Destroy the thing." Alaysi said, frowning. Medean came to his feet slowly and waited until some of the fire left Alaysi.

"Arhahnis is loath to destroy that which he does not comprehend. You expect everything of Arhahnis and in this you are not alone. But you must remember Arhahnis is the brother of the Gods just as we are brethren to one another. Would you destroy a powerful gift from me without knowing its purpose?"

Alaysi stepped close to Medean and tilted his head. It was not often he gained a small victory over the titanic mind of the mystic but this time he felt certain he had him dead to rights.

"Then you *will* become Talsaiyr," Alaysi said.

Medean hesitated. He stared at Alaysi with a complex expression of ardor, surprise and mirth.

"When you enter the palace you will find that Danis and Tius have abandoned their Tajaen names to become your avowed brothers. Ah! I note your shock but it is true. The ceremony was conducted in the presence of Lirea and Iskanye *before* they departed for the Dome temple."

Poor Alaysi could only stand in silence while Medean patiently waited for the reality that the Talsaiyr had gained two new family members to sink in. At last, Alaysi shrugged, shocking Medean with his taciturn acceptance.

"I see. Ammanmus will be furious. He'll have another reason to decry Arhahnis for his rash actions but this is a shrewd move and long overdue," Alaysi said, glancing at the palace.

"The primary strength of the Arhahn lies in his ability to make rapid decisions. House Talsaiyr needs the minds of Danis and Tius. You should be relieved, you have help with their presence," Medean explained and Alaysi turned slowly to level a wry smile at his friend.

"Help for me? How novel."

* * *

When the Dartship was safely within the Sphereworlds, Moniah poured Tealos brandy for he and Saeonar with quaking hands. He snorted, shaking off a memory of Icrass.

"What a desolation that place is," Moniah said, tossing his cloak to a seat. Saeonar hesitated before accepting the drink from Moniah. He sipped the brandy and made a final check to ensure the ship was on autopilot, bound for the night side of Auros Prime.

"True spoken, Moniah. Poor Litos."

The Dartship bounced through turbulence and Moniah leaned down to glance out a window but Saeonar merely yawned, removed his Coracle-diant and laid it over his knees.

"Did you see the fear in their eyes? What a tragedy to have our best Wizans resigned to Sine-Togan. At last I understand Ammanmus," Moniah said, rubbing moon silt from his face.

"Litos is a powerful Wizan, Moniah. I fear for anyone who crosses him but tell me, do you think Ammanmus had anything to do with these Taen Arhahns?"

"No. His heart will break when he learns of such an obscene cult."

Saeonar moved his wand to a cushion beside him and reached for the decanter Moniah held while gazing wearily but triumphantly at the forward view. Saeonar sipped from the flask and reached out to hand it to Moniah who took it and swallowed twice, pointing to Saeonar's Wizan wand.

"What happened?" Moniah said.

"Oh, I see what you mean…I believe the Coracle reacted to electromagnetic energy I felt in the Orb chamber. Litos had a rather severe shock of static electricity, confirming my suspicions of the presence of elevated magnetic fields. Moniah…my hair was on end in there and my toes lifted from the floor."

Clearly agitated, Moniah drank more of the brandy.

"Something is in the air; the Oscileans sing of it. They nest high in the mountains as if…they seek escape from proximity to us." The Dartship engines startled them, dropping in pitch. The Shuttle buffeted in turbulence. They were now flying through nocturnal storms. Saeonar leaned forward toward Moniah, his eyes sparkling with hesitant curiosity in the muted light of the passenger cabin.

"Wisdom, since you went up to the mountain holy place, you have been sad and, forgive me—less than patient. Tell me of it."

Saeonar jerked forward and to the left as the ship rattled and bounced severely. Moniah set his hands on the seats next to him to steady himself while Saeonar hurried to the flight deck then lumbered back down the aisle seconds later.

"I can't fly this soup better than Kaylon's autopilot. Forgive me, Wisdom, I intruded." Moniah reached out and steadied Saeonar into his seat as the ship jumped through turbulence in the air.

"You cannot intrude, Saeonar. In the past, Arhahnis has always gone to the holy place alone. I was moved deeply when he insisted I join him. At the summit, by the torch I beheld entity Necontis."

Saeonar shook his head in awe, bit his lower lip, sipped and nervously swallowed more of the wine. Without words and eyes riveted to Moniah, he demanded *and begged* for more.

"I encountered Necontis only one other time, centuries ago, when the sphere plate constructor factory ships were completed," Moniah said, pausing to collect his thoughts.

Clearly, Moniah was having difficulty articulating his feelings and thoughts and, during a pregnant pause, Saeonar moved to the edge of his seat, willing the First Lord on.

"I saw Necontis issue to Arhahnis a message I cannot yet fathom. Most of the song of Necontis was clarity itself, yet much of his energy boomed a music that, although I sensed meaning, I could not fully interpret? Anyway, let me have more of that, please."

"Automatic landing sequence engaged. Location: Sumae-Thumaen," the autopilot interjected and Saeonar frowned waving dismissively with an unconscious gesture in the direction of the flight deck. He handed the decanter to Moniah, who partook of it slowly, wiping his mouth with the back of a trembling hand.

"Please, go on," Saeonar said.

"Afterward, Arhahnis was weak. I helped him to the torch, wrapping him in my cloak. During the descent from the summit, he leaned heavily on me and we never spoke of the encounter but just before we reached you and the others at the camp, he turned to me, advising that I should prepare my heart for the future, as *he* must. Now I understand how he moves through time but I do not forgive him for making me his secret instrument."

A chime sounded from the flight deck, startling Saeonar.

"Augment," he said and the voice of Alaysi rang through the cabin speakers.

"Haolae. You are directed to land at the temple garden due to security issues with the wind. Ah, the wind that wavers from the ash of the void, see it storm and quake. Anyway, welcome back! Arhahnis commands me to inform you that Tius Derat and Danis Resto are now avowed brothers of the Talsaiyr. Despite the late hour, Himself tasks you to make yourselves available to greet our brothers who await you in the Gold hall. Change keeps the heart—" but Moniah punched a button to silence the speaker. He leveled a look of such contempt at Saeonar that the Wizan recoiled.

"This is good news."

"It is not the news or the deed but again, Arhahnis acts for the Tajaen of his own will, always his will. He he pushes us and the councils. Sometimes he is more a stranger to me than the stars in the void."

Saeonar capped the decanter and stood slowly. He made adjustments to the cabin lights and Moniah grasped his arm.

"Thank you for clarity, my friend. As always, you've insisted we settle to the heart of matters."

"I sense Arhahnis' purpose will be revealed to you soon, Moniah. The Arhahn has always been a soul removed from us. He cannot act with consideration for anyone else. His nature forbids it. I advise we trust the seed of our destiny."

Moniah threw his cloak over his arm and stood.

"I will let Ammanmus rage, as he surely will at this new act of nepotism," Moniah said as the Dartship landed.

* * *

Arhahnis strode down the elliptical staircase within the palace of Sumae-Thumaen. He passed the throne hall and nodded to Wizan guards who bowed their heads as he continued under a cupola containing the palace chronometer, itself the size of a small building, comprised of intricate gears and discs detailing the year, month, day and second. A hall of black marble led to a golden door with no handle. As Arhahnis approached, the door sang out a clear tone and slid up revealing a large dimly lit chamber. Inside, Ammanmus, Tius, Medean and Meliphor awaited on a cantilevered platform beneath a large dome that shone with holograph images of stars, constellations and nebulae.

Naturally, Arhahnis made no excuse for his late arrival. Meliphor smiled and took his arm and Arhahnis merely nodded to Ammanmus with whom he had argued late into the previous night. Ammanmus walked to a large control board and made adjustments. Above them, a section of the stellar cartography display zoomed to show an image of a magnified field. Tius joined Ammanmus to make a critical adjustment of focus and while this delay caused Arhahnis to pace, Meliphor approached Medean.

"Thank you for helping last night," she said, taking his hands in hers. Medean offered a slight bow from the head and smiled, noting that Arhahnis stared at a solar system in the magnified display area.

"My pleasure, Aswarie. Moniah will return. His anger is short-lived and I suspect it was due to his distress over the mission to Icrass," Medean said quietly, while Meliphor eyed Arhahnis whose concentration on the stellar display begged her to join him. The Parsec grid zoomed into another calibration and Ammanmus stepped back from the control board as Tius' hands flew over holograms, until a single solar system locked into full view.

Arhahnis motioned to Medean and Meliphor and they joined the others on the raised area from which they could see three-dimensional images of nine planets and sixty moons surrounded by a large asteroid field.

"The candidate planet, Infinite," Tius said, breaking the silence.

"It has but a single star. A golden furnace," Meliphor chuckled, while Arhahnis studied the image of the system as it focused on the third planet of the system. Meliphor linked her fingers with Arhahnis, each of them gazing at a world of white clouds, blue-green seas and ochre brown landmasses. A graphic display at the right side of the image provided detailed breakdowns of the planet's dimensions, chemical, and atmospheric composition. A separate image presented aspects of the candidate planet movements in relative space.

"Planetary rotation, 86164.1 seconds. Orbital duration and velocity around local star, 86400 seconds."

"Beautiful," Medean said, crossing his arms over his chest.

Tius refined the image of the candidate planet to sharpen focus of a series of the planet's quadrants in alternating views.

"The topography varies; it is more akin to Simatos than Auros Prime in this regard. You see here vast forests, two great oceans and deserts interspersed in a majority of temperate regions," said Tius, while Ammanmus stared intently at the image.

"And the native species?" Arhahnis inquired with a subdued concentration. Tius glanced at Medean who nodded and Tius touched another control. The image of a biped appeared. Meliphor gasped and

Arhahnis leaned forward, his hands banging against the control island.

"Gods..." he muttered in astonishment.

"Your children, Infinite," Ammanmus said.

"It is a strange mirror," Arhahnis said. At this Tius chimed in, "I concur, Infinite. With the greatest respect, no defining proof can be made that the Arhahn is responsible for the creation of the beings on the candidate planet."

Ammanmus scowled at Tius.

"No proof. By the gods look, at the native species!"

"I agree," Medean interjected pointing to the screen. He added "see, delicate barometric pressures, a vibrant topography and diverse aquatic signatures—and every biochemical reading an exact match to your molecular structure."

"How far?" Arhahnis snapped.

Tius worked the controls and the planet diminished in view while the hologram withdrew their view out of the system.

"The third planet revolves around its star at thirty clicks per second and the solar system travels through the local galactic parsec at two hundred and fifty clicks per second. I calculate the third planet's distance from the Sphereworlds and Suum Nebula at three hundred spectrum years."

"What does that translate to in terms of duration of void travel?" Arhahnis said. Meliphor rested her head on his shoulder. Not to be stymied, Tius pursued his lips and lifted his face for a moment then looked at Arhahnis.

"At our present capability, about five months, Infinite."

"Only five months, five months..." Arhahnis muttered as he stepped off the control area platform, glancing back at the stellar display, which was still retreating through star systems and voids of empty Space.

"It is vital to consider that our studies show Aurocearian physiology will be changed– if, in fact, we chose this candidate world," Tius said.

"What do you mean, specifically?" asked Meliphor.

"The content of the planetary atmosphere. Our minds will not function precisely as they do on worlds within the Sphere," Medean responded and Arhahnis stared at the hologram image retreating through space where it now arrived at the Nether Suum nebula.

Arhahnis was lost in silence, directing a fathomless gaze upon Ammanmus. Meliphor looked to Arhahnis then Ammanmus. The two Aurans appeared to be on a similar mental wavelength, as though lost in memory, considering some obscure fact.

Medean took pity on her.

"The bipeds of the candidate world although strikingly similar to us—are very primitive," Meliphor's eyes lit up.

"The mountain canticle!" she said. Arhahnis glanced at her and then at Tius, noting his confusion.

"Necontis revealed to me that we shall become as one with the successor," he said and Tius visibly shuddered. A brilliant scientist, he could still recall vivid memories of the nearly-forgotten garden time but the candor of the Arhahn and his revelations unnerved him.

"All of Aurankind?" He asked.

"The explorers shall become as *they* are," Ammanmus said looking at the hologram dome.

"Do we dare impose our destiny on others," Arhahnis muttered to himself.

"We will have to act quickly to secure council affirmation, Infinite," Tius said and Arhahnis turned to Meliphor, his lips parted but, before he could speak, Medean did.

"More importantly, it is time for Wizan cooperation."

"Medean is correct. Moniah must return, regardless of his distractions," Ammanmus said.

"And what of Lirea? Such a fate before her," Meliphor said quietly, her face glowing in the soft blue light of the control consoles but Arhahnis remained motionless under the planetarium avoiding the entreaty of her eyes.

"Tius, prepare to convene grand council. I will speak with Meliphor and Medean now," Arhahnis said. Ammanmus and Tius bowed and took their leave. When the brass door closed behind them, Arhahnis took Meliphor by the hand.

"My love, your candor is too revealing," he said. She sighed and lifted his hand to her lips.

"Forgive me."

Arhahnis turned to Medean who was inspecting his fingernails.

"Truth which we held in such esteem must now be parsed out in careful increments. We must know the ship will be ready," said Arhahnis and Medean's normally beneficent smile faded at the corners of his mouth.

"If I go, the word will spread. I was followed here by the Quattral."

"What about Alaysi?" Meliphor said.

By Will of Annevnos

Core members of the Quattral, led by Cieyos and Seratt, raced toward a remote Constructorbot city operations station in the inner space Sphereshell, two hundred million miles from the Portal. They flew in small lightning quick "speedships" that barely reduced flight speed before gliding over the inner sphere circumference, guided by magnetic tracks. The speedships roared down connecting to tramcar tracks where they blended in with fleets of automated Constructorbots moving at hypersonic speed.

The ship ducked into a conduit leading into the skin of the inner sphere shell and soared toward an intersection of million mile-long service corridors, where mammoth banks of Constructorbots clung to their berths. Here the speedship came to rest. While it was packed into a cubicle by a robot, Seratt took a moment to study his brother in arms. Cieyos had the look of a changeling—his eyes danced with emotions so that he had to look away from Seratt in a futile attempt to conceal his anxiety.

Once inside the relative safety of the station, Seratt approached Cieyos who leaned against a small window studying armies of Constructorbots waiting for deployment in a continuous cycle of maintenance errands throughout the shell's immense inner boundaries.

Gazing at the interconnecting plasma tubes fueling the outer sphere igniters, each hundreds of miles in diameter, created a hypnotic tapestry of inverted cones and sub stations, fooling the eye into a false sense of horizon. The perspective made Seratt shiver as he attempted to discern a horizon in the Sphereworlds inner circumference.

"You have a scent of mountain greens and wind, Cieyos, forget your experience at the mountain. Arhahnis Talsaiyr is a trickster. You've always been the eyes and ears, Cieyos, it is this openness and vulnerability pulling you into the miasma that is Taen and Wizan. I see the hypnosis in your eyes."

"You were not there," Cieyos said without looking at Seratt.

Gradually, the others arrived. There was the hyperactive Mertoos, frantic as always—gazing raptly at the machinery and corridors and the Aurie, Jange, huddled in the folds of a luxurious cloak, wary of being in the world of the machines. Together with Seratt and Cieyos, they waited as patiently as they could for the master, huddled in groups around an inert repairbot, within the gloomy space of the Constructorbots sub station. An enervating place to be, pressure doors holding in a cold but livable atmosphere while beyond the walls the sound of moaning wind lost in endless miles of corridors was punctuated by echoing clangs of machinery or screaming tramcars.

"As you know, I do not trust in the old ways," Annevnos said causing everyone to stare toward a gloomy corner where his outline could barely be seen before the door to the hangar sealed behind him leaving white hair and shining gold eyes in the dark. Nervous laughter softened as Annevnos moved into the light and closer to the group.

A huge crash brought cries of concern from the group as the floor vibrated deafeningly; even Annevnos looked over his shoulder in fear.

Jange covered her ears and stumbled. Cieyos took hold of her. The terrible vibration trailed away, moving through the sphere shell like a wave and Annevnos spread out his hands.

"Machines begetting machines," he said. Some of the others snapped questions to each other.

"Gravity displacement?"

"No. It was a factorybot, probably disengaging detritus."

Cieyos smiled reassuringly at Jange, he saw she was cold and handed her his small glow orb.

"I am confident that planet wide mind speech has all but vanished among the greater population," Annevnos announced, demanding attention.

"With the exception of the Oscilean beasts, lord Prime," Jange said glancing at Cieyos.

Annevnos lifted an eyebrow while setting a small case he carried onto the hulk of the miniature constructorbot, its many laser and tool appendages fully extended as if it had been short-circuited.

"Wizans and Greenrobe mystics communicate telepathically as they have since the garden time," Annevnos said, glaring at Cieyos who glanced nervously around at the others Auran faces among whom he found no allay save for Jange.

"How is this still possible?" The gruff Mertoos exclaimed while he searched the room for eavesdroppers with a hand held scanner.

"It must be an augmentation of Wizan adepts," someone else

postulated, stepping closer into the dim overhead light source. Doctor Onothi leaned onto the ruined machine.

"But we were certain the neurotransmitters enabling mind speech decades ago."

The issue became a debate and Annevnos would have none of it, his voice thundered above the murmurs.

"I have conducted research, having suffered of fools in unrelated events. I am certain the so-called inmade spark and soul of mind is become a thing of the past for the Taen and Wizan, as it has for the greater population. Save for certain aforementioned practitioners whose method we shall soon have no interest to conquer."

The chamber became deathly silent. Annevnos opened the case he had brought and nineteen heads peered at its contents. Seratt and Cieyos were the exception, being already familiar with the mysteries therein. The interior of the case contained a soft tray of pill-sized capsules, each glowing red. Annevnos lifted one to the light.

"Once ingested, this bead will dissolve, releasing micro transmitters programmed to travel through arteries to the brain."

Annevnos began dispensing the beads, one to each.

"The transmitters will interlink each of you to me. We will then communicate—as Seratt and Cieyos already do—via this means."

All eyes shifted to Seratt and Cieyos, and then scrutinized the beads. The Aurans' and Auries' many-faceted pupils glittered and sparked with fascination in the dimly lit area.

"Magnificent. We have been outmaneuvered by Wizans and their use of song speech but these will even that equation," a delighted Doctor Onothi announced, his orange-gold pupils sparkling. Seratt raised a finger to his chin.

"Lord Annevnos, one matter disturbs; once we make greater use of this technology Wizans might be able to hear us." Annevnos smiled, never a comforting expression and gazed into the rapt faces huddled around him.

"Our communication, of artificial nature, will be undetectable to the Oscilean creatures. It follows that if the air beasts cannot hear us, their Wizans will be deaf to our purposes."

Silently the Quattral operatives swallowed the bead pills. Annevnos watched his cohorts for reaction, and then placed his hands onto the Constructorbot.

"All chronometers are to be synchronized to mine. Do not underestimate the Observatore fleet of Moniah Talsaiyr. He has secured the aid of Danis Resto who cajoled the council to empower Moniah with complete control over all ship movements," Annevnos said, wiping dust from the Constructorbot.

"I shall denounce this in the Awclotan council," Seratt chimed in and Annevnos paused before replying, "I give you leave to raise the issue as a political concern but Tius supports Moniah, so do not expect a reversal of the decision. Now, to our immediate purpose…"

Mertoos, the eccentric physicist, danced a gigue, his hands in the air.

"Ah! Poor Moniah—that megalomaniac. What do the Talsaiyr have that we do not?" He said, singing the latter part in a parody of Wizan song speech devoid of mirth at which Doctor Onothi stepped away from the overhead light in mock astonishment.

"What! Are we not all the children of Arhahnis?"

The room exploded in the laughter of dread. Even Annevnos threw back his head, adding his staccato cackle to the cacophony.

* * *

By the time Alaysi reached the ship foundry at Valcecosti, he had traveled by such a circuitous route that he could hardly stand to sit another instant. As his Satarship sped closer to the cloudy atmosphere of the planet Costi, Alaysi threw down his light stylus onto a pile of sheets scribbled with poetry. He glanced out of a portal to scrutinize a world heavily guarded by vessels commanded by Admiral Sey. The shipbuilding facility itself was far below, occupying ten thousand square miles of a series of deep caves in the temperate western hemisphere.

The Satarship slowed in its approach and Alaysi caught sight of one of several constructor platforms in geostationary orbit, its long elliptical shape illuminated by windows and alternating navigation lights of red and green.

The Satarship bounced through the turbulence of thick clouds and Alaysi gathered his things, leaving a trail of papers while he hurried to the shuttle pod.

"By land, sea and air go I, a fleeting glimpse in a Quattral eye," he sang strapping himself into the pod seat. In another instant, the pod jetted from the larger craft and dropped quickly toward the bulk of a huge vessel. Alaysi clapped one hand over his mouth and swooned as the pod banked hard and slowed dramatically to crawl within the hangar bay of the Admiral's command ship. When Alaysi reached the bridge, he found Admiral Sey, Moniah and Kaylon huddled over a hologram display.

"Haolae, lord Alaysi," Admiral Sey said and Moniah looked up from the hologram and, seeing the pallor of his brother, came toward him.

"Greetings to you Admiral, I must si…" Alaysi stumbled and Moniah grabbed hold of him. Kaylon hurried over and they settled Alaysi into the navigator's seat.

"What happens here? Are you ill?" Moniah demanded placing his palm on Alaysi's forehead.

"My stomach is in the wild yonder," Alaysi said. Kaylon offered him a piece of Kamis root.

"Why do you think I eat so much of this," he said, "I apologize for the pod craft. It is designed for speed." Alaysi examined the root as though it was an alien object.

"Fast and terrible, why are we all hurtling around at such terrible velocity these days?" Alaysi said, averting his face from the Kamis root.

"Clear the bridge, please," Admiral Sey said, and he smiled at Alaysi, handing him a decanter.

In a moment, only the admiral, Moniah, Kaylon and Alaysi remained. Alaysi took a swallow and then another and nodded indicating his wits were returned. Moniah gestured for him to join him at the blisterdome forward view. The ship was well below clouds and they could clearly see four large constructor platforms each attached to a large bulk of metal. Here, an unfinished clamshell; there, a tapered hull; an observation dome trailing attachments, girders, and a molecular engine array.

From their height it was impossible to gauge the girth of the disparate pieces but in comparison to the platforms, the pieces were quite large and clearly comprised sections of an incomplete ship.

"You can truthfully report the ship is near ready," Moniah said.

"That is near ready?" Alaysi blurted indicating the hull work with his drink container.

"When completed, this vessel will be the pride of Aurocearia," Kaylon interjected, ignoring Alaysi, lifting his chin while he surveyed the massive parts.

Admiral Sey smiled. Moniah studied the platforms quietly.

"Very clever. It appears as nothing in so many parts," Alaysi said. He cleared his throat and added, "Medean has reason to believe the Quattral are preparing to seize control of the Awclotan council."

"They have tried this before," Moniah said, unmoved. Admiral Sey and Kaylon exchanged a worried glance but Alaysi would not relent.

"Moniah, please return with me."

"I am needed here."

"With respect brother, what remains here is well cared for. Your place is with Alaysi now. Both of you must attend the council," Kaylon said and Alaysi smiled at him, turning back to Moniah whose face was set in steel.

"If we are not already too late," Alaysi said and Moniah turned away to pace. While the others held their breath, Moniah placed his hands on the hologram display and stared into glowing design schematics.

"Then I must go. Kaylon, send us out," Moniah relented and Alaysi turned to Kaylon, tugging him gently by the sleeve.

"But not on that horrible pod, I beg you." Unable to resist, Moniah flashed his beguiling grin at Alaysi.

"Not even for the Arhahn?"

Alaysi shook his head, noting that Admiral Sey did his best to conceal his amusement while Kaylon appeared insulted. Moniah noticed Kaylon's resolve and shrugged in the face of his Seal Bearer's adoration of Arhahnis. It was an awkward moment.

"None of you remember what it is to have your feet on solid ground," Alaysi replied.

* * *

Throngs of Aurocerians converged beneath the towering doors of the council hall and waited patiently to climb the terraced steps. It was a beautiful day spin on Auros Prime. The air was sweet with honeyflower and high above, the planets Ves, Detate and Ermiat filled the azure blue sky along with Oscileans whose songs drifted on gentle breezes above the multitude.

Within the council hall, three tiers of windows lining either side of the upper clerestory nave opened to allow Oscileans to enter while, far below, an overlapping sea of voices wafted up in muted echoes from the thousands of Auries and Aurans moving toward the throne dais so that others could enter behind them.

For the benefit of late arrivals, two huge floatscreens descended at opposite sides of the dais to magnify the images of the Talsaiyr for those standing a full mile away at the rear of the hall. On each screen the date 18.5003.12 was illuminated in glowing red. The dais held two vacant places for the floating thrones of Arhahnis and Meliphor as well as five other permanent thrones for Moniah, Lirea, Alaysi, Ammanmus and Iskanye. Additional space had been made for three additional thrones for the newly avowed Tius, Danis and Kaylon but the artists had not yet finished them.

With Kaylon at Valcecosti and no place for them on the dais, Danis and Tius contented themselves in seats of honor in the council stalls adjacent to the dais. While Tius busied himself in discussions with the governor of Auros Prime, the incorruptible Eutimos Lorra-Sers; Danis made the rounds, raising his voice over the din of voices as he pressed the flesh of his colleagues.

As gregarious and sharp of mind as he was tall and powerful, with shoulders as wide as a bull, Danis was a perfect example of the physical type Aurocearians called, Abraxon. He stood in perfect contrast to the aesthete Tius with his cautious, scholarly disposition.

The roar of a thousand Oscileans from high overhead silenced confusion and the hall reverberated from the strains of the giant Orglatrompettas over the entrance at the opposite end of the dais. Wizans robed in blue and crimson cloaks of the Maetie guard entered the nave escorting the floating thrones of Arhahnis and Meliphor while the assembled throng sang the "Deshale Arhahni", an ancient anthem of loyalty.

Lirea, Ammanmus and Iskanye followed the thrones on foot and Lirea turned around occasionally, as did Iskanye. Ammanmus leaned toward Lirea, reassuringly patting her arm.

"Moniah will be here," he said, while they progressed past bowing heads. As the thrones reached the half-way point along the aisle, there came a roar of fire from the clerestory galleries five hundred feet above when the Oscileans let loose streams of flame. The smoke that drifted down upon the Quattral delegates from their incendiary salute smelled of incense.

Mertoos wrinkled his nose and tapped Cieyos on the arm. Cieyos waved away a draft of smoke, his attention fixed upon the imperial thrones as they reached the dais.

"Where is the First Lord, I wonder," Mertoos said through a yawn while he glanced around. Every planet was represented by contingents of engineers, priests, poets, architects and artists. Cieyos ignored the question. He studied the council stalls carefully.

"Every member of the Awclotan council is present. The Talsaiyr have something significant planned this day," Cieyos said.

Mertoos placed one hand on his mantle.

"Look around! Why do you suppose I directed our brothers and sisters to wear their mantles? After all, we must present ourselves formally to the Arhahn in the custom he requires."

Cieyos smiled and chuckled surveying mantles reflecting polished brass light from the shoulders of a thousand stone faced Quattral behind them.

There had been a time when Annevnos forbade the priest-created custom of the mantle but as the Talsaiyr dynasty gained power and the ranks of the Quattral swelled, Annevnos countermanded his decree so that Arhahnis could appreciate the numbers of those who increasingly disavowed his authority.

* * *

Annevnos flew a route that kept his speed-ship masked by planetary motion. Alone in a swivel seat in the observation dome above the bridge, he enjoyed a rare moment of quiet to appreciate his handiwork. Inner sphere space spread out before him and for all purposes one could not tell one was within anything. He rotated the seat to view a reverse angle and could barely perceive what appeared to be a large pink moon -- actually the portal to the Sphereworlds beyond which pink plasma gasses of the Suum Nebula glowed invitingly.

As Annevnos studied a passing moon circling the mostly unpopulated planet of Ermiat, he activated a hologram and the planet of Icrass appeared.

He studied the moon.

"What mysteries do you contain?" Annevnos muttered and added "Computer, describe."

A glowing image of the moon enlarged, with a half sphere grid on one side of Icrass, representing the curvature of the outer sphere shell.

"ICRASS SATELLITE: A MOON. DIAMETER; FIFTEEN THOUSAND MILES, ATMOSPHERE: ONE-SIXTEENTH GRAVITY, NO VOLCANIC ACTIVITY. STATUS: INERT. A TAEN FACILITY WITHIN A FORTIFIED BLERMETAL CAVERN. ONE ACCESS. RESTRICTED. THE FACILITY CONTAINS A DEFLECTOR CAPABLE OF SURROUNDING THE MOON IN A G CLASS STASIS FIELD. THE FIELD PROTECTS THE MOON DURING OUTER SPHERE IGNITION. POWER SOURCES: FIVE SAEN MOLECULAR CONVERTERS LOCATED TWO MILES BELOW THE SURFACE. TOTAL POWER OUTPUT ESTIMATED AT ONE TRILLION-"

"Cease," Annevnos said as Seratt climbed a circular staircase to join him.

"We shall arrive as scheduled, lord Annevnos."

Annevnos leaned back in his seat staring at the frozen image of Icrass. Inner sphere planets reflecting from outside the dome shone in his black eyes and gold floating pupils.

"What do you hold for me, Icrass?"

* * *

The council hall rang with voices as Moniah and Alaysi strode up the long aisle. Moniah stared at one of the large floatscreens in which he could see Danis trying to quiet a harangue from someone in the Awclotan council. Alaysi paused by an Aurie he knew well, standing near the aisle.

"What happens?"

"It was just revealed that the Aswarie's, Lirea and Iskanye, returned from a secret meeting on Simatos in which they attempted to persuade the surrender of voting proxies so that a new agenda could be put forth today," the Aurie said. Alaysi kissed her hand and ran off to catch up with Moniah.

"Tell me," Moniah said and before they reached the dais he not only knew what he had missed but what he might expect.

"I call a salute and pause to proceedings upon the arrival of the First Lord," Danis announced and he stepped away from a speaker's podium to consult with Tius while Moniah approached the throne dais. He leaned forward to address Arhahnis and scowled at Lirea who put her hands on her lap and set her mouth in a line.

"I do your bidding and return to find you have sent my lady into secret negotiations!" Moniah said through clenched teeth, facing the Arhahn. Meliphor did her best to appear as though Moniah was simply paying homage but her eyes darted away from his potent scrutiny of Arhahnis.

To his credit, Arhahnis made no attempt to derail the anger of his brother. Moniah interpreted the Arhahn's blank expression as capitulation. He sneered in mild disgust but at that moment, Arhahnis replied.

"Thank the gods you are here." The statement arrested Moniah.

Something in the voice of Arhahnis triggered a sense of pity in Moniah.

For the first time in his memory all the trappings of Arhahnis, the magnificent robe and mantle, the splendor of the floating throne—could not abate a sense of immense vulnerability the emperor presented to his public.

Moniah turned to face the capacious surroundings and strode to the speaker podium. Overhead, Oscileans sang out to him and he waved to the creatures and the sea of tiny heads of the Wizans. Somewhere up there was Saeonar, watching one of the large float screens in which Moniah suddenly came into view.

Careful Moniah, he told himself and waited until the hall became as silent as such a huge space could be while collecting his thoughts.

"I understand why many of you feel uneasy that it appears your voices have been circumvented to create a new agenda. But Arhahnis has never led you into tyranny and he does not begin that path today. You seek his wisdom and now he gives it, for I was with him in the presence of Necontis whose words echo from his mouth," Moniah said and stepped away from the podium to give his full attention to the floating throne while anxious murmurs arose from the assembly.

The droid cameras focused on Arhahnis whose image now dominated the floatscreens. He did not stand but the clarity and power of his voice carried to every corner.

"My brothers and sisters, eons ago voice entity Necontis commanded us to nurture the delicate properties of the Nether Suum nebula.

We thought the task might never end but all of you spread across the worlds we brought in close nature to one another within the sphere must now know that we succeeded.

And though the sphere has shut out the stars, the Suum that enriches our lives is stabilized by the mighty properties of energy imbued into it from the sphere," Arhahnis said. Cheers arose and more than a few chants began but Arhahnis raised one hand with a palm facing out and silence returned. He continued.

"Did we imagine we would be free of a larger destiny? Why then did we come into mortal being? I will tell you. Only the Sphere itself causes us to appear insular, confining our lives within its artificial boundaries. This year we are given a new directive. The Gods compel us to explore the cosmos."

No sooner did the words echo into the hall than a surge of Aurans and Auries swarmed toward the dais but this was no rabble. Even Quattral delegates were among them, applauding vigorously.

As Grand Ambassador of the councils, Danis raised his hands calling for order but his echoing voice was lost in the din of a spontaneous demonstration until Arhahnis stood from his throne to walk closer to the edge of the dais. Alaysi chewed his lip, surreptitiously motioning for the Maetie guard to form a perimeter around the lower steps of the dais.

"I demand to speak," the voice of Mertoos rang out and suddnly his image was magnified at the podium. Danis looked to Arhahnis who nodded assent before returning to his throne.

"This is a day for celebration," someone called out and Danis smiled.

"We will hear the Quattral representative," he commanded. The delegates who had come to the podium returned to the nave proper murmuring excitedly. On his throne, Moniah reached out to touch Lirea's hand. She met his loving gaze with a complex expression of tenderness beseeching forgiveness.

"I had to help. Arhahnis needed us to put the agenda before the council," she whispered. The muscles in his jaw flexed and his eyes roamed over her passionately but then Moniah smiled and gently touched her chin.

"Remember my love, the council between our hearts is paramount, even above that Arhahnis requests."

Mertoos placed his hands on the podium, bowed his head in the direction of the dais and looked out into the nave.

"No one denies our cause for elation. However, it is difficult for the mantles of the core Quattral to join whole-heartedly in celebration. Why? The reason for our hesitancy should be obvious. The First Lord controls all aspects of our fleets. Are we to assume the Talsaiyr and their Wizan colleagues will now command this vague exploration enterprise to the exclusion of other interests?" Mertoos said, raising his voice over a sea of protest from the Wizans and braying Oscileans. Confusion reigned as Quattral members faced their protestors with ardent applause. Moniah stood from his throne and walked toward the edge of the dais with his hands outstretched in a silent gesture for order because no one was listening to Danis demand the same.

Suddenly Iskanye leapt from her throne and before Ammanmus could stay her, she joined Moniah.

"Templar," she called out to a Wizan guard "step forward." The Wizan mounted the dais whereupon Iskanye seized his Coracle-diant from his holster. A veil of silence ensued as all eyes glued to Iskanye.

"Moniah, take the Coracle in hand," she said and Moniah, stunned and in no position to refuse without causing further confusion, took the wand from her. He stared at Iskanye who aimed the Coracle at her own chest amidst gasps of astonishment. From somewhere high overhead Moniah could hear the distinctive tone of his Oscilean, Prestant, moaning.

From his throne, Alaysi changed the focus of the droid camera to center on Moniah and Iskanye. The priestess stepped back two paces from Moniah at dead aim of the Coracle-diant. Moniah fixed her in a leveling glare. Ammanmus virtually squirmed in his throne while Lirea's hands flew to her chin.

"There are those of the Quattral who infer that to disagree with the Wizan invites their wrath. Once and forever let me allay your fears," Iskanye said and turned to meet the iron eyes of Moniah.

"What are you about Iskanye?" he whispered in the ancient Wizan tongue he knew she understood, but Iskanye merely lifted her chin defiantly.

"Lord Moniah, if there is fury in the Coracle summon it now, call forth lightning and destroy me," she demanded.

A flicker of light danced in his eyes and Moniah took his stance aiming the Coracle at Iskanye's heart. The Coracle wand emitted a hum and issued a thin but impossibly bright beam of red light that flew toward her but the light beam failed, dissipating to a fine mist.

Cheers went up but Mertoos regained the speaker's podium and the droid cameras swiveled automatically to present his image.

"A dramatic gesture by her Holiness but Moniah is her long-avowed brother Talsaiyr. What test is this?"

Instantly, Moniah turned to face Mertoos and took aim upon him. Now a helix of red and gold light issued from the Coracle-diant, it spun toward Mertoos but, again, only a foot from his chest the light energy dissipated. Without violent provocation, a Wizan cannot harm a living being. Mertoos collected his wits while Moniah slowly lowered the Coracle-diant, handing it back to its owner who took possession of the wand as though it were a gift from the Gods themselves.

Mertoos could only walk away from the podium in silence as the council hall erupted in the ancient chant of loyalty to the Talsaiyr. It took hours for the Talsaiyr to take their leave of the assembly, progressing slowly amidst the presses of Aurans and Auries who crowded the nave aisle to offer fealty.

CODEX: CONFIDENTIAL ARCHIVE OF MEDEAN:

"Arhahnis announced the first exploratory mission to a distant world will take place in the near future. This had the desired effect, for Aurocearians, unable to create children and blissfully unaware of death or illness, are discovering a greater purpose in the form of a mass sociological movement, wherein we strive to obey the canticle of Necontis to achieve the fullness of destiny. This is largely an unconscious, non-articulated desire to augment our exploration of other worlds by finding a successor, a planet of children if you will, to inherit Aurocearian knowledge. Essentially, the matter is now a foot race with Arhahnis and Annevnos competing for ultimate power. All the subterfuge preceding the council, now threatens to tip the scales of social order into anarchy while the fates of Arhahnis and Annevnos converge into a cosmological ordeal."

Where Dreams Sleep

Now look at our number: Moniah, Lirea, Iskanye and myself, Alaysi, Kaylon, Tius and the good-hearted Danis. The avatars of mortal creation, Arhahnis and Meliphor have united priests and ministers in the Talsaiyr dynasty. Balance is lost in a subjugation of my design. – Ammanmus Talsaiyr

The royal shuttle gained its cruising altitude to pass over the outer environs of Rentu-Treaur, bound for the Wizan regions a half-days journey away, nestled in mountains partially shrouded in mists rising from a network of lakes, ponds and dense forests. Inside the forward salon, Meliphor poured Soffa for Iskanye.

"Tell me of Elanrar, I saw it last when we toured the inner realms," Meliphor said, her eyes sparkling in anticipation, for the Empress who loved to travel had not visited the planet in question for centuries.

Iskanye removed a maroon cape and lifted her feet onto one side of a soft divan. Graceful and lithe, Iskanye did not possess Meliphor's legendary beauty but her soft features, brown and blue eyes and tresses of golden-silver hair created a loveliness of surpassing quality. Whenever Meliphor, Lirea and Iskanye were together, their combined beauty captured the attention of even the coldest of heart.

Iskanye gathered her hair behind her shoulders.

"Elanrar is breathtaking. You recall it was one of the last planets to be aura formed," she said, sipping a cup of Soffa.

Meliphor leaned forward, gently blowing steam from her cup.

"It is a world of striking contrasts. The mountains are steep and so rich in minerals they sing in color under daylight."

The shuttle trembled in mild turbulence. Meliphor set her cup down, nodding to Iskanye.

"And there are hills which glow with fire moss. The one ocean is a blue light enough to rival the finest Beron silk," Iskanye said, glancing out of one of the ornate windows. They were flying through a light snow flurry. A soft hissing sound turned their attention to an oval door inlaid with ormolu and cloisonné that opened as Lirea entered.

Meliphor turned her body fully around to face Lirea, her cup frozen in place on the way to her lips and Iskanye put her feet back to the floor. Lirea's expression was set in stone, a crinkle on her brow.

"Come and have Soffa," Meliphor said and Iskanye patted an embroidered cushion next to her but Lirea drifted toward one of the forward windows where she stood with her arms folded tightly across her chest. Meliphor set her cup down and, with Iskanye, joined Lirea at the windows.

"What is it Lirea, why so pale?" Meliphor said, tenderly moving a tendril of Lirea's hair.

"You must tell all," Iskanye teased, trying to elicit some sense of light-heartedness from Lirea. But the First Lords' consort only blinked and, without meeting their eyes whispered,

"I will not be left behind."

Meliphor squeezed Lirea's shoulder gently.

"But, of course not."

Lirea angled her face to Meliphor and Iskanye.

"You *knew*," she said and Iskanye glanced nervously to Meliphor, she was not about to speak before the empress. Meliphor cocked one eyebrow and lowered her face to meet the flashing eyes of Lirea.

"We have all participated for a purpose," Meliphor replied, her tone gradually moving toward an official voice. Lirea slid past them to the table and divan. She poured Soffa for herself but held the cup to her lips untasted. Meliphor and Iskanye joined her.

"Arhahnis should have waited until we reach Moniah," Meliphor said. Some of the fire in Lirea's eyes quieted.

"I concur. This must not stand," said Iskanye.

"Then let us have no more of it until we reach the Dome temple." Temporarily satisfied by the loyalty of her friends, Lirea smiled at Iskanye.

"I regret I could not join you on Elanrar. How did the Oscileans take to the planet?" Lirea asked. Iskanye sat next to her, lit an Ol stick and took in a draught of smoke.

"At first they sniffed about the ground but soon they took wing. A Wizan, Erfros, implored me to tell you that a hatching occurred just days ago, so it seems a success."

"Another planet for the Oscileans," Lirea enthused, showing something of her happier self.

"Strange, though, while on Elanrar, I experienced a feeling, a usic I sensed from the Colomeran," Iskanye said. Her fingers trembled and she set the Ol stick into a sand cup.

"I have heard this. Moniah tells me it is a bonding of the planets," Lirea replied.

"There was a discordant range in this music, something not true," Iskanye explained wistfully as if she were still trying to discern what she had experienced. Lirea settled back in her chair.

"Moniah will know. He will make it right."

The salon door opened; a Templar Wizan entered.

"Aswarie Meliphor, the Arhahn asks for you." Meliphor stood and followed the Templar guard into a connecting hallway and up a gentle rise of stairs to a larger cabin. Inside, Arhahnis, Medean and Ammanmus were seated around a large table.

"Meliphor, please tell the others we will be landing at the Dome temple before nightfall," Arhahnis said, extracting himself from a council session.

Meliphor smiled at Medean and Ammanmus but stayed put. Arhahnis stood, excused himself and approached Meliphor.

"You are angry I have prepared Lirea," He said reading her expression.

"Prepared her?"

"It is my opinion she must not risk the expedition."

"In our haste to win the day, beloved, I counsel against cruelty," Meliphor replied discreetly.

Arhahnis reflected for a moment, a brief fire lit his pupils.

"Time which we have luxuriated in, no longer affords me the tact I would prefer to use with regard to matters of State."

"If doubt should replace faith even among us as it does our enemies, where does that leave us?" Meliphor said, turning on her heel.

* * *

Dragonflies the size of birds buzzed over sapphire ponds with surfaces as smooth and untroubled as opaque mirrors. Above the still ponds, near the rolling summit of Mount Kese, the Oscileans Prestant and Montre, bearing Moniah and Saeonar—soared toward the largest and most ancient Wizan Dome temple. Its ground floor, sturdy pillars and thick marble walls grown over with fire moss and vines supported a marble dome streaked with the weathering hands of eons.

Prestant and Montre braked airspeed with sudden upbeats of their wings to land within oval openings along the upper circumference of the dome. Inside, the beasts gazed down into the temple proper from one of a series of concentric galleries overlooking a fire pit. The place resounded with grumbling Oscileans and Aurocearians, many of whom were still dismounting the beasts to see to the watering and feeding of their winged creatures. The entire stone temple interior, carved with intricate detail in reliefs of gardens and forests, danced in the glow from the fire pit. Smoke and incense wafted up to an open oculus at the dome's apex.

Moniah patted Prestant and made certain the water trough contained clean water. The water was so pure that, at first glance, it made the trough seem empty.

He met Saeonar on one of the ramps and they strode down to the temple floor to converge with the assembled Wizans around a single throne dais of carved marble. At either side of the dais were two silver Oscilean statues, in seated postures, their wings upswept, heads lifted toward the sky.

Each Wizan tossed a handful of incense offering onto the fire while, overhead, their beasts looked down from the circular galleries. The Oscileans sniffed the incense and began to sing, their voices reverberating around the dome.

Moniah moved closer to the fire pit, lifting his hands and the temple fell silent.

"We summon our leader, Tetra-Lachaen, the secret one," He intoned and stepped back, bowing to the fire pit.

As one force, Wizans lifted their Coracle-Diant wands high into the air and from each a ray of gold light poured forth while the Oscileans in the galleries roared flame into the central fire pit. The Wizan light and Oscilean fire merged over the pit until from the converging Oscilean fire and Wizan energy the figure of an Auran took shape. The Auran rapidly coalesced from the brilliant flame and light, his body appearing as though from a blinding flash.

The Auran floated down from the light, his glow dissipating when his feet touched the dais. Moniah and Saeonar were at his side instantly, Moniah urging him to drink water while Saeonar checked his pulse. The other Wizans remained expectantly silent, craning their heads as they drew closer.

Moniah steadied the Auran as he took seat on the throne, his body flashing with residual energy. Yet, here he was, the secret leader, the "Tetra Lachaen" of the Wizan, the Auran called Erfros. He breathed out a sustained breath of steam, cooling his body, and the glow radiating from him lost its luster. Erfros smiled, holding a hand before him in a clear signal he was on the verge of knowing he was whole and all was well. He smiled and the Wizans heaved sighs of relief. Erfros pulled on a robe and shivered, then he smiled again and clasped arms with Moniah, raising his hands.

"I am with you, the transference is complete," Erfros announced and the Oscileans sang out in triumph.

He beckoned Moniah and the Wizan watch commander to approach. Moniah brought forth a box containing a holster and Coracle wand. Erfros leveled his blazing green and gold eyes upon Moniah.

"The storm of change comes like the speed of high flight my brothers, Lord Moniah…you are now Tetra-Lachaen," Erfros said, reaching into the box. He lifted the Coracle holster, staring at the Wizan implement with longing and, amidst gasps, handed it to Moniah.

While Moniah hesitated, the Wizans balked. Some even hissed for it was understood that the First Lord, already empowered with royal authority, should never become Tetra-Lachaen. Moniah suffered ridicule in the pregnant pause while the others reminded him of the harsh irony that he had in fact, as the first Wizan blood, decreed that Erfros should be the leader.

"Wisdom! Your strategy is high on the Arhahn's path, haven't we enough nepotism?"

"Hear him, my lord."

"Does Moniah recant his oath?"

Erfros sliced the air with his hand and his voice rang out a curse.

"Moniah's design maintained Wizan independence from outside meddling. Think how long this has served us while the First Lord remained the decoy, his life at risk, with the Quattral certain it is he who leads the Mysterium."

"It is true. Aswarie Iskanye met Erfros on Elanrar. She never suspected the humble Wizan who supervised the new colony of Oscileans on that world was the most empowered of them all," Saeonar said but Moniah cut him off with an impatient expression when the Wizans returned to arguing.

"I cannot accept," Moniah blurted out but Erfros' bushy eyebrows shot up and he took Moniah by the collar, staring into his eyes.

"I see the deep reaches of space in your eyes, Moniah Talsaiyr." Prestant slowly walked part-way down the ramp with Montre but the Oscileans' grumbling turned to snorts under the withering glare of Erfros.

"There is no time to debate. We sweep the past aside to meet the challenge of the Quattral. First Lord Moniah knows that a Taen priest, one Atep, has transgressed and held the Orb of Necontis. Atep glimpsed the storm time. Our safety, our *continuance* will be sustained by Moniah as Tetra-Lachaen. In time, all of you will see the wisdom of my decision," Erfros said turning to meet all the other faces.

While the others debated, Erfros leaned toward Moniah and Saeonar, lowering his voice to a confidential level.

"Once, we could fly with the moon turns but now the moon you and Arhahnis cast out of the Sphereworlds beckons Annevnos." Saeonar glanced at Moniah whose eyes flared with anger.

"Icrass," Moniah hissed.

"You will soon travel in the void."

"I will refuse this command."

"No. You must be the source of reason on the world Arhahnis has chosen. This is the wisdom I have foreseen," Erfros said. Moniah rubbed his lips with his knuckles—events were moving too quickly. Erfros saw into his mind, realizing that Moniah would not leave the Sphereworlds while danger threatened.

"The wheels of your mind spin loudly," Erfros grumbled and before Moniah could react, Erfros made his purpose iron-clad. He grasped Moniah and, stunned, Moniah was locked into a vortex of plasma energy exuded by Erfros.

"Sto-o-o-p!"

Wizans surged forward, their excited voices causing the Oscileans to moan. Erfros placed his hands on Moniah's head and raised his voice above the confusion.

"I give you, Moniah Talsaiyr," Erfros' wavering voice sang in the humming of the plasma light and Moniah slumped to the dais, trying to maintain his balance. He tried to speak but only a smoky light emitted from his mouth. Erfros removed his hands from

Moniah and the loud humming vanished with the light. Someone turned their head and hurried out, vomiting. Plasma light trickled from the fingertips of Erfros, flowing over Moniah. The First Lord moaned and fell to one side, Saeonar rushed to steady him.

Through clouded vision, Moniah saw Erfros sway on his feet. His hair turned white in an instant while everyone backed away, averting their eyes.

Then, as if defying the gravity his body had balanced against in life, Erfros floated up. A Birthfire orb of energy none had seen in centuries claimed the body, surrounding it in a sphere of watery gold plasma.

"Gods," Saeonar cried sinking to one knee while steadying himself by leaning against Montre. The Erfros Birthfire orb rose up, up—to vanish through the round oculus of the dome.

A deafening silence pervaded the temple. The Wizans gathered around Moniah. Death, in the form of self-immolation had come to Aurocearia and Moniah looked out upon a swarm of pale faces.

Slowly, Moniah lifted the Coracle of Erfros into the air. All eyes fixed upon the instrument of the high Wizan. Moniah closed his eyes and a beam of golden light from the Coracle traveled up through the dome oculus into the air and still higher through mists and clouds as a beacon to the royal shuttle, which banked gracefully to land quietly on a broad terrace outside the dome temple. Wizans emerged from the temple with their somber Oscileans watching expectantly through mists wafting up from the forests below. Moniah and Saeonar approached the shuttle, a gentle breeze, tickled with snow, moving their capes and hair.

Maetie guards emerged from the main hatchway over which the Talsaiyr symbol gleamed in a shaft of passing daylight. Medean stepped out and looked at Moniah with a knowing expression. The Mystic bowed deeply to Moniah whose face carried a new weight of deep responsibility.

Auruaii

Although the assembled Wizans expected to see members of the house of Talsaiyr emerge from the royal craft, they were not expecting Arhahnis himself. Lirea stepped out of the hatch and, seeing Moniah, her face lit like a spring morning as she hurried into his embrace. She leaned back, taking in the dancing fire in his eyes.

"Oh gods," she muttered holding his face in her hands. One look at Saeonar and the others seemed to confirm a perception for she hugged Moniah tightly and wept into his shoulder.

"My love, I am here now," Lirea said. Moniah turned to Arhahnis who approached through a throng of bowing Wizans. Lirea tensed in his arms and Moniah immediately sensed her anger with Arhahnis, who noticed the Coracle wand Moniah wore.

"Brother, this day is marked upon you," Arhahnis said, placing his hands on Moniah's shoulders. Saeonar, Medean and Ammanmus gathered Iskanye and Meliphor around them. It was almost unheard of for the High Taen to visit a Wizan dome temple.

"I am now Tetra-Lachaen," Moniah said to Arhahnis, taking Lirea by the hand. Arhahnis cast his eyes down assessing this new fact while Meliphor and the others looked to one another for guidance.

"You know why I have come," Arhahnis said. His voice carried a new deference and Moniah could sense a quiet anxiety in his brother.

"For the first time, you've succeeded in surprising me with your swiftness to action," Moniah replied. Arhahnis smiled, tentatively.

"And you have the occasion to surprise me in a manner I would never have expected. We are equal in our duplicity."

Moniah led Arhahnis to a balustrade of the broad, curved terrace from which they overlooked a horizon of mist and snow-enshrouded mountains and forests. Above them, Oscileans peered down from the outside ledges of the Dome Temple galleries.

"I am relieved to see Medean," Moniah said while Arhahnis gathered his thoughts. Arhahnis cupped his hands together.

"The counsel of Medean is vital to us," Arhahnis said, lifting his chin and revealing by his posture that he had capitulated to the desire of the Mystic. *It must have galled you to be commanded by Medean,* thought Moniah, but there was still time for farewells and he needed to consider what he had experienced with the passing of Erfros.

"Admiral Sey is en route with the Auruaii ship," Arhahnis said flatly.

The Arhahn's shoulders dropped, having been relieved of a terrible burden. Moniah felt admiration for the sheer audacity in the way Arhahnis succeeded in turning what should have been a request into a command. So, time was denied him again, Moniah mused, and he closed his eyes to feel the snow on his face and enjoy the pungent, sleeping scent of Maulin trees.

"I was not aware Sey had conducted flight tests."

"I directed him to proceed," Arhahnis interjected, meeting Moniah's pensive expression with resolution. Arhahnis added, "My heart quakes to interfere with your command. Forgive me Moniah. I am pressed to action. We do not know what the outcome of a struggle with the Quattral might bring but I fear it is inevitable. Once the Auruaii ship arrives, time will be of the essence. I must at least attempt to implement the directive of Necontis. Perhaps we can subvert conflict. That is my hope," Arhahnis said, wearily.

Moniah's jaw flexed but there was no disregarding the drawn countenance of the emperor, who was doing his best to fulfill the needs of mortal Aurocearians while obeying ethereal demands. Still, the implication was clear that Moniah's actions had accelerated matters.

Arhahnis sighed. For the first time Moniah saw a flare of desperation in his magnificent eyes.

"You are my right arm but I must have you take leave of me now." Moniah recalled the words of the strange, blinded Taen Atep, who had prophesied, "Nothing will stop the changing."

"You have taken the fleets from me and I have gained the Wizan only to lose myself in stars," Moniah said, and looked at Lirea, who studied him carefully while Meliphor tried to comfort her. Moniah motioned to Arhahnis and they joined the others. Medean touched his sleeve.

"A hope for the future."

Moniah ignored the enigmatic statement and put his arm around Lirea's waist. There was one final aspect with regard to Arhahnis' dealings he must remedy. Before he could address it Arhahnis spoke.

"Moniah will journey to the candidate world." Lirea glared at Arhahnis.

Moniah winked to reassure her and she restrained her fury. "Lirea, we travel to the stars," Moniah said. Medean smiled. Bewildered, Arhahnis mis-read the situation as he spoke.

"I wonder as to the wisdom of this Moniah," he said, but it was Medean who interrupted with a steadfast resolve.

"Infinite, to ask the First Lord to leave that part of his heart he would only long for is cruelty. How can we journey to the candidate world and impart compassion and wisdom if we arrive in sorrow."

Shocked, Ammanmus looked to Medean, then to Arhahnis, while Iskanye muttered thanks to Medean. Arhahnis turned his head as though he had heard a new sound, as if he were aware he was losing control of history in that instant.

"One cannot grip for eternity," Moniah said under his breath. An Oscilean bleated in the distance, its voice muffled by snow.

"My concern is for her safety," Arhahnis replied, but Lirea had had enough. She stepped forward in a fluid grace of fury.

"How can you speak for me? How can you decide what risks I am to take? Infinite, you rule Auros but you do not rule my destiny."

"I stand with Lirea. It is her right to be with Moniah in all things," Iskanye said, while Ammanmus stared at her as if she had just threatened the life of Arhahnis, who turned to Meliphor.

"We must reflect the true nature of Auros. Moniah and Lirea are one. You must surrender your desire to bend us to the will of males," she said. It was an electric moment. For centuries, Auries had removed themselves from conflicts their Auran males were determined to escalate but they had paid a price for bliss by creating a void of power.

In the process of refining political power Arhahnis and Ammanmus filled that void, shutting out dissent with their iron will. Now, in this moment, three Auries overwhelmed the loss of centuries. In the silence, Saeonar saved the day.

"Where Moniah goes, so do I," he added, "If he will have me." Moniah clasped arms with Saeonar and paused to take in faces dusted with snow.

"And where we go so do Prestant, Montre and their mates."

Saeonar grinned ear to ear. "To fly new skies my friend."

Ammanmus moved closer to Arhahnis.

"Do you intend to permit this? How can it profit the expedition to include Oscileans?" Ammanmus asked, arms folded, leaning toward the Arhahn, his eyes searching the will of the emperor. Arhahnis glanced at Lirea, who held hands with Meliphor.

Arhahnis waved away an offered hot drink. "You mean of course how can it profit the Taen to permit such a potent *Wizan* representation to the Beings of a new world," he added, "We have exacted a great toll from Moniah. How can I refuse his demand—made in the presence of the Wizan?"

* * *

Dawn broke in clear skies upon snow-laden trees. Through soft but heavy snowfall, the royal party converged outside the Dome temple, all eyes fixed to the whiteout of leaden skies. Like a large metal cloud, over a mile in length, its silvery-white hull camouflaged by winter skies—the enormous ship *Auruaii* descended over quiet misty forests to the cry of Iln Kites. In the muted light, the hull of the ship gave the illusion of being covered by a silver liquid, dappled by dark blue heavily-tinted portals and blister domes.

"Behold, the *Auruaii*," Moniah said to Saeonar, raising his voice over the subsonic hum of the engines as he placed one arm around Lirea's waist. A higher pitched whine announced the approach of a Satarship, which swept into view at high speed, dwarfed by the immense form of the *Auruaii*.

The vast ship emitted a low steady pulsing sound from its antigravity engines. Wizans stared in awe, pointing to various features of its streamlined bulges. Its long clamshell prow rose up to a clear bubble-dome bridge area, where scattered rays of sunlight gleamed on its hull, high over their heads.

Moniah studied the gleaming silver hull that not long ago had floated in sections over Valcecosti. The Satarship slowed to hover near the temple terrace, extending a ramp under its side hatch from which Alaysi and Tius emerged, craning their necks to take in an unobstructed view of *Auruaii*. Wizan fliers circled the area in the distance, on the watch for intruders.

"Look at it! An island of metal afloat in the ether," Alaysi said, hurrying to Moniah, while Tius made his obsequious bows to Arhahnis and Meliphor.

"Our flying home," said Saeonar and Alaysi scribbled a note to himself. Lirea lifted herself on her toes to kiss his cheek.

"Admiral Sey reports the *Auruaii* traveled without incident. Although our flight here today was swift—I am reasonably confident we were paid little attention," Alaysi said in confidential tones to Moniah as they stepped away from the others. Moniah touched his chin.

"Comforting on the surface but if Annevnos monitored the flight of the *Auruaii* he would not reveal it," Moniah said, watching a ramp extend from the underside of Auruaii's prow. Admiral Sey strode down the ramp, waving to Moniah.

Alaysi glanced up at the passing shadow of Prestant. The Oscilean was enjoying a leisurely morning flight. Nearby, Montre could be seen perched on a colonnade of the temple, scrutinizing *Auruaii* with a steadiness of wonder and hesitation as she rocked gently from side to side.

"Everything you would have requested is in the Satarship. Shall I off-load it?" Alaysi said jerking a thumb over his shoulder. Moniah waved a hand before him.

"Have floatdroids do it. We'll need to inspect the ship."

"I hope you will forgive me Moniah. Arhahnis demanded that I prepare your things," Alaysi said, wringing his hands. Moniah chuckled.

"You were powerless in events, Alaysi. Stop fretting brother, you've done well."

Alaysi turned to Lirea. "I have packed your things."

"The gods must love you Alaysi, I certainly do," Lirea said bussing his blushing cheek.

Montre grunted, instinctively ducking her head, though the hull of the ship was nowhere near her or the temple. Prestant landed near her and they sang excitedly, sniffing the air. Moniah signaled to Saenoar who took his leave of Admiral Sey to hurry to Moniah.

"I must choose a crew," Moniah said, and they strode toward the temple.

* * *

Within the ship, Moniah clasped arms with Kaylon and gazed at the onlookers from the flight bridge.

"We've sufficient provisions for two years. I have Constructorbots and a supervisory team overseeing conversion of the hangar into a compound for the Oscileans," Kaylon said, while they watched a screen imaging the hangar and, sure enough, in the screen, Wizans were busy loading in sacks of feed and grain while Constructorbots welded water and food basins to the bulkhead. Moniah turned to Kaylon.

"Arhahnis will desire you to remain here."

"My place is on this mission," Kaylon insisted.

Moniah glanced at Saeonar who gave a broad smile. *Relief?* Moniah chuckled and looked back at Kaylon who tapped his chest.

"You need a flight specialist. I am he."

Lirea entered the bridge, dusted her hands and, finding Moniah, joined he and Kaylon. Daylight flooded the spacious interior. "The medical facility is better than I expected," she said to Moniah, who cocked an eyebrow at Kaylon.

"Kaylon, you will have to submit to a medical examination before flight."

Kaylon frowned. Lirea laughed.

"Follow me," she said.

"But, Aswarie Lirea, I am in perfect health." Lirea took his hand, winking at Moniah.

"First of all, you are Talsaiyr—no need to call me lady Lirea—we're family. Secondly, my lord, Moniah is the commander of our adventure. Come thee hence and fear not. I am a skilled physician." She led Kaylon away.

As afternoon arrived, *Auruaii* buzzed with activity. Kaylon supervised Aurans and Auries checking systems while the giant Oscileans Prestant, Montre and their mates Wholestep and Halfstep were allowed to enter their new temporary home. The beasts paused just inside the hangar, snorting and thumping their giant claws on the deck, while anxious Wizans including Moniah and Saeonar looked on.

"So we too…sing in the metal beast," Prestant sang, sniffing the floor, which was now covered with a thick carpet-like substance.

"It is wondrous…smells of Keln nuts," Halfstep warbled. Wholestep studied Montre as she carefully inspected the large chamber, flexing her large wings, which did not come close to touching the high bulkhead ceiling.

"The metal beast is rigid," Montre intoned. Moniah turned to Saeonar whose pensive expression showed his concern for the creatures.

"Let's to the bridge while they find their way."

* * *

Delayed due to Moniah's insistence on taking the Oscileans aboard, the time for departure finally arrived. A light rain fell through mists upon Arhahnis, Meliphor, Alaysi, Tius, Ammanmus, Iskanye and Medea, all gathered on the terrace facing the ship's ramp, from which Moniah, Lirea, Saeonar and Kaylon gazed back at them.

"The time has come," Medean said to Arhahnis, who nodded with a quick jerk of his head. He stepped forward with Ammanmus, who coughed into his palm.

"Remember, our studies indicate your mental abilities will be altered in the atmosphere of the candidate world. This is…unavoidable," said Ammanmus. Lirea nodded and Arhahnis met the determined look of Moniah.

"Moniah, find beings with love in their hearts—all else will come as time needs," he said.

"Infinite, if you will have me, I am prepared to become Talsaiyr," Medean interjected, electrifying everyone. Arhahnis turned to Medean with a look of utter relief but the mystic raised one cautionary hand and smiled at Moniah.

"With the caveat that I join the expedition."

Alaysi clapped a hand over his mouth, barely stifling a yelp of surprise. Tius straightened his spine, looked first to the Arhahn then to Moniah, and finally to Meliphor, who reached out to take Medean's hands in hers.

Ammanmus appeared ready to speak and then simply smiled while Iskanye glanced over her shoulder at the many witnesses.

"Brilliant," Moniah muttered. Medean was offering Arhahnis and Ammanmus a balance. By letting them send the most powerful Greenrobe, he was making sure that the expedition would no longer be dominated by Wizan influences. The begging eyes of Ammanmus conveyed as much to Moniah, while Arhahnis stared into Medean's eyes.

"I will be at loss without you," Arhahnis said quietly, then turned to face the others raising his voice to its imperial tone.

"Medean, declare yourself to these witnesses," he said and Medean, without hesitation, did just that.

"With an open heart, I seek to become Talsaiyr."

All the Talsaiyr followed in chorus. "Haolae, brother Medean, come within." And the customary phrase of greeting took on a literal meaning as Medean walked up the ramp to join the expedition members.

Moniah took Medean by the arm. "Welcome aboard, brother Medean." He added, "Have you all that you require?" Medean lifted his hands, shrugged his shoulders slightly and smiled. "All that time permits."

Arhahnis and Moniah approached one another and the Arhahn took Moniah's hands in his own. There was not a sound to be heard as the titans measured each other in a peace they had never known.

"You have seen it is a beautiful world Moniah. Study the databases with care. I give you the fullness of my heart. I believe these beings are the mirror of our souls. Never forget it," Arhahnis said. He let go of Moniah's hands and stepped back, his eyes welling in tears. Meliphor and Iskanye held each other. They waved, but could not speak.

"Lord Moniah, I transfer command of this vessel to you," Admiral Sey said, with a bow, and stepped off the ship's ramp.

"Fare thee well. When the time comes I will send Taens," Ammanmus promised in parting. The ramp closed and *Auruaii* began to rumble in a deeper rhythm. Moments later, it lifted straight up, backing as it did to put distance between the bow of the ship and the temple terraces. The vibration of its engines shook snow and leaves from nearby trees.

* * *

Moniah, Saeonar and Kaylon focused their attention on flight instruments The Wizan region appeared to be no more than a topographical map far below.

"Inertial dampeners and redundant systems online, Moniah," said Kaylon.

"Very well. Saeonar?"

"Directional auto navigation systems operational, all atmospheric and redundant systems fully functional."

Moniah led Lirea to take seat in his command chair while he scrutinized holographic displays.

"Accelerate to inner sphere flight speed." Suddenly, the dark blue of Auros Prime's upper atmosphere gave way to the black of inner sphere space. An opaque filter transformed the observation bubble dome around them to a gray field through which Auros Prime's star, emerging from its far side, glowed warmly.

"Portal passage in ten minutes, lord Moniah," Kaylon said.

Auruaii sped past the planets and moons of inner sphere space. In the quickly diminishing distance, a single pink orb glowed before them. Moniah pointed it out to Lirea.

"The portal." She leaned forward following the direction of his gaze.

"From here it appears to be a solid object."

Moniah joined Saeonar and Kaylon at the navigation station.

"Any sign of Quattral Activity?"

"Not in our vicinity. Two Observatore ships to our port side at ten thousand and thirty thousand clicks," Kaylon said, scanning a console.

"Initiate molecular engine drive to supra-light velocity the instant we enter the portal circumference," Moniah said, calculating something in his mind and turning to glance at Medean at the helm station.

"Understood," Medean said quietly. As *the Auruaii* approached the portal circumference, Lirea came to her feet, her gaze fixed on the portal to outer space. A tense silence fell over the flight bridge. Moniah leaned toward a speaker plate.

"Weapons crew, prepare Saen cannons. Await my signal."

Auruaii reached the portal. Moniah chewed his lip. Sweat tickled his back. This was the critical time. If operatives of Annevnos activated the outer Sphere shell igniters before the ship could gain sufficient distance from the Sphereworlds, *Auruaii* would be consumed in flaming defeat.

"Moniah, portal control contacting us for identification confirmation," Saeonar reported.

Lirea reached behind her to find the command seat and sat down again with eyes glued to the widening maw of the Sphereworlds portal.

"Ignore it! *Now* Medean," Moniah said, his voice cracking. The ship hummed at a higher pitch, the sound quickly escalating above audible levels. They had only a fleeting glimpse of the Suum Nebula as starlight within it smeared into red and blue shifts. Moniah's shoulders sank two inches. He wiped his brow.

"Thank gods. Kaylon, please convene a crew meeting in the bridge conference room," Moniah said and Kaylon immediately announced the command over the ship's address system.

* * *

Two large oval windows curving with the shape of the aft bridge area revealed the passing star-shifted light. Four Aurans entered through an automatic door to join Moniah, Medean, Kaylon and Lirea, who gazed at the stars.

"For the ship's log. We have departed the Sphereworlds. All systems are nominal," Moniah said, indicating chairs to the four Aurans who chose seats and settled in.

"Brother Wizans, for the duration, think of me as your captain rather than First Lord. Saeonar is First Officer and Kaylon—Flight Specialist. Our esteemed Seer and now brother, Lord Medean serves as Navigator and Lirea, physician to the crew."

"As I am the sole Aurie aboard, I hope you will not overwhelm me with masculine powers," Lirea teased.

Moniah was clearly taken aback. The open surprise by Moniah genuinely amused his crew. Moniah chuckled; charmed by the obvious but effective tactic she had employed to put everyone at ease. A floatdroid hovered up from the center of the table, revolving to offer Soffa cups, water a series of fresh fruit and what appeared to be protein cakes.

Moniah began to look more relaxed and took a cup of Soffa, gesturing to the four Aurans.

"Report status please."

"Wizan Vetaeos, molecular drive. Drive is fully operational," he said, acknowledging Lirea with a bow of his head, for he had not seen her in years.

"Rete, Saen weapons. All weaponry is nominal."

Moniah angled his chair to face the other two Aurans. The first cleared his throat. "Uletis, Hyper drive, fully functional."

Saeonar commented, "Were it not we would be a slow-moving vessel."

Moniah frowned at Saeonar, who sighed as he chose a piece of fruit from the revolving floatdroid. Saeonar added, "Thank you for the fresh provisions Lirea but I hope you will be prepared when this is replaced by gelatins and foul void foods."

"Caras, hyperbolic chamber and chief engineer. All systems nominal, my lord."

"Questions?" Moniah said, relentlessly adhering to the formality he had learned from Admiral Sey. Lirea folded her hands on the table. She touched his hand and raised one finger. Moniah winked at her.

"By what means will we be able to communicate with the Sphereworlds in an efficient manner? The Saen pulse?"

Moniah leaned back, nodding to Medean.

"Medean?"

"We have learned that the very fabric of the void, that which appears to be empty black is actually dark matter."

Lirea frowned and joined her fingers on the table.

"This matter is substantial."

Yes, we use supra-accelerated light as a carrier for transmission of image, voice and data. But, Aswarie, we have also learned that the dark matter helps accelerate this carrier signal. We will bounce signals from the magnetospheres of surrounding stars, planets and other space bodies to focus and further accelerate the transmissions. In this way we can communicate over long distances in real time."

Lirea smiled and leaned toward Medean, who read her mind. Nonetheless, she said it anyway.

"Just Lirea, my brother."

"With velocity at full molecular drive, we should reach the planetary system in five months," Kaylon said, declining a cake offered by Saeonar.

"In one month's time we will enter hyperbolic sleep spheres. Caras, are you certain the Oscilean hangar is fully prepared for the duration?" Moniah inquired, leaning forward again to sip his Soffa.

"Yes, my lord."

Moniah nodded. He smiled and, to the relief of the others, he softened his stern manner and put his hands on the table.

"Anything else?"

"A request," Lirea said, raising her hand. Moniah cocked an eyebrow, his eyes twinkling at her.

"I would like a tour of the ship, would the Captain deign to escort me?"

Saeonar stood. "That will be all for now."

Alone with Lirea, Moniah sighed as she stroked his brow with her fingertips.

"You're tired my love," she whispered and he took her into his arms and onto his lap. They stared out of the portal at passing stars.

"Do you know what I am feeling? The ship will make us new by the time we reach the candidate planet," Moniah said softly, kissing her cheek.

"New?"

"Yes, after that much distance, living in this traveling city. We'll emerge new Beings."

"Through it all I will love and trust you. Now, come with me. You must rest," Lirea insisted, standing up and tugging Moniah to his feet.

"Yes, Doctor Lirea."

* * *

In his command center near the Sphereworlds Portal, Annevnos watched the *Auruaii* defy confirmation procedure and disappear as it jumped to light speed.

"So much the better," he muttered, viewing a small section of the Portal still under construction where grid work of sphere shell material arced out for thousands of miles, its varying end lengths fixed with millions of beacon lights. Annevnos closed his eyes; he could see a blurry image of the face of Seratt in his mind's eye.

"Who else besides our illustrious First Lord and his minions have defied their own laws?"

"We believe the Greenrobe, Medean, was aboard," came the voice of Seratt.

"Then Medean is now an avowed Talsaiyr. Arhahnis screams his intentions. Disperse all operatives to assigned locations," Annevnos commanded.

* * *

Arhahnis met with Tius at the palace of Sumae-Thumaen, where the Arhahn took surcease from the strain of his emotions in his favorite music chamber. Word had spread rapidly that Medean was now Talsaiyr, and a darkened mood filtered through the populace for it smacked of a desperate move to consolidate factions. Arhahnis tapped his fingers against the keys of the instrument then executed a smooth glissade across two of the five manuals of the Sieuwan console, filling the hall with the quivering sound of the long vertical harp-like strings and clear bell tones of the tuned spheres.

"Any reply from the Quattral regarding my command for a council session?" Arhahnis asked quietly as the scales faded.

"To my knowledge, no response has been forthcoming, Infinite. There is grave unrest regarding the avowal of Medean but, more urgently, you never revealed to the Awclotan council the departure date of *Auruaii*," Tius said, taking seat near the Arhahn, who tried to pick out a quiet tune.

"And Annevnos?" Arhahnis said without looking up.

"The whereabouts of Annevnos remain a mystery."

"It is a time for loss and gain, Tius." Arhahnis struck a chord and stood. He waved a hand absently over a hologram droid as he passed it and the robot presented an image of the *Auruaii* traveling along its parabolic flight path to the candidate planet. Tius cleared his throat.

"It gives me comfort, you see," Arhahnis said, taking seat across from Tius, who opened a box and filled an Ol pipe.

"So, the consensus is I have prevented others from partaking in the expedition," Arhahnis said, at which Tius frowned but nodded, his face partially obscured in smoke.

"I fear that is true."

"What is more, it was my intention to do just that."

Tius coughed and lowered the pipe slowly into his lap. His pupils flashed like embers in his green eyes.

"Why?"

Tius regarded Arhahnis with open scorn but the Arhahn was unfazed, lowering his golden pupils to the hologram display of the *Auruaii*. Only then did the hard flashing edge leave his eyes.

* * *

Moniah paced alone in the upper observatory, smoking his Ol pipe. For some reason the air scrubbers worked better here than on the bridge, where smoke bothered Saeonar. The silent glory of passing stars calmed Moniah, reminding him of all the centuries he had spent gazing into the space outside the Sphere shell during its construction.

In the past, he had wondered what it would be like to be given a chance to explore the Suum Nebula. He had never conceived that his wish would be granted in a way that would see him traveling light years beyond the inviting mysteries of the planetary systems at the doorstep of Aurocearia.

Now that his destiny conveyed him far into the void, he felt a subconscious trigger of dread tugging at his heart. He settled into a swivel chair, tipped up his collar against a chill and pressed a button on the armrest.

"Personal log: this date by the Colomeran calendar, nineteen point five thousand five point twenty-five. Morale is high but our departure was…difficult emotionally. Since then, an unspoken rule is at work in which none of us are comfortable speaking of Auros." He leaned back to gaze at the stars and to enjoy his Ol pipe, one finger depressing a pause control as he gathered his thoughts to continue. The quiet lulled him for a moment into the lethargy and silence of space.

"The farther we progress the more I long for home. The smoke ponds, Wizan regions, Ves…the ship is spacious and even luxurious but it is a mile long and four hundred feet across at the widest beam. A small world for those accustomed to life in the expanse of wonderment. I am concerned that Medean is privy to information I do not possess. He is always quiet, keeping his own council but we have a bond and, although I wonder what motivated his avowal into the Talsaiyr, I must admit his timing was impeccable. I hope he will confide in me when a way is clear before him."

An intercom beeped. Moniah pressed another button.

"Yes?"

"I am loath to inform you that I am lost, *again*," Lirea's voice blurted out. Moniah activated a ship's diagram and subdued his laughter.

"Find a ship schematic and activate your portable comlink."

He watched the schematic diagram but no sign of Lirea appeared.

"Oh…I left it in our quarters," came a tepid reply, Moniah touched controls on the schematic.

"Computer: locate the Aurie Lirea by genetic signature."

"Processing request," the computer responded. A small flashing light appeared on a screen in the armrest. "Aurie Lirea is on deck forty-seven, D section, aft," the machine reported.

* * *

Meanwhile, Prestant and Montre lumbered toward Saeonar and the Wizan Caras as they inspected the Oscilean hangar deck.

"The void beast is rigid…no flight to be had," Montre complained. Saeonar shrugged.

"No more rigid than the stone and metal floors you have all been accustomed to on Auros Prime."

"How long…with no flight?" Wholestep sang out from a large beam overhead.

"Only a few weeks until sleep," Saeonar assured him.

"Saeonar, what if we reduce gravity in the hangar? They can float about, rest, or at least have a semblance of flight," Caras suggested, wiping grit from his hands. The temperature gauges in the hangar had been giving him trouble. The Oscileans purred a rumble of happy thought at the suggestion. Four huge heads turned to Saeonar.

"Very well, can you adjust the water and feeders to be zero-gravity efficient?"

Caras smiled.

"Give me a few hours."

* * *

Moniah found Lirea examining the open door of a turbo-elevator. She blushed when he approached and paused before her with hands on his hips. Lirea pretended nonchalance, resting one shoulder against the soft gray material lining the curved wall.

"What if someone was ill and needed you?" Moniah said.

Lirea glanced into the turbo-elevator.

"It gives me a feeling of suffocation to go into these things. So I have tried to walk the ship but…"

"All the more reason to wear your portable link." His own beeped at that moment.

"Come see what we have done for the Oscileans," Saeonar's voice said. By the time Moniah and Lirea reached the hangar, the entire crew was present. Saeonar rubbed his hands together, approaching Moniah. "We've fixed an oversight."

Moniah regarded Saeonar with a bemused smile. Caras was huddled over the water and feed dispensers in the Oscilean hangar. He deactivated a small constructorbot welding torch, threw off a clear face guard and wiped sweat from his brow.

Saeonar patted his back and Caras turned around, his ruddy face grinning. "All done?"

Caras stood up. The two Auran's inspected his handiwork.

"Now they can drink or eat in zero G," Caras explained.

Halfstep half flew, half jumped from her perch to join Prestant, Montre and Wholestep at the newly re-configured feeder area.

Prestant stuck his massive head into a rubberized flexible seal affixed to the water trough while Kaylon and Vetaeos looked on.

"A simple vacuum," Kaylon said approvingly, turning to Vetaeos, who pinched his nose to retard a sneeze.

"This should have been done to begin with in case of sustained atmospheric system failure," Vetaeos said and Kaylon nodded agreement.

"Shall we conduct a test? Go ahead Caras," Saeonar said.

Caras activated a control worn on his waist sash. There was a brief scent of ozone, and then everyone was floating. Moniah grabbed Lirea and laughed.

"We fly!" Lirea cried, locking her arms around Moniah as they spun higher. Saeonar put his hands straight up, reaching for a distant cross beam. Medean folded his arms across his chest and simply ascended while the muscular Vetaeos tucked his arms and legs to his chest and tumbled end over end.

Kaylon grabbed hold of a stanchion and pushed forward with his legs, launching himself across the width of the hangar. Uletis took hold of a crossbeam, twirling around it like a trapeze artist, while nimble Caras grabbed Uletis by the ankles and soared around the cross beam with him.

"Very healthy, I heartily recommend this distraction," Lirea said to the others from Moniah's embrace.

"Much for comfort…wings are light," Montre sang.

"Who is in command?" Kaylon asked flying across the hangar.

"The ship," said Saeonar and they all laughed.

Still gorging with his head in the rubber tube, Prestant's huge body lifted up, rear end first. He grumbled a deep shuddering sound while the other Oscileans undulated their wings slowly as they floated and turned upside down singing a cacophony of music intermixed with the snorting laughter the beasts made when amused.

Kaylon tumbled by Moniah and Lirea.

"Perfect for exercise!" Moniah smiled at Kaylon and held Lirea close while they revolved slowly in a circle, locked in embrace at a forty-degree horizontal angle to the deck.

"I can think of a better use for such delight," Moniah whispered to Lirea, amidst laughter and puffs of gray smoke from the snorting Oscileans.

* * *

Within the Sphereworlds, Annevnos gazed at the sky from the surface of the planet Anceria. He could see Auros Prime, which appeared as a vivid blue and white orb, directly above its ascent over the green water moon Ves. His mind engaged in artificial telepathy.

"Anceria will reach perigee to the Portal in five hours," the mind of Cieyos informed him.

"Perfect. Command Seratt and the others to seal all entrances and exits to Quattral areas," Annevnos ordered while he methodically destroyed pulse discs in the Quattral library.

* * *

On Auros Prime, the floating thrones of Arhahnis and Meliphor moved majestically along the long nave aisle of the council hall. Rarefied brilliant daylight of a clear winter day streamed down through the clerestory windows, two and four hundred feet above. Every inch of the council hall teemed with Aurocearians and the Awclotan council stalls were filled to capacity.

Normally the place would resound with the thunder of the "Deshale Arhahni" anthem but today the singing was not robust and the Musemaun used all his stops to cover the unimpassioned voices, lost in the peel and rumble of the Orglatrompettas.

Danis stood by the speaker podium, his wide shoulders and broad chest heaving under the weight of his robes as he frowned, taking in the abnormally large numbers of Quattral in attendance.

Seratt stood quietly among his delegates, ignoring the music. The floating thrones reached the dais and revolved slowly to face the assembly beneath a gigantic triple orb seal of the Talsaiyr. Danis signaled Alaysi and two enormous holographic screens floated out from concealed niches at either side of the throne dais to settle into position.

Ammanmus and Iskanye appeared distracted, flanking Arhahnis and Meliphor. Tius never moved an inch. He had inherited an uneasy throne and his eyes darted about while his hands gripped and released the armrests repeatedly. Facing the throng was obviously a new and not entirely pleasurable experience for him.

The Spherewar

The face of Arhahnis appeared on floatscreens and holograms throughout the Sphereworlds.

"First Lord Moniah and his fellow explorers departed our worlds aboard a vessel bound for a planet which, through the intercession of the Gods—might hold the future of Aurocearia."

No sooner had he made the announcement than Auries and Aurans of the councils leapt to their feet demanding the podium while the delegates in the nave created a cacophony of astounded anger.

"So, it is clear only the Talsaiyr are privileged to participate in the expedition." The Quattral Aurie, Jange, announced from her place in the council stalls. Ammanmus stood from his throne but another Auran stepped out of the stalls pointing to the dais.

"True spoken. We were informed the Greenrobe Medean joined this select crew. Apparently he too is now an avowed Talsaiyr!"

"Four Aurans chosen of the Wizan Mysterium are part of the crew," Ammanmus said but his clumsy revelation elicited guffaws from the Quattral.

"Poor Kaylon and Medean, how, I wonder, will their objectivity, to say nothing of empirical procedures, fare in the face of a crew dominated by and *commanded by* Wizans?" the Quattral Mertoos cried out. Danis pounded his tall staff on a sonic amplifier, trying to regain control by using procedure.

"Remember the injunction of Necontis; to discern if these beings, our brothers and sisters in the void, are fit to partake in our legacy," Iskanye said, but the angrier factions seized on the word "fit". The word went round the assembly, repeated and scorned in an ash heap of her intention to suggest the risky nature of the expedition. Even the loyal governor of Auros Prime, Eutimos Lorra-Sers came to his feet in what was fast degenerating into the most calamitous assembly in memory.

"Is lord Moniah commanding an expedition or leading a colonizing effort?" he asked. Tius stared at him with obvious shock and Arhahnis spoke but, for the first time in anyone's memory, his words betrayed him.

"Brothers and sisters, we live in wonder as to our own continuance in mortality. We must therefore heed the directive of the voice entity."

Seratt could hardly contain his glee and strode to the podium while an electric atmosphere of discontent evolved around him. His face filled the floatscreens.

"Who is arbitrating these terms? Fit? Continuance? The time has come to challenge your dreaming mind Arhahnis Talsaiyr. Taen and Wizankind subvert diversity of all Aurocearian purpose, inspired by their secret gods, hiding behind them while manipulating *us*. It is nothing less than the domination of Aurocearian destiny," Seratt roared, redeeming himself to his Quattral cohorts. Meliphor reached out to grasp hands with Arhahnis while echoing groans and hisses from Oscileans and Wizans filtered down from on high. The Council Hall was so tense in sweat and anxiety that daylight streamed down into the nave from the clerestories through a haze.

An Auran of the Awclotan council jumped into the fray.

"Treason! The miracles of *witnessed visions* cannot be dismissed by those whose purpose recognizes only Quattral science."

By now, Seratt had stepped down from the podium and joined his cohorts. He nodded to Mertoos and Cieyos and then he spun toward the dais, firing a small weapon from which a red laser light struck the top of the Arhahn's throne.

Pandemonium ensued and with his first act of rebellion, the long-held tension between factions erupted. All the private battles of Annevnos and Moniah were now realized in open hostility as Wizans and Quattral squared off. The Quattral unleashed a battery of sonic thrusters and Saen lasers, firing at the dais and council stalls while stunned Wizans hurriedly took a defensive stance using their Coracle-diants to create plasma shields.

A confusion of lights arced around the vast area, scattering most of the Aurans and Auries in a stampede of panic while others, too stunned to accept what was happening, simply stayed put. Sonic weapons and lasers tore through an Auran caught in the cross fire in the aisle. His chest robe, running in blue-silver currents of his blood, his face a spasm of agony, reflected from his mantle. Screams of panic filled the air like furies. The Auran turned to face the dais, lifted his arms beseechingly toward Arhahnis before he fell forward, dead, onto the steps.

Alaysi threw himself before the Arhahn throne while Maetie guards crouched on the dais, shielding the Talsaiyr as best they could while smoke and black, filmy embers filled the air.

The Oscileans took wing, flying down to spew fire at the Quattral while council members stumbled from their stalls, forcing their way toward side exits. The council hall was lost to anarchy. Screams and echoing thunder commingled with hot blood and sweating light, hissing through a stinging haze. Saen lasers ricocheted from stone and marble—transforming the seat of government into a nightmare melee.

Danis clenched his teeth, one hand clasped over his other, bleeding, arm as he lurched to grab Governor Lorra-Sers, dragging him behind the light shields of the Maetie who averted their faces from the Quattral fury unleashed upon their cordon of energy. Stray arcs of electricity flew up from the confrontation.

"Say again, I cannot hear you," Alaysi screamed into a portable comlink. Arhahnis remained on his throne, too stunned to move while Meliphor, Ammanmus and Iskanye begged him to escape. One of the floatscreens turned to face Arhahnis and the face of Annevnos appeared.

"Arhahn, your delusions die today. I will bend the sublime articulation of matter itself to assail the doors of heaven," Annevnos hissed, his black and gold eyes flaring pistons of hatred. Tius led Governor Sers toward an exit where Alaysi frantically pointed to an arch to the right of the dais while Ammanmus tore a piece of cloth from his robe as makeshift dressing for Danis.

"Infinite, we must leave. *Now*," Danis thundered. The floatscreens crackled in static.

Arhahnis could not speak. He stood on uncertain legs and was led by Danis and Alaysi to the exit where doors opened to a terrace. Alaysi and Danis peeked outside.

"There!" Tius cried out, pointing to a group of Quattral rushing upon them firing weapons. Airborne Wizans swooped around the back of the council hall. The Oscileans unleashed a torrent of fire, reducing the Quattral assailants to ash. Meliphor screamed and Arhahnis grabbed her arm, spinning her away from the horrible sight of smoldering bodies as they dropped to stained marble.

Alaysi pressed his comlink to his ear, hurrying everyone to the royal shuttle, which was landing at the far end of the terrace. As the Talsaiyr raced toward the ship, they beheld a Capital in chaos. Random explosions dotted the landscape, a constant roaring sound filled the sky as Quattral ships careened amidst vessels commanded by Admiral Sey.

Danis reached the shuttle first, storming into the flight deck where a Wizan pilot was in communication with the Admiral.

"Report, Evstenos," Danis said, addressing Admiral Sey by his first name. He winced, knocking his arm against the co-pilot seat and slumped into it, wiping sweat and blood from his brow.

"Detec…ting…intense Quatt-activity," The Admiral said, his voice lost in a sea of interference.

"I sent him away, *I* sent him," Arhahnis berated himself in the shuttle salon and no one questioned to whom he referred, it could only be Moniah. As the shuttle lifted into the bosom of a fleet of escort Satarships, Arhahnis gazed in horror at Quattral platforms surrounded by protective light domes, hovering above Rentu over key centers. Cloudy skies teemed with Oscileans over Treaur as Wizans fought to maintain control of the temple and palace complex.

"I have failed the entity Necontis. My hubris is destroying us," Arhahnis moaned and Meliphor threw her arms around him, weeping.

All the machinations between Moniah and Annevnos, the Wizan temple and Quattral guild had exploded and the irony was that Moniah had been sent on an expedition he was dubious to command, leaving the Sphereworlds bereft of his abilities. It was all the more terrible a defeat for Arhahnis because in the absence of the First Lord, Arhahnis was hopeless to thwart the birth of a new and terrible reality—War.

The royal shuttle was dark and silent under the sway of a huge Satarship. The echo of a subsonic explosion made glasses clink and the shuttle vibrated severely, toppling a serving cart. Meliphor sobbed quietly in the lap of Iskanye and Ammanmus stood before one of the observation windows, staring. His shoulders heaved in spasms of grief he would not reveal by facing the others.

Alaysi, Tius and Governor Lorra-Sers huddled before a floatscreen that was showing images of the palace, the Colomeran cavern, and a blurry image of a station in the portal.

"We are a sea of tears," Alaysi said, burying his face in his hands.

* * *

On the tranquil planet Anceria, a world of tropical forests and islands, most of the population was still assimilating the horrors unfolding on Auros Prime. Dumbstruck Aurocearians gathered in hushed groups in their council hall staring silently at a floatscreen, unable to believe what their eyes beheld. A sonic boom shattered their stupor and scores raced outside to point in terror at the exploding Quattral compound from which a massive fireball soared into clear skies.

Rising from the smoke, a single gleaming black ship, streamlined as a thunderbolt, ascended then veered sharply. Its engines kicked into full speed, sending a concussion wave to the ground that shattered windows and generated an ear-splitting sonic blast.

Aboard his attack ship, Annevnos touched a finger to his left temple. It was difficult to concentrate on telepathic communications with so much occurring. He smiled, listening to reports as the ship vibrated in the liberating power of G-forces.

"Activate the Sphereshell resonators," he commanded through the telepathic enhancers and opened his eyes to monitor the ship as it broke free of Anceria's grip. Blue sky transformed to black and, directly ahead he saw the Portal. A glaring image flooded Annevnos' mind. He could see Seratt, mortally wounded, outside the council hall on Auros Prime.

In the vision, Seratt stumbled against a massive pillar, blue-silver blood dripped from a corner of his mouth, his robe smoked and charred in the chest area. Seratt raised a fist.

"Annevnos...to God," he muttered then crumpled. As he fell, his bead implant interlink with Annevnos faded and the mental image blurred to darkness.

Annevnos leaned forward and waved a hand over a section of the large console control board.

"Trajectory: Icrass," the ship computer said.

* * *

Within the Sphereshell, thousands of Quattral Constructorbots spewed from hidden bases. They overran control stations, activating a series of resonators unfolding from concealed compartments to interlink with the outer shell igniters.

Plasma waves danced up from the outer sphere shell, issuing titanic bursts of electro-plasmic energy into the pink clouds of the Suum Nebula where a tremendous wavering rift began to form in space only twenty thousand miles outside of the Sphereworlds.

The attack ship streaked at full speed—dangerously close to the outer Sphereshell—toward Icrass. Annevnos held himself firm against the turbulence, his attention fixed to screens showing the Sphereworlds itself, pulsing with energy.

"Time is mine," Annevnos said, his voice vibrating with the ship.

Just as in a naturally formed star, the Sphereworlds' outer shell burned lighter to heavier elements. Annevnos intended to create sufficient energy with the resonators to drive the Sphereworlds through the rift he created with this energy, punching a hole through the space-time continuum and propelling the entire civilization into the hyper-plane of existence, back to heaven itself.

* * *

"When I hold you again we will be four months older and light years away from today," Moniah said taking Lirea's face in his hands. Her eyes danced with fascination and a hint of apprehension. He kissed her.

"To wait in cold sleep, isolated from your arms," she said hugging him tightly. Nearby, Kaylon, Medean and Saeonar huddled around a control console in the center of the sleep chamber.

"Very well, then, I approve of the modifications. All is ready," Kaylon said, standing to his full height to stretch his back.

"Excellent," Saeonar said, tapping a control to check on the hangar deck and the Oscileans who had been nervous earlier.

"We shall awaken as you wish Moniah, at one week's approach distance of the candidate world," Medean said, turning to inspect his sleep compartment.

"Lord Moniah, bowshot interlink with Auros Prime in five minutes," Vetaeos reported from the other side of the chamber. Moniah smiled and turned to Caras who was chewing a protein roll while engrossed with Saeonar with the hangar deck view.

"Caras, we'll wait for hyper sleep a few minutes until we see the council session," Moniah said and Caras wiped his fingers on his robe and touched a series of controls. A floatscreen lowered from the ceiling, imaging a warm-up field of soft blue with a running series of written Aurocearian characters. While they waited, Lirea supervised the others as they took turns placing a palm on a holo-reader to scan for slow viruses and to check pulmonary rates for pre-sleep muster.

The floatscreen locked into a signal from Auros Prime and everyone froze in horror at the scene of riot unfolding before them. Fires burned in Rentu-Treaur, Oscileans fell from the skies, incinerated by Quattral ships while Aurans and Auries in the Quattral compounds ran for their lives, many little more than staggering limbs of flame from the fury of retaliation of Oscilean fireballs. Lirea flew into Moniah's arms.

"No, no," she repeated until her eyes, awash in tears, could no longer process the images and she buried her face in Moniah's shoulder, her hands clenching his robe. Moniah closed his eyes for a moment, shutting out a spectacle too dreadful to witness.

Saeonar smashed his fist against a bulkhead. Kaylon turned away, bumped into Caras and slumped to his haunches. Medean lowered his face and settled slowly down to sit on the edge of his sleep-control console. Vetaeos covered his face and wept.

"Icrass," Saeonar said looking up to lock his watering eyes with Moniah whose mouth, set into a line, trembled in fury.

"Hyperbolic sleep chambers nominal. Awaiting final instruction," the computer announced calmly.

* * *

On the moon Icrass, Annevnos' screamship blasted the outer airlock doors to the Taen fortress while inside the ship Annevnos stepped into a shielding room and spread his legs and arms. A flexible web of interlocking metal armor surrounded his frame. He stepped forward and lifted a massive weapon from its cradle.

Commander Litos and his Wizans took aim at the Blermetal airlock doors that glowed red-hot. They fixed breathing masks to their faces and gravity clamps to boots. The Blermetal doors sang in a high pitch and melted away and the interior of the fortress temple roared as precious air screamed out.

"Hold and fight," Litos roared against a hurricane of wind. Six Taen priests screamed in terror as they were sucked out into the unforgiving atmosphere of the moon while Litos and his Wizans fought with all their might to hold onto walls and fixed objects. Around them, papers, glow orbs, chairs, tables and a rain of dust and detritus followed the unfortunate priests into oblivion.

A single Auran, hidden in a protective suit of silvery metal comprised of connecting armor plates, strode into the fortress. He carried what looked to be an enormous Saen polarizer, four feet long with a wide muzzle. The barrel of the weapon was connected by a cord to a large, oval, backpack. The invader stepped inside the massive frame of the doors just as emergency blast doors creaked into place and the storm of escaping atmosphere subsided.

"Fire!" Litos commanded and the Wizan wands unleashed a torrent of light beams at the figure whose suit glowed in a protective bubble of light. The invader lifted his weapon. A massive white-hot helix beam of plasma issued from the muzzle, spinning plasma at the Wizans, consigning them to history as their stricken forms evaporated.

A Taen ran toward the intruder commanding him to stop but he was thrown aside by a sweep of an armor-plated arm.

Litos retreated up the stairs and Annevnos moved steadily toward the staircase, following the retreating Wizan commander. Inside his suit, Annevnos could see a small projection-screen showing him a beeping source of energy.

His polarizer weapon dripped liquid fire from its muzzle as he trudged up the stairs. In the corridor above, elite Templars formed a line and as one, fired their Coracle-diants at Annevnos, who swayed, then braced his footing and raised the polarizer to fire. The hellish weapon unleashed a steady torrent of death upon the Templars, scattering them into blazing forms burning so hot they soon crumpled into shapeless mounds of cinder.

Litos pounded on the door to the outer shrine.

"I cannot open up, you will destroy the orb," the Provost replied from within. Litos stepped back and blasted the door with his Coracle-diant. Inside, the Provost stared at Litos defiantly while his adjutant braced himself before the statue of Necontis.

"Stand away or I will destroy you along with the Orb," Litos thundered, sweat pouring down his soot stained face. A blast from behind knocked Litos to one knee. Annevnos entered.

"There it is," he whispered, as the small screen in his suit helmet flared with a constant beeping light source. The priests maneuvered themselves before the statue.

"Leave this place, it is forbidden," The Provost said as Litos grunted and lurched to his feet. He spun to confront Annevnos, raising his Coracle-diant. Annevnos lifted the polarizer. Coracle light shot forth, Annevnos stumbled back but plasma screamed from his weapon to conjoin with the Wizans power.

For an instant Litos held sway but the polarizer field overcame Wizan energy and Litos erupted into a ball of fire. Litos the brave, died without a sound.

Annevnos aimed the polarizer at the priests and the statue.

"You would defile a shrine to Necontis," the adjutant Taen said, averting his face from the smoldering heap that had been Litos.

"Who is Necontis but myself made immortal," Annevnos replied, and fired. The Provost threw his hands up to shield his face and the priests melted into the golden statue, which transformed into molten pools, revealing the Orb Chamber.

Annevnos stepped over blobs of gold and bones and fairly stumbled into the shrine chamber, pulling off his helmet to gasp air, his white hair matted with sweat. Around him statues of the Talsaiyr faced the coffer, their hands out-turned in a silent gesture of warning. Annevnos spit at the statue of Arhahnis and then, eyes flaring, used all his strength to lift the lid from the Orb coffer. The lid slid off and crashed to the floor, raising dust to float in the reduced atmosphere.

Inside the coffer, an orb, of three feet in circumference, glowed like a small star of delicate azure blue. Plasma lines within it swam about creating iridescent flashes of gold and silver that stung the eye but were irresistibly beautiful. Annevnos pulled off his gloves and held his hands near his face, his black eyes watering, and golden pupils flashing ecstatically. His hands trembled above the Orb.

"A spark of eternity, I feel it, I feeeeel it," he said, for the first time laughing with true mirth. Minute traces of electromagnetic energy flared from the Orb to caress the statues of the Talsaiyr. Annevnos activated his comlink. His voice trembled over a pulsing musical sound the Orb generated.

"Cieyos, bring all resonators to full power." He punched a control on his forearm and wiped the blood of others from a small screen transmitting an image from the portal. Outside the Sphereworlds, the rift created by the sphere resonators collapsed gravity, drawing the Sphere toward it.

Annevnos ignored the excited voice of Cieyos in his mind. He activated a generator in his suit connecting it to the master resonator signal and then put his gloves on. He lifted the Orb, which issued smears of white-hot light, smoldering Annevnos' thick gloves. Gravity in the shrine relaxed, dust whirled about like snow to commingle with the long strands of his hair.

The signal beam Annevnos wore directed plasma at the Orb. Annevnos smiled in triumph feeling the current around his armor suit. He had to avert his face while holding the orb at bay.

"Embrace me," He moaned sensually and the Orb sang out a clear tone as Annevnos laughed in delight while he pulled it to his chest. As he did, the Orb music changed, clanging out a fearsome discordant noise. The Orb exploded into smaller spheres that raced around Annevnos whipping up dust, scorching him with electric charges.

Annevnos bellowed in pain, averting his face as shards of the Orb fixed to his suit where the pulse beam connected him to the resonators of the Sphere shell. The connection shorted. Annevnos grasped at it, desperate to disengage the signal while his body convulsed with powers he could not possibly contain.

His gloves disintegrated into ruined bits revealing charred hands, which he raised in a beseeching motion as music filled the chamber. The remnants of the gloves whirled away and the music vanished. Annevnos screamed in fury as plasma released from the Orb fragments swam over him, his suit melted away and his skin glowed in flashing hues of red, orange and white. Some of the orbs spun around his feet emitting charged particles that crackled in bursts of electrical discharges. Annevnos lifted his arms and looked down, his mouth open in a silent scream. The titan found his voice, bellowing to the Gods with all the fury he had suffered in mortal time, "NO!"

As the transforming energy overcame him, Annevnos sensed his end. He would be denied the Godsrealm. His fearsome mind summoned all the power of his immortal soul.

Fighting the power of the Godsrealm, Annevnos took on a new form of being, his eyes emitting gold and black rays. His legs dissolved into tentacles, desperately grasping the bases of the Talsaiyr statues.

"I will not die," he cried. The transforming orbs whirled around Annevnos' frame. As his mind splintered into a parody of the manifestations of Diasentue, six heads on long necks sprouted from his shoulders, each an expression of his fury, greed, fear, madness, lust and envy. The transmitters in his mind fused, evolved, and, capturing his fear of death, his own determination acting with the polarizer weapon diffused transforming energy to create a black vertical prism around him. Annevnos beat at it with his fists, his heads darting about in search of escape. But the prism contained him and floated up, crashing through the roof into space.

The prism hummed in energy, surrounded by a thin yellow polarized field of light as it soared away from the fortress moon toward the spatial rift. Within the rift, a pulsar of brilliant golden plasma appeared, expanding to an oval of silver light, in which the face of Necontis took form. The faces of Annevnos, able to see out of the black prism, screamed as one.

"Necontis!"

The entity face glared at the prism then shattered into fragments of dissipating light.

As the face of Necontis vanished and the rift disappeared the gravity it created was lost, causing the Prism to veer back toward the Sphereworlds. Sensing devices within the

Sphereworlds shell scanned the prism, interpreting it as an aggressor and the outer shell igniters flared to life. The vast corona flames, creating a mammoth solar wind, propelled the prism away from the Sphereworlds at fearsome speed, into deep space.

Alive and sentient within his prism, Annevnos watched the Sphereworlds retreat behind him as he absorbed life-sustaining energy from the void itself. Too powerful to die, Annevnos was now an entity, his divided consciousness surviving in the form of the manifestations he had forged from the fury of the Gods. Removed from time, the fluidity of a new existence dawned upon Annevnos and the entity hibernated in the shell of his prism, assimilating, drawing strength from plasma and solar winds.

A god spark of demon seed by his own design, Annevnos struggled through grief and defeat in an abyss of loneliness that would have shattered even his previous and formidable brain. But he was no longer slave to the constraints of Aurocearian reality. In fact, he was a new titan, born of the Godsrealm and his own enduring prowess, mastering the powers of the prism, utilizing its unique properties to search for a new home.

Metamorphoses

In the final moments of his challenge against civilization, mechanisms within the Sphereworlds shell and almost certainly augmented by the Orb of Necontis—rebelled against the entity Annevnos, ironically perceiving him as an invasion force just as they had been programmed to do by Annevnos and Moniah.

With the spatial rift failing, the outer Sphereshell igniter-transducers that alternated energy from the inner Triune stars in conjunction with the Sphereshell's cold fusion heat, created a balance, forming a new resonator to maintain the constant nurturing force within the heart of the Suum Nebula.

Annevnos had believed the Sphereworlds would act as a vast resonator to create a velocity and dimension of sufficient force to tear at the very fabric of space itself. Who can know if the device might have worked but it appears the Gods dissolved the rift and that proved to be the folly of Annevnos and the core of his defeat.

The civil war continued primarily because the Quattral gained the support of the populace because Arhahnis moved ahead with the expedition into space without allowing other Aurocearians an opportunity to participate. However, when Annevnos vanished and his plan to transport the Sphereworlds into the Godsrealm fell to ruin, so did the war.

-Danis Talsaiyr: Report to the Awclotan Council

Safe within Admiral Sey's command ship, the Talsaiyr converged around Arhahnis, who sat motionless, his arms folded before him while he surveyed the drifting smoke of the passion of war.

"I will step down from the Awclotan throne," Arhahnis said quietly, amidst debate. His words stilled the others. Danis set down an auto stylus. Tius put his chin to his chest and stared at the governor Lorra-

Sers who shook his head while Ammanmus approached the emperor.

"Brother, what are you saying? The capital is secure. Look upon it," Ammanmus said. His tone, though animated, was not in itself persuasive but a floatscreen he indicated presented scenes of quiet streets and pavilions in the twin cities. Auries and Aurans milled about or embraced one another. Arhahnis remained frozen as a statue.

"Danis and Admiral Sey have won the day," Alaysi said in the background, but everyone ignored him. Arhahnis unfolded his arms and rose wearily to his feet. It was true. Through the efforts of the Grand Ambassador and the Admiral, order had been returned to Auros Prime and peace prevailed from the core planet to all the other Sphereworlds.

Arhahnis turned to Admiral Sey, who placed one hand in the breast fold of his robe.

"The inner realm is free of strife, Infinite. Our vessels report total calm," he said.

"Much of the fighting occurred on Auros Prime. If Quattral operatives loyal to Annevnos remain in force, they are nowhere to be seen," Danis concurred and Tius lifted his face to offer a pensive smile. He moved closer to Arhahnis, offering him an Ol pipe. Meliphor wiped her eyes and placed her arm through Arhahnis'.

"Brother, it is vital for us to return to the palace. Show yourself to the populace. Then make whatever decision you feel prudent. If you abdicate, it could engender a resurgence of animosity," Tius said.

"True spoken, Tius," Danis said, slamming his hand on a table.

Arhahnis studied each of the faces gathered around him, taking in their sweat-laden brows and soiled robes. He turned to face Admiral Sey whose lips were pursed in concern.

"Take us to Sumae-Thumaen."

* * *

Diasentue perceived the war and lamented. Pride and degradation of spirit overwhelmed the Aurocearian mortals. For the sake of the future, it would be necessary to exercise a creator's prerogative, to implement changes for future purpose. The bliss of love manifested itself within Diasentue and the godhead responded. The unified signature of electromagnetism and the nature of the Aurocearians was reconceived to unite Aurocearia with the new direction of the Gods Intention.

* * *

Crowds of Aurocearians holding gloworbs and torches raised their combined voices a million strong, chanting the Taen canticle of peace from the acropolis pavilion, cheering Arhahnis who stood with Meliphor atop the royal gardens of Sumae-Thumaen palace. A light breeze carried the scent of flowers and from somewhere in the temple garden a steady whir of Constructorbots making repairs to the damaged temple was the only remaining indication of physical conflict in the royal precinct.

"Do you see, they love you still," Meliphor said, stepping back to allow Arhahnis the full measure of the crowd's devotion but he stayed her and, touching the lower part of her back, pushed her forward to share the affections of the populace. His hand trembled and she glanced at him curiously and then turned to him in concern for the Arhahn's body was trembling. His shaking fingers lifted to his brow and he gasped, staring into the sky where a burning sphere resembling an enormous balloon of fire burned through the atmosphere.

The core of the burning sphere flashed with golden currents of electrical plasma.

"The Orb," Arhahnis croaked, with dreadful recognition, pointing to the sky and Meliphor swung her eyes up to gaze in awe at the fiery sphere as it hovered over the acropolis, casting a shadow onto the crowds, stifling their praises. Ammanmus ran out to them and halted. Arhahnis faltered. Meliphor cried out and steadied Arhahnis with the help of Ammanmus, whose face drained of color as he gazed upon the furious engine of the Gods.

* * *

Three miles above the city, Admiral Sey jumped out of his command seat, dropping a cup of Soffa. His right hand quivered and he snapped his fingers in panic.

"Scan and identify," he said, peering into a hologram. Impatient with the small image, he dashed to the forward blister to look down upon the continent. Waves of light emanated from the burning sphere, creating a hypnotic corona of sound and light, infusing the atmosphere with lightning while dark clouds formed around the radius of the sphere.

"Nothing penetrates this orb."

"All scans are reflected."

Admiral Sey gulped down his fear and hurried back to his command seat. There was no sign of abnormal ship movements in the atmosphere of Auros Prime. He punched a control but the inner realm showed scenes of normal space transports, shuttles and Satarships throughout monitored planets. Quattral facilities were silent, appearing abandoned and devoid of energy spikes.

* * *

Acting on instinct, Ammanmus grabbed Meliphor when Arhahnis' body emitted a sonic pulse wave and then glowed with a faint iridescence as though he were lit from within. Both barometer and catalyst of divine energy, the Arhahn's glow pulsed in time with the burning sphere, whole note, half note, and quarter note. Meliphor tore away from the priest and threw her arms round Arhahnis.

Unknown to the Aurocerians, the transforming will of Diasentue manifested over them. Bliss in love sang its lament but the godhead energy stormed over its children.

Meliphor braced herself and stepped back from Arhahnis. She whimpered and moaned. Iskanye stumbled to Ammanmus, one hand on her belly.

"I cannot feel my body," she cried, her eyes alive with fear. Arhahnis reached out to Meliphor but she retreated, studying her hands, running them over her face while Ammanmus held Iskanye by the hands, desperately searching her eyes. He palmed her forehead trying to find a medical reason for what the Auries were reacting to and then he winced as Arhahnis issued a wail of torment.

Below them Aurans and Auries milled anxiously, pointing to the palace and the glowing form of Arhahnis. A sonic wave boomed from the burning sphere and plasma issued from it, spewing golden rays that fanned out rapidly to every corner of the city amidst gasps of awe and terror.

Suddenly, Auries everywhere emitted the same incandescent glow as Arhahnis.

"The Quattral!" someone screamed. No other male save for Arhahnis appeared affected by the manifestation. Ammanmus grabbed Arhahnis by the shoulders.

"The gods' vengeance," Arhahnis cried and suddenly the glow quit his body, but the strange plasma energy danced around and through the Auries. Arhahnis tried to embrace Meliphor but the instant they touched he was attacked by the energy, which drove him to his knees. Panic seized the emperor. Gold and red spheres of light, some as small as droplets of rain and others as large as melons, whirled around Meliphor but she no longer appeared to be afraid. Indeed, she seemed to *luxuriate* in the energy.

Arhahnis ran to the balustrade where he stood shaking, for the crowds were dotted by glowing forms he knew to be Auries, engulfed by the same energy affecting Meliphor and Iskanye. Ammanmus sank to his knees before Iskanye, grasping her legs but he, too, was physically pushed away from his beloved by a violent charge of electricity while her body faded into a hazy apparition of its mortal form. Ammanmus screamed.

* * *

Within the confines of the sleep chamber aboard Auruaii, Lirea's transforming energy glowed so bright that Moniah and the others had to shield their eyes from the glare. Moniah gasped as he was thrown away from Lirea, whose voice resonated with amplified power. Some terrible realization showed in her expression.

"Beloved, I am always with you," she said.

Moniah struggled to his feet but he and the other Aurans' bodies were overtaken with currents of electrical energy. Saeonar faltered, his hand moving to his sash but his Coracle was half a mile away in his quarters.

Kaylon stumbled across the room. Uletis sank to his haunches while Caras grasped the central control station and Vetaeos slumped to the deck. Only Medean remained still, his eyes closed, accepting the energy, feeling its current transform him. With shuddering effort, Moniah raised himself to his feet and dashed for Lirea while the others looked on helplessly.

Lirea's body floated up, transforming into a brilliantly illuminated Birthfire orb of golden light while she ascended.

"No!" Moniah bellowed reaching out to her but what had been the mortal Lirea disappeared through the upper bulkhead. Panic stricken, Moniah staggered to an imaging screen -- a view of space appeared but there was no sign of her.

* * *

More helpless than he had ever been, Arhahnis cried out with impotent fury. "Necontis!"

But the power of his rage and voice were as nothing compared to the singing tones that encapsulated Meliphor and Iskanye, whose bodies were now barely discernible as ghostly illuminated forms within their Birthfire orbs. As he looked on through flows of sorrow what had been Meliphor and Iskanye, ascended into the skies. Grabbing the rampart balustrade for support and gasping through tears, Arhahnis beheld a sight that turned his blood cold. The air sang with Oscileans flying about in confusion while around them, rising into the skies were millions of red and gold Birthfire orbs, the tears of Auros, flowing up to the Gods, and in each vessel, a transformed Aurie.

The ascending Auries presented a terrible yet beautiful vision within their Birthfire orbs, imbuing the day with millions of small stars. Oscileans flew in circles crying forlorn songs while wails from the helpless and enraged Aurans assailed the Gods.

What Annevnos had longed for and failed to achieve, the Auries gained as they unknowingly rode the ether back to the Godsrealm, transporting half the race of Aurocearia to its original state of being -- beyond mortal cares, removed from time's clicking tyranny.

* * *

Admiral Sey ignored the frantic Aurans, unable to tear his eyes away from the silent, tragic spectacle of millions of Birthfire orbs rising ever higher through the atmosphere of Auros Prime. When they reached the inner realm of space, the Birthfire orbs' glowing light diffused and they simply vanished one by one, through the awful mercy of the Gods.

The ship computer voice droned on amidst the sobs of the crew.

"Interrelational anomalies decreasing. Anomalies scanned at coordinates zero one, three point nine, degree parabolic..."

The voice stopped as an Auran roared in fury, smashing a control on his station with his fists. Silence draped the ship and the Admiral collapsed into his command seat. Hearing muted reports from another ship, he turned to see his communications specialist hunched over his console, oblivious to his duty.

* * *

Moniah felt a hand on his shoulder. He let Medean help him to a seat. The First Lord gazed at the others, their expressions frozen in weariness and dread. He lifted his head to stare at the ceiling then his tears came and Moniah buried his face in the arms of Medean and wept.

There were no words spoken. Moniah lifted his head after a passing of time, stood and walked absently to the automatic doors, which hissed open. He continued down a corridor aimlessly, the words of Necontis searing his consciousness, "You are bound by peace," the entity had warned Arhahnis; then he thought of the blinded "Taen Arhahn" heretic in the fortress of Sine-Togan on Icrass. What had he said? "Nothing can stop the changing..." He found himself at the Oscilean hangar and entered. Prestant moaned and rumbled toward him and Moniah held the giant face of his winged beast in his hands, pressing his forehead to Prestant's. The Oscilean's breath washed over his face, stinging dried tears, but Prestant could not sing. His mind voice echoed with silent confusion and sorrow.

Moniah searched for anger, mentally cursing Arhahnis, blaming him for failing to understand the predictions of Necontis. The Arhahn had caused a war and brought the wrath of the Gods upon them. What a cruel wrath it was but as soon as the fires sprung within Moniah they were cooled by what remained of his rational mind, for the bitter truth was that they had all failed.

Arhahnis had betrayed them by seizing all temporal power under one roof. Annevnos had sowed hatred in his envy and malice for mortal being; Ammanmus had chained the passions of Aurocearians to the strictures of his unbendable Taen edicts and Moniah…what about himself? Had he not made the Wizan a secret community and thereby brought suspicion upon the errors of his brothers? A ship speaker interrupted his inward scrutiny.

"Hyperbaric chambers ready for subjects for sleep duration," the ship computer announced for the hundredth time. Moniah lifted his face from Prestant's to gaze at the female Oscileans, Montre and Halfstep. Montre lifted her head, twitching her nose in his direction but Moniah turned away and she lowered her head back to the deck, letting her tears fall.

* * *

Two days later, Moniah finally unlocked his cabin door. Medean found him seated at the edge of his bed holding one of Lirea's robes to his chest. His gaze fixed to the bulkhead where his Coracle-diant, given him by the transcended Erfros, rested in a special niche.

"The others are ready, brother," Medean said and Moniah cleared his throat. He gently placed Lirea's robe on the bed and stood. Medean stepped aside and the cabin door opened. Without another word exchanged between them, Moniah exited. Medean glanced back into the cabin, shuddering before he followed the First Lord to the crew conference chamber.

The Aurans stared at the conference table around which they sat, or looked at Moniah with a weary fathomless abandon. He took seat, placing his hands on the table.

"I have communicated with the Sphereworlds," Moniah said, his voice muted gravel for lack of use.

"Arhahnis and Ammanmus believe…our Auries did not suffer. It seems they have transformed in a state of grace," Moniah paused, wringing his trembling hands. By now they had all viewed images from Auros Prime transmitted by Admiral Sey.

"The concept of a future for Aurocearia seems a dream," Saeonar said pushing back from the table.

"Future? We are cursed!" Rete hissed.

Moniah raised his face and leaned back in his seat. He stared at an empty chair and shifted his gaze to Saeonar who looked at him with such pity that Moniah struggled to maintain his bearing. Medean poured Soffa and slid a cup to Moniah, who picked up the cup and drank it as though it were the last nourishment he would know.

"We will proceed with the mission," Moniah said, stunning the others.

Kaylon slammed his fist to the table and stood to gaze into space. Moniah turned his face slowly toward Medean.

"We cannot return to the past," Medean said.

"What purpose does our journey serve, why ***not*** return?" Caras interjected, his voice a steely void of emotion. Medean upturned his hands and responded, meeting each of their faces calmly but with obvious determination.

"My brothers I vow to you the full purpose of Diasentue has yet to be revealed and therefore our resolve to fulfill the mission must not waver."

Kaylon returned to his seat. He studied Moniah and glanced around the table then folded his arms over his chest. Moniah leaned forward and spread his hands out on the table.

"If there is a future, we are probably the key to it. I must concur with Arhahnis. The directive of Necontis ***must*** remain in our hearts. I believe Lirea and the others would want it thus," he said, his voice trailing to a whisper.

"How do you know?" Caras asked quietly. Moniah looked at the Auran.

"I feel it," he said, tenderly. "Medean, I wish private word with you." The others took leave and Moniah moved closer to Medean.

"Brother, did the Wizan bring death to Auros?"

"No Moniah. The Tetra-Lachaen Erfros surrendered his life for you. The war which threatened the peace of heaven was intolerable to Diasentue." Moniah straightened his back, his face set in steel.

"The wrath of the Gods is intolerable." Moniah replied, fire in his eyes dimming to sorrow.

"Look again upon the images of the Beings on the candidate world, Moniah."

"Arhahnis called them mirrors of our souls…they are remarkably similar to us."

Medean stood up and gazed at Moniah, his gentle green-purple eyes and golden pupils twinkling.

"Perhaps there is a future on this new world. One your grieving heart has yet to consider." Slowly, Moniah looked up at Medean, a faint promise of hope glimmering in his eyes. Medean turned away and walked through the automatic doors, leaving the First Lord with his thoughts. If he had succeeded in providing any ray of hope for Moniah, he had truly served his brother in the face of cosmic tragedy.

* * *

Moniah inspected the sleep compartments, inside each of which the other Aurans, what remained of his crew, slumbered in hyperbaric rest. In the Oscilean hangar deck the beasts drifted about, unconscious and unaware of the new universe they would awaken to or of the presence of Moniah who, wishing to take one last private journey into his memories of Lirea, sought out the last place where they had shared joy.

"We shall proceed, in desperation if we must, what else is there to do?" Lirea had once consoled him. Her words were as precious now as the memory of her embrace that he fought to recall and Moniah floated in the hangar deck, arms gently folded over his chest, his robes and hair undulating about him, a placid smile in place as he savored memories drawn over the fires of passion that had stretched across centuries.

When he finally entered his own sleep compartment, Moniah was at peace. A longing that would never waver, firmly rooted in his being but conjoined now with a sense of excitement, of wonder and--most important for the well-being of his soul—the promise of accomplishments, yet to be realized, consoled his dreary spirit. The most important motivation was a selfish desire he embraced that he should never lay eyes on Arhahnis or the Sphereworlds again.

Moniah could not conceive of his home worlds in their new incarnation. What it must be to live in worlds with half their history erased in the course of a single day. He longed to walk in the Smoke Ponds with Lirea and be free of *Auruaii* and the mission.

Whatever horror the final moments of mortality had revealed to Annevnos, Moniah desperately hoped that they had defined the meaning of suffering. Finally, Moniah stepped into his hyperbaric chamber and sleep without boundaries deepened his subconscious in whose merciful embrace he found disjointed visions of Lirea. Treasuring the dream of happiness, Moniah drifted deeper into hyper-sleep.

* * *

Halfway between the Sphereworlds of Aurocearia and the candidate planet, *Auraaii* hurtled toward a small solar system consisting of two dead planets, some moons and one gas giant. At the dawn of Aurocearian time, as Moniah had seen in his trance, Arhahnis as catalyst of the gods endowed Aurocearia with life. But his divine energy had not been limited to the home worlds. What Moniah had not seen was the bioplasma Arhahnis had emitted into space, which long ago had found its way to the gas giant system.

The substance of the Arhahn's bioplasma was a quick seed in the gasses of the giant planet where a new design articulated sentient life to suit the environment.

The mind strain bioplasma had conceived a race of vast intellects whose corporeal forms consisted of gas orb bodies of hydrogen, oxygen and genetic sub-strains of the Arhahn bioplasma. Although the beings appeared delicate and easily harmed, due to their semi-transparent bodies, they were resilient, powerful and swift in harnessing a rich and inexhaustible supply of energy sources from which they created floating cities and high technology.

Because the technocracy was a cousin of Aurocearia, it developed as quickly as its progenitor, although the two civilizations were widely disparate relations in form and purpose.

While traveling the void, Annevnos did not perceive the gas beings and his prism sped deeper into space, drawn to the energy of a large orange star. Though entity Annevnos did not discover the gas beings, he would have found their purpose to return to immortality akin to his sole and driving need to return to his god-like state.

The gas beings had long studied the Suum Nebula, whose properties they recognized as the origin of their being. In their beautiful language they called their world "Exciluea" and themselves, the "Excilue." For ages, the Excilue had trained powerful airborne telescopes upon the Suum to focus on the giant, erratically flaring star at the heart of the nebula cloud.

It was fascinating to the Excilue that the star could apparently simply turn off its energy, revealing itself as a sphere, its vast outer surface as smooth as a bearing, shifting in inky shades of black and silver. Of equal fascination, there appeared the occasional glimpse of a solitary portal on the sphere and within viewed through the portal, stars! Stars that had once shone *outside* the sphere and, around the stars, their planetary children. When agitated, the sphere emitted pulses of fire from billions of ignition sources, forming its heroic coronas.

Much improved from earlier models, the new great lens focused on the Sphereworlds with delicate precision. It had been a challenge to align it with Hybora but now that the city floated in calmer regions of the thousand clouds, it worked perfectly.

Numbers of Excilue took turns floating around the lens, their translucent bodies flashing colors while they conversed, their topsails quivering so that they created a constant moving ring around the lens.

It seemed that the vertebrates in the Sphereworlds star must be the incarnate Aurocearian originators of life. This revelation evoked great joy and tranquility throughout Exciluea.

Already the first vessel was ready for flight. To visit the creator!

"A spectacle to daunt the imagination of the mind of god," *Careful Watch* sang to the leadership representative *Bold In Love*, whose body pulsed a series of vibrations from the pink spectrum.

"Your poetry rings true," it said sending out one of its prehensile trunks from its topsail to seize a water globule and taste the water pod contained inside.

"I think this must be as exciting as when we first created the city," said *Careful Watch* whose radial eyes blinked in a stream of lights as it noticed something in the far distance.

"Anything?" *Bold In Love* pulsed.

"Residual storms."

"Shall I instruct control to shift the city to counter orbit?"

"Yes, do so now."

"What a vision the lens offers."

"I have seen enough. Let us go down to the dense depths and inspect the ship." Singing a response *Careful Watch* followed *Bold In Love* as it folded its topsail close to its body, releasing lifting gas, and sank quickly past the lens, plunging through the nesting arcade, past the water baths and out of a portal into the gas atmosphere. Here they picked up speed dropping ten thousand feet in as many minutes to then slow as they approached a large curved form of metal.

* * *

The Excilue ambassador was a strange creature, like a jellyfish come to hover before the floating throne. The invertebrate being was a large translucent oval sphere ten feet in circumference. It was a bioluminescent orb whose, interior convulsed in alternating pastel shades that seemed to augment its thought and emotional patterns. On the top of the orb-shaped body, a graceful topsail of soft gray flesh-like substance undulated in a regular motion. There were what seemed to be respiration gills under the fluke of the topsail. When it spoke, the body colors twinkled and the clear voice projected calm and intelligence.

"We sought your communications, created then a syntax of your speech," the Excilue Being said, evidently still mastering spoken Aurocearian. Arhahnis studied the ambassador with Ammanmus at his side while Danis and Tius whispered to Admiral Sey nearby.

"Ambassador Bold In Love, you must forgive our preoccupied thoughts. Auros has of late suffered a metamorphosis which leaves our hearts devoid of joy," Arhahnis said, at which Ammanmus nodded agreement, tapping a finger to his chin while he continued to scrutinize the beautiful alien.

Bold In Love radiated a quick pattern of red, purple then red, and green light within its sphere shaped body. On signal from Ammanmus, a Taen near one of the floating stones scanned the being as surreptitiously as possible.

"Infinite one, Exciluea grieves for Aurocearia. In this transformation, what purpose you send in the void of interest to us?" the Excilue said and Arhahnis leaned forward. The court fell silent around him and Admiral Sey moved closer to the throne dais.

"Purpose?" Arhahnis said, his tone moving from diplomacy to suspicion while glancing to Ammanmus, whose expression hardened while Tius examined the body of the being with open fascination.

"Forgive, Infinite one. I offend. Aurocearia—our source, our longing," *Bold In Love* replied.

Utterly confused, Arhahnis tapped the armrests of the floating throne. Ammanmus remained silent, aware that Arhahnis although confused was assimilating some inner realization as to the nature of the aliens while he studied them.

Looking at the Excilue being was agonizingly similar to seeing a Birthfire orb; very disconcerting after the awful experience of witnessing so many similar orbs transport the female population to eternity.

"If there was only a face to see, an expression to read on these strange creatures," Danis whispered to Alaysi.

Obviously, the Excilue were extremely advanced, having arrived in a sophisticated vessel, but Aurans were a wounded lot, trying to pick up the pieces, standing behind the disciplines of their various intellectual pursuits to stave off collective madness.

Few Aurans cared what was occurring beyond the Sphereworlds at the present and Moniah's mission was regarded as something for priests to ponder.

However, the Excilue ambassador and its kind evidently thought enough of the mission to risk sending one of their own to worlds that had just experienced a terrible war, its population of Aurans in the throes of a mass sociological depression. Why risk coming to the unstable Sphereworlds now?

The journey to Aurocearia seemed a great deal for the Excilue to risk, for Arhahnis correctly perceived the Excilue to be a cautious and secretive race. The Taen who had scanned the Excilue whispered urgently to Danis, who discreetly waved his hand over his chest in signal to Ammanmus, who, in turn, leaned toward Arhahnis in private council.

Arhahnis came to his feet, offered a dim sketch of his former smile and, without missing a beat, ended the audience.

"Ambassador, please accept the pleasures of our palace while I attend to other matters. We will meet again, soon."

The Excilue flashed soft pink and blue colors throughout its body, its sail undulated and it floated back, away from the throne. While Alaysi escorted the Excilue from the throne hall, Danis, Tius, Admiral Sey and the Taen hurried to the dais.

"Tell him," Danis said to the Taen.

"Infinite, the Eek-sy-luu, forgive me, possesses a residue of spectrum energy!" the priest said.

"This is revelation? All creatures are found to possess this energy," Arhahnis said, rising from the throne in exasperation.

"All beings and creatures in *Aurocearia,*" said Ammanmus and Arhahnis turned slowly to meet his eyes.

"This confirms that the catalyst creation energy you projected to all living beings was not confined to our worlds. The Excilue see *you* Arhahnis, as the master of their destiny," Ammanmus added. Arhahnis listened quietly and then strode away, leaving the others confused. Danis frowned and started off to pursue Arhahnis but Ammanmus stilled him with a touch of his hand.

Arhahnis continued into a solarium where he meandered to a wall on which a mural showed Meliphor and him walking across clouds, her foot stepping to the Mountain of Beginnings summit.

"These aliens could not have prevented the war," Ammanmus said from behind him. Surprised by the intrusion, Arhahnis swung around to confront Ammanmus.

"You do not have the power to substantiate what you suggest. Your words are scant comfort to any of us. Think, Ammanmus. Had these Excilue come to us before the struggle their presence would have thrown the Quattral into disarray."

Ammanmus stepped deeper into the room while Arhahnis paced, wringing his hands.

"You cannot know this for certain brother. It is a time for loss and gain, remember? Your words are the living prophecy of Auros."

Arhahnis swept an arm across a table hurling delicate firestone sculptures to the floor where they smashed into iridescent fragments.

"Get out," Arhahnis thundered. Ammanmus strode away. Arhahnis stood entirely still, silently, his breath heaving and then he lifted his face to the ceiling.

"*Why* could they not have come before the war?" Arhahnis cried. His voice ringing to the ceiling where the memory of Meliphor gazed back in painted likeness.

Planetfall

From Earth, the titanic sphere shone as a bright star, dominating its neighbors within the iridescent nocturnal smear of the Milky Way, inspiring legends for primitive man. In Asia, priests dubbed it a cosmic dragon while in the west it was perceived as "Alcoyne," daughter of the gods and the most spectacular light in a pantheon residing in the constellation later known as the Pleiades.

On nights such as this, while gazing into the cold clarity of a heaven chilled by oncoming winter, elder Zoimon, was hypnotized by Alcoyne's brilliant beauty of silvery light made all the more stunning by the lack of the moon Goddess and her sibling, whose celestial bodies would soon rise to herald the advent of winter solstice.

A gust of wind seized his breath and the sudden whimper of his eldest hound convinced the wizened old Zoimon to return inside and take his place at the hearth chair.

"A chill from the Atlantic brings the death of bones," he said, pulling a ragged cloak about his neck, turning to glance within his simple dwelling. Gathered around the hearth were the welcome faces—and unwelcome aromas—of what remained of the city leaders. None of whom, apparently, paid heed to his advice concerning the importance of hygiene. Zoimon squinted into the night.

"Be safe in the comfort of the Gods, Clovis," He said lifting his head to gaze into the sparkling firmament.

The year was 828 AJ, after Julian, the Roman Emperor who had restored the pantheon of the classical gods and whose long reign had secured a miraculous recovery of Attic culture resulting in the saving of the library at Alexandria. This had led to an expansion of sea-faring trade and exploration by Europeans in the year 400.

A hundred vessels of the Atlantean design had arrived on the North American continent in 402, disgorging hearty travelers who settled along the eastern seaboard. The journey had been arduous at best but the European fleet brought hundreds of eager settlers whose habits and customs so unnerved the Native Americans that they fled to remote locations, deep in the continent.

What had been a period of relative tranquility was now changing. In the unexplored regions of South America, the Mayan culture was in decline while in Europe the Langobard struggle with Byzantium had finally ended in 796.

The Emperor Charlemagne was losing the ancient realm to hostile invaders while in Spain the Omayyads established an anti-Caliphate. In Asia, Pala Kings ruled eastern India and the Tang dynasty controlled China while Japan entered its Nara period establishing a permanent capital and driving out Chinese influences. In Africa, Ethiopia reached its zenith.

In the winter of 825, the settlers of North Amernius lost touch with Europe as trade retracted due to political unrest, harsh winters and stormy seas.

Since it was before the advent of advanced science for humanity and, therefore, no one on earth possessed a telescope, terrestrial stargazers could not study the depths of space or discern the difference between the artificial star and its naturally occurring neighbors.

During nights that the star glowed, whispers of mystery abounded as to the purpose of Alcoyne and what were perceived as her fiery messengers streaking across the sky. The people of the continent called Amernius were unaware that their world was being bombarded by meteors and, like their counterparts in other lands, the people were shrouded in the dark ages of pre-feudal history. They could only reach for comfort amongst the legends of the ancient gods.

Zoimon gathered his tattered cloak about his neck.

"The goddess keep you, Clovis," he said and paused in his doorway to scan the streets before hurrying inside. He bolted the door and waited, finger to his lips, ear pressed to the door but, hearing no creeping footsteps, he moved away from the door waving his arms and smiling.

"Me-thinks we are alone here," Zoimon said.

Around the fires of his crackling hearth, old Zoimon, elder of the priest cult of Diana, the Moon Goddess, sat down to allay the fears of his people.

He coughed, shooing a mewling cat from his feet. Grimy, rapt faces gazed at him intently, seeking comfort and reason in what was an age where the myth of nature overwhelmed empirical knowledge.

Zoimon scooped a wooden cup of hot tea from the hearth kettle, stretched his aching leg and rubbed his beard. A night bird settled overhead in the rim of the hearth hole in the ceiling, decided the wilds of the night were preferable to smoke and fire and fluttered away.

"The battle tore us asunder. Zoimon, what say your portents? If Alcoyne angers our father the sun, this fathoms why there are storms from heaven and why cursed fire rains in the sky. We failed to heed and now Acadia is fallen," a man's voice put forth, to grunts of assent. Zoimon peered into the gloom beyond the hearth's glow, above them, through the hearth hole, a shimmer of moonlight appeared.

"Claudius, you've a keen enough mind but yer unschooled in sacred truths. The city did not fall of heavenly wrath," Zoimon said. Muffled agitations arose from the people; a child cried. Its mother rocked the babe quietly, gazing at Zoimon with eyes alive in wonder and dread. Zoimon smiled reassuringly.

"The sun is the father of Diana. Diana's son, Trehoomena, the second moon and the issue of herself, rises in the mid gloom twice in a month, *protecting* us from the demons of the outer darkness." Zoimon paused to sip tea, coughed, then gazed up through the large smoke hole and consulted one of his many scrolls.

"Trehoomena rises. Come now," said Zoimon, standing feebly.

"Is this wise?" Claudius asked but Zoimon smiled and refused the aid of an arm offered for support as he led the small group outside.

"There! Behold the crescent of Trehoomena in the south, and in the glow of the dancing lights to the north be Diana herself." Buffeted by a frigid wind, Zoimon accepted his walking staff from a youth. Leaning on it with both hands he stared at expectant faces, taking time to meet the glistening eyes of each as he spoke.

"See, then, as the ancient wisdom foretells: we of Gaia are led through the glorious firmament by the protection of the father sun, his daughter Diana and her son, Trehoomena, the rider of dawn. When fireballs streak the heavens, it cannot harm us. What few crash down to land are the hapless defeated of the Gods."

The group jumped as a wavering glow and footsteps approached around a corner but sighed as they recognized the priestess Elria, escorted under torchlight by her guards who held the flames at arms reach to prevent smoke from sullying her robe. Elria touched Zoimon tenderly.

"Goodly Zoimon, you are teaching under the stars?"

One of her bracelets chimed against another in the silence. She turned to the people.

"You truck with despots and this raises dread within you. Take comfort in the wisdom of Zoimon and leave him to peace then," she said. Zoimon lifted his face to carry his voice over a stirring breeze, his tone softening in order to provide comfort.

"Sleep now my friends. The winds of winter are soon upon us and work has yet to be borne." A dog barked and, slowly at first, then as a single movement, the people dispersed. Zoimon smiled, nodding to the occasional bowed head or whispered praise. A mother gave Zoimon a loaf of bread and a cured cutlet and he kissed her brow in thanks. People hurried to the relative safety of their homes, inspired to take their leave by stronger gusts of cold.

"Zoimon, get thee in, you tremble and the night is not safe. Raiders are still about our precincts," Elria advised, her gentle voice suffusing into the wind. Zoimon turned to regard Elria's luminous green eyes. He paused to luxuriate in the beauty of her shapely features, a pang in his heart lost to younger days.

"Be now forgiving. The people's only guilt was to trade with Canelor. Varrick cares only to conquer. He'll leave us to peace, now," he said, gazing into her sacred green eyes. Elria smoothed her hands over the soft mink lining of her velvet robe and smiled.

"If there is ever a day dawning without your counsel good Zoimon, I shall be alone in a land of fools. To your bed with thee and sleep well," Elria said, and nodded to her burly captain. Zoimon watched until she was safely away in the comfort and safety of her guards.

Once more Zoimon turned his gaze to the night sky where Alcoyne flared in dancing, twinkling light. He made the peace symbol in the air with a trembling hand and with cautious movements returned to the warmth of his small house, where he rolled his bed makings to the center of the room beside the fire, chuckling while his dogs nuzzled him, tails wagging, happy he was at last taking to bed.

Dying embers glowed in the grate and Zoimon gazed up through the round smoke hole into night. He scratched one of the dogs and kissed another.

"The wind is safely held without, the warm fire within, and you, my truest friends, close at my side. These are blessings." He blew out a candle, sighed and groaned as he lay back.

Quickly enough, the old priest's eyes fluttered closed. An elder hound nuzzled under the covers at his elbow, another at his feet. His heart beat in rapid time and he turned quietly, uttering a quiet moan, and fell into the arms of Morpheus, who would never return him to mortal consciousness.

* * *

Gentle breakers, illuminated under the glow of the moon Diana, rolled into shore from the Atlantic, carrying a cold breeze over the distant battle-weary city of Acadia. Clovis rubbed sandy grit from his face, studying his former capital under the moon glow while taking care to keep his body hidden in the tall reeds on the dunes.

He glanced over his shoulder where his wife, the deposed Queen Marina, did her best to make suitable comfort of her bivouac, huddling close to a small fire hidden deep in the tall reeds and trees. Marina held an infant, gently rocking the child while she stifled a yawn as she stoked the fire. An owl hooted. Clovis came into the reed clearing to scan the horizon. Only the steady lulling sound of gentle waves stirred the night.

"Come, sleep now, Clovis," Marina urged, reaching up to touch his thigh.

Clovis swatted a marsh fly from his face. He groaned as he sat down beside his wife.

"Look at the heavens, Marina, so bright! The Gods' souls shine upon us. Who would know I lost our world? " he said. Marina sighed, unconsciously twisting her last valued possession, a ring, round and round on her finger.

"Acadia is too rich a prize for any one people to possess," Marina reflected, wistfully, gathering her shawl tighter around her baby, kissing his brow.

Clovis smiled wearily at Marina. Her face, though careworn, was still lovely and devoid of hatred and her dirtied hair shone under the moonlight. He leaned over and softly kissed his baby's hands.

"The tyrant of Canelor is too powerful; he sweeps across Amernius taking what he will," Clovis said, tossing a stick into the reeds. He pulled a fur skin from a sack, and then rolled the skin into a ball as a pillow for Marina.

"Rest now; I shall keep watch," Clovis said and Marina lay back, cradling the child. Silent shooting stars hypnotized Clovis but he chewed pepper twigs to remain awake. His eyes became lead weights and he rubbed sand into his cheeks as the creep of night progressed and the hours passed. When the fire lay in embers, Clovis heard a low rumbling sound that droned in his ears unlike anything he had ever experienced. He rose to his knees.

A flock of nested birds took wing, piqueing his interest. Clovis looked around. Marina awoke.

"What is it, that sound?"

"It comes from on high," Clovis whispered, but only darkness and the silent glittering of stars were perceptible in the gloom.

Confused, Clovis put an ear to the ground.

"Could it be Varrick's army? If so, why would they move at night?"

The rumbling grew louder and lowered in pitch.

"I feel it in my teeth," Marina said, keeping one hand on the child's coverlet. Clovis found her eyes in the gloom. They stared at each other for a long moment.

"What is this new terror? Mercy of Diana, it shakes my stomach, Clovis!" Marina cried, her voice quaking with fear.

"It is a deep humming such as a million bees or the rumble of the quaking earth." He splashed water on his face and stood, wincing, as his aching back and legs rebelled.

Clovis towered above Marina, his head darting about, searching for danger. Then, the stars above Clovis vanished slowly. Marina blinked, "A cloud," she muttered. She gave out a startled cry and cringed, instinctively guarding the child.

Clovis waved his hand frantically.

"Shh, be still," he hissed and then his eyes followed the direction of her trembling hand, which pointed straight up.

Marina's palpable fear showed as goose flesh on her skin. Clovis looked straight up to gaze at the darkening sky. The stars were gone. His teeth chattered from the subsonic humming it made—whatever *it* was—hovering above the treetops. The floating thing filled his field of vision. It seemed to be solid and as large as a city. Clovis squatted to his haunches and spun about, fingertips in the sand, taking in the dimensions of the enormous object.

"It is longer than a mile," he gasped shaking his head as if to awaken from a vision his mind refused to accept. Bright lights shone out from its underside, brilliant unwavering beams that scanned a parcel of ground and then went dark; all without a sound.

An owl screeched and took wing. Other birds flew away, scared from their night roosts, and deer scampered into the nearby forest. Marina inched closer to Clovis; her breath, foggy from the cold, gasped in short spasms while her body quivered against him.

* * *

Moniah leaned back and away from a scan screen while Saeonar and the others studied an infrared floatscreen image. The ship digested a plethora of information concerning everything from atmospheric readings to soil samples and, most importantly, the three native sentient beings.

"I detect bioplasmic readings, very minute to be sure but here and here in the lower spectrum. This confirms the Arhahn's presence," Caras said. Moniah frowned, switching a screen to infrared he looked out upon a mature world of beaches, trees and small, primitive cities.

If Aurocearia had seeded this world then it had evolved as rapidly as the Sphereworlds, yet these beings lived in a manner Aurocearians had never known, devoid of high science as if a strange parody of the Garden age were in place. Medean approached Moniah.

"I see your mind, brother. Consider, what we know as years in the fluid realm of time, which the Gods alone command, could be a reality consisting of centuries for these beings."

"Five thousand years to us, five thousand centuries for them," Moniah said and Medean simply smiled. While the others concentrated their scrutiny on the three beings, Moniah weighed the ramifications of this revelation--or was it merely a speculation?

He had risen from hyper sleep with a renewed sense of purpose for the mission. After four months in the deep sleep of suspension, the Sphereworlds seemed to be a place as distant to him as the amnesia of the eternal Godsrealm. Was it possible? Could he have lived so long with Lirea in his former life?

"What was our reality has no relevant construct to this world," Medean said, and turned away.

"A male, a female and, according to the genetic signature—their offspring," Kaylon said, adjusting a spectrometer.

"An issue of the adults?" Rete said in amazement, his fascinated gaze locked on the floatscreen. Kaylon stepped aside, allowing Saeonar and Rete to peer closely into the three -dimensional image.

"See for yourself. The offspring is clearly related to the adults. It is a male and is in all measures a smaller version of them. Note the structure of the brain, organs and blood vessels. Here. See the lungs and heart?"

"A child," Medean interjected, locking eyes with Moniah.

"Their respiratory functions are highly agitated," Caras said, stepping down from the flight bridge. Moniah stroked his chin.

"They are terrified," Medean said and Moniah hurried to his command seat. Finding his Coracle-diant, he returned with it to a large Saen array control center near the helm and navigation stations.

"Caras, disengage the Saen weapons from the forward underside cannons. Rete, I will infuse my Coracle into the Saen beam," Moniah said as he unsheathed the Coracle of Erfros, carefully examining its golden and platinum engravings. Saeonar frowned. He moved slowly toward Moniah while the others, bewildered but obedient, carried out the order.

"Moniah, what are you planning?"

Moniah ignored Saeonar and moved toward the Saen array control station. He unscrewed a cylinder and set his Coracle-diant into an aperture.

"We must calm these beings."

"With the spectrum of Wizan!"

"Yes."

The bridge doors opened and Vetaeos entered, hurrying down the flight bridge to the science stations where he paused, taking in the scene. Moniah and Saeonar stared at each other while Caras, Rete, Medean and Kaylon looked on.

"Oh! By the Gods, the Oscileans are still in sleep," Vetaeos said, seeing the pulsing, humming image of the aliens. Moniah nodded to him distractedly, and then turned again to meet the unwavering glare of Saeonar.

"You tread on dangerous ground," Saeonar said, his voice a whisper but heard clearly by all.

Saeonar glanced at Medean beseechingly and Medean swallowed apprehensively and spoke with a soothing, almost condescending tone.

"Moniah, is this prudent? The Wizan spectrum carries in it properties unique to Aurocearia. Saeonar gives wise counsel in advising caution."

Moniah tossed his hair as his head jerked to one side. His eyes flashed. He motioned to Kaylon, who quickly brought up an image of the three beings on the largest floatscreen.

"Look at them, their hearts beat like drums, the offspring, the…child, screams. Whatever else our purpose is, we have not come here to strike terror into their hearts. I will hear no more. This action is my command." Moniah set a steely gaze upon Rete.

"Ready, lord Moniah," Rete said.

Saeonar folded his hands over his chest and stepped back. Moniah placed his hands on his Coracle-diant and closed his eyes. In a few seconds, the Wizan wand glowed with a soft golden light that streamed into the Saen array control aperture.

Moniah opened his eyes and stepped back as the Coracle-diant energy subsided. The bridge was utterly silent. Kaylon cleared his throat and, with Rete, checked the spectrometer screens.

"Infusion complete," said Kaylon, and Rete smiled at Moniah. Medean sat down and sighed while Uletis, Caras and Vetaeos studied the mystic as though expecting him to protest.

"Confirmed: their respiratory functions are calming, cardiopulmonary rates stabilizing. Well done, Wisdom," Rete said, addressing Moniah in Wizan title. Moniah's blue eyes watered, his silver pupils flashing softer, slower patterns. He walked quietly to the blister dome and looked out to the glittering moonlit sea.

"I will go down and face these beings," he said, so quietly that Vetaeos could not hear him. But, when the others sprang to action, checking temperature, barometric pressure readings, airborne pollens and viral scans, Vetaeos dashed to his station to assist Medean in conducting a final bacteria survey. Medean joined Moniah near the blister dome.

"The moment you breath the air outside, history will change for us," Medean reminded Moniah, whose eyes raised slowly to the full moon in the northern sky. Beyond the moon, Moniah felt sure he could see the location of the Suum nebula and Sphereworlds.

"But Medean that reality occurred the moment we arrived."

* * *

A warm light, abating the chill of night, flooded over Clovis and Marina. Clovis stood to his full height. He reached for Marina and she came to her feet, rocking their child in her arms. Clovis looked up into a golden shaft of light. He had no understanding of how long he was hypnotized by the light but it soothed his cares like a numbing drug.

"We are dead, Marina--painlessly, my love. See? Opens there above a portal to heaven," Clovis said, letting his broadsword slip from his fingers as the light bathing them diffused around a large, round, transparent sphere that descended through the shaft of light. Inside it, one could make out a form.

"An angel," Marina cried, tears drying on her cheeks in the warmth of the light.

The light beam softened in intensity and the sphere settled to the ground directly in front of them. It made a soft shimmering sound as the glass of the sphere disappeared into two hovering disks at either side of the angel they could now clearly see.

The angel wore a fabulous robe of dark blue, hemmed in gold that appeared to be a type of vine leaf. The hair of the angel was long, nearly to his waist, midnight black and shining clean. The face was that of a man, handsome and strong of feature but his *eyes* were large pools of beautiful blue and where the round pupils should be, there were sparkling flecks of shimmering silver as if tiny lights floated within them.

"Are we dead? Do you want us to go with you great one?" Clovis asked.

Moniah stood before them, as stunned by their similarity to Aurans as they were awed by his presence. He restrained himself from wincing because they smelled a fright. Their voices, however, were calm and they spoke clearly and, apparently, with some intelligence, albeit in a thick accent full of hard vowels. The sounds were not musical and wavered from a contralto to a baritone register.

"Medean, route the aliens' words through all translation protocols, musical phrases, phonetic matching. Begin a database. It's too much to expect they will learn even a rudimentary form of Aurocearian so we need to learn their language as soon as possible," Moniah said into his hand held comlink.

"Beautiful. Does it speak Latin? There is music in its voice," Marina said, through happy tears. Clovis swallowed nervously, wiping his beard, and put his shaking arm around Marina's waist to steady her nerves.

"Look there! It holds something, something of rare metal, into which it speaks." He said and he looked up at the *Auruaii* and its clamshell-shaped prow, towering over them.

"A floating city. A heavenly city where other angels dwell?" Marina said, hugging her infant to her bosom.

While Moniah studied the aliens, they gazed back with trust and patience. A subtle change occurred in Moniah as his perception and senses attuned to an awareness of earth and the scent of pine and sea, the sounds of crickets, of the aliens language, even the sound of their breathing. The male continued to speak in short phrases. There was an air of intense curiosity and supplication in the tone, proving intellect, and, Moniah hoped, sheer stupor at the overwhelming image he must seem to them. Any sign they perceived him as divine must be quickly averted. There would be nothing like the Taen Arhahn sacrilege allowed on Earth.

Moniah studied the humans. The male was strong of limb, with an open countenance, and strangely enough wore hair on his face. His clothes were badly soiled and his eyes were small, difficult-to-read brown orbs with an iris and lens that resembled that of an animal! Moniah moved cautiously closer and the female gazed at him longingly, as though her life, hard lived, was eager to surrender to him. Moniah reached out and touched her cheek. Her face, young but careworn, softened, her eyes closed and she smiled. The male cried silent tears of joy as a night bird flew past.

Moniah activated the travel sphere and the native family looked about, startled, as the plasma glass spread out from the discs to enclose them. The female jumped as the glass formed under her tattered shoes and the male crouched to the floor, smoothing his grubby hands across the curved, striated glass.

The infant awoke but merely yawned and turned its head to nuzzle against the female. When the travel sphere lifted, the male cried out but the female continued to stare at Moniah longingly.

Moniah noted that as Clovis and Marina stepped into *Auruaii*, Clovis touched his stomach then the face of the female and child as if confirming their physical person still existed. Moniah led them through pristine corridors where Clovis seemed fascinated by lighting sources, pausing several times to peek up into recessed alcoves of lighting bays. At one point, Clovis reached up with a shaking hand then, drawing it back, smelled his fingertips, apparently satisfied that he was not burned.

They came to polished metal doors, finely wrought and inlaid with intricate carvings that opened to reveal another chamber.

"Look, other angels," Marina said, huddling near to Clovis, her dozing child held tight to her chest. Medean stood near a holoscreen while Kaylon, Rete, Caras and Vetaeos looked on from the other side of the room.

"These too, are men angels. Behold these lights, without fire but warm and steady as the sun like the others we saw," Clovis said, blinking at the more intense spotlights of the hospital bay. He and Marina followed Moniah very closely, sticking to his side. Moniah turned to them gently and touched his chest.

"Mo-neye-ah. I am Moniah," he said. Clovis chewed his lip and wiped grimy sweat from his brow. He glanced at Marina who nodded and Clovis repeated the name, impressing Moniah with the fact that the male could repeat the sounds and form the word. Clovis turned to Marina.

"Mo-neye-ah, the angel's name." She smiled and coughed, then grunted and shook her hand before her as if trying to impart something. Moniah smiled. She relaxed, smiled in turn with a quivering lip, touched her chest then Clovis', and hugged the child close.

"Marina, Clovis and our son, Darius," she said. Medean approached them, patting two of the hospital scanning beds as he did. Clovis looked to Moniah, who indicated that they should lie down on the beds. Clovis helped Marina to the first bed.

She smelled the clean bedding and sighed then smiled at Clovis, who carefully sat on the other bed and then reclined, his eyes as wide as saucers, darting from Moniah to Medean to Marina.

"What a stench!" Vetaeos said, but Moniah raised his hand, never taking his eyes from the male and female on the beds.

"Return to duty stations. Begin, Medean," Moniah said. Medean scanned the alien family using a non-invasive, overhead Saen beam unit.

"Marginal nutrition. The female has a virus. This is why she sneezes. The child is healthy but undernourished. I would recommend inoculations for the virus and bacilli we determined hostile to them upon arrival."

Moniah nodded approval and walked away for a moment.

"Moniah, please do not stray too far, they are more comfortable when you are near," Medean said.

"What can we do about the smell?" Kaylon said, pinching his nose as he followed the others out of the bay. Medean cocked an eyebrow at Moniah and paused. Moniah smiled at the aliens then turned back to Medean.

"Simple enough: we clean them. They are riddled with bacteria. The child has parasites in its hair. Minor scrapes and bruises on the adults and here, a scar on the male."

"A battle scar," Moniah said, examining an overhead screen. The ship comlink beeped. Moniah raised a finger to the family, indicating a pause. Clovis smiled and mimicked the gesture.

Moniah moved to a wall speaker plate.

"Yes."

"Saeonar wonders if he should awaken the Oscileans." The listless voice of Uletis crackled into the room, causing the aliens to look about. They saw a hologram on the far side of the room depicting the face of Uletis.

"Sprites!" Marina said, pointing to the hologram.

"No. I will personally give the order." Moniah said. He returned to the aliens, who regarded him with trusting, loving faces.

"This will not hurt you," Moniah said, and led them to showers where they luxuriated together removing filth, blood and insects. They laughed with such delight that Moniah chuckled as well, listening on the other side of a partition as he fed their malodorous garments into a recycler.

Robed as Aurocearians, deloused, fed and inoculated; it soon became apparent that the primitive family suffered from debilitating exhaustion. In Moniah's quarters, they fell asleep in moments as Medean and Moniah looked on from the doorway.

"Remain and monitor them. Tell me when they awake," Moniah whispered, and then left Medean alone with the snoring family, who held each other tenderly, even in sleep. Medean settled into a chair to study his medical scans; occasionally peeking over his records to make sure the primitives were resting peacefully.

* * *

Moniah entered the bridge to find everyone converged around the master-scanning console.

"Look at the water buoyancy in this lake. It is perfect.

Auruaii will float," Caras was explaining to Saeonar.

"Why submerge the ship?" Moniah asked, joining them to study a holographic map of the land in the immediate vicinity.

"This large city due east of us is a short distance away. When the day breaks everyone will see us. If we do not *wish* to be seen as yet, I suggest we put down in the lake," Saeonar said, and Moniah studied the map. The lake in question seemed remote enough from the city, guarded by rocky foothills and surrounded by forest.

"The city is undoubtedly the home of the alien family. There appears to be conflict within its environs. Note the random fire damage and sonic scans revealed what sounded like screams and fighting. It is quiet now," Kaylon added.

Moniah sighed and rubbed his forehead. "Perhaps we have found our first destination," he said. He turned to Uletis, who oversaw the hyper-drive. With Lirea gone and Medean serving double duty as ship's physician and navigator, the Wizan engineer had also been serving double duty with the chief engineer, Caras. Uletis had fared badly after the metamorphoses. Refusing nourishment, he had spent several days in the care of Medean, suffering from a desperate depression after emerging from stasis sleep. Since then, Uletis had been consumed with his work and was only now evidencing some interest in the mission.

Once, Uletis had reminded Moniah of Alaysi, with a similar buoyant sense of humor and an open, easy manner but, though he had emerged from depression, aside from work, Uletis was socially removed and distant to the point of being sullen. Looking at him, Moniah wondered how Alaysi might be but he shook off the thought.

"Uletis, what is our energy output?"

"Nominal my lord. Anti-gravity molecular inducers are functioning perfectly. We could hover for weeks, even months if need be."

"Yes, but what effect is our output having on the environment?" Moniah pressed.

Uletis pointed to a graph at the side of the master hologram.

"Forgive me, I misunderstood. We are inducting oxygen and nitrogen compounds and expelling same after re-conversion to thrust." Moniah glanced at Saeonar, who nodded agreement, though he was still suspicious of Moniah because of the Wizan tranquilizer agent he had used to calm the native family.

"We do not adversely affect the planet," Vetaeos interjected, offering Moniah a cup of Soffa.

"Very well. We shall float. Kaylon take the helm. Medean is with our guests." Kaylon smiled and threw himself into the navigation station while Moniah sipped his Soffa, taking stock of the mood of his crew.

In the dark before dawn, *Auruaii* moved over the chosen target. Kaylon expertly centered the huge ship over the water and lowered the ship gently into the lake. *Auruaii's* anti-gravity engines pushed a stream of water from its underbelly in radial waves. The ship settled into the water and then floated with only the upper third of its streamlined structure visible above the surface.

* * *

Unaware of his own weariness, Medean fell asleep. While in repose, his mind connected with the aliens and, in so doing, despite disjointed and often frighteningly barbaric images—*by dreaming within their minds*—he learned their language. He awoke to find Marina smiling at him.

"Marina," Medean whispered.

Her smile brightened, she held up a hand and chewed her lower lip, struggling to articulate. Her posture stiffened as she nursed the infant with a formula Medean had given her, which she had repeatedly tasted.

"Mead-ean," she said triumphantly.

"Yes, I am Medean."

Clovis stirred, then sat up and winced and smelled his skin. He smiled at Marina and rocked the child in his arms while Marina accepted fresh swaddles for the child from Medean.

"Angels in mortal form, come to make us whole," Clovis said, and Medean lifted a brow to Clovis who sat stunned as the two beings recognized one another's words.

"Angels?" Medean said. Clovis bolted forward, searching Medean's eyes as if trying to find something. When Medean smiled, he nodded having discovered in the expression of the Auran what he could not read in his wondrous orbs.

* * *

By midday, Medean, Moniah and the aliens were huddled around a table littered with food. The classroom worked efficiently with Medean translating to Moniah and Moniah in turn repeating the new words. A hologram showing images of objects and life forms on the new world boosted the learning curve exponentially.

"Tree", "Rock", "Deer", "Horse", "Water", on and on until evening. Moniah adjusted the hologram and a picture of the planet as seen from space came into view. Clovis and Marina pursed their lips, leaning toward the image with furrowed brows.

"Beautiful," Clovis sighed.

"Let us provide a perspective," Medean said, and readjusted the image to show the horizon. Clovis opened his arms, tears glistened in his eyes and Marina simply stared in wonder, rocking her cooing child.

"Earth," Clovis said.

"It are beautiful," Moniah said but Medean wagged a finger at Moniah correctively.

"It *is* beautiful."

The look Moniah fixed upon Medean made Clovis laugh and, for the first time in months, Moniah laughed as well. Clovis clapped his hands, thrilled that he could connect on an emotional level.

The child cried out and Marina hurried to its improvised crib. She lifted the child and sang to it as she sat in a chair facing away from the group to breastfeed. Moniah and Medean became wistful at the sound of her feminine lullaby. Clovis studied the Aurans and Moniah stood up and discreetly wiped moisture from his eyes with his robe sleeve. Then he jabbed a button on the table.

"Caras, I have a job for you," he said, excitedly, winking at Clovis.

"I will help," Clovis said.

"You already have, my friend," Moniah said, and Clovis stood up to straighten his robe. He came around the table, extending his right hand to Moniah. Moniah mimed the gesture.

"Friends," said Clovis and Moniah reached out and shook hands with him.

"Friends."

* * *

Bright morning light shone through blue skies into the bridge blister dome, warming Moniah's face. Across the lake, deer stared at the ship while wild horses lazily chewed grass. The beauty of the new world entranced Moniah. Hearing the sound of the bridge door opening, he turned around to see Caras and Kaylon enter.

Caras proudly held a small tray for Moniah's inspection. On the tray were small devices no larger than a pea.

"The interlinks?" Moniah asked as he lifted one to scrutinize, holding it up to the light.

"The devices fit comfortably in the ear. I have given two to Clovis and Marina, who were quite amused," Caras explained, rubbing his hands.

"Medean is wearing one now. He's been up since dawn with the Marina alien," Kaylon said, while making a check of control stations. Moniah continued to examine the device.

"We are the aliens, brother, and they are called people." Caras nodded, carefully forming the word.

"Pepple."

"Almost. A bit more practice with pronunciation." Moniah chuckled, glancing at Kaylon.

"How do they function?" Moniah asked, tapping the tray. Kaylon sat down facing Moniah and lifted one of the devices between two fingers.

"Simple. The transmitters fit into the ear; we hear what the alie-uh, *people*, are saying," he said, adding, "Each time a word is spoken that we do not understand, it will translate to Aurocearian, we then simply ask what the word means."

* * *

A Satar shuttle emerged from the *Auruaii*. It pivoted away from the half-submerged ship and flew just above the trees following the coastline. Inside, Moniah listened to Clovis point out landmarks. The poor man was a bit green in the gills despite his obvious glee. Kaylon and Uletis huddled near the flight deck, peering past Saeonar, who piloted.

"It is a magnificent world."

"Painfully so. So much of it looks like Auros Prime."

"But look at the city…squalid and mean."

Clovis watched the landscape speed by beneath him as the Satar shuttle followed the coastline, rounding a cliff to reveal a vista of a curved bay surrounded on one side by miles of open fields, townships and, bordering the bay, a large city of wood and stone buildings.

"Acadia!" Clovis said, pointing to the city, but his expression darkened as they approached the outer boundaries.

Soldiers rode through the streets. Even from his safe vantage in the air, Clovis braced and hissed as though he could still feel the tyranny they imposed. Moniah touched Clovis on the shoulder.

"Clovis, where do these invaders come from?"

Clovis pointed due west toward the horizon.

"Canelor," he said, with contempt.

Moniah patted his shoulder. The shuttle was now over the city proper and some people pointed up in terror while others stood stunned, with mouths agape.

"The temple and my council seat," Clovis said, indicating a small plaza near the heart of the city.

"Saeonar, put us down in the plaza," Moniah said. He led Clovis toward the rear cabin where Uletis and Kaylon were securing arms to their waists. A gentle nudge and the Satar shuttle landed. Saeonar stood from the pilot seat and joined the others. Clovis watched the Aurans strap on holsters. Moniah, Saeonar and Uletis carefully holstered their Coracle-diants. Saeonar noticed Clovis smiling with a grim determination, his eyes darting to the holsters he must assume were weapons.

Saeonar turned to a box, threw open the lid and lifted a Saen pistol. He extended the weapon to Clovis but Moniah's arm shot out, slamming the pistol away from Clovis.

"My first act will not be to put weapons in the hands of these people," Moniah said.

Cowed, Saeonar nodded agreement and Clovis glanced at the floor dejectedly. Moniah met the deposed ruler's eyes. The man lifted his face, his mouth set in a line of determination and…regret?

"Clovis, trust me," Moniah said. Clovis smiled. Moniah took in a deep breath and then paused, tilting his head, his eyes staring at the bulkhead.

"Saeonar, what is the date?"

"Fifty two point five zero zero six point forty."

Uletis grunted and moved his cloak to conceal his Coracle-diant holster while Kaylon assisted Moniah in fixing the clasps of his shoulder mantle to his robe.

"It is spring on Auros Prime."

Clovis pointed to the First Lord's mantle.

"Armor?"

* * *

Those who had not entirely lost their wits at the sight of the landing shuttle ran to the small courtyard of the priestess near the temple. Elria was brought forth and hurried to the plaza with a frightened mob while soldiers—torn between duty and terror—tried to keep order. When the ship's outer door opened, some of the soldiers threw down their swords and fled. People swooned, children wept and then a collective gasp arose from the crowd, followed by stunned silence, when Moniah appeared in the doorway.

"Clovis, stay between myself and Saeonar." Moniah said, and followed by Saeonar and Clovis he stepped out of the door into the cool clear air that smelled of the sea and the smoke of hearths and of war.

"The king returns with gods!" a man yelled. A soldier backhanded the man and lifted his sword but Moniah drew his Coracle-diant and took aim. The Coracle unleashed an electric arc that struck the sword and the Soldier screamed, dropping his weapon in terror. Men surged forward to stare at the sword that now glowed red with heat and, as it cooled, steam arose from it. The soldier grabbed his groin and as his face flushed in crimson, he wet himself. He covered his mouth but stumbled away vomiting as he shoved his way through the crowds who abused him with stones and spit. An elderly woman dropped to her knees.

"Praise the gods, praise them," she said. Saeonar smiled awkwardly at the woman, waving his hand, indicating she should rise, but this served only to make her grovel further. In the confusion, Kaylon leaned close to Moniah to carry his voice over the fray.

"Medean reports that the Oscileans need to be awakened. Their vital signs are too debased to continue in sleep."

Moniah frowned, hesitating, and Kaylon held the comlink out to him.

"Medean. Let them awake and stretch their wings."

Saeonar scanned the crowds for signs of hostility. A tense silence ensued. The priestess summoned her courage and stepped out of the crowd.

"Elria," Clovis said, beaming happily, and gestured that she approach Moniah. It was difficult to concentrate for the crowd coughed, sneezed and snorted, craning their heads, pointing to the Aurans while their hushed but incessant jabbering competed with dogs, and scampering fowl. Over the confusion hovered a mephitic stench of unwashed bodies. Most of the people wore a style of clothing, also soiled, similar to what Clovis and Marina had been rescued in. Crude tunics and breeches, heavy leather belts and furs. Children huddled close to their seniors, sucking thumbs, crying or staring. Men and women pointed to the Aurans then to their own animal-like eyes. Moniah stepped forward, attempting to smile, though he was still unnerved with what had transpired with the soldier.

It was obvious that the priestess was doing her best to maintain a confident front, though her hands shook visibly and her soft features paled.

The priestess was lovely, with soft, emerald eyes. Her tresses, gathered in gold fixtures, tumbled over gentle shoulders. Her full lips trembled and it was apparent that she had to summon strength from within herself to look into the eyes of Moniah. She glanced at Clovis then at Moniah and swallowed, nervously raising a hand to finger a necklace shaped in the form of a female goddess set in gold.

"Mo-neye-ah, this be Elria, our priestess of the temple of Diana," Clovis said. Moniah smiled and Elria bowed her head. Her eyes lifted again to Moniah.

"Perhaps you have already met," Clovis said, innocently, and Kaylon chuckled but Moniah did not turn away. He glanced at Clovis. Elria's puzzled eyes ran over the ship but she looked back to Moniah and Clovis, understanding that she could communicate with the tall handsome deity who had come from the clouds.

"My lord, you save us," Elria said, quietly.

"I am given the title of First Lord but we are come not as lords," Moniah replied, as gently. He turned to the crowd.

"Stand with us as equals."

The people muttered in confusion. Kaylon went to the groveling woman, and extended his hand. She looked up and tentatively reached out. Kaylon helped her stand and smiled at her, immediately securing her an honored place among the other people, some of whom touched her or bowed to her.

"This shall be a complex ordeal," Kaylon observed to Moniah in Aurocearian, which was not translated. Elria and Clovis exchanged a confused glance and Moniah smiled reassuringly.

A few brave souls crept closer to the edge of the Satar shuttle to peer at its smooth metal skin. A young woman saw her distorted reflection in the ship and jumped back to the safety of the crowd.

Saeonar tapped it with his hand and nodded to a young man who reached out slowly then touched the ship and then laughed. He mimed Saeonar, who ran his hand slowly over the surface indicating it was safe to touch.

"May I speak with you…privately?" Moniah said to Elria. She gestured toward the courtyard. Moniah took Saeonar aside while Clovis and Elria spoke hurriedly to each other. Elria touched Clovis's otherworldly robe as her eyes darted to Moniah.

"Remain with the ship. Kaylon, dispense food to the people, they look hungry."

"Yes, brother."

"Uletis, stand guard at the gate."

"With respect my lord, you should remain in our sight," Uletis said, scanning the crowd. Moniah glanced at Elria and the courtyard. Almost all of the stone and thatch-roofed structures were plain and crude and none of them, save the temple itself, were more than two floors high.

The temple was a simple rectangle with a brass door turned green from the weather, framed on either side with Doric columns. Immediately adjacent to the temple was the domain of the priestess, a simple residence made of stone with a small forecourt garden.

"I will be just inside that building," Moniah said, and then turned to Elria who stood waiting at her gate.

A commotion from somewhere nearby shattered the moment. People ran into the plaza, shouting, and surged toward the Satar shuttle where Saeonar shielded his eyes to peer into a street Moniah could not view from his position.

"The soldiers attack!" Clovis screamed and Moniah reached for his comlink as he hurried back toward the ship. A bearded man pointed to the sky and jumped up and down.

"Behold, the gods come with dragons!" he bellowed, shaking his hand at the sky. All eyes turned to look up to where Vetaeos and Rete could be seen riding Prestant and Montre. Elria hurried back to the ship and, seeing the Oscileans, covered her mouth while muttering something Moniah could not possibly hear in what was now total confusion. People shrank away from the Aurans and Moniah instantly surmised that they were terrified of the Oscileans; it was all too much for them to process. A squad of mounted soldiers thundered into view along the street, hell bent for the plaza.

"These creatures are our friends, they shall help you." He spoke into his comlink, "Vetaeos, Rete, disable the warriors' weapons."

"What are those wondrous creatures the men ride, marvelous."

"Now Vetaeos!"

"Understood, disable only," Vetaeos' voice replied.

Saeonar closed the ship hatch and strode to Moniah who reached out his hand to Elria. She did not shy from him.

"What are drgins?" Saeonar asked Moniah, who prayed he could find an end to impressing the people with violence. It was not at all what he had envisioned despite Clovis's and Marina's admonitions and warnings about the state of affairs.

Moniah heard Prestant rumble with joy, feeling his wings stretching at long last in the open sweep of air.

"Wind is sweet," Prestant sang to Montre while Vetaeos spoke into the comlink with Moniah.

"Not the people…stink," Montre rejoined. Beneath them people raced into doorways or hit the dirt as the attacking soldiers tried to steady their horses. Prestant snorted in surprise when Vetaeos fired his Coraclediant at the soldiers whose swords melted in their hands or, turning into molten metal, slipped away from leather scabbards. Spears disintegrated into ash. In moments, the Canelorians were in full rout, galloping away, their foot soldiers left to run along behind.

"Land near the ship," Moniah said into his comlink and, purposefully, strode to stand with his arms held out, inviting the people to watch him receive the landing Oscileans. The people cowered but most of them did not flee although, to a man, they kept a wide berth from Moniah.

People shook their fists at the escaping soldiers and one mother dashed to her children to pull them away from kicking the dust and the charred shape of what had been a lance.

Prestant and Montre sang loudly and joyfully to Moniah and Saeonar and landed as gently as they could, carefully folding back their tapestry-like wings to keep from unwittingly striking anyone nearby. The Oscileans' scales glistened in the crisp sunlight, refracting green, gold and brown iridescent shades. There was utter silence all around as Moniah hugged Prestant around his neck and chuckled while the happy beast nuzzled and licked him.

"Let them see your loving heart Prestant," Moniah sang to Prestant. Elria stepped closer, gingerly, trying to listen to the strange melodic language Moniah spoke to the dragon.

"Not of effort…my heart to you great one…sadness in the void," Prestant rumbled and Moniah knew he sang of Lirea for his large eyes watered and he moaned, then lowered his long face to nudge Moniah in the chest, nearly toppling his master.

"Be easy, cause no alarm. I cannot sing of Lirea…not now," Moniah sang, wiping a tear from his eye. He chewed his lip and turned to the people, keeping one hand on Prestant's forehead. Prestant licked his head, pulling Moniah's long hair over his head, covering his face. People laughed and Moniah gently threw his locks back from his face and smiled. A boy giggled pointing to Saeonar, who had fallen to the ground laughing as Montre licked him repeatedly, her sandy tongue swiping his face. Montre gently tugged at Saeonar, lifting him to his feet with her mouth.

Clovis regarded Moniah with astonished joy while the crowds converged nearer to the Oscileans as Saeonar encouraged them to approach the placid creatures. Prestant snorted, angling his long neck toward Moniah to study him with an expression that Moniah knew conveyed displeasure of the malodorous smells he was being subjected to. Montre lifted her head high, wrinkling her sensitive nose. Moniah chuckled and followed Elria into the courtyard.

Uletis took up station at the garden gate once more, folding his arms over his chest when Kaylon approached.

"Some of these poor beings, these people, are too ill for Taen or Wizan remedies. Look how they eat, like ravenous beasts. Sad. And see there that one…male or female it is hard to tell but such wrinkled flesh—many of them are so afflicted," Uletis said.

Kaylon waved to the ancient crone who had thrown herself at his feet as she pressed her hands together thanking him for the food her family was devouring.

"This is not illness of itself, Uletis," Kaylon said.

"But there are many of them with this malady and see how it makes them infirm? That one shakes and there, that one is nearly bald of hair with a deformed leg. Pitiful."

Kaylon flexed his jaw. A cold snap lifted his silver blond locks and he too folded his muscled arms over his chest, very unaware that women were already enamored of the tall blond god who had been young before their ancestors were born.

"What we see here is not a sudden catastrophe to their bodies but, I suspect, a slow death, draining them, drawing them to stoop and bend. It reminds me of creatures on Auros, preparing for death and transfiguration," Kaylon said, while his eyes roamed over a young man who helped one of the wizened elders to pet Montre's flank.

Moniah took a last look around and then entered the residence of the priestess as Clovis bowed to him, holding open a wooden door. A scent of pungent incense greeted him, which was not a surprise, given the fact that Elria was obviously very clean of her person. The room was spacious, with rough-hewn wooden beams painted bright green and red, whitewashed walls. There were few furnishings: there was a table where she poured water for Moniah; there were two chairs that would have been miserably uncomfortable without the large burlap and velvet cushions; there were several candles on a large mantle that was darkly stained with creosote. The mantle had a cooking arm with holders for two pots. In one corner, near the only window, a small one, a crack ran to the floor and a vine struggled to enter the house. A bucket with a large brush made from wood and the hair of some beast was placed near the crack, and one could see the evidence of newer plaster near the window ledge where repairs were in the process of being completed.

Moniah accepted the cup and unobtrusively scanned it with his hand-held comlink before drinking. The link flashed once and he sipped the water. It was sweet and pure. He sipped again, tasting its goodness and only then becoming aware that everything aboard *Auruaii* was marked by "Auruaii flavor," as Prestant had complained.

"Will you sit?" Elria said, and it suddenly occurred to Moniah that the people had called the Oscileans by a name. He felt a chill on his skin. He sat and only then did Elria sit, too, while Clovis remained standing near the door.

"Elria, what is the name your people called the sky creatures?"

She glanced at Clovis and then at Moniah as if he should know the term.

"Dragons."

"Yes, dragons."

Elria rose to her feet and gestured for Moniah to follow. She parted a curtain and led him through a covered hallway into the temple. In the sanctuary, his eyes adjusted to its gloomy and, for the most part, barren atmosphere. The interior area was larger than it appeared from the outside, with two rows of columns leading the eye to an altar from behind which a statue of dark bronze surveyed the rectangular room.

Elria pointed to one wall and then he saw it. A mural on which, among other images, were faded depictions of what could only be interpreted to be Oscileans. Moniah strode toward the mural and the closer he got the more gooseflesh rose on his skin.

The creatures depicted in peeling and faded primary colors were not as beautiful as real Oscileans and their expressions seemed ferocious but there they were. Moniah turned to Elria, who had just dipped incense onto a brazier near the altar. Moniah followed her gaze up to the statue of a woman wearing a tunic and sandals and who carried a sling of arrows. On either side of the statue were two brass moons, one full, the other a crescent. The moons were affixed to the one wall of smooth, polished marble behind the altar.

Moniah offered a slight bow toward the statue. Elria stepped back from the brazier, looked at the mural of dragons, then at Moniah. Clovis appeared in the hallway arch and placed his hands on his chest, bowing his head, but he did not enter.

"Elria, dragons are not evil. As you and Clovis witnessed, they are beloved to us and we speak to them," Moniah said.

"There is much between us, my lord," Elria said, glancing at the mural and then turning her soft green eyes back to Moniah.

"Moniah."

"By your command, Moniah," she said, bowing her head. Unconsciously, before he could stop himself, Moniah reached out and lifted her chin gently to meet his eyes.

"Not a command, a request."

He felt her tremble at his touch and her cheeks blushed, but she stood firm and looked into his face with a complex expression of wonder, expectancy and admiration. When he pulled his hand away, she reached up quickly and held it to her cheek.

"Your touch is a comfort to me, Moniah, it is strong, warm and true," she said, transfixed by his eyes of stars in blue pools.

To her, Moniah was a tower of beauty and reason. He was handsome and strong, immaculate of his person in a land of brutes. He was not a man. Even more intriguing, he was clearly a superman, and she saw in his hypnotic eyes every possibility, fear, mystery and passion she had ever dreamt.

Moniah gazed upon a sweet creature of elegant frame with long brown tresses. In the half-light of the Temple her eyes softened and appeared less small and vulnerable so that his flesh rose in goose bumps and he sighed, "Lirea".

* * *

The Hugherni clan fortress was a shell, sacked and ruined. It was not fit for winter quarters but Clovis insisted that if he was to be restored as King—the ceremony would be in the family Keep. It was a stone oval of battlements, facing onto a softly rolling moor. The walls rose gradually to a height of only forty feet above the narrow and fevered streets of Acadia. With a light snow drifting through the remains of a scorched great hall, Clovis looked out from his throne while Elria placed a small crown of brass on his head. Her necklace and jewels, Marina's ring and the Hugherni crown were the only treasures remaining to Acadia after the looting by the soldiers of Canelor. Moniah and Saeonar stood next to the throne, by invitation, and tried not to appear awkward, though it was plain that they bestowed their blessing on the event.

"I suppose we have put the right man in power," Saeonar said to Moniah in Aurocearian. Moniah smiled at Elria.

"We restored what existed."

"It is hard winter that comes on for them," Saeonar said, while pulling on gloves.

"Our winter. We will use the *Auruaii's* provisions to help feed the people; their food stores were decimated by the army of Canelor."

"Using *Auruaii's* resources will deplete our own," Saeonar reminded Moniah, while watching Marina hold up her son to the cheers of the people, whose collective breath filled the hall with a cloud of fog as if from broken steam pipes.

"We shall have to eat of this world Saeonar," Moniah said, and joined Medean and Kaylon at the throne dais at the urging of Clovis, who beamed like a child aware that the world lay at his feet.

Goddess of the Moons

"The sky people are most wondrous beings to behold, as tall as a man bearing the measures of earthly bodies and as powerful as warriors. They are given to long hair, which is lustrous but their eyes captivate. If a person's eyes are windows to the soul then surely looking into the eyes of an Auran transports one to the very cosmos as though you gaze at a clear night sky ablaze with stars."

-King Clovis Hugherni, earth, circa 828 AJ

Water cascaded from *Auruaii* as its enormous bulk lifted from the lake. Inside the bridge, Uletis and Caras rocked back on their heels when the bow rose up.

"Residual suction; we're leveling now," Uletis assured a bewildered Caras, who settled cautiously into the command chair. A floatscreen above Uletis showed an image of Medean's face.

"Arrival?" Medean asked, glancing down out of range of the imager, probably to check his chronometer.

"Ten minutes," Caras said, and Medean smiled approvingly. The floatscreen folded back into its niche. *Auruaii* glided over trees, raining water onto the forest below as its gleaming enormity cast a mile long shadow over singing birds and scampering creatures.

When the ship cleared the treetops of the hills around the lake, the forward view from the bridge presented a vista of broad flatlands and meadows surrounding the city of Acadia. Near its eastern gate, a huge half-moon bay provided a natural port for the eastern perimeter of the city.

"There must be thousands," Caras said, magnifying an image of crowds gathered at the bay.

* * *

Moniah, Medean and Elria waited for *Auruaii* on a large broad stone dock the ship's Constructorbots had created. The human masons continually inspected the dock with fascination. Kaylon and Vetaeos kept a discreet but watchful eye on the crowds while Rete blew the chill from his hands as he spoke to Clovis, who, judging from his gesturing to

Marina, appeared impatient to point out the floating city to a close circle of dumfounded lords and ladies. Moniah checked his chronometer, shielding his face from the sun with his hand to peer in the direction of the lake.

It seemed the entire population of Acadia and its environs was gathered near the dock, stamping their feet to keep warm against the cold of a clear winter's day.

"There it is," Moniah said calmly, pointing. Elria pulled the fur collar of her cloak tighter against her neck and followed Moniah's gaze to the south, where a huge glistening silver object floated above the trees. Rarefied winter sunshine reflected from the long graceful silvery form of *Auruaii*.

As she watched spellbound, the object as large as her recently-saved city, floated quietly toward them.

"Water falls from your sky city," Elria said to Moniah, who handed her a glow orb. She caressed the glowing grapefruit-sized orb. It made her shudder with its soft warmth.

"*Auruaii* has been floating, the water you see is from the lake," Moniah said. He tapped the glow orb.

"We will create more of these onboard *Auruaii* to dispense to the people." Behind them, amidst the crowds, Clovis could be heard shouting.

"There! There is where we lived for days." Astonished sounds rose up from the crowds who pointed toward the approaching ship. As *Auruaii* drew closer the people quieted to stunned silence, watching the vast ship pivot over the bay waters, casting a large shadow onto whitecaps.

"It is beautiful, with the graceful form of a fish or bird," Elria said, in wonder. Moniah pointed to the ship as *Auruaii* lowered into the bay, eliciting startled gasps from the throngs. The ship settled into the water and came to a stop alongside the dock, extending a ramp to the levee from its starboard side cargo door. Medean, escorted by Clovis and Marina strode onto the dock with assurance. Hesitantly, people followed them. Moniah smiled, waving encouragement with his hands, signaling that they should follow, while Kaylon asked the people to form two lines abreast.

The people would do anything for the charismatic Seal Bearer who often found flowers or herb sachets in his pockets along with adoring notes from his many anonymous admirers. Moniah clicked on his comlink, raising his voice slightly to be heard over the sloshing of water between the dock and the partially submerged hull of the ship.

"Caras, Medean is on the ramp with Clovis and Marina. What is your status?" Elria searched Moniah's expression, he smiled at her, they did not speak but much was transmitted between them in silence. "We have enough to inoculate thousands. Ship's processors are making plenty of food," the voice of Caras explained.

Moniah whispered to Elria.

"Would you like to see the inside?"

She nodded without fear and brushed a tendril of soft brown hair from her face, her green eyes danced with contained excitement.

"Caras, set the autobots to making as many portable glow orbs as there are people, one each and open the aft cargo bay," Moniah said, taking Elria by the hand to lead her to the aft entry. Kaylon waved to one of his many admirers and inched his way to Medean, who was never far from Marina or Clovis.

"What is he about now?" Kaylon said in Aurocearian, jerking his head in the direction of Moniah and Elria, while pulling the interlink from his ear to prevent his words from being translated.

Medean removed his interlink and lowered his voice.

"Elria has not encountered the Oscileans."

"She is the only human in sight who has not."

"The preparations for the reaffirmation of Clovis and Marina held her attention. Anyway, Moniah is now presenting the Oscileans to Elria," Medean said, placing his interlink into his right ear. Kaylon scanned the long lines of men, women and children queuing up to receive inoculations against various diseases Medean had learned plagued the people and for which he had prepared cures from blood samples provided by the king and queen.

"I suspect Elria will do anything Moniah requests," Kaylon said, and Medean removed his earplug again to look deep into the eyes of the hard handsome face of Kaylon, who was studying Saeonar, who in turn was laughing about something with the jovial Vetaeos and the normally more subdued Rete.

"If Moniah finds happiness, who are we to disapprove of it," Medean said, and Kaylon shrugged, replacing his interlink.

"I disapprove nothing Medean, I simply observe."

"Observe less, participate more."

Elria took a firm hold of Moniah's arm with one hand while lifting her gown away from her feet with the other as they crossed a metal ramp into the aft cargo bay. She paused at the threshold, her curious eyes roaming over the interior.

Moniah patted her arm leading her inside the ship. She stared awestruck at what to Moniah was a boring and mostly barren interior of metal floors and bulkheads, in the center of which lay Montre with her long neck draped across the forelegs of Prestant who licked her face as she dozed.

Elria reached out slowly, she pulled her hand back and Moniah chuckled.

"He will not bite, I promise."

"Nor spit fire?" Her expression of delight and concern made Moniah throw back his head and laugh. Montre sat up and drew herself away while Elria clung to Moniah. He took her hand in his and together they reached out to Prestant. Elria looked up at a compassionate face longer than a table. This was not the ferocious countenance depicted on the temple walls. Prestant lowered his head cautiously toward her.

His breath sounded like a fireplace bellows but did not smell. She and Moniah petted a large nose which, for the most part, resembled that of a horse, except for the long whiskers extending from its chin. The eyes of the dragon, augmented by long lashes, looked very friendly and wise at close range.

"He has the eyes of a horse," she said, and Moniah led Elria along Prestant's side. She stroked the long neck with its mixture of skin and scales, its color shifting with the light.

"A dragonfly's hue," she muttered.

Prestant extended his wings and Elria stepped back, grasping Moniah's hand. The wings were amazingly wrought tapestries like those of a huge butterfly of blue, red, green, brown, and a mixture of orange and umber. Prestant yawned a deep rumble one could feel through the vibration of the deck. He turned and lumbered away toward a water tank. His clawed feet, as large as a cart, thumped across the flat smooth floor.

Prestant snorted and turned to face Moniah and the female alien.

"This place…smells of sour," the beast sang out. Elria's eyes grew wide at the sound of the dragon's musical voice though she was unable to decipher what it communicated. Moniah stepped forward, speaking to the dragon in a flowing voice, musical itself but resembling more of an incantation.

"The people. I have told you they will learn to be clean of body," Moniah sang to Prestant, moving closer to the beast. "We wish to sing…in the air, Moniah. This craft…not our home," Prestant sang.

"I have a place in mind in the mountains. There we can make a home for you and the other Oscileans. It will be as it was on Auros Prime," Moniah chanted in reply. He smiled at Elria, winked, and stroked the dragon behind the ear.

Prestant angled his long neck to look at Montre, Wholestep and Halfstep, gathered around a feeding bin. The other dragons snorted then sang a chorus in response that reverberated around the hangar deck. Elria covered her ears.

Prestant flapped its wings once, its long neck swept back to face Moniah.

"This…sings true," Prestant sang.

"I am not…another day…in this metal beast," Wholestep added and Halfstep shook its body. The motion flowed from its shoulders to its head like a dog throwing water from its body.

* * *

Auruaii's portals and blister domes glowed with light, illuminating the last long lines of people who waited patiently in the night and cold to receive food and medicine. Those already processed, moved away from the ship, their glow orbs creating a lovely string of lights along the causeway that dwindled into wavering dots in the distant streets.

Moniah and Elria observed this silent parade from the observation bridge, where a floatdroid hovered before them, offering tea. Moniah enjoyed watching Elria eat. She was not gluttonous or ravenous like so many of the others he had been appalled to witness shoveling handfuls of food into hungry mouths. The priestess benefited from her privileged rank, which not only guaranteed her comfort but also had obviously protected her from the fate of her fellow citizens at the hands of the Canelorians. Besides, Elria was a lady and, even if reduced to rags, Moniah was certain she would comport herself with dignity.

"What does the name of your land, Amernius, mean?" Moniah said, handing her a cup of tea. She had been staring at the softly-lit control panels of the bridge. Elria sipped her tea.

"It means, land of many peoples. The city name Acadia, uhm, is the sea, or, the garden by the sea." She said and watched as Moniah nodded, mouthing the words and meaning.

In the quiet light of the bridge, his large blue eyes resembled large pools that flickered hypnotically with silver flecks.

"Tell me of R-eu- y?" Elria said moving closer to Moniah.

"It means, that which travels of Auros," Moniah said while lighting an Ol pipe.

"Auros, as in you are an Aurocearian."

"Yes, exactly."

Elria waved a hand delicately about and glanced around the bridge. "Then this *Auruaii* is not your home. Auros is?" she pressed, her eyes searching his.

Moniah set his pipe down and met her curiosity head on. At last, this was the meeting he had prayed would take place, not that the fervent devotion of Clovis and Marina was unwelcome, but here was true communication.

"You are very perceptive, Elria. That is true. This is a conveyance. It travels through the void."

She frowned, her lovely eyes flickered, trying to form an image, to understand, and Moniah pointed to the stars above them beyond the blister dome. "The void," he whispered.

"You have seen Diana and Treehoomena in the void," Elria said, enthusiastically and Moniah's mind went blank. Then he recalled the twin moons of Earth and the belief that they were the incarnation of the mother goddess and her son.

"Yes, we have seen the golden orbs, just as you see them here." She did not pursue the subject; her eyes roamed over him. Elria ran a hand through her hair and she looked away nervously and then moved her eyes courageously back to Moniah. Her voice was so muted he leaned toward her to hear.

"Do you…" she began, then sighed and seemed to become even more nervous. Moniah smiled but, perplexed at her agitation, he took her hands in his.

"Please, ask me anything."

"Do you love, Moniah?" she said. Moniah flexed his jaw. His eyes danced with light and he sighed deeply, with resignation.

"Forgive me," Elria blurted, fidgeting, but Moniah squeezed her hand, shaking his head. She could tell he was fighting an inner battle and, though her own hand quivered with tremors, she squeezed his in return.

Moniah could feel her courage, if this woman who had resisted savagery, held her people in safety during oppression and was capable of sitting here with him and speaking intelligently of worlds beyond her reach—if she could do all this, then he owed her the utter truth.

"Love survives in my worlds. I say survives for we Aurans are transformed beings."

As he spoke Elria's concentration poured straight into his eyes, the blue pools deepened into space itself and his silver specks of pupils became stars that transported her to the planet of Auros Prime, eons earlier…

Elria could see Moniah's mortal body glowing with silvery phosphorescence. He stood naked atop a vast wind-swept mountain surrounded by pink and white clouds. His powerful body, normally concealed under robes, was revealed to her in this vision of the past. Other Auran beings she could not recognize emerged from glowing dissipating spheres of light and fire, they gazed upon an Auran whose hair was a fiery red, streaked with black, who stood alone amidst wondrous swirls of green and gold liquid forms while flashing red, purple and blue lights danced about him in the wind, like blots of ink dropped into water.

"My brother Arhahnis, beloved of the gods," the voice of Moniah spoke into Elria's mind. The Auran Arhahnis' eyes flashed with forty beams of light, she could see them, like sunbeams that shone through clouds and in each of the beams it was as though some spirit dwelt, for she could discern ghostly forms which appeared as Auran in nature although their wavering images were difficult to behold for the light that radiated from them was both alluring and painful on the eyes.

"Manifestations of Diasentue, our gods," Moniah's voice whispered into her soul while in trance.

Elria watched Arhahnis raise his hands high over his head, golden light poured from his fingertips into the air releasing streams of brilliantly glowing orbs, millions of them, billions of them, which then floated to the ground across the breadth of that far away primal world. Where the bio-orbs fell, pools of liquid bubbled into life releasing crawlers and flying insects while other orbs bounced into the air and burst like popcorn to form birds.

Seedlings exploded from the soil, shooting up roots and branches. Animals scampered from the emerging plants and trees while other creatures twisted up from the ground where the light orbs rained upon it. Glowing spheres burst like pollen spores and still other creatures and insects exploded into being. Purple globs became large flying insects or birds. Pools of liquid bubbled into fish in a nearby ocean while seedlings and branches shot up from the ground. Leaves and flowers unfurled, and, seeing through Moniah's eyes, Elria gasped as inches from his face a smoky sphere of gas, smelling of resin, evaporated into a puffball of smoke, leaving a small bird creature to beat its spinning wings into existence.

Around her, in the far away then of time, she could feel the brine-like wind tainted with a faint scent of sulfur and other entirely new olfactory sensations.

Elria could feel tears of joy on her cheeks. The Arhahnis Auran-man floated above the mountain in a trance. His hands lifted to form an arc above his head and then, as her soul filled with love she could not express, as though waking from a dream with only the memory of music too marvelous for mortal life, Elria witnessed the totality of the Aurocearian miracle.

Arhahnis raised his arms from his sides in two arcs moving them closer, ever closer, to join above his head. As he did this, crackling spits of lightning jumped between his arms and hands. Far below him, in the sea, white water churned and frothed, sending salty spray high into the air. Then, a thunderclap reverberated through the air and Arhahnis became a splendid pillar of light.

Too intense for her human vision, she saw again through the eyes of Moniah and there was Arhahnis, his hands meeting above his head, causing the thunder and, instantly, the sky that had only contained a few stars, erupted into life. Meteors of light hurled away from Arhahnis; stars suddenly blinked into existence. Elria felt her soul race through space itself. She saw planets burn into shape, forming from colorful nebula clouds. Arhahnis was the dance of creation.

On one large world, she saw round balloon-shaped creatures, their songs echoed in her body, songs born on the wings of vast gaseous expanses and clouds.

Her mind raced back to the worlds of the Aurocearians where the Arhahnis Auran slowly floated back to the surface of the summit. Around him, the planet sang with life, rains fell and the Oscilean creatures took form from the very clouds.

Thunder echoed across Moniah's world. She saw him and others approach the Arhahnis Auran, carefully, lovingly holding him while rainbows of gas and light, which seemed to be made of water, danced around the summit.

"In our love, a longing from our hearts merged with that of Arhahnis."

Elria saw the creation of the Aurie's. She could sense Moniah's powerful mind, feel it call to a place beyond time. Spheres of light Elria knew to be "Birthfire", each large enough to contain a single Auran, descended from the sky. The Birthfire orbs opened like flowers, revealing female Aurocearians. She saw Arhahnis laugh in purest joy as Meliphor came to life.

The Aurie slipped from the dissipating Birthfire sphere and her body appeared to cool from hotter temperature as she descended into the arms of Arhahnis.

"Meliphor," Elria heard Arhahnis call her. Wind whistlers buzzed around them and then Elria saw Moniah open his arms to another Aurie, Lirea. Suddenly the vision retreated as though through a tunnel. Moniah's voice echoed in Elria's mind, calling a name, "Lirea, Lirea…" and back came Elria through the nebula; she passed stars that morphed into atoms, then into blood and living tissue, becoming a speck in the glittering eyes of Moniah.

Elria trembled and her eyes opened wide as she blinked. She uttered a yelp and her arms jerked forward as she grasped frantically in the air at nothing visible, one hand slamming onto her chair seat. Her head jerked from side to side.

"Where? Where?" she said, coughing."

"Here with me, shhh. You are here in *Auruaii*."

Moniah recognized panic. The vision had overwhelmed her nervous system. He took hold of her, firmly but gently, and rubbed her arms, soothing her, then he took an ice cube from the hoverdroid and rubbed it quickly and lightly over her lips, across her forehead and under her jaw at either side of her face. Elria's breath quieted to a more normal rhythm but Moniah held her, rubbing her arms more slowly. He palmed her forehead where her silken hair was matted to her brow with dew. He yanked the hoverdroid closer.

"Chilled water," he commanded and the droid lid opened, revealing a basin of water into which Moniah plunged his hands. He then used his dampened hands to caress Elria's face and neck. Much better, her color was returning. She let out an exhausted, meek gasp and wept, falling forward to lay her head against his shoulder.

They sat for long moments in mutual comfort with only the quiet hum of the control stations around them. Moniah looked up at the stars of Earth and fought to restrain his tears.

Elria sensed his mood. She lifted her head from his breast and Moniah lowered his face. He trembled and Elria reached out to touch his chin. Moniah lifted his face and she saw a tear run down his cheek. The tear sparkled like incense flaring on a brazier and dried to a fine dust before her eyes.

"You saw through my mind," Moniah said, his voice quavering with emotion. Elria nodded, words at present impossible for her.

Moniah stood and gathered his wits. He lit his Ol pipe and wandered over to a porthole to gaze at the last groups of people to leave *Auruaii*, their glow orbs stragglers of pearly light filing off the dock into the night. Elria stood, paused to gather strength in her legs and joined him at the blister dome.

"You are of the ages, Mo-neye-ah?"

"Many turns of your sun," he said, turning to look at her with a weary attempt of reassurance.

"You have shown me paradise. There is no death--in Aurocearia?"

Moniah's face darkened. Again, she could sense some inner pain within him.

"I beg forgiveness for I have hurt you," Elria said and Moniah explained the war that had caused the mortal extinction of Aurie's. Elria backed away in horror. He continued to describe a feeling he sensed that Lirea and all the Aurie's were now, once again, living in the eternal Godsrealm.

This explained the fascination the Aurans had with human children and it was now very clear why the Aurocearians did not have females within their floating city.

"For all the wonder and awe I feel for thee, Moniah, and for wise Medean, loyal Saeonar and the other brave Aurans…my heart aches for you."

"Death came to Aurocearia," Moniah said, and he thought of Wizan Erfros, who transformed in the Dome temple, leaving Moniah as High Wizan. It seemed an empty title, Tetra-Lachaen. What good had come of it? Was death to serve Moniah?

"Even if we die and leave no heirs, perhaps we shall impart some good for all mankind," Moniah said, tenderly.

Elria could not resist an urge to comfort Moniah and her arms went round his shoulders.

"Great lord, you gave peace to our land," she said.

Moniah raised his arms slowly; he paused then closed his eyes, embracing her. Now, in the quiet exhaustion of the bizarre afterglow of trance, Auran and woman gained silent strength from one another. It was the language without words, their hearts beat in time and a bridge across the stars gave comfort from Earth to the wounded soul of Moniah.

A thousand memories of Lirea coalesced into the scent and feel of Elria. And, for Elria, a love she could never have imagined began to take hold of the fiber of her heart.

CODEX: ARCHIVE. SHIP CHRONOMETER: 048.5007.56:

Envoys from the far outlands of the continent Amernius recently converged on the city of Acadia. The ruler, Clovis Hugherni, has renamed the city Renthia-Acadia, "The new city of many peoples", which is partly a derivative of our capitol Rentu, on Auros Prime. The human city is a focus study in cultural phenomena, aside from our presence, due to the emerging artistic nature of its citizens to whom, by direction of Moniah Talsaiyr, we are parsing out rudimentary but efficient technology. Quite wisely, First Lord Moniah has determined that humanity is not capable of or prepared for introduction to the "high sciences" such as molecular motion or plasma energy. Application of these spectra will remain mysteries for the foreseeable future. However, he has allowed Caras and Uletis to create heat and light sources using natural gas and even, in some cases, battery- powered electricity. Auruaii's fleet of constructorbots assisted native artisans and craftsmen in transforming dirt-floored, windowless houses and buildings—into insulated relatively hygienic structures. At my direction, we have created sewage plants andclimate-controlled food storage areas. Saeonar and I have introduced Taen bio-farming techniques to arrest and curtail waste and inefficiency with regard to livestock and grain. (Humans are wanton omnivores.)

-MEDEAN TALSAIYR, ARCHIVE CLOSURE: SECURE

Moniah enjoyed his morning walks through the city, which he made into habit over the course of several months, taking a different route each day. Either Saeonar, Rete, Caras, Uletis or Vetaeos would accompany him, so there would always be another Wizan with the First Lord. But, so far, there had never been so much as a harsh word exchanged between Auran and Human, with the exception of the initial problems with the occupation forces of Canelor.

Moniah and Saeonar strode through the market streets to visit the library Medean was eager to show them. People haggled over their goods in the familiar language as well as in some dialects still unknown to the Aurans. As they rounded a new paved street curving up from Market Square, Moniah paused to look at the harbor. Constructorbots were completing augmentations to the docks and causeways and, anchored around *Auruaii's* partially submerged bulk, were half a dozen trading ships.

Moniah took binoculars from Saeonar, who automatically handed them to Moniah without request since he was so accustomed to the fact that Moniah was forever peering into the distance or surveying the harbor.

"Three of the ships fly the flags of Europa."

"Are they staring at *Auruaii*?" Saeonar asked, suppressing a yawn. He coughed and sighed with boredom for it was always the same. Moniah studied the crews on the ships. They in turn converged at the rails pointing to *Auruaii*_with obvious fascination. Scents of delicious foods wafted up to them. Beyond the north gate, a caravan of wagons with brightly-painted murals headed into the city. Saeonar rubbed his belly.

"Ah, smell that Moniah."

"Your stomach rules you Saeonar," Moniah said, and swung his binoculars around to the west to view the source of satisfaction for Saeonar's hunger. Outside the western gates was a large encampment of tents and huts.

"We have tried to invite them to come within the city but most of those people are from the deep western regions near Canelor--they fear us," Saeonar said. He added, "There is still a bite in the air." Moniah grunted and spun around to face the harbor. On a deck of one of the ships, a man wearing a feathered cap held a large pad before him as he furiously sketched.

"Wonderful! See, that man in the cap? He is rendering an image of *Auruaii*," Moniah said, pushing the binoculars into Saeonar's chest. Saeonar frowned and reluctantly lifted the eyepiece to look in the direction Moniah pointed.

"Uh, interesting." Saeonar lowered the binoculars to scan the streets below. He paused and adjusted the focus on three men who had disembarked from a skiff.

"And there, my lord, see the captain there? Another searcher."

Moniah took the binoculars and found the subjects of Saeonar's interest. Sure enough, there were three sailors pacing excitedly through a street.

Judging by the fine coat, sandals and breeches, one of them was the captain. The men asked frequent questions as they entered the market square and some of the locals pointed in the direction of the hill. These sailors were called searchers because they always behaved in the same manner, anxiously seeking out Aurans so that they could behold the mysterious "sky people" at close range.

Since none of them ever saw *Auruaii*_fly, they dismissed stories of the arrival as fantasies for they could not make any sense of what *Auruaii* was? Only a few skiffs ventured close enough to the void ship to examine it more closely and they would soon row away as if relieved to keep a safe remove from the long, strange metallic whale-shaped city with its one-way portals that seemed to be mirrors from the outside, at least.

"Kaylon is at his best again," Moniah said, chuckling as a masted skiff rowed away from *Auruaii*. The void ship was emanating a subsonic field that disturbed the water and created a mildly unpleasant sensation designed to discourage those who intruded too close to the ship. It had also been Kaylon who reprogrammed the ship's hull portals into one-way filters after waking one morning to discover a cadre of filthy faces peering into his cabin at the water line.

Saeonar looked over Moniah's shoulder just as Moniah swung the binoculars to the west again, and Saeonar had to duck away to avoid being crowned.

"It's the Oscileans. Everyone outside the city fears them," Moniah said, and Saeonar held out his arms and lifted his head to the sky.

"You mean, of course, the Dragons!" Saeonar said, with a mock quavering voice, shaking his hands to mimic fear. Moniah punched Saeonar in the arm.

"Ow."

"Let's get to the library, unless you prefer to wait for the searchers to find us and harass us with questions."

"Gods, no." Moniah chuckled and they proceeded up to the library hill. The library was very much an Aurocearian building, marble and stone with a dome, intricately carved with Ol leaf patterns as well as leaves found among the flora of Earth. Inside, the walls of the great rooms sloped inward and under the dome they found Medean, reading.

People of all ages were seated at tables surrounded with upholstered chairs; a gas fireplace pulsing heat against the chill. A stationary servodroid sat ready to serve refreshments. As the students caught sight of Moniah, they came to their feet in a sign of respect. Medean turned about, saw Moniah and closed the book he held.

"Hay-oh-lay, lord Moniah," a teenage girl said, measuring her words to sound out the traditional Aurocearian greeting. Moniah repeated the greeting and smiled at her.

"That shall serve for today. Thank you," Medean said, and as the class dispersed, he led Moniah and Saeonar through an atrium garden to his private office which faced the western regions and distant mountains.

"I am besieged with queries about the Oscileans," Medean said, pouring Soffa, offering a cup to Saeonar. He added, "To the degree that I am making slow progress through the marvelous human scrolls and tomes."

"Did people make this?" Saeonar asked, sniffing the cup.

"One of my students, yes," Medean said, handing another cup to Moniah, who studied the surroundings then set his gaze toward the mountains.

"No, thank you," Saeonar said, setting his cup down. Moniah sipped his, paused and sipped again.

"It has been months since Prestant requested a permanent home outside *Auruaii*. I think it is time for us to deliver on that promise," Moniah said, with his eyes still fixed on the distant vista.

"The Oscileans are a distraction, Moniah. I assume none of you are prepared to delve with the people into the mysterium of Wizan?" Medean correctly surmised. Moniah nodded and Saeonar lit an Ol pipe.

"Astute and to the point, Medean," he commented, moving a pile of scrolls and tomes from a chair to sit. He saw a mouse scamper away and looked about his feet.

"I see you need minor Sonics in here to discourage these rodents."

"The Oscileans have ventured about the surrounding areas. They are very fond of the high areas there…to the south-west. The place is lush and fertile and the mountains are quite steep," Saeonar said, pointing out of the large window.

Medean joined Moniah at the window.

"There are fern glens and the misted crags remind them of Auros," Moniah said, thinking better of partaking of any more of the Soffa drink made by humans.

"It seems to be a perfect home for them but I remind both of you that the tribes in those mountains are not pacifists. In fact, we know very little about them," Medean said.

Moniah stretched his arms and smiled at Medean as he leaned against the windowsill.

"Well, teacher, all the better reason to meet them, hmm?"

"With respect, Moniah, I suggest we make some diplomacy with the Canelorians. We know they incite terror and regularly attack caravans from the hinterlands," Saeonar said, scratching at a wax stain on the table before him.

"True spoken, the greater regions west all the way to the Pacific Ocean are cut off from us due to the despot in Canelor," Medean said, gently taking an ancient scroll from Saeonar while Moniah ruminated. The First Lord paced to a sealed door. He tapped it and smiled.

"One hopes this opens to a wine cellar."

Medean followed Moniah to the door and opened it with a comlink lock. Saeonar heaved himself from the chair and joined them to peer into a small but immaculate chamber containing a floatscreen desk, glow orbs and a portable computer link.

"Last night I found Montre and Wholestep sitting atop *Auruaii* staring toward the mountains," Moniah said, as he leaned forward to study the floatscreen that contained images of the local people as well as of other traders and sailors.

"Why not show these images to the people?" Moniah asked, pulling the desk chair out to sit. Medean shook his head in the negative.

"It is my discovery that many people are dubious with regard to transmitted and permanent photographed images. This is, I believe, due to their religious and various sociological experiences."

"The images frighten them," Saeonar said, and Medean nodded. Moniah scanned the database of languages, customs and faces.

"Perhaps it is time to make a report to Auros," Medean said. Moniah abruptly stood up. He glanced at the screen, and then turned to Medean.

"No. We are in a formative stage. Kaylon informs me that matters are stable on all of the inner realm planets. No emergency signals have been received and I am not prepared to speak with the Arhahn. But, you're correct—do not present any more technology to the people. They are still assimilating what we have done thus far," Moniah said, then exited.

Saeonar shrugged and both he and Medean followed Moniah back into the larger antechamber. Medean resealed the door.

"The winter frost ceremony is soon upon us. If we can found a city for the Oscileans, make peace with the mountain tribes and be back to participate in the winter ceremony, as requested by Elria, good work will have been done," Moniah said, confidently.

Medean looked to Saeonar whose eyes sparkled with amusement while Moniah gazed out of the window to the west and toward Canelor.

"It is my belief that we will have no more struggle with man. Let our words and deeds spread and you will see. The good Canelorians will come to us, freely and openly."

Saeonar shook his head, sighed and chuckled.

"Well, as usual my friend, you ask for so little."

* * *

Elria discreetly wiped away a tear discreetly. Moniah winked at her, then checked his saddlebags while Prestant flexed his wings in preparation for flight.

"If I came with you, mayhaps the mountain people would find it easier to accept you?" she said, her eyes pleading.

Moniah glanced over his shoulder. Saeonar and Vetaeos were already mounted on Montre and Halfstep.

"Do the mountain people know of your ways, Elria?" Moniah asked patiently.

"They are nomads and we are strangers to them," she confessed.

"Then it is too dangerous for you. Stay here with Medean. Caras, Rete and Uletis will assist you in whatever you need. Kaylon is in command in my absence," Moniah said, as gently as time would permit, for he wanted to reach the mountains before dark. He waved, then paused and blew her a kiss. She reached out and grabbed air, then pulled her fist to her chest.

"Eveet!" Moniah commanded, and the dragons surged into the air. Elria watched them soar over the city boundaries, rapidly growing smaller, for they flew more quickly than she remembered. The dragons reflected sunlight on each upbeat of their large, beautiful wings.

People on rooftops and in the streets waved and yelled cheers to them, children danced about, beating their arms to imitate flight. Elria heard someone approach from behind. She turned to see Kaylon, whom the people called "the golden one" because of his long blond hair.

"Clovis tells me some of the encamped people have come into the city. Would you care to meet them with me?" he asked.

Elria smiled and accepted. She turned once more to look at the vanishing images of the flying dragons. They could have been large birds at this distance. Before turning around to be escorted by Kaylon, she lifted a lock of Moniah's hair and, with eyes closed, took in its fresh scent. Then, she carefully put the lock into a fold of her velvet robe.

* * *

"There's a fine landing, just ahead," Saeonar's comlink squeaked. For safety's sake, he had taken the lead in case there were dangerous beasts of the air yet undiscovered, other than the many species of birds. The dragons banked into ravines of the Allegany-Sierra Mountains, landing on a gentle hill covered in moss, fern and wildflowers. The air was quite cold, as expected, and Moniah wondered if he would succeed with the goal of the expedition before the onset of deep winter.

A brook gurgled nearby, which the dragons sang to in delight, sampling its pure cold goodness with their tongues and then drinking deeply.

"They love it here," Vetaeos said, lifting his chest to enjoy a deep breath. Moniah checked the saddlebags.

"You are certain the seedlings you brought will not interfere with existing foliage." he asked of Saeonar, who removed ten small pods.

"These are Oscilean favorites—"

"Call them dragons. It's easier for the humans to comprehend and eliminates the need to explain history," Moniah said, waving his hand.

Vetaeos continued.

"Yes of course, we created hydroponic variations which thrive here and are totally benign to existing vegetation. It can be cultivated as it was, *is*, on Auros."

Moniah shielded his eyes from a bright shaft of sunlight that broke through clouds.

"Perfect, now if only the mountain people will allow us to remain," Moniah said, scanning a surrounding density of forest. The hour was late and the wind picked up again. Montre and Prestant nudged two large boulders into a clearing while Saeonar scraped weeds away from them with his boot. He pointed the Erfros Coracle, aiming it at the boulders. A red beam hissed forth and Saeonar held the beam steady until the large stones glowed with radiant heat.

The Aurans camped through the night, to be awakened at dawn by the dragons who could "smell" a number of humans nearby. On wing, Moniah spotted the mountain people first, moving along a high dirt trail by horse and wagon, heading down through a pass into a valley, no doubt to escape the more severe aspects of winter.

"Demons!" someone screamed.

Moniah winced. He waved and smiled but the damage was done.

"By the gods, Dragons! Hide the children, hide them." Someone else bellowed. The mountain caravan degenerated into panic, wagons were abandoned and terrified horses stampeded headlong into the forest, spilling food, pots and clothing as they trampled underbrush. One of the horse teams pulled a wagon at breakneck speed toward a curve beyond which the hills plunged into a canyon.

"Fools."

"Saeonar, stop complaining and follow," Moniah yelled over the wind.

Moniah spotted a mother in the back of the careening wagon, clutching children and an old man, all bouncing and jostled while another man at the reins screamed and yanked back on the taut straps with all his strength. Prestant swooped down so that he flew just over and ahead of the wagon. The grimacing man at the reins yelled in terror.

"Prestant, put that horse to sleep," Moniah sang, and the dragon uttered a loud song. The galloping stallion slowed to a trot and then stopped short, nearly throwing the driver forward. The dragon sang again, the horse lifted its ears, looked ahead, then to the right, then ahead and abruptly settled down on its haunches.

Prestant landed on the trail followed by Montre and Halfstep. Moniah dismounted from Prestant. He walked several paces into the trail and halted. The people remained utterly still, like statues.

"Yes, they're in shock," Vetaeos muttered, stifling a yawn. A man on a horse trotted forward. He wore a long dirty tunic, beard and was built like a bear.

"The chief?" Saeonar whispered to Vetaeos, one hand resting on the handle of his saddle.

"Undoubtedly." came the bored reply. The chief raised a spear, though his hand trembled noticeably. Accustomed to human ways, Moniah held his open hands out before him and to the sides, turning once fully around. The chief lowered his spear and dismounted. The burly man approached Moniah slowly, chewing his mustache while his eyes twitched.

"You saved me house," the chief said. Moniah silently thanked Medean for his database augmentations to the interlink translators.

"I would rather have died myself than cause you harm."

The chief's eyes studied the dragons with awe. He pointed at them with a tremble he tried to conceal.

"You command these demons?"

"These dragons are not demons," said Moniah.

The chief considered this. Behind him a man sank to his knees. Saeonar pointed to the kneeling man.

"Yes, I see it. Again, we receive obsequious fealty," Vetaeos said, placing his Coracle wand over his lap at the ready. Suddenly inspired, Moniah stepped back to pet Prestant on the nose.

"The dragons live in the high reaches of these mountains. We bring them to you on this day so that you may see them incarnate from legend. From now on, they will protect you." he said, improvising on the spot.

"You live in the high mountains," the chief said, while the others murmured with astonishment. The chief leaned close to Moniah, watching his eyes while he grimaced and tilted his head from left to right.

"We do," Moniah said, and the chief sank to his knees as well.

"Now you have done it," Saeonar hissed at Moniah in Aurocearian. Moniah spun around and checked himself, though his eyes glared.

"Get down and dispense food to these people."

Saeonar looked to Vetaeos, who shrugged and unfastened his saddle straps.

"It is always food, *our* food."

* * *

To augment his role as friend to the mountain people, Moniah made a weekly trek by foot to their nearest village. He brought glow orbs, medicine and food, arriving weekly with a fleet of Constructorbots that traveled late at night without warning beacons to be as invisible as possible.

On one of his visits, Moniah elected to venture to a village that suffered "omens". He arrived to find that the place was scarcely more than a few tattered log buildings with little sign of life. Though Prestant grumbled, Moniah dismounted at the outskirts of the village and proceeded on foot. It was quiet and his feet, cracking twigs, brought forth bird song.

In a flash, Moniah heard a hissing sound and was suddenly knocked to the ground by a man who had jumped from the roof of a hut.

The assailant was strong and grimaced with blackened teeth, pushing a short but deadly knife toward Moniah's throat. Moniah fought desperately, his own hands locked onto the blade handle.

The man recoiled from Moniah's eyes but it was only an instant of hesitation and Moniah could not throw him off. Filthy sweat dripped from the man's yelling face and Moniah roared from the sting of it in his eyes.

* * *

Elria lifted incense to the statue of Diana. The nightmare of the previous night haunted her waking hours and she could not rest until she tried to do something.

"Diana, goddess of the moons, your sons, protector of Renthia-Acadia, hear my plea. Save Moniah, protect his holy spirit and cause no harm to befall him. I pray thee," she intoned.

* * *

Moniah felt his strength going. In a moment of panic, the past came rushing into his mind. He could hear Ammanmus warning him that once on the candidate world, Auran's would become as the people. Was he now only as powerful as a man? The blade inched closer. It nicked Moniah's neck, a trickle of blue-silver blood dripped from the wound. Empowered and enraged, Moniah managed to bring one knee tight against him, shoving against the attacker's chest. The man flew back and stumbled. He had lost the knife, which Moniah refused to pick up.

The man sneered and yanked another knife from his waist but Prestant stomped into view, crushing small trees and bushes around him. The Dragon lifted the man by the scruff of the neck but the man reached behind him and cut Prestant's nose. Prestant rumbled and the man fell from his mouth. He spun around and lifted the knife to throw it at Moniah.

"No!" Moniah yelled, with his hands outstretched before him.

* * *

Elria pinched incense onto the altar brazier. It flared into a bright red flame. She knelt with her arms outstretched before the statue, her face enveloped with incense.

"Hear me goddess. Hear the priestess of thy temple."

* * *

The human assailant roared and threw the knife. Prestant reared back and issued a terrible ball of fire, consuming man and knife.

Moniah heaved a sigh and sank to one knee, wiping sweat from his brow. Prestant nudged him and he reached up to pet the dragon, which gently pulled at his robe collar, helping him stand.

"Angry?" Prestant sang, and Moniah stroked the beast lovingly while he struggled to steady his breathing.

"You saved me."

"This place…is ghosts…only bones here," Prestant sang, and it was then Moniah noticed the village was, in fact, abandoned.

"This event is not a song to tell," Moniah panted, still catching his breath. He mounted the dragon. As they ran for the sky and Prestant took wing, it was the dragon rather than Oscilean Prestant, who cried out a grave song to wildflowers and the crazy man they had left behind.

* * *

The Aurans chose the uppermost crags of a mountain for the location of their Wizan fortress. Saeonar named it, "Myzinos-Wur". The remote location provided a fabulous view of the low lands including Renthia-Acadia and the bay. Due to the eagle eye vantage and severe cliff faces, the new Wizan fortress was virtually inaccessible to the mountain people, lending privacy for the ceaseless work of the Constructorbots as well as for the dragons. The high vantage provided another spectacular view of the mountain range and flatlands to the northeast and of the gently rolling cliffs due south of the city where Moniah decided to build his residence.

The singing of laser torches cutting designs into carved stone carried across the evening as Saeonar and Moniah inspected the fortress temple.

"A Dome Temple, on Earth," Saeonar said, pausing to make certain a round Constructorbot pivoted to properly apply a cutting laser. Earth's yellow sun was setting into crimson skies. Vetaeos appeared with a warm mug of the delicious drink humans called, "Tea." Moniah took it into his hands and breathed the fragrant vapors. He had been riding Prestant and his hands were chapped from the wind.

Around them, sunset presented dramatic purple-red symphonies of color. Eagles flew nearby, their cries echoing into ravines.

"If there were planets in the sky, we could be looking upon the Wizan regions of Auros," Saeonar whispered and Moniah closed his eyes to blot out a memory of his home worlds.

"Lirea would have loved…" Moniah started to say something but his words trailed into silence.

"She still does, somewhere, my friend," Saeonar said, patting Moniah's shoulder. Vetaeos emerged to join them on the rampart.

"If time is space, then surely our Aurie's are nearer to us than we can perceive," Vetaeos suggested. Moniah moved closer to the rampart to watch a Constructorbot lift a square stone block into place.

"What happened to your neck, my lord?"

"Nothing Vetaeos, an insect," Moniah said, wearily.

"There are frightful bugs on earth it's true. I was bitten in the glen by a yellow creature with stripes. The insect raised a welt on my arm," Saeonar said, lifting his robe sleeve to show Vetaeos.

Another eagle flew by, calling out into the growing twilight.

Varrick, the Hammer

Elria emerged from the temple of Diana into the courtyard. A dove landed only a few feet away from her, flapped its wings once, looked at her and flew away. It happened so quickly that Elria's acolytes, gathering morning offerings of food and flowers, did not notice the omen.

In that instant, Elria knew Moniah was safe and no demon from the nightmare realms would harm him, or haunt her nights. As usual, handsome Kaylon was fending off the attentions of women and men; she could see him politely refusing offerings while he crossed the square. She opened the courtyard gate.

Kaylon waved to Elria and almost tripped as a child threw flowers in his path. The people were acting increasingly familiar with him in the absence of Moniah in what amounted to a public courting.

"Will you smile at me, lord?"

"Come to take supper, honor our house."

"I love you. I will *serve* you." They whispered to him and he smiled but continued into the safety of the temple garden where no one would dare enter without invitation from the priestess.

"We have to do something about this fawning," Kaylon said, with mild frustration, for even he found it somehow irresistible.

"You are too beautiful, lord Kaylon, I fear my powers do not extend to matters of the heart," Elria said, while opening the gate wider. Kaylon gave her an ironic glance and pulled a flower from his golden locks.

"I have just come from Clovis; his scouts report a great deal of activity in the west," Kaylon said, whispering thanks to an acolyte who handed him a glass of water.

"Canelor?" Elria whispered.

"It is hard to tell. Clovis thinks it could also be tribes moving into their winter lands in the valleys west of the mountains," He said gesturing to her home, and she led him within her abode.

"I have other news, for you," Kaylon added, with that touch of wry amusement so many found entrancing. Elria lifted her chin.

"Moniah is returning."

"He is," Kaylon said, warming his hands by the fire. He turned around about to speak and caught sight of Elria standing before her small window with her hands on the panes, staring into the sun with a radiant smile on her face.

* * *

It was so clear that one could see far out to the Atlantic Ocean and, looking east, the city of Renthia-Acadia, its new buildings gleaming in the sun. Overhead, Prestant and Montre flew over the dome temple, singing to the beauty of the day.

"We will use the shuttle. Let Prestant remain here with you," Moniah said, turning away from the telescope to face Vetaeos. Below them, on the esplanade balcony, Saeonar was pointing out the spectacular views to Rete who had arrived days ago to visit the first dome temple of Earth.

They noticed Moniah waving to them and hurried along the balcony to a gentle rise of stairs leading to the higher portico balcony.

"Wizan Vetaeos, you are now the watch commander. Rete, I appoint you second in command as Templar warrior," Moniah said, stuffing fresh Ol into his pipe. While the effect of his words and command sunk in with the Wizans, Moniah took Saeonar by the arm.

"The Ol crop is sweet. Excellent work."

"I am happy you approve."

Moniah put his arms over the shoulders of Vetaeos and Rete.

"Myzinos-Wur is only accessible by wing or shuttle. The mountain tribes will not trouble you but it is your duty to meet with them."

"True spoken. I advise that you let the Oscileans take the air freely and fly on scout, as they are wont. If they report trouble, take action. Remember, if you find yourself in conflict, disable their weapons and *mediate*," Saeonar said, while Moniah fumbled in his robe to find his buzzing comlink.

He ambled a few steps before responding, watching his comrades sip ale, and partake of the evening. There was a relaxed, easy manner about his Wizans and for some reason Moniah thought of Clovis in a comparative way. Odd. Strange that a primitive man Moniah had only recently encountered could now be compared on a sociological level with himself and his fellow Aurans.

* * *

CODEX: WIZAN ENTRY:

Vetaeos and Rete have met in council with the mountain dwelling tribes. Wizan

Vetaeos assures me these mountain people love us and refer to us as "The brave ones." They are a proud people who idolize our strength and dominion over "dragons." The humans have even sworn oaths of loyalty to Wizan and are apparently overjoyed to learn the science of greenhouses for growing winter food as well as a more efficient manner in which to store grain. Upon return to Renthia-Acadia, Moniah directed a fleet of Constructorbots to a location on the rolling green cliffs south of the city, in order to begin construction of a palace. Although Kaylon expressed doubts about moving the First Lord out of the safety of the ship, I think it is a brilliant stroke, for the project brought forth fine artisans and Moniah welcomed their skills.

Moniah has named the palace, Maethus-Dia. It is intended to be a place where people may freely assemble, petition and secure help from us as well as the local native authorities King Clovis and Queen Marina. The palace project moves quickly—as doall things under the guidance of Moniah.

Constructorbots have raised a mighty and beautiful structure perfected by the skills of stone carvers and masons. Gifts arrive from across the world. Tiles and carpets from the East! Marble from Omer and Italia, gold and silver from Indra! From the Far East, ornamentations and intricate wooden panels. Great stone columns were carved at a quarry in a mountain range located to the south of the palace site. Medean and Elria—with help from eager students—set about making a garden and reflecting pool. This is a triumphant year for the mission. I can scarcely describe something so wondrous in such a dry word. If the Arhahn and our brothers in the Sphereworlds find any fault with what we have accomplished on Earth, let them say it to me!

A concern, I have noticed my communication with Montre and the other Oscileans diminishes in the long distance song-speech. Uletis has noted his memory is dulled and it is difficult for him to recall precious accounts that date back into the reaches of his life on Auros. I will study the report created by Ammanmus and Tius that describes expected biological alterations in Auran physiology; though, in truth, I am more concerned how these physiological alterations may have been accelerated when Moniah first encountered the people! As to Uletis, it is my opinion thatUletis can stand to forget some and thus suffer less but in truth, my own memory is blurred where the great years stretch back to the garden time. Medean assures us this "bio-assimilation" was expected. As an experiment, I conducted a spectrum resource of my Wizan capabilities and find that I am still adept in transferring and capturing ambient energies for use through the Coracle-diant. However, there are elements in the higher spectrum I cannot attain. Moniah describes this as "evolution."

-WIZAN SAEONAR OLASHI, ARCHIVE CLOSURE: SECURE

* * *

Moniah walked through the solarium with a spring in his step. The palace smelled new with a unique combination of mortar, freshly polished stone and a tinge of residual ozone from the army of Constructorbots' lasers, cutting, carving and polishing devices.

As he swung open the solarium doors to proceed into the Great Hall, Moniah paused to run his fingers over a mosaic from the Far East and, below, it a wainscoting frieze depicting Oscilean heads in profile. It occurred to him that it was unfortunate he had never met the shaman priest Zoimon, whose extensive library had served to provide detailed drawings of architectural styles from all over the world.

Zoimon had died on the very eve *Auruaii's* arrival on Earth. Whenever Elria described him, it was with loving and tender terms, as though he had been a dear friend and paternal figure in her life. Because of the rich and extensive nature of the deceased shaman's library, Maethus-Dia took on a unique characteristic of a form of high Byzantine style in the main structure, augmented by classic influences of Attic ornamentation. The people loved the palace and Clovis remarked that it reminded them of the legends they grew up with of far away places in the ancient lands of their ancestors.

As Moniah made his way to his meeting, he considered the concept of traveling to other parts of the world but, as quickly as it occurred to him, he reconsidered the idea. Had it been Ammanmus or Tius who expressed concern about colonizing versus coexisting? No matter, Arhahnis had said it best, "Avoid wanderlust and find a place that welcomes you..." This was wise counsel, better to create a land of dreams where everyone was welcome than to fan out across the world, diluting energy and eliciting concern as to the true intent of coexistence.

The human New Year approached and Moniah was anxious to set down substantial policy. He opened a large window to smell the garden and watch Constructorbots laser the finishing touches on a small but elegant Taen temple. Satisfied, he continued through a Moorish portico and on through two highly polished brass doors that opened into a very large hall with windows facing the garden on one side and with a partially completed fresco on the opposite wall.

Moniah hurried into his seat. Two wagging-tail pups yelped and cooed with excitement, careening toward his feet.

"There you are!" Kaylon announced. Medean activated a floatscreen, while Caras and Uletis turned their attention from a beautiful but empty dais to face the First Lord.

"Please, be comfortable; this will not take long," Moniah said, cheerfully, while reaching down to pet the pups, which gamboled about, sniffing and playing. The floatscreen's blue field transformed into the faces of Vetaeos and Rete.

"Reports? Kaylon?"

"There is an army amassing at Canelor. The tyrant controls all the lands from the mountains west and a good part of the northeastern hinterlands," Kaylon said. Moniah poured Soffa from a servodroid.

"You refer to the one called Varrick, yes? Well…I believe the wonders we have wrought will overcome this adversity." Moniah gestured at the floatscreen where Vetaeos could be seen in front of a panorama of the mountains.

"All is well, Wisdom Moniah, we have established several varuette— excuse me, farms. The mountain people are content and prosper," Vetaeos explained.

"Superb news," Moniah said, studying Medean while lighting his Ol pipe. Kaylon glanced at Medean with something less than affection, which the mystic ignored while he studied a pulse disc on his portable computer link.

"Tell him about the plants," the voice of Rete said, and Vetaeos moved closer in the floatscreen image.

"Ah yes. You recall my lord you were concerned about the invasive nature of seedlings we transported from Auros?"

"Yes, yes."

"No such problem exists."

"Excellent. But keep an eye on this, Vetaeos, life is aggressive and we have to be careful of mutations and hybrids. But, very good!"

Rete stepped into view in the screen and Moniah noticed that Medean was staring at the empty dais. He felt the eyes of the First Lord and met them squarely.

"My lord, one thing, I urge caution when eating of a certain plant we will ship to your kitchens. It is a form of, what? Oh, yes, it is called pepper," Rete said and Moniah laughed and signed off, terminating the link.

"Is this a throne hall, brother?" Medean asked.

Kaylon leaned back from the table placing one foot on the tabletop, his eyes flashed at Medean and Moniah relit his pipe. Everyone was finding their purpose and Medean was educator of the people. His influence with them was so profound that many even took to wearing green robes, which in itself did not disturb Moniah as much as the hints he had gained from Kaylon that Medean might be dispensing too much detail pertaining to Aurocearian history. Kaylon and Medean were growing apart and Moniah realized his instinct to stabilize policy was a bit overdue.

The dispensation of knowledge to the people of Earth was a core directive of the mission but it was also a delicate matter. So far, only Elria had shared a unique vision of the Aurocearian past with Moniah, but the priestess, as far as Moniah was aware had never divulged a word of her visions with Moniah to others. She seemed to appreciate the private nature of what had passed between them.

Moniah shifted in his seat, then stood to pace.

"I will speak with Medean in private." When the others had gone Medean turned to Moniah.

"My lord, I sense your thoughts."

"That is part of my concern, Medean."

Medean smiled and came to his feet. Moniah puffed on his pipe, staring at the empty throne dais and then turned at the sound of Medean's computer powering off.

"People learn, Moniah. They do not function in the mind as you and I. You and Elria share a special bond of love and, by so doing, your memory transferred to her. But my students and the humans who teach under me do not possess the far sight. Or, what may be called in Elria's case, supreme intuition."

"You know I trust you, Medean, more so than Arhahnis himself but we must not convey details of our history," Moniah said, offering his Ol pipe to Medean who, for the first time in Moniah's memory, accepted it.

"Our minds change and Medean smokes."

"We are a world made new. For example, this palace Maethus-Dia, the guarded realm? An unusual name," said Medean, while pacing toward the empty throne dais. He cautiously partook of the Ol pipe.

"Unusual?"

"It implies secrets but I suppose we are incarnate secrets."

"That is not my purpose in naming the palace. Kaylon is concerned that you reveal too much to the people but I cannot fault you. You know that Elria…"

"Experienced trance, yes, and I understand, brother," Medean said, calmly. He added, "I have constructed a brief but highly edited version of our history which you may peruse." Moniah stood in the center of the throne hall, his glance roaming over the large room and empty dais.

"Arhahnis will come to earth, Moniah," Medean said, very quietly, and the simple revelation stunned Moniah, although he wanted to hear those very words. He scrutinized the mystic, who had stooped to gently lift the pups. There were other concerns brewing within Moniah but he suppressed an instinct to press Medean.

As a Wizan, Moniah dealt with reality as it transpired. True, he could summon powerful forces from the elements of nature around him but a mystic possessed the power of "Far Sight". It was as if the Greenrobe mystics existed on another level, one most Aurans, especially after the metamorphoses, did not care to deal with.

Medean chuckled as the pups licked his chin and he wandered toward the doors leading to the temple and garden.

"We are home, Moniah, in one form or another." he said, without turning around. For some inexplicable reason this simple observation in Far Sight raised the hackles of Moniah.

*   *   *

Moniah loved to stroll the high walls of Maethus-Dia, ruminating over his view, planning. It occurred to him that in a literal sense, the name of the palace fit perfectly, for Moniah had created a high wall surrounding the structure for protection against the wilds and because in most of the architectural renderings he had seen, rulers on earth had deemed it prudent to surround their domiciles with defenses. But Moniah's intention for the wall ramparts was not so much for protection as to enjoy a spectacular view.

To the west, forests and distant mountains. To the north, the great snow peaks where the dome of Myzinos-Wur could be seen on clear days. To the south the coastline descended into reeds, meadows, and the great bay of Renthia-Acadia and to the east less than half a mile away, the rugged cliffs overlooking the Atlantic.

However, none of these views could be seen from the ground due to the forest being in the way so the rampart wall was an inevitable decision for Moniah. Besides, the First Lord had seen the aftermath of what the humans could inflict on each other with the attack of the Canelorians on Renthia-Acadia, which suffered from its low and virtually unprotected city walls.

He met Saeonar on the eastern rampart where they gazed out toward the city.

"Renthia is a sprawling mass," Moniah sighed, as he grasped the stone ledge. He jerked his head in the direction of the city.

"Despite his promises, I must wonder exactly what Medean professes in his library school." Saeonar strode toward Moniah and tossed the remains of a cup of Soffa over the rampart.

"Even Moniah cannot control all things. You built this palace for the future, for the Arhahn, yet you wince at the thought of his coming," Saeonar said and Moniah turned away but his friend was undaunted.

"Now you worry over Medean. I have been to his school and there is nothing to fear. Are we not come to Earth to impart, to participate?"

Moniah lifted a hand beseeching silence.

"True enough, but we must measure out our time, Saeonar." Saeonar huffed in rebuke. He put his hands together before him and squeezed them into a ball. "Moniah, you pine for the past. This is why you want what we made here to *freeze* in time. To unfetter barbaric minds we must evolve into the future with these people, no matter the outcome," Saeonar insisted. Moniah raised his cloak collar up around his neck. The wind had taken a nasty chill.

Moniah looked into Saeonar's unrelenting countenance and sighed, lifting his face into wind heavy with the salty brine of the sea and the scent of pine from the forest.

"When do you propose we transmit to Auros? To date we have received several communications," Saeonar pressed, and something in his tone infuriated Moniah.

"I have replied to all of the communications."

"Only in a cursory manner, the Arhahn—"

Moniah sliced the air violently with his right hand. His eyes danced with light and Saeonar coughed, adjusting his waist sash.

"After the winter frost celebration and not before. *I* command this mission," Moniah all but thundered and stormed away, leaving Saeonar to cool his own temper. Saeonar slapped the wall ledge with his hands and turned away to gaze into the west.

* * *

In the immense forest regions of Canelor, King Varrick, called the "The Hammer" by friend and foe alike, reposed with his generals in the great hall of Canelor Keep. The old castle had all it could do to feed the army commanders and warriors Varrick summoned to his feast.

Goats, chickens and pheasants ran a merry chase from the sweating serfs who suffered the guffaws of the generals while they stumbled about in pursuit of the cackling birds. At his table, Varrick stabbed a ham with his grimy short knife, taking two gluttonous bites from the glazed meat.

Although Varrick could not conceive the idea, he was the last of his kind on the continent Amernius. His well-worn, muddy boots kicked away chickens and mongrels which pecked at crumbs fallen from the beaten table on which Varrick abused even the crude dining manners of the day. Varrick chuckled ominously while his warlords grabbed at serving girls, spilling ale and wine in clumsy half-witted attempts to steal embraces from overworked and wary servant women.

Lances, swords and shields were heaped beside two huge doors because Varrick had learned long ago to allow no one at his feast bearing arms. The king surveyed his scarred and dirty lot. His cold, blue eyes glared from deep sockets as he wiped grease from his beard and unkempt mustache onto worn leather forearm guards, stained with the dried blood of his latest victims.

The place reeked and the smoke from the fire pit choked the air. Varrick stood up to his full height, nearly seven feet tall. This was usually enough to command attention, but when his daunting presence failed to foster silence he pounded an already bent flagon on the table. Still, they roared.

Varrick smirked and held out the flagon toward a servant girl who filled it but, seeing it was hopelessly bent, Varrick grabbed the jug from her so fiercely that he drew blood from her fingers, knocking her against a wall in the process. The servant girl threw back her dirty hair and wrapped her bleeding wrist in her soiled sackcloth apron. She pushed a dog from her feet with her knee and cowered away.

Varrick pounded his fist on the table before him and waited until he could hear only a few coughs above the crackling fire.

"We've gained all the forces needed. The time is nigh to march on the city of the sky people and take what we will of 'em." Varrick bellowed, for he rarely spoke. A crusty arm shot up, a general stood, spit at a dog then lifted his chin.

"Winter is on and remember these sky people scattered our occupation forces at Acadia," he said, glancing about while the others grunted assent. Someone else stood unsteadily, struggling with a girl whose red-stained eyes trembled with fear as she struggled to escape.

"They've the dragons. How do we fight these?"

"No one has seen the dragons for some time. I say they were illusions!" Varrick said, gulping ale. A young man wearing a breastplate came to his feet at one of the senior tables near the fire. Varrick grimaced. His eyes squinted to study the upstart.

"But, great lord, many beheld the round metal balls that fly in the air. The sky people command these comets. What fight do we have against such armor?"

Too many voices groaned agreement. Varrick strode toward the mantle, hefted a spear and, in one terrifying motion, sent it flying at the young warrior.

Women screamed. There was a loud clanging sound, immediately muffled. The young warrior coughed and wiped his mouth, surprised to find blood on his hand. He stepped back and reached down to hold the spear in his chest. The weapon had pierced his armor plate. He choked and fell dead. For a moment no one moved.

A girl cried and tore at her hair. She ran weeping from the hall into the arms of a tired matron who gathered the distraught girl in her arms. They wept, slumping onto a campaign chest.

"All armor can be breached," Varrick thundered, as two serfs pulled the fallen warrior from the hall, leaving a thick red stain in his wake. One general glared at Varrick. He trembled and started to stand but another reached out to grab his arm.

"Stay your hand."

At last, there was real quiet. Varrick strode forward, paused and raised one dirty fist, his gritty teeth clenched.

"These sky people'll bleed mortal blood. I say their powers are akin to nothing. Recall the Indians, their *medicine* will fell us, we was told. But what did we find with 'em? Mere trinkets, bows and arrows and skulls and now they be a fortnight's march sulken in the wilds to the great west." Silence, then all arms shot into the air with a roar so deafening even the mongrels fled the din of war.

As the warriors settled again into gluttony, an old man in a tattered robe entered the hall. His hands trembled from palsy as he wandered to the huge soot stained fireplace.

"The sky people do only good around the land," he said, as loudly as he could. The hall quieted.

"In all the lands, no voice brings news of harm at their hands," the old shaman added. Blinking, he reached out to support himself with the stone mantle.

Varrick eyed the old shaman and, disgusted, shoved his plate of food away.

"They be gods," the shaman announced with assurance. Some laughed, but others eyed him carefully over their plates. The old shaman ran a shaking hand down his white beard.

"Gods? Gods who fly on winged serpents? And bring their hateful creatures to our lands! You're a fool Mayron," Varrick shouted, noting that some of his generals seemed infected by doubt. Mayron flailed his arms desperately.

"No. What wisdom tells us these winged creatures are evil? Did not one of them save a child from drowning near the rapids at …?" Varrick slammed his fist to the table. He bolted to his feet and stomped his boot.

"A wive's tale, tole by women with dreams in their noggins," Varrick said, twirling a finger around his ear. The generals laughed uproariously, unaware of the scowls of women huddled in a doorway. Mayron seemed to shrink. His shoulders, already hunched, curved even more under the onslaught of ignorance he felt powerless to enlighten.

Again, he lifted his shaking arms and the robe sleeves fell away from his thin forearms, revealing tattoos marking him as a shaman. An uneasy silence prevailed.

"Listen to me," Mayron croaked, as forcibly as his ancient voice could sound.

"You have made Canelor great, in *terror*. Today we are feared and obeyed throughout the forests even to the western mountains but, I vow to thee, these sky people are gods. They bring wisdom to the land and cures for pestilence. If you march upon them, you shall be consumed." All eyes turned to Varrick who tilted his head and rubbed his face.

"You are talk, old man. Even you says we rule the greater area than any before us. Your heart longs for old ways, shaman, and times of your power." Varrick sneered, pointing at Mayron who stepped away from the mantle, his chin jutted out in defiance.

"And you are a beast, Varrick. Your hammer has beaten down our souls and your crown is stained in blood. Fear and destruction are the watchwords of Canelor. How I long for the days you speak of, when Ciros ruled," Mayron said, and coughed, accepting a wooden cup from the same girl Varrick had wounded while snatching ale from her. Utter silence reigned.

"Now we have fear, fear and bloodlust," Mayron sighed, thanking the servant girl. His energy spent, the old man settled down to sit on a barrel. All attention reverted to Varrick, who many were certain would kill the old shaman outright. Varrick chuckled drunkenly.

"Your time of foolishness and sorcery is gone out the world, Mayron. I have made Canelor great and it'll be greater the still. Ready the men to arms!"

Mayron hobbled out of the hall, covering his ears. He started up a flight of steps where a lovely young woman awaited. She smiled bravely at Mayron, reaching for his arm to steady him, but Mayron suddenly spun around, moaning as the grip of Varrick's huge hand seized his arm.

"Old man, when I come back, what lies remaining here will end its days." The young woman threw her silken gown behind her and marched down the few steps to put herself between Varrick and Mayron.

"Release him, Varrick." Varrick let go of Mayron. He rubbed his chin, eyeing the woman and smiled his dirty grimace.

"I've always loved thy spirit, Corina. Take your father's fool upstairs and say his grave prayers. He won't survive me return." Mayron fought back the pain in his arm to level a steady glare at Varrick.

"The sky people will know you are coming, Varrick. They will know and they will crush you." Varrick turned on his heel and Corina helped Mayron up the curving stairs.

"He will not harm thee, Mayron. If he does, I will curse him to the people," she said, her pretty oval face flushed in anger. Mayron patted her hand and huffed as they went around and up the stairs.

"You're sweet and brave, Corina, like your father. The house of Ciros has never bred evil or dullards." Corina opened a door and helped Mayron into her chambers. The old shaman collected his breath and Corina parted a tapestry and shouldered open large shutters to reveal a parapet.

Mayron joined her and they watched generals in the lower keep mount horses while, beyond the walls, soldiers gathered young men.

"If they do not obey and fight, he kills a member of their family and then kills them," Corina muttered, her expression resigned with depression from too many years lived under the brutal warlord.

"Varrick is keen of mind in his tyranny, despite his infamous stupidity. But his mind is that of an insect to the gods who have come to us," Mayron said, shaking his head. Hope softened Corina's features.

"Travelers tell tales that the sky people are beautiful to behold," she muttered, gazing at the forest.

"This I know, they have eyes like pools with stars in them and the bodies of the finest warriors," Mayron replied, stumbling back inside to attend a teakettle. Corina came within.

"Has anyone beheld their women folk?" Corina asked. She sat on a high-backed bench, nervously fidgeting with a woolen shawl.

"Not that I am privy to, but who could blame them for keeping their delicate ones safe from such as we," Mayron said, chuckling ironically as he bent forward to poke at a stew pot on the cooking fire.

"Mayron!"

Corina jumped at the dreaded bellow of Varrick. The shaman pursed his mouth and, with help from Corina, they returned outside again to the parapet.

In the Keep below, Varrick sat atop his huge horse, regaled in a bear cloak and armor. He glared up at the parapet.

"Rest easy, old man, for when the sun shines on us home returned, I'll soon see to it you join Ciros." One of the generals laughed and spit on the hay at his mount's hooves. Corina pulled her shawl around her shoulders and Mayron tilted his head and put his hands on the lintel.

"If thee escape that you deserve, I will fall on thy sword willingly," Mayron said, with a steady voice. Rebuked, Varrick locked eyes with Mayron as he spurred his horse.

* * *

During the long march, Varrick's mind replayed Mayron's warning, *They will know you are coming* the old bastard had warned, and it occurred to Varrick there might be truth in this prophecy. A new plan formulated in the despot's mind, one that would make use of a strategy he had learned from legend but never, until now, employed. As the march progressed to Acadia, there was no doubt that they had started the new campaign in a heady resolve to conquer. Winter was never a good time to lay siege.

The particular lethargy peculiar to winter was making the men sullen and ill-prepared for battle. Varrick kept them busy at the hunt and drill but he determined to avoid all villages and towns, keeping to the dense forest.

While mulling through his strategy, Varrick ordered a halt in the winter caves just inside the western pass of the Allegheny Mountains. As his troops made camp, Varrick leaned over a fire where a slain deer was spit-roasting to lock eyes with his senior generals.

"Now, lend heed ta me, this be our way to triumph. We will not storm Acadia."

The generals looked about in confusion and Varrick jabbed the toes of his boots into the coals. He waited a moment while the steam arose from the leather and pulled them out again.

"Tis best we examine the sky people from afar," his senior General said, ripping meat from the turning spit. Varrick sniffed and wiped his nose on his bear cloak. He wagged a grimy hand at the general and yanked meat from the bone. Outside the cave, wind gusted through the trees and a large branch laden with snow cracked and fell into the camp, spooking the horses. Varrick jabbed a thumb over his shoulder and his serf trundled out to help. Varrick gestured for his men to move closer to the fire.

"That is not me wisdom. We'll examine sure enough at close quarters. Acadia is rife in bounty and trade from winter caravans. Fat 'en happy. Heh? But these sky people have won the hearts en minds of Acadia *and there's* the start of defeat. We shan't win that over. Naw, that's legend and stuff for dreamin' girls and heartsick boys wantin' adventure en glory. You there! Bring that here ta me. Look now close on, this is a feat I learned from one 'a ole Ciros' books."

The generals crowded closer and Varrick jerked his large head around making sure no one but his close circle could hear or see.

As the others huddled around him, Varrick seized the cloth sack from an aide and filled it with pebbles. He drew a rough line in the snow and scribbled a large A in the center of the line. Then he placed the sack just outside the lines and squeezed the sack until the pebbles spilled out.

* * *

So called, "Watch fires" were a tradition among the people of the eastern seaboard. The custom of creating bonfires had begun with the advent of seafaring trade and segued into the popular festival known as "Winter Frost", which heralded the New Year. One of the primary locations for a watch fire was the cliff where Moniah constructed Maethus-Dia. The First Lord took advantage of the occasion to open the palace to Clovis and his court.

A thick covering of snow covered the mall greens surrounding the palace, which, lit by lanterns and glow orbs, combined with its surroundings to create a magical spectacle for adults and children alike. Already, fires burned near the cliffs, stoked by cheery maids and men whose laughter and song filled the cold breezes in anticipation of the moon festival. The evening was clear of clouds and, toward the north one star in particular dominated the purpling firmament. It was a perfect, even enchanted, evening, and Moniah was elated with his timing to open the palace during such a celebration.

Clovis and Saeonar warmed their hands around the largest fire, situated adjacent to the palace on the east mall. The king had grown a bit gray of late but his eyes shone as he clutched a mug of mulled wine, watching his son dance around the fire. Nearby, Marina and the acolytes of Diana prepared a portable altar for the priestess Elria. Trumpets blared a fanfare and all eyes turned to the opening gates of the palace from which Moniah, Elria, Medean and Kaylon emerged to cheers.

Jovial songs slowly transformed to a more subdued chant when Clovis bowed to Elria. On this night, at least for the duration of the ceremony, he would defer his power to the priestess. Clovis's son ran to Moniah, who sank to his haunches to receive a handful of pine wrapped in twine.

"Thank you Darius. Look how you have grown!" Moniah chuckled, standing to ruffle the boy's hair. An exclamation of wonder from the people turned Moniah's attention to the crowd near the fire and the altar where everyone was looking up at the brilliant star. The sky was now black and the star outshone all others.

"Alcoyne dances in the night my lord," Clovis said, wiping wine from his chin.

"Alcoyne?" Moniah said, intrigued.

"One of the daughters of Atlas, Moniah," Elria interjected, while they made their way toward the altar. The pulsing glow of the star made Moniah's skin prickle. He glanced at Kaylon, who silently mouthed the word, "Auros".

Children and young adults called out excitedly and Moniah saw them crowd around Medean. The mystic shook hands with them and then put a finger to his lips and gave his attention to Elria.

* * *

At Renthia-Acadia, Uletis accepted a cup of the warm mulled wine all the humans were partaking of. He smiled, thanking the lady whose bright eyes and rosy cheeks conveyed the joy of the season. She bowed, giggled and hurried away from the gate ramparts with a group of young girls.

"Nothing to concern ourselves with here, the streets are quiet; unless you have caught anything unusual," Caras said. He paused to light an Ol pipe.

"I see a dove perched on the pitch of a roof. I think the creature is about to lay an egg and if she does…there will be mourning doves crying soon thereafter. A good many people are at Maethus-Dia and the harbor. Look, you can see at least twenty fires from here," Uletis said.

"*Auruaii.* You see its nearly covered in snow," Caras said, indicating the vast ship, still partially submerged in the deep waters and the ice, at its special dock. A stone garrison house near the ship glowed from within. Caras lifted his binoculars.

"There is ice around the ship." He handed the binoculars to Uletis.

"I'll go down later and run the outer hull magneto field to melt it." A door opened at the gatehouse and a tall man wearing fur skin boots and a thick cloak approached. He waved.

"Ah, Haolae Robert, any news?"

"Hey-o-lay, lord Caras, lord Uletis," Robert said, sniffing the air. He adjusted his broadsword and smiled as Caras offered him the binoculars.

"Agh! Give up the titles Robert, we've names like you," Caras said.

"All gates report a quiet winter frost eve, praise the goddess. One of my sentries tells of a group of men who took lodging at the south quarter, nothing unusual." Robert said, peering toward Maethus-Dia.

Uletis reached over to activate the infrared device on the binoculars and Robert jumped back.

"Great moons of Diana! This is fascination," he said, while Caras chuckled. Robert handed the binoculars to Caras, who blinked to refocus his vision.

"When the fires are put down for the night, it is tradition to take feast. The men and I would be honored if you should join us," Robert said, huffing steamy breath into his hands.

"And so we shall, Robert," Uletis agreed, feeling secure.

In fact, all was quiet, yet foreboding, for Varrick's men had been steadily making their way into Renthia-Acadia for days. Provisioned with cured meats, pelts and minerals, they were easily mistaken for winter snowbound traders from the far north who, along with other caravans, went unnoticed.

Varrick took advantage of the Winter Frost season to bring in his Trojan horse. The fact the city had tripled in size only abetted the strategy of the tyrant.

* * *

Elria approached the altar on the mall outside Maethus-Dia. She was radiant in a white gown with a midnight cloak and scarlet hood. She lifted her hands and everyone fell silent.

"Goddess of earth and of the night, whose majesty turns the tide and lights the bleak hours, hear me, thy servant. Across the lands of Amernius, thy children stand at watch fires to herald your coming, full and measured, to mark the turn of winter light."

Moniah shifted his feet as cold from the ground crept up his legs and he pulled his long cloak about him to retain heat. A soft breeze blew at Elria's copious gowns, her hood fell but she was engrossed and appeared immune to the cold. Marina held up a tray and Elria took a handful of substance from it tossing it across the watch fire blaze. Colors erupted.

"Earth mother, Diana, from time before time thy children have marveled at thy transformations and now again, we herald thee with supplicant hearts as you rise to heaven."

"Hear us and grant anew," the people chanted response. Clovis smiled, some people began to talk but stilled again as they saw Elria was improvising the litany.

"We give thanks for the Aurans who bless us and keep us, who have come from on high and—with their powers—relieved our burdens," Elria intoned. She bowed to the fire and to the small statue of Diana on its portable altar.

Moniah gazed straight ahead as the people turned their focus to he and the other Aurans.

"Praise their presence among us," the people said proudly, smiling. Saeonar cleared his throat and lifted a hand to his mouth to cover his words.

"Not comfortable with this."

Moniah reached behind him and through his robe, elbowed Saeonar in the ribs. It was cold enough now to steal one's breath away.

Elria lifted her hood as Marina held an incense brazier up so the priestess could wave its fumes toward her face. Seconds later, the moon, Diana, rose above the sea. Elria turned to smile at Moniah.

"What now?" Kaylon whispered. Saeonar simply shrugged, his ribs still aching. Moniah met the determined and beatific expression of Elria. She extended her hand and he stepped forward to join her at the altar.

"Great lord of the skies, honor us and stand with me as we greet the goddess and her son incarnate, Treehoomena," Elria said, in a public voice. Moniah nodded assent. Elria's lovely green eyes sparkled at Moniah and he smiled gently in return. Although he loved her, he was quite aware she was using him. The tribute of honor was real but conjoined to it was a subtle and potent political maneuver. Just this once, he would allow it.

Elria gently nudged Moniah and they shifted to face east where the second moon peeked over the horizon.

"Rejoice, oh children, behold Trehoomena, son of Diana, the incarnation of dreams," Elria said, with a loud, happy voice. Elria embraced Moniah, who felt his arms come up to embrace her. Sackbuts, lutes, fifes and drums burst into a merry gavotte and the people danced and sang around the watch fire.

Meanwhile, the second moon, Trehoomena, arose as a silver crescent in the eastern skies. Around it, silent auroras danced against a back-drop twinkling with stars.

"Can we eat now?" Saeonar muttered to Kaylon, who flexed his jaw and ducked as a bouquet of winter pines and berries sailed by his head to land at his feet.

All joined together in a ring of linked arms and the merrymakers hurried into the palace; their cheers, laughter and music resounded around tables laden with food and drink. Dance music filled the air and Saeonar rubbed his hands as he dove into a servodroid tray of candied fruits. Moniah and Elria danced a gavotte while nobles of Clovis's court clapped in time around them.

"The dragons are here!" Clovis announced, nudging his way into the circle, his brow sweating under a crown of Holly. Moniah stopped in mid step and, still holding Elria by the hand, swept her out of the circle to join a mob hurrying into the capricious expanse of the Great Hall.

Prestant's' song echoed into the palace and Moniah ran out under the portico to find his winged friend trumpeting in the night. Prestant sniffed the air and caught sight of Moniah and lifted his head to the sky, issuing a fireball that glowed against the faces of astonished merrymakers before dissipating like spent fireworks in the snowy dark.

With a thud, Montre landed on the snow nearby. Saeonar paused in the doorway. He dropped a glazed apple and—opening his arms wide—hurried to hug the neck of his bleating familiar. Clovis and Marina welcomed the Wizans Vetaeos and Rete, taking their gloves, handing them mulled wine.

"What an excellent surprise!" Moniah beamed, clasping hands with Rete and Vetaeos.

"We are only the messengers of a gift, my lord," Rete said. He paused, doing a double take as the child Darius helped bring a water pail to the dragons. "The *infant*?" he asked, indicating the child.

"The same. So tell us what is this message?" Moniah demanded, impatiently. Rete and Vetaeos exchanged a smile, Vetaeos folded his arms over his chest and Rete lifted his hand to Prestant saying.

"Have you not wondered why Halfstep is not with us? Look at Montre's belly!" Moniah's lips parted but he said nothing, moving expectantly to Prestant, who lowered his eyes on Moniah while the corners of his long mouth lifted. The dragon smiled.

"Our mates…rest in nesting," Prestant sang to Moniah and Saeonar. Elria jumped as Moniah clapped his hands together in triumph. Saeonar reached his broad arms to touch each of the dragon's necks, pulling them closer so that the huge beasts had a time of it with their wings.

"Great Diasentue, you will raise hatchlings on Earth. Oh, I am proud of you, both of you." Saeonar said, wiping tears from his eyes.

"So…alive with emotion." "They are…as people now." The dragons sang to each other over the confusion of joy.

* * *

The Dawn of 832 of the human year brought a flurry of activity to the palace as those who, having enjoyed its shelter during the night, awoke with blurred minds to a quiet morning. The revelers prepared to depart on horse back or by boxcar wagons. Moniah accepted Elria's invitation to accompany her to Renthia via her own unique wagon.

The conveyance, pulled by a team of twelve horses, was a splendid presentation of her unique status. Brightly painted and carved with flowers, vines and birds, it groaned along the dirt road to Renthia-Acadia, attended by a phalanx of mounted guards. At their present pace, it would take hours to reach the city but Moniah had grown to appreciate slower, if not necessarily more leisurely, travel.

Within the warmth of the capacious wagon, Saeonar and Moniah luxuriated on silken divans surrounded by tapestries, woven carpets and rosewood carved walls inlaid with ebony and mother of pearl.

"Do you think we are spread a bit thin?" Saeonar asked then whispered thanks to Elria as she handed him a cup of hot tea. Elria handed Moniah a cup then set the tea service on a table and took seat next to Moniah, who gazed out a window.

"My lord?" Saeonar asked and Moniah, aware he was distracted, readjusted his posture to face Saeonar.

"Hmm? No, I do not think so. Rete will see to it Maethus-Dia is secure. Clovis will remain there with his court until I return."

"But that leaves only Vetaeos to return to Myzinos-Wur," Saeonar said, inspecting a scone.

"Granted, but the dome temple is remote and the mountain people are a friendly lot. Let us, uh, converse in the people's language," Moniah said, sipping his tea, patting Elria's hand.

"You have a point. It is time for other Aurans to come to Earth," Moniah said, in the Amerniun language.

"Is it true, Moniah, will your great one arrive with them?" Elria asked, her eyes sparkling with excitement.

"My brother, who is emperor of Aurocearia, has always desired to come to Earth," Moniah said, smiling.

"High time, too," Saeonar muttered, before biting into a scone he had finally determined deserved his special attention.

"The Auran, Arhahnis himself?" Elria whispered with awe and added, "The worlds within the sphere." Moniah took her hand in his and searched her curious expression.

"You might visit our home, Elria." Elria's mouth parted in wonderment, Moniah lifted his eyebrows.

"Yes, I could take you there."

"To fly among the stars with you," Elria said, dreamily. She snapped back to reality, adding, while clasping Moniah's hand. "How long would such a journey take?"

"Five months. Part of the time we would sleep but we would be partially aware of our surroundings in the void. *Auruaii* has the capacity to, to, how do I explain? The ship *describes* things about space to our minds as we travel. I could even speak with your mind whilst we slept," Moniah said.

Elria hung on his every word, her eyes delving into the worlds Moniah's eyes contained.

"Five months," Elria muttered.

Saeonar cleared his throat. "If we were to journey at the speed of your fastest horses, it would take millions of years to make the same trip," he said. Elria looked at Saeonar with a trace of fear darkening her expression. "Longer than human history has been writ," Saeonar added, quietly. Moniah sighed and shook his head, quickly and correctively, at Saeonar, which Elria did not see. Elria ran her hands over her face and pulled her hair from its headdress confines. She smiled at Moniah and coughed then reached for her teacup while Saeonar studied her.

Feeling agitated, Moniah patted his robes for his Ol pipe and, seeing his waist sash holster and pouch on a sideboard, he stood. An indescribable moment passed between Elria and Saeonar. She could not quite fathom the mixed and guarded expression Saeonar fixed upon her but she was familiar enough now with Auran eyes to recognize the darker reflections of their souls. Was Saeonar somehow taunting her?

Moniah fumbled into his pouch for his Ol pipe. He glanced up into a mirror and froze in place. His face was not changed but, in the cold light of day, he could clearly see that his once raven-hued hair was now subtly streaked with white. The eyes reflecting back had more than a trace of a nameless weariness. Somehow, he sensed an internal mechanism was ticking down and it occurred to him how strange it was for such apparent youthfulness to cohabit with a sudden onslaught of age. Suddenly, the many faces of the human elderly he had seen while on Earth took on a new and disturbing personal meaning. Was aging itself part of what Necontis had foretold in terms of becoming one with humanity?

The logic of life assured him that this revelation was accurate but he wondered what relevance oncoming age had for the gods' experiment in mortal cares. Was Aurocearia as finite as one generation? His blood ran cold. The product of love that burned between he and Elria had never produced a child and the capricious gods had removed all Auries from mortal existence so why should it be a surprise that he and all Aurans could become extinct.

Moniah lit his Ol pipe.

Elria stood wearily and gazed down on Saeonar.

"Lord Medean teaches us that the heart is a place for the future," she said. Saeonar did not respond and, exhausted from two days with virtually no sleep, the priestess retired to her bedroom at the rear of the wagon while Moniah chose to sit by a leaded glass window to watch the passing of snow-laden trees. Saeonar studied his liege and friend with compassion and sadness. Saeonar loved Moniah with all his heart but he could not relate to Moniah, who had known a love spread across millennia. Saeonar's own feeling of loss was a mixture of subdued rivalry directed against an alien godhead that commingled with sadness and longing for Aurocearia, and was therefore a more abstract frustration.

As the wagon rumbled along, Saeonar suffered for Moniah, whose revelation he sensed had come cruelly at a moment when the First Lord was happy in a realm of love. Saeonar felt isolated and transparent in remembrance of an age forever lost and it gave him chills to realize that time had no healing for such measures. Only new challenges and experiences quelled the fear of Auran minds what could that mean for the denizens of the Sphereworlds, trapped in a magnificent but rigidly unchanging environment?

The Lord of Dragons

Moniah sat down slowly into his command chair in the bridge of *Auruaii.* He looked around as though he were in a new and strange place, noticing a thin coating of dust on the spatial interlink control as it rose up from the floor near his right armrest.

"Computer, initiate communications sequence, codex Auros Prime, audio-visual," he said, and a large floatscreen unfolded from the bridge ceiling. Static on the screen changed to a rapidly flowing matrix consisting of numerals that resolved into an intricate three-dimensional field of blue.

While the spatial interlink configured, Moniah traced a pattern in the dust of his command seat armrest with his finger. He looked to the right out of the blister dome, watching lights and fires illuminate the city as it prepared for another cold night.

"Clearance, bowshot molecular energizer engaged," the melodious voice of the computer announced. A chime sounded, indicating real time communication and, for the first time in years, Moniah beheld his brother. Arhahnis gazed at Moniah from his throne, resplendent in a robe of forest green and deep blue with gold Ol leaf embroidery. Moniah could feel and smell the luxury of Aurocearia as if he were standing in the throne hall of the floating stones.

"Moniah! My brother," Arhahnis said, his voice cracking with emotion. Moniah bowed his head briefly. Now that he saw the Arhahn, he felt a stir of tender emotion in his heart, dissipating his former bitterness.

"Arhahnis, my heart is warmed to see you."

Behind Moniah the doors to the bridge opened and Kaylon, Saeonar and Medean entered. The Aurans immediately sank to one knee, seeing the image of Arhahnis on the screen. Himself raised one hand.

"Rise, brave Aurans and let me behold you," Arhahnis said.

Moniah noticed the red-black hair of Arhahnis was also streaked with white. Moniah looked over his shoulder, motioning for Kaylon, who came to his feet and stepped forward.

"I am transmitting a new and full report of the *Auruaii* log as well as data concerning our experiences with the people," Kaylon said. Moniah leaned forward in his seat.

"Every Auran shares in pride with your accomplishments on eartos," Arhahnis said and, despite himself, Moniah chuckled.

"Earth," he corrected, gently.

"Earth," Arhahnis repeated, luxuriating in the word.

"How can we assist the mission?" Arhahnis asked, his golden pupils dancing with joy and excitement. Moniah nodded to Medean.

"Infinite, Taen assistance is needed in order to implement our medical priorities."

"Is there danger, are any of you ill?" Arhahnis asked, so tenderly that Moniah placed one hand to his chin and studied his brother as if he were a stranger, for he had never heard him speak with such vulnerable compassion.

"My own database and that of the Taen ship's hospital facility created by Lirea, is adequate but requires resources," Medean said, unhappy that he had mentioned Lirea. Arhahnis nodded to someone off screen and Ammanmus stepped into view.

"This brings our matter to hand," the Taen high priest said. Silence ensued as each Auran, both those on Earth and those light years removed, considered the uncertain fate ahead of them.

"Studies indicate our bodies evidenced sub-molecular transformation, which is traceable in residual plasma gene."

Moniah looked to Medean and the mystic nodded agreement. For several months, Medean had conducted his own secret physiological studies of his and Moniah's tissue and blood chemistry and the results matched the findings of Ammanmus.

"Brothers, I believe Auries will join with us in a time of Transmaking and we shall see a new generation of Aurocearians," Ammanmus said.

Moniah sat up in his chair, while the others muttered in astonishment behind him.

"How do you come to this conclusion, Ammanmus? Auries *joining* us?" Moniah said, and the others crowded around him to stare at the floatscreen. A rift of static distorted the face of Ammanmus but quickly cleared and Moniah saw in the face of his brother a quiet certainty that took him back to a life when his own trances and visions shaped his being and resolve. Hope, it seemed, really did spring eternal, as the people of Earth so often remarked.

Ammanmus held up what appeared to be small glass vial. Everyone aboard *Auruai* leaned forward to stare at the object and Medean hurried to stand directly under the floatscreen so that he could scrutinize the object at the closest possible range.

"I hold a container of the Arhahn's blood. This sample was taken from him recently. A spectrometer reading of its contents shows a remarkable presence of Meliphor's blood chemistry."

"Gods," Kaylon whispered, glancing at Moniah, whose gaze was riveted to the floatscreen while he absent-mindedly wrung his hands. Ammanmus sighed and lowered the vial out of sight.

"Precisely, Kaylon. We believe that during the metamorphoses, the gods changed our physiology to comprise aspects of the transcended Auries," Ammanmus said, then he paused to mop his forehead.

"Could this presence of Meliphor be a residual chemistry from the garden creation time and therefore unique to Arhahnis?" Medean asked.

Ammanmus angled his face down to respond.

"This possibility was taken into account and, thus, Alaysi provided samples as well. Since Alaysi never enjoyed the love of an Aurie, we felt his sample would be conducive to developing a more wide-reaching hypothesis. What we found is that our brother Alaysi's sample also contains traces of biochemistry unique to Aurie physiology."

Saeonar paced the bridge while Kaylon gaped in open astonishment and the others murmured excitedly. Moniah waved his arm over his head and they quieted.

"I concur with your findings," Medean said and turned to Moniah.

Moniah felt a sliver of hope among his confused emotions in the light of this scientific exploration. The fact that Ammanmus was in the presence of Arhahnis reinforced a certainty of mystical truth. The floatscreen image refocused to image the face of the Arhahn.

"We are changed in the length of a single year," Arhahnis said.

"Each human generation grows old; youth passes to age and only birth continues their lives. If Aurans stand at the brink of extinction, at least we have transmuted wisdom. I pray it will somehow live on. Ammanmus, I believe I speak for all of us when I thank you for giving us the hope unique to our beloved home worlds." Moniah said.

"Another generation of Aurocearians will prove your hope, Moniah. Even the Excilue believe we are at the brink, not of extinction but of continuance," Arhahnis said. Then the Emperor paused and examined the backs of his hands. He added, "Though I will never walk upon Earth, I have foreseen my successor will do so."

Moniah relinquished his unspoken question as to what, if any, might be the fate of Aurans outside the Sphereworlds, for a resignation to fate was brightened by hope.

"We will initiate contact again in one week," Moniah said, clearing his throat.

"Should we find this impossible for any reason, let me salute you, brave brothers." The Emperor stood from his throne and sank to his knees, offering an unheard of sign of respect to the earthbound Aurans. Saeonar covered his face with one elbow, to avert his eyes from the kneeling Arhahn. A second later, the floatscreen signal terminated into black.

* * *

Outside Renthia-Acadia, Varrick observed the city. The giant tyrant could see his breath in the cold gloom of the early hour. He stood up in his stirrups, angling his body to look right, left and then behind in order to make a visual check of where his mounted troops were positioned.

Varrick spun around to peer at the city again, still steeped in darkness. He had sent in a scout at midnight and now only an hour remained until dawn, a perfect time to strike.

"Where be the damned signal?" he hissed and, as the words spit to his beard, he saw it: a torch waved from a rooftop. Varrick grunted, yanked back on his reins and raised his terrible hammer high over his head.

A thunder of horses erupted from the forest on three sides of Renthia-Acadia. As the mounted army galloped toward the city gates, Varrick sneered in contempt of the sky people. Where were they and their fearsome dragons? Where was this fabled floating city?

* * *

Elria met Moniah as he disembarked from *Auruaii*. Something seemed to have taken the best of him for he appeared weary and though the hour was very late, she sensed the hour itself was not at fault, though in a strange irony she was not privy to, time itself, was in fact, the issue.

"My lord, what troubles you so?" Elria asked, taking Moniah by the arm. He gazed at her; deeply touched that she had roused herself at such an early hour to be with him. In this way, she was so much like Lirea, who had always known when to join him.

Moniah was tempted to tell Elria the substance of his communication with the Sphereworlds. He had always vowed to impart an "utter truth" to her and the people but he had already corrupted that vow many times, arbitrarily electing when to reveal this truth and when to subvert or edit it.

Cries from the city diverted Moniah's attention. Soldiers, followed by a crowd, were running toward them.

"My lord, we're under attack!" Clovis's man-at-arms shouted, while struggling free of his woman and children, who wept in fear, turning to Moniah beseechingly.

For a heartbeat, Moniah was too stunned to move. Shaking himself to action, he spun to Kaylon and Saeonar.

"Let as many people into *Auruaii* as you can," he thundered above the sounds of confusion, while the streets filled with people and the temple bell tolled.

"Look, yonder. There and there!" a woman gasped to Elria. Fires dotted the city amidst shadowy forms scurrying around.

Moniah cursed the insular melancholy he had allowed himself to indulge in. His leadership lulled by years of trusting peace was remiss for he had ignored the threat of Varrick and, though no one yet mentioned that the invaders were from Canelor, the sinking of Moniah's heart and the terrible look in Elria's eyes announced the fact.

Bells and gongs sounded in the predawn and Saeonar covered one ear while talking into his comlink. Kaylon mounted a horse.

"I will ride in," he shouted and angrily spurred the steed. Moniah paused to take hold of Elria. "Go into the *Auruaii* with the others."

Panic threatened to seize the people as a mob of women and children and the elderly clambered onto the dock.

"I would remain with *you*," Elria begged, jostled by a woman in tears carrying her infant. "Help us, great one." The woman cried to Moniah, who pulled Elria toward him.

"You must stay here and do what you can. You cannot be harmed within the ship. I will come for you." A young soldier hurried toward Moniah with two horses in tow. Moniah mounted the horse. He leaned down to Saeonar, who seized the reins of the other horse.

"I need you here with the ship," Moniah said, but Saeonar refused, cutting him off. "No. Elria can seal the hatch, she knows how. My place is with you." Saeonar threw his leg over the saddle and patted the horse's head and off they went into chaos.

"Can we use the sonic arrays of *Auruaii* and put the warriors to sleep?" Moniah yelled.

"With their metabolisms, easily done but we could kill children and the elders using that power in such close quarters," Saeonar bellowed in reply, leading them toward the main garrison.

* * *

At dawn, Corina found Mayron on the south ramparts of castle Canelor. He sipped slowly from a steaming mug and peered into the distance.

"What is it, Mayron, what do you see?" she asked, excitedly. The old shaman pointed toward the mountains to the south.

"Behold, the sky people's dragons."

Corina peered into the sky and there, sure enough, were the forms of two large, winged creatures, flying due east.

"The dragons are bound for Acadia," Corina said, and hugged Mayron.

"No, that is the *old* name, they are going to *Renthia*-Acadia," Mayron corrected her gleefully and he sang with joy then hobbled into the castle, seizing a shield bearing Varrick's coat of arms from the wall. Mayron threw the shield to the floor.

"This is the end of Varrick!" he sang and Corina, infected with a sense of triumph hurried to join him. Mayron stomped a foot on the shield and began to hop up and down on it. Corina laughed and joined him. As they jumped on the shield, Mayron giggled like a boy, lifting his arms into the air he chanted.

"The hammer will fall and down will come Varrick, greed and all!" Mayron and Corina held hands and laughed so loudly that the queen's ladies and pages stormed into the room where they stood transfixed in confusion.

"Majesty?" One of the women asked timidly.

Exalted from their joy, Corina threw her arms around Mayron, ignoring the servants.

"Are you certain Mayron?" Corina said, breathlessly. Mayron heaved a sigh to catch his breath and puffed out his chest replying.

"Of course, I have foreseen it."

"Bring us hot water for bath and open the wine and ale cellars to the castle," Corina instructed her servants. She swept out to the parapet where starlings and bluebirds already heralded the sweet welcome of spring.

* * *

At the dome temple dragon Keep of Myzinos-Wur, Montre and Vetaeos stood over the giant reposed form of Halfstep, whose belly was fecund and ready for labor. Rete rattled his comlink at his ear but all he heard was confusion on the vox channel.

"Rete, what in Hades is going on? We need you. Here, bring that sulfur compound," Vetaeos said, lifting his ear from Halfstep's heaving side. Her breathing was regular and Montre cooed to her with birth song.

"What is Hades?"

"Don't confuse the issue. Whatever it is at Renthia'll keep, now come here with that compound." Montre leaned her face down to Halfstep who rolled her eyes at the nervous bickering of the Aurans.

"Aurans are forever made…as foundlings when birth song," sang Halfstep.

"Prestant flies to join Moniah…great sadness in the human city."

"Our eggs…warm to remain at Myzinos?"

"This place is sweet…I hear…new music in the Aurans."

Vetaeos ran his hands gently over Halfstep's flank. Her scales reflected the morning sun and she lifted her head from the straw to lick Vetaeos, but he rubbed sweat from his brow and jerked to his full height.

"Now, Rete!"

* * *

Wispy clouds parted and the Oscileans moaned at the sight of the city in rout.

"Changing comes…hear it sound," Prestant sang to the dawn. Wholestep smelled the air, wrinkling his nose at the smoke and soot wafting up from the city as they passed over the palace.

Clovis watched the dragons, Prestant and Wholestep, soar toward his besieged city. He sealed Maethus-Dia, trying not to look into Marina's frightened eyes, and rode off with his guard.

* * *

Robert "the tall" took aim with his arrow and let fly. He then jumped back behind the safety of the rampart tower while Uletis and Caras barked orders at the other commanders, pausing only to take careful aim with their Saen pistols. Able-bodied men and boys clustered at every garrison, taking bows, spears and swords and hurrying back to the streets where the battle for the city raged block by block. Varrick galloped through the streets, wielding his hammer over his head, first right then left, hurling people to the ground or against walls under its terrible blows.

Moniah felt his soul sing with power but it was not the bloodlust of war and he gritted his teeth with rage as they galloped toward the new and larger central plaza.

"Not now, not now!" he roared, sensing a turn of his biological inner self.

"Look! Oscileans," Kaylon said, pointing up as his horse reared on its hind legs. Moniah shut his eyes tight and sang to Prestant.

"Fire, my son of winds. Bring fire on the invaders."

High above, Prestant and Wholestep arced over the city, issuing fireballs of death. Varrick caught sight of a dragon as he galloped toward the central plaza. He crouched in his saddle as one of the creature's shadows passed over him. Screams from his personal guard spun his attention to the rear just in time to see a meteor of fire strike them.

* * *

Medean climbed to the roof of the library. Around him in every direction, the city was evenly divided between conquest and melee. Medean closed his eyes and connected to the beasts the people called horses. Careful to picture in his mind only those horses ridden by Varrick's men—he sent out disruptive thoughts.

Varrick's mounted troops were suddenly torn between battle and the effort to control bucking and rearing horses. Moniah saw Medean standing on the distant library dome, his green robe a solitary sentinel of peace amidst the war. Prestant and Wholestep took advantage of the mind song Medean transmitted to land near Saeonar and Moniah who dismounted the horses to climb onto the Oscileans.

"Mind song of Medean…loud in pain," Prestant sang to Moniah.

"It must be my friend, try to block it," Moniah chanted. Kaylon reared in his horse, a spear sang through the air over his head and he turned to fire three rapid pulses in the direction of the arrow's origin. A garden wall exploded revealing a Canelorian soldier, who ran stumbling away.

"Kaylon! Signal the *Auruaii*. Have the Constructorbots activated," Moniah yelled. Kaylon paused then took out his portable comlink. His hands trembled but he worked quickly, keying in commands.

"Hold this ground, I am going up to take a visual," Moniah said to Saeonar, singing, "Eveet!" to Prestant and the Oscilean beat his wings with might, taking them quickly higher. Hovering above the city, Moniah scanned the situation. Varrick was pressing from west to east, driving everyone to the harbor. It looked as though ninety percent of the population had gathered on the stone docks and levees around *Auruaii.* The ship must be teeming with refugees, Moniah thought, realizing that, if Varrick succeeded in reaching the harbor, it would be a slaughter.

"Fly down," Moniah commanded to Prestant, who sang in reply. "'Tis better…here." but, dutifully, the great creature obeyed and down they swooped through acrid skies.

* * *

Light years away, Arhahnis entered the temple of Surrant-Wonder to stand before the vast altar-wall dedicated to the voice entity, Necontis. The Aurocearian emperor and his generation had lived thousands of years and Arhahnis prayed for the merciful intercession of the gods so that his race might continue beyond the time of Birthfire which, each Auran sensed, was at last seeking to transform the nation of Aurans yet again.

Behind him, the temple filled with Aurans who chanted while Arhahnis gazed up at the forty starburst golden orbs representing the manifestations of the godhead, Diasentue. Golden wisps of plasma energy surrounded Arhahnis.

"Meliphor?" he said, in trance, and lifted his arms to his sides. Birthfire plasma sang to life around him and coalesced with the golden plasma to form a transforming sphere around his body, just as it had done millennia ago to transcend him to mortal life. Arhahnis floated a few feet above the marble floor. He looked up and saw another orb of intense radiant hot light in which the face of Meliphor smiled upon him.

The Arhahn transcending Birthfire orb floated up to the high reaches of the temple like a miniature star, radiating pulses of gold, green and purple light that danced from the walls in crackling electrical currents. Ammanmus fell to his knees before the altar and wept with joy. He lifted his arms as the transcending Birthfire energy possessed him.

* * *

People still crowding into *Auruaii* for safety paused to watch in fascination as a fleet of round Constructorbots suddenly emerged from the aft hangar and—sounding like a swarm of bees—flew into the city just as Varrick made it to the central plaza where the bulk of his forces confronted the city soldiers.

"Where be this mighty host?" Varrick grunted. He could only see one dark-haired sky being atop a dragon. The commander?

Saeonar—distracted by guarding Moniah until he landed and covering Kaylon while he sent commands to the ship's robots—never saw the spear Varrick's adjutant launched. Moniah heard a guttural sound followed by the roaring wail of Wholestep.

Saeonar leaned forward in his saddle and fell from it to topple to the ground. Moniah was unaware of his own movements; in a blur he was at Saeonar's side, his eyes refusing to take in the sight of the spear protruding from Saeonar's chest.

Moniah cradled the Wizan's head. A thin stream of blue-silver blood trickled from Saeonar's mouth.

"You glow, Moniah," Saeonar wheezed.

"My friend, No!" Moniah wailed, lifting his face to the sky. Tears flowed and he could see them strike Saeonar's awful robe, fluorescent drops evaporating in a mist as his very essence prepared to transform.

Saeonar winced. He handed Moniah his Coracle-diant.

"Remember when you became Tetra-Lachaen? Take my Coracle, keep it always," Saeonar said, grunting in pain.

"Yes," Moniah gasped and the body of Saeonar began to glow. He squeezed Moniah's hand.

"You have cast the die on Earth, a world of Wizan. I have, ugh, a trick of my own," Saeonar said, attempting to smile as his blue-bloodied hand grasped the Coracle to cover Moniah's fingers. Saeonar's eyes emitted a fine misty light and he whispered.

"I loved you." With the last of his strength, Saeonar infused his Coracle-diant with his life force. The marvelous lights of Saeonar's eyes went dark and his body swirled suddenly into a myriad of colorful streams of warm light, infused with red and golden plasma that dissipated like a fog in the sun. Moniah felt his hands empty and he stared dumbstruck at the empty robes that had contained Saeonar.

Kaylon, Medean and Uletis had come into the plaza with the outlying garrisons. Everyone backed away from the Aurans and their glowing bodies of cascading radial light. The fighting ceased and all eyes fixed on the stranger apparitions the Aurans presented to an exhausted and stunned assemblage of sweating and blood stained humans.

A few of Varrick's cornered men tried to run from the plaza down an alley but they halted and ran back to the crowd as Caras appeared, his body pulsing blinding golden light.

The glowing Aurans sent Varrick's men into a panic. Prestant fixed his eyes on Varrick and reared back, a terrible fireball erupted from the Oscilean's mouth and Varrick threw himself from his horse as it struck. The tyrant bellowed in fury, his cloak and chainmail melting in flame.

Instantly, people crushed in on Varrick and one of his own generals drew his sword and stabbed the giant.

"There is deliverance for my brother," the general, Erik, thundered, spitting at the stunned face of the dying Varrick, whose son he had murdered at Canelor. A squadron of Constructorbots flew over the plaza, utterly terrifying what remained of Varrick's forces. Most of the exhausted soldiers stared at the Aurans in wonder, their weapons clattering to the ground.

"They *are* gods,"

General Erik muttered, dropping to his knees. Moniah came to his feet wearily. He held Saeonar's Coracle-diant wand in a steel grip. Kaylon gathered up the transcended Saeonar's bloodied robes. Silence prevailed, no one so much as moved. Moniah looked around at the blurry images of the battle worn citizens and defeated warriors then inspected his glowing hands that pulsed light with each beat of his sorrowful heart.

A New World

An eerie, silent procession of glowing Aurans walked alone toward the *Auruaii.* Overhead, Constructorbots buzzed through the air en route back to the ship while the Oscileans flew circles above their masters, keeping a watchful eye on the humans.

No one spoke to the Aurans. Exhausted citizens mourning their losses and relieved to be free of menace had not yet processed their grief although cheers could be heard from those not directly affected who, energized by the new miracle of the radiant Aurans and aware of victory, were driven by mania to celebrate.

When Moniah reached *Auruaii*, the ship was surrounded by hundreds of milling people as the crowds poured from inside it to praise the victory. The praise quickly subsided to whispers of awe seeing the Aurans approach. Elria caught sight of Moniah. She struggled through the crowds but she caught only a glimpse of him as he entered the hangar deck before the Blermetal doors closed, sealing the ship.

Within *Auruaii*, the Aurans' bodies were literally singing with Birthfire energy. The clock of mortal life was nearing its end and transforming plasma poured out of Moniah, Medean, Kaylon Caras and Uletis, surrounding their bodies in the orbs of plasma light and swirling gases each Auran had known at the moment of his birth on Auros Prime, eons ago.

Plasma waves driven by the energy winds of the Auran Birthfire orbs hurled discarded baskets of food, clothing, clubs and other detritus left behind by the people against the walls of the hangar deck. The Oscileans lifted their wings and sang in response to the music emanating from their masters.

Moniah's heart released the anger he felt against all humans, gone was the disgust for their needs, which had killed Saeonar. As his mortal coil unwound, for a moment—or was it a lifetime, Moniah yearned to behold Elria, if only to bid her farewell.

Throughout the Sphereworlds as on Earth, Aurocearians ascended into the air within Birthfire orbs. Diasentue beheld the majesty of his first mortal children with compassion and the godhead entity manifestations of love and tolerance conjoined in the cosmic mind to conceive a future for Aurocearia. The godhead Diasentue determined to renew Aurankind from generation to generation through intercession with the Auries who existed beyond mortality in the Godsrealm. Mercy manifested in Diasentue during the time of Transmaking, and Aurans were reunited with their Auries to create the new generation. The godhead reconceived Auran lifespan; never again would Diasentue allow his chosen mortals to live for millennia. Auran genetic code was altered, programming a two hundred year lifespan into the Aurans. Within the cosmic mind this evolution became reality and manifested…

Moniah floated above the hangar deck, his physical sensation dulled in a pulsing of love light while he commingled with Lirea. Moniah beheld the universe of the Godsrealm and his eternal consciousness remembered his heavenly home. Together he and Lirea became a new entity. The Moniah Birthfire orb split into two equal portions by a process of chromo dynamic interaction and Moniah transcending evaporated from mortality as his son, Moniah incarnate, took mortal form.

Within the confines of his mind, Moniah beheld images and memories from his father entity. As his body took shape and Moniah incarnate lost all sense of communion with the Godsrealm, his own unique expression took hold of mortal flesh and his spirit burned down into corporeal consciousness.

* * *

Outside the *Auruaii*, crowds converged on the waterfront and harbor. The citizens of Renthia-Acadia, along with the former invaders from Canelor, watched the ship expectantly, hoping for a sign, a word from Moniah or the other Aurans they had come to love. There were no enemies at Renthia-Acadia now. The invaders and native citizens were past caring about the tyrant Varrick. He was a memory best forgotten, leaving a weary peace to reign.

At midday, food was served and musicians even played as the crowds milled to and fro waiting for their sky people friends to emerge again. The hour moved on into afternoon and still no sign of life could be seen in the ship.

Elria and Clovis huddled together, sharing a glow orb in the chill of late afternoon, ignoring speculations overheard around them.

"The Aurans glowed in fury."

"Nigh! They were blessed in victory."

At last, the sun began to set on the longest day in memory, its dying rays bleeding red streaks in the western sky. Elria gazed determinedly at the observation bridge domes and blister windows. Sunlight reflected from the gleaming hull of *Auruaii* but the vast ship remained inert, silent and somehow no longer accessible.

* * *

Mortal time meant nothing to the entity Annevnos. Safe within his traveling prism, the monster determined that he could never physically return to Aurocearia. The vengeful Gods had transformed his chemical and molecular composition, in effect magnetizing him, so that, in his present incarnation, he comprised one field with Aurocearia as the polar opposing field.

In the silence of deep space, the prism had traveled near other worlds, testing their limitations and, while none of the worlds visited thus far had proved to be inhabited and were, therefore, unacceptable for Annevnos to make landfall upon…had he willed to do so there would have been no preventing him. The black, vertical prism sailed on through solar winds, its sonic pulses tasting uncharted realms.

Had it been years or moments since Annevnos heard the *Auruaii* progressing through the void? He dimly recalled trying to follow the ship but it had moved too swiftly under the power of engines some of his minds could recall helping design in another, terrible life.

When the velocity of the *Auruaii* carried it beyond reach of his senses, Annevnos turned his attentions to other structures within the void until he locate a faint noise within the solar system of a giant orange star dominating two planets and a moon. His prism orbited the largest planet, where the noise magnified with the voices of savage and primitive intellects.

From within the prism, Annevnos studied a world of sand storms and dense but dry forests from which grunts of barbaric voices revealed the name of the primate world, Selos. Annevnos descended through skies thick with the orange glow of the large local star.

Above the silver-swept planet of Selos, Annevnos sensed the former Aurocearian generation transcending. One of his six heads, Envy, wailed in lament, its mind aware that all it had known was gone and the gods had renewed life. The central mind of the entity rejoiced for it realized Birthfire was now an irrelevant aspect of his biology and the prism was its own unique protection against mortality. Annevnos continued to hover over the planet Selos, his six heads peering into a window facet of the prism interior that presented magnified images of life below. The heads darted and preened while Annevnos used his hands and the tentacles that had been his legs and feet to rub the prism interior, changing views, scrutinizing everything.

Annevnos discovered a world whose humanoid inhabitants fought a daily struggle for survival. Ferocious storm winds assailed the Selosian cities, hurling silver dust and pigment so that the material, although a treasure on earth, was a constant nuisance to the Selosians.

The Selosians learned to grow their moldy crops within heated caves as arable land knew only a scant season and was rare and widely scattered across a world where the best water sprang from underground streams. The planet's proximity to its giant orange star had long exacerbated harsh living conditions on Selos by evaporating much of its one large ocean.

During a mild winter orbit, which reduced the silver storm's severity, allowing the Selosians to enjoy brief excursions outside their ornamented but crude structures, the black prism of Annevnos finally descended to the surface.

The humanoid natives observed the strange, singing prism, descend from the firmament to stand vertically, with no visible support, on one of its tapered ends, just outside the boundary of their largest city. Tall and powerful, their skin stained silver by the constant ingestion and permeation of silver pigment, the Selosians were beautiful, if not imposing, people. They dwelt in a world of feudal kingdoms and were a fearless lot but they had never seen anything like the prism.

It towered fifteen heights of the tallest warrior and its midnight surfaces gleamed as if wet but each face of the prism was so black as to appear like a sliver of the darkest reaches of space. The impenetrable prism pulsed a humming tone that beat time like a heart and each pulse revealed an outline of sickly, yellow light. Inside and invisible, entity Annevnos studied the few brave souls who dared approach his traveling prison. From their minds, Annevnos gathered their history, of wars and farming, and also images of dirty temples where sacrifices were made to silver and stone idols.

Could they have heard the cacophony of his many cackles, even the brave onlookers would have retreated. Annevnos' heads showed mirth, glee, wanton lust, inspiration, calculation and patience. It would be easy enough for Annevnos to appear as the greater warrior god and sweep the petty idols of the Selosians aside. There would be time enough for all his plans but, for the present, Annevnos simply observed, learning their boisterous brutal language through which he sensed their fears and their unbounded ignorance of all but the crudest rudiments of applied sciences.

Even so, Annevnos perceived that the planet was a powerful resource of elements. Elements the keener minds of Selos would be trained to harness and fashion.

* * *

Moniah incarnate awakened to find himself in the lap of the Oscilean, Prestant. He was aboard the void ship *Auruaii* and the creature was dozing, one enormous paw curled up, gently holding Moniah in place. Long hypnotic rumblings of breath like the coming of a storm wind issued from Prestant's nostrils and mouth. The exhaled air blew Moniah's hair and it was this tickling sensation of hair on his face that had roused him from dreams.

Moniah sat up, dimly recalling trying to walk in the first moments of life and of feeling very cold until Prestant nudged him toward the discarded robes of his father. Prestant's large eyes fluttered open and he watched Moniah incarnate carefully crawl down to the deck where he wobbled on strong but untried legs.

A tear fell from Prestant. It seemed so cruel of the maker to deny the children any sense of nurturing from their father beings. These new Aurans were obviously the progeny of their transcended ones and fully mature physically but they were also unique children who were brilliant with inbred understanding and knowledge. Their minds swam with songs and memories of the past and they were having much difficulty with emotions. Indeed, with all the sensations being born fully mature cascaded onto them.

* * *

Auruaii had sat silent for so long, life around the giant space ship revolved with only the occasional glance of curiosity. A large sailing vessel nearby creaked as its rigging caught wind and a few children fishing at the levee gathered up their catch baskets as the fishing boats came into the harbor for the night. The wind was calm and only a few gulls could be heard in the still of a warm eventide.

A clang, followed by a hissing sound, caught the attention of one of the fishing boys near the aft hangar door. He set down his basket to scamper along the levee where he could see the large oval door rising slowly to reveal a soft glow of light. The boy whistled to his friends, who began to shout and race about drawing the attention of adults.

People threw down their cooking utensils to hurry toward the wharf. Someone rang the temple bell and soon the levee was crowded with onlookers. A single Auran form appeared in the hangar doorway, shielding his eyes from the setting sun. Young prince Darius Hugherni, son of King Clovis, rode onto the scene atop his mare and all but jumped from his saddle to run up the long dock to where he saw a blond-haired

Auran standing serenely amidst a gaggle of stunned anglers and merchants.

"I am Kaylon Talsaiyr," the Auran said, and a few people cheered him, at which the Auran smiled bemusedly. He seemed disconnected from his surroundings and hesitant as he studied the curious people.

People gathered around Kaylon, studying him with the perplexed realization that he was a stranger to them, yet also familiar. When he announced his name, it only served to elicit further consternation.

"Nigh, yer a spittin image of the lord Kaylon tis true but our Kaylon was a devil of a handsome thing. Naught to say you aren't comely me lord, but surely you are…" a woman replied, moving forward to take a closer look.

Kaylon smiled at the old woman, she winked at him and he shifted uncomfortably on his feet. The crowds parted to allow Clovis a clear path to the dock. Clovis gestured to his guards who turned to the crowds.

"All right then, please all of ye move back a bit now. That's it."

Clovis approached Kaylon with caution. He coughed and leaned forward studying the Auran carefully.

"My lord?" Clovis said, searching the Auran's face. As far as he could tell he wore the mantle of Kaylon but seemed a bit less powerful of frame as well as somehow more subdued than the heroic Kaylon he remembered.

"Not the same sparkle," Clovis muttered to himself.

"You are Clovis Hugherni, King of Renthia-Acadia?" Kaylon said, in a smooth melodious voice.

"I am he, lord."

"Will you come within the ship, please?" Kaylon said. Clovis indicated that he wanted a moment alone with his son. He took Darius by the shoulder and led him a few paces away. The eyes of the young prince remained fixed on Kaylon.

"There is a certain distance about this Auran. He bears the same name but I must needs to venture within the sky ship to find answers. Remain here and send word to Elria to come forth from her prayers."

Darius lifted his shoulders and wiped sweat from his brow.

"Mayhaps her prayers are answered," Darius said, pulling his tunic sleeves up to his forearms. Clovis fingered his goatee and ruffled Darius' hair. The prince blushed and immediately ran his hand through his curly locks.

"The imaginative mind must remain receptive. I have an idea about what has happened but how, I wonder, could they have changed so much from whom we knew?"

"Mayhaps they are not your friends. I will send for the priestess."

"Yes, and be quick about it."

* * *

Elria maintained her vigil over the *Auruaii*, hoping to glimpse any sign of Moniah until her spirits sank and she retreated to the temple of Diana and the only source of emotional comfort that remained to her. As time passed, she avoided the harbor as much as possible.

Finally, just a week before Kaylon emerged from the ship, an acolyte awakened her at dawn and reported that the dragons had been seen flying away from *Auruaii*.

"They must be returning to the mountain city," Elria correctly surmised. Then, when news came that Clovis was seen hurrying to the harbor, Elria was quick on his heels but she was hard pressed to make her way through the crowded, narrow streets that had grown increasingly overloaded in the new age of peace. She found a scattered crowd milling about on the broad stone quay but saw no sign of Clovis or Moniah. Frustrated and depressed, Elria took shelter from the setting sun under the portico of the Harbor Inn. The heat and the ocean breeze lulled her as she gazed at flower bees until a commotion stirred her attention.

"They be comin' out priestess!" a fisherman called out to her, his sun-wrinkled, happy face grinning like a schoolboy caught in mischief. The port was very busy in springtime trade, fish and farmers markets, not even counting those who, like Elria, were simply loitering to see what would happen next. Once again, Elria was frustrated trying to make her way through the confusion and crowds.

"Stand aside!" she commanded, impatiently. This time she would employ her authority to clear a path, determined not to miss seeing Moniah again. In her eagerness, she had failed to summon her guards, whose mere presence would have cleared a wide girth.

Queen Marina and her ladies joined Elria at the main crossway of streets nearest the *Auruaii*. The Queen took hold of Elria.

"Come under my parasol," she said and their combined presence helped clear a direct path to the ship. Just as they reached the *Auruaii* dock, one of its shuttles sped out of the aft hangar. The crowds were thinning as though leaving a sporting event. Clovis waved to the women excitedly as he approached.

"They have gone to Maethus-Dia," he said.

"No one has been there since the battle. I trust we left it in right order," Marina said, chewing her lip. Elria gazed at the shuttle as it grew ever smaller and Clovis placed his hands on her shoulders.

"I have much to tell you," Clovis said and Elria's mood brightened. She brushed a lock of hair from in front of her eyes.

"When might I see Moniah again?" she begged to know, searching the face of Clovis as though he held the key to her every desire.

Stellar Seas

Moniah incarnate walked the halls of his father's palace on Earth. The *Auruaii* vessel, a safe place to undergo Birthfire Transmaking, was ghostly and sterile but here, at Maethus-Dia, he could sense the dream-memory of Moniah transcended and feel in the beautiful chambers, a greater connection to his ancestor.

Though he studied shipboard databases of images of their transcended "fathers", Moniah found that he enjoyed even more looking at the murals in the Great Salon, which pictured Moniah transcended and his *Auruaii* crew making landfall, their first encounter with humans, the revelation of the Oscileans, the dome temple. It was a lovely museum of illustrated history that warmed his heart in the emotional vacuum created by the fact that he never knew his father.

Morning sun shone through clear prisms of leaded glass windows onto a mural depicting Moniah and the man, Clovis, standing around a bonfire surrounded by dancing people and, in the painting, he could see who Moniah transcended truly was and feel his presence on Earth. Moniah incarnate reached out to touch the mural, while Kaylon and Medean looked on.

"Strange to know only a part of oneself. Forgive me, I have been too preoccupied with my past," Moniah said, turning to Kaylon, who studied the murals with a wounded, yet distant attitude, as though he gazed upon a painful memory.

Medean smiled tenderly, his calm and patient gaze swept over the mural and he touched it gently.

"I understand your feeling, Moniah," he said, and added, "The others are waiting."

Moniah looked at Kaylon, who stepped back from the mural as though he had intruded. Moniah regretted the moment somehow because he wanted Kaylon to feel secure in his presence and continue serving as Seal Bearer.

"We are privileged to possess elements of their memories and skills," Kaylon said, referring to the transcended Auran generation, while they made their way into the Great Hall and up its broad curving staircase. Kaylon noticed Medean scanning Moniah and himself with a hand held medical array.

"Are we fit, Medean?"

"I apologize for intruding, brother, but I wanted to ensure your cardio pulmonary rates have stabilized from yesterday. This device is most effective when the subject is unaware of the process since that facilitates a more natural reading," Medean said, deactivating the scanner.

"You are both in superb condition," he assured them, and Moniah took hold of Kaylon, pausing at the entrance to a high, barrel vaulted corridor, at the end of which a set of brass doors were open, leading into the private office chamber Moniah had had made for the Arhahn. The room was seldom used but future history would see it crowded with the struggles of empire.

"Kaylon, I pray you will wear the mantle of Kaylon transcended, as Seal Bearer," Moniah said.

Kaylon flexed his jaw. His brilliant blue eyes watered and he glanced at Medean before replying.

"Yes, brother, perhaps our lives shall be long enough for me to earn the title," Kaylon said.

Medean sighed. The three proceeded down the corridor toward the doorway and Moniah considered the bitter irony of Kaylon's words carefully.

"One thing the transcended ones never suffered…a biological clock ticking away inside," Medean said, as they reached the doors. Moniah paused as if he were going to comment but thinking better of it, he led them within.

Inside the spacious chamber were: confident Vetaeos, enjoying a view from the single stained glass window he had opened to gaze at the ocean; Rete, who was a bit of a nervous soul and who fairly leapt to his feet upon seeing Moniah; Caras, who was seated with his head tilted back, still suffering from allergies. Also present was the bemused Uletis, whose soulful eyes begged for confirmation that a new promise had been born from the saddened heart of his transcended father.

"Haolae my friends," Moniah said. He winced for a moment, seeing in his mind's eye a mercifully brief yet dreadful image of a dying Auran, the missing Saeonar.

"Moniah?" Kaylon said, studying Moniah. Moniah avoided meeting his eyes. He coughed, waving his hand as he rounded behind a large black desk near the window.

"I think I might have a bit of this sinus affliction poor Caras suffers from."

"Then I pray for you," Caras said, accepting a medicine inhaler from Medean.

"Please sit and be comfortable. Medean, how long before interlink commences?"

"A few minutes yet, brother," Medean said, activating a floatscreen that lowered from the beams of the ceiling. While the device came to life with the customary blue field and focus correction matrix variables, Moniah put his hands flat on the midnight-dark desk and scanned a pulse disc report.

"I want to express my utmost appreciation, Vetaeos and Rete. You have done exemplary work in securing the Dome Temple of Myzinos-Wur," Moniah said.

Vetaeos gulped down water and wiped his mouth. He blushed.

"Forgive me. I still cannot seem to slake my thirst."

"I will correct your electrolytes," Medean said, and Vetaeos leaned forward to turn his attention back to Moniah, who was checking his own pulse by holding the fingers of his right hand against his left lower jaw.

"Wisdom, my lord, Moniah. We thank you. The Oscileans are in good health despite their incalculable age but they are depressed. This is particularly acute in the case of Montre," Vetaeos said.

Moniah tapped his chin with his fist.

"Perhaps her mood will improve when the eggs hatch. We'll encourage her to spend as much time as possible with the hatchlings," Rete said, dabbing his nose.

"Spatial interlink initiation sequence engaging," the floatscreen computer said and Moniah touched the Coracle-diant of fallen Saeonar, which was resting on the desk. He looked up at Rete.

"I felt like a hatchling of Prestant during my first days, he guarded me and saw to my needs. Please assure me that he is free of any disease or harm," Moniah said.

Rete deferred to Vetaeos.

"Prestant thrives."

The floatscreen chimed and all eyes turned to the screen. Until now, the Terran-dwelling Aurans had communicated only once with the Sphereworlds, when Moniah had convened them aboard *Auruaii*_during the first days. For weeks afterward, the second incarnate generation within Aurocearia and those on Earth had spent the better part of their time acclimating to life and awakening the culture of Aurocearia from its short but devastating pause into regeneration.

During their first communication with the Sphereworlds, the Earth-dwelling Aurans

had learned that a sociological consciousness in Aurocearia evoked the traditions of the transcended generation. The talents of their forefathers manifested into the second dynasty, who discovered mortal purpose by instilling the collective society with resolve and dedication to the past while propelling a need for new endeavors.

The new Auran generations were as individual in many respects as their transcended forbearers, inheriting powers of communal telepathy that had begun to fade in the last millennia but which was still part of Aurocearian mental capacity. This power was augmented by a new phenomenon of "dream memory", in which the young Aurans experienced vague but potent visions of the past. The result was that, although each young Auran was his own master, essentially free of regrets, comprehensive memories, struggles and aspirations of their past lives, they were not entirely free to awaken their own destiny.

At last, the screen flashed to an image of Arhahnis seated on the Awclotan throne. He was petting a miniature Oscilean, which reposed on his lap looking dolefully at the master of Aurocearia.

"Haolae. I am very pleased to see each of you again so soon. Are there any medical anomalies that require immediate attention?" the Arhahn said, and Moniah gestured to Medean.

"Fortunately no, Infinite. Ammanmus and I have maintained a daily vigilance and our physical and mental eccentricities are found to be in common with those experienced in Auros," Medean said, glancing at Kaylon, who cleared his throat and pointed to Caras. Medean lifted his right hand.

"One matter, Infinite."

"We are brothers, dispense with the title."

"Yes, brother. Our chief engineer suffers from an apparent onset of a condition the humans refer to as hay fever. My research indicates that this condition is, in fact, a reaction to pollen and other plant life emerging to flower. He also has a difficulty in eating solid food."

Arhahnis' golden eyes actually fluoresced from the light of his pupils.

"Ammanmus shall transmit a chemical formula that is easily duplicated aboard the medical facility of *Auruaii*. The formula is an anti-agent to this all-er-gee ailment. As to the other matter regarding Wizan Caras, I too suffered from a disability to process foods. This is a common complaint in the Sphereworlds. We have devised a nutritious drink that eases the system. Ammanmus will transmit the recipe this day."

"I thank you, Infinite," Caras said, coming to his feet and sitting again with a bow of his head. Arhahnis nodded. One could hear the small Oscilean in his lap wimper and the Arhahn stroked the beast.

"The Awclotan council has reconvened with a unanimous decision to support the government structure. Arhahnis transcended has been named the angelus by the temple triumvirate. His laws will be upheld. We govern a peaceful realm. Hence, I have determined to fulfill the ambition of the angelus and make all preparations to journey to Earth."

Moniah listened to the Arhahn with singular concentration. He was elated to learn that his small group would not have to carry the weight of the mission but he was openly surprised that the Arhahn would make the journey to Earth in the infancy of his reign.

"We shall arrive five months hence, Haolae," Arhahnis said, and the miniature Oscilean in his lap perked up and stared into the screen as the transmission terminated. Caras stood up and ran from the room into the corridor where he vomited into a planter despoiling a fern. Medean hurried after him.

"Somewhat over-reactive, I think," Kaylon said.

Moniah stood from the desk and faltered. Kaylon cursed under his breath and helped steady Moniah, while Uletis sneezed in fits and Vetaeos comforted Caras. Seeing the First Lord stumble, Medean ran to join Kaylon in helping Moniah toward another chair.

"I am well, just my legs."

"Let us hope we find a better start before the Arhahn arrives," Kaylon said and Medean placed his medical reader to Moniah's brow.

"Your temperature is normal. I recommend gradual and increased exercise periods, once a day."

Moniah nodded impatiently and insisted on standing up.

"It is close in here, let's to the ramparts for air."

The three Aurans proceeded out of the room Moniah called the "Elevan Study". They stopped to check on poor Caras and, assured he would recover himself, continued on to an adjoining transept hall and out onto the ramparts.

It was a perfect day, warm but kissed by a cool breeze of salt air from the Atlantic. Azure blue skies filled the horizon. Moniah breathed in deeply, unaware that with each breath he was changing and, by doing so, fulfilling prophesy. He lifted his face into the sun while Kaylon ambled toward the rampart ledge.

"We must make the people welcome here again," Moniah said,

measuredly. He opened his eyes to smile at Medean and Kaylon, who pointed down over the rampart to the mall green below.

"Judging from the caravans approaching and the crowds below, me thinks you will have to make little effort in attaining that goal."

Moniah chuckled, amused by the mime of Earth-speak and joined him at the rampart to gaze upon a crowd of people who saw him and cheered. Farther along the dirt road leading to the city, three large painted wagons drawn by horses kicked up dust as the court of Clovis arrived to pay its respects to the "son" of Moniah.

* * *

The Imperial fleet increased to flank speed for the final leg of its journey toward Earth. Nestled among its escorts, the mammoth flagship *Maethuean*, a sister ship to *Auraui*, dominated the center of a formation of six Intervoid class vessels. Hundreds of decoy "dronepods" hurtled around each of the main vessels and around the fleet as a whole, intercepting micro meteors. The overall appearance of the support vessels and the *Maethuean* royal ship in convoy resembled a whale attended by dolphins, all surrounded by darting and cavorting minnows.

Within the central chamber of *Maethuean* the images of stars being passed at near lightspeed streaked by outside two large oval windows at either side of the chamber spanning the two hundred foot beam. Arhahnis, in his floating throne, waited for his colonial lords to assemble while he spoke with Danis and Alaysi.

"All vessels report nominal operations, morale is high, Infinite," Danis said, lifting his ample chest with pride.

Arhahnis smiled and gestured to Alaysi.

"I am curious about this residence Moniah transcended created."

"It is a beautiful, if somewhat primitive, edifice. Here is an image," Alaysi said, activating a small hologram. Arhahnis studied it while the other Aurans muttered.

"See how green."

"Look at the ocean!"

"It appears capacious and pleasing," Arhahnis said.

Danis stepped closer, accidentally crushing Alaysi's foot with his bulk.

"Oh! Forgive me, brother. Why, it seems to be a delightful place." Alaysi winced and rubbed his sore foot with his other.

"Apparently the people are accustomed to being welcome at the palace. Moniah reports some of them even function in it as guards," Alaysi said. Suddenly, Arhahnis' mood darkened, he waved an impatient hand, abruptly silencing Alaysi.

"Convene," Arhahnis muttered to Danis, who cleared his throat and turned away from the throne to address the court.

"My brothers of Star Council, attend the Arhahn."

Two hundred mantles glistened on the shoulders of the Aurans attending the Arhahn, whose miniature Oscilean climbed down his robe to sit at the base of the throne at his feet, where it stretched and preened its wings.

"I will not detain you long as there is much to accomplish pending our arrival at Earth. I am creating Danis Talsaiyr to the mantle of Colonial Fleet Admiral for the time being. I trust you support my decision with your vote in this matter."

Muttered discussion followed until one Auran stepped forward and bowed.

"We so agree, Infinite."

"My reasoning in this decision is to provide us with…shall we say, *reassurance* while we journey into uncharted seas. And, we are certain our government is secure in its bureaucracy, give or take a mantle," Arhahnis added, eliciting chuckles of amusement.

Without voicing their concerns, the Aurans in the fleet had felt a collective vulnerability as they left the familiar Sphereworlds farther behind. Despite Auran coherence into a new generation, Quattral fury with the Awclotan Order had been reborn because of the nature of Auran dream memory, which rekindled animosity as well as talent and aptitude.

There was a living faction in the Quattral whose warped interpretation of memories recalled from deceased minds blamed the Taen priests for the Sphere war. The hard-liners of the Quattral decried the Awclotan regime for its tenacious manipulation of society to maintain socio-political power.

The belief survived in the Quattral fanatics that the Taens of the angelus generation had played a cruel trick on the Aurocearian natural order by using their skills to project false "divine" entities, the Auries. With this rationale accepted, the Quattral were enraged that their fellow Aurans had been so cruel as to smite the race by destroying the Auries and, in so doing, release a virulent disease that nearly exterminated Aurankind..

The myth could only be propagated by mortals who had never known a living Aurie and thus had no true sense of the reality of Aurocearian culture prior to the metamorphoses. Refusing to accept the past was a mortal curse. Concern for which, Arhahnis was happy to leave behind in the Sphereworlds.

For the indefinite future, the Quattral social misfits had elected to participate as loyal citizens for the greater good. They felt that they would need time, possibly centuries, to expose the crimes, mass delusions and evil experiments of the Taen and Wizan. The same discipline of hierarchy and social structure Arhahnis, Moniah and Ammanmus transcended had struggled to create for the good of the society, now served to dampen emotional healing.

In spite of their extraordinary mental prowess, Aurans were suffering from the denial of acute emotional distress. They were children without parents, catapulted into fully mature minds and bodies with the developed knowledge to command a vast technocracy. The core Quattral lived in contempt of mortal creation itself, and so the pain of continuance into a new generation was intolerable without finding a new myth that could be used to undo the priestly regime on which they hung hatred, desperation and a long-suffering renunciation of mortal purpose.

None of the Quattral or other Aurans thought much about Annevnos, chiefly because most of the Aurocearians who knew him had perished. The misanthrope designer of the Sphereworlds and Quattral founder was believed to have died centuries ago during the war, and, therefore, no Aurans possessed a dream memory connection that would reveal he lived on, transformed. It was also convenient for the Quattral and for the Awclotan throne of Arhahnis, for disparate reasons. For the Quattral, discussion about Annevnos was related to resounding defeat and distracted from future purpose. For the royal regime, Arhahnis and Moniah transcended had failed to guard the powers of the Gods, nearly resulting in catastrophe. The books of Taen were therefore also closed on his legend.

Arhahnis motioned Ammanmus to speak.

"Each of us has barely drawn sufficient breath to know our own worlds and now we venture to a new horizon, where the very air of Earth itself will alter our physical lives. In this exciting opportunity we ask you to prepare to become, in new awareness."

Danis lifted his chin and tapped his ceremonial staff which bore the triple orbs of the Talsaiyr ensign.

"This council is adjourned."

Arhahnis locked eyes with Danis.

"Make it known that we repudiate servitude from the people. All labor of such description will continue to be fulfilled by servodroids. I will handle the matter with our brothers on Earth."

As the shipboard council dispersed, Arhahnis stood and gathered up his pet Oscilean.

"You have spoken the pith of the matter beautifully. We are but young explorers and, as such, we prosper to live out the purpose of our ancestors. Auros is not so much a home as a new realm and so our having no real longing for Auros creates the perfect generation to establish the next phase of co-existence with Mankind," he said to Ammanmus.

Meanwhile, Danis was eying the last of the Aurans to leave the spacious throne chamber, in the process, catching the conclusion of a conversation.

"But what of brain wave alterations?"

"Taens will monitor for severe anomalies."

Danis frowned and turned back to study Arhahnis and Ammanmus on the throne dais, his expression which had once been relaxed with anticipation now clouded with apprehension. Later that same 'day', according to ship's time, *Maethuean* and her fleet arrived in the Terran solar system and soon approached Earth itself. Arhahnis entered the observation bridge to gaze at the Earth and one of its moons.

A few feet below, on the flight bridge, Aurans were busy checking final approach velocities and vectors. Comscreens connecting vessel command centers glowed with images while many voices spoke over each other. Arhahnis consulted an overhead analyzer depicting parabolic orbits of the Earth and its moons. He frowned and his eyes sparkled while he studied the image. Nearby, Ammanmus and Alaysi pointed to a magnified image of the planet.

"Such diverse beauty. Are you excited to command your new palace, Alaysi?" Ammanmus asked. Alaysi lifted one of his bushy eyebrows.

"Our palace, brother. Think of it, we shall meet them soon," Alaysi said.

Arhahnis slapped the rail of his observation bridge but contained his temper. The arrival of the fleet had not been calculated correctly and the system was now in danger. Danis was preoccupied with efforts to supervise the fleet while the crew at large struggled to follow a precise vector, slow the fleet, avoid collisions and monitor their instruments. Still, the damage was done.

"Ammanmus, inform Danis I will be in the lower refractoscope Saen array," Arhahnis said and departed amidst bowing Aurans. Still fuming, Arhahnis entered a cabin occupied by a single large command chair. He took seat in the chair, quickly activating controls that lowered the chair into a blister dome on the belly of the outer hull of *Maethuean*. The belly blister dome extended a hundred feet below the ship.

"Infinite, we are secure from molecular drive, preparing for station keeping orbit over Renthia-Acadia. Forgive me, brother, but why are you in the extender arm? It gives us concern. That is a vulnerable location," Danis transmitted from the bridge.

"Hold present coordinates. Revert all Saen controls to my command," Arhahnis said, impatiently. On every ship of the fleet, Aurans waited in silence. What had happened? Aboard *Maethuean*, Arhahnis fired a laser resonator at the primary moon and waited for return data.

"This cannot be," he muttered, but when the data displayed, it confirmed what he had noticed on the bridge.

"Computer, how long before the primary moon collides with Earth?" Arhahnis said, quietly.

"Seventy-four years, ten months." Arhahnis readjusted the ship Saen molecular manipulators and ordered the ship to face the moon in question.

"Plot the required correctional data to return the moon to original parabolic solar orbit and project the information," Arhahnis commanded, moving his hands rapidly over holographic controls. Display screens around Arhahnis projected a series of quantum equations. Arhahnis activated the Saen devices and beams of Saen tractor energy plasma fired from the ship, striking the moon. Slowly, the moon began to move as night settled over the continent below.

Arhahnis entered the bridge amidst whispers of concern.

"What occurred?" Danis asked, hurrying to join the emperor.

"I have corrected an oversight which should endear me to the astrophysicist guild," Arhahnis said, while Aurans of that same body argued among themselves.

"Who was responsible for fleet deceleration?" Arhahnis asked. Poor, harried Danis' broad shoulders sank a full inch.

"Lord Serati."

"Demote him. The misalignment of the moon was set into motion by the fleet's proximity to the planet's magnetospheres," Arhahnis said, cutting him off without mercy. Danis wiped a patina of sweat from his brow but Arhahnis patted his arm.

"You did admirably brother, make no issue of the demotion and place Serati in an appropriate level of responsibility. We are all pushed to weariness," Arhahnis said, in a confidential tone, his golden pupils flashing a more tranquil pulse of light.

Danis forced a smile and Alaysi came to his rescue.

"When shall we make landfall?" Alaysi asked.

Arhahnis looked to Ammanmus.

"Moniah is waiting at Maethus-Dia, Infinite."

"The time is at hand, prepare all craft." In that instant, the mistake was put to rest as word went round to make landfall.

* * *

Anxious crowds filled the mall greens surrounding Maethus-Dia. Dancers and crowd charmers wound their way through happy throngs while Elria, Clovis, Marina and

Darius converged around Moniah and the other Aurans. Elria found it hard to restrain herself from staring at Moniah. She knew what had happened, thanks to an exhaustive and tender recounting by Clovis, but the sight of the raven-haired Moniah incarnate, so closely resembling his transcended father, tugged at her heart strings.

"He *must* be my Moniah," she whispered to herself. Though others declared that Moniah was dissimilar to his ancestor, Elria denied it. When Moniah met her eyes, she was certain his love, like his new body, had been reborn. Under a clear night sky people, whispered in awe while Moniah pointed to a series of large, silvery, glowing objects.

"There is the fleet of the Arhahn," Moniah said, happily.

"Ships of the void, like *Auruaii*?" Elria asked and Moniah turned to smile at her for the first time.

"Precisely. Come closer, join us."

She moved closer to the group of dignitaries, blushing at a wink from Clovis. Everyone craned their heads to stare at the glowing ships, their faces kissed by the light from lanterns and glow orbs but, suddenly, people cried out in panic, they lurched about and many spun toward Elria, pointing frantically at the bright dots Moniah called ships.

Moniah felt his blood run cold. He watched in dread silence as the largest vessel, clearly the *Maethuean*, fired Saen beams at the moon, Diana. It was inconceivable!

"What is this?" Moniah managed to hiss through half-choked words. Kaylon and Caras leaned toward him. A few feet away, chattering people surrounded Medean. The mystic did not respond but remained perfectly still, staring into the night sky.

Elria was clearly horrified; she watched the goddess moon struck by the same glowing red streaks she knew Aurans could use as terrible weapons. Above her, Diana moved away from Earth. She could actually see it happening.

"There must have been some orbital damage to the moon when the fleet arrived," Kaylon whispered to Moniah.

"I concur, Wisdom," Caras added.

Uletis stepped closer to Moniah, pressing the bridge of his nose with his fingers.

"If only this did not resemble an attack."

"The moon must have posed a danger to Earth," Kaylon insisted. Moniah was at a loss as to what to do but he heard Medean soothing the crowds.

"Good people, hear me," Moniah said. He looked to Elria, who watched him with fear and other emotions he had never seen in looks directed at him, anger and even contempt showing in her expression. He started to speak to her but Medean raised his voice over the confusion.

"There is no harm to the goddess. Our emperor has communicated with Diana and, you see, she lives yet, sailing the firmament," Medean explained to a hushed audience.

Thank gods that nothing else was happening in space above Earth, Moniah mused. His eyes roamed over the grumbling crowds and he turned to study Elria, who regarded him steadily.

Moniah moved toward Elria, his hands held out before him. It was a gesture she had seen many times and now, in the darkness, he seemed so like the Auran she had loved.

"Have we ever harmed the people of Earth?" Moniah said, simply.

"Oh no, he begs," Vetaeos muttered, obscuring his mouth with his hand.

"Be still. We need a miracle of diplomacy," Kaylon muttered.

Elria locked eyes with Moniah. She raised her hands and turned to face the crowd.

"Lord Medean, the wise, speaks true. Be still and comforted for you have witnessed miracle," she said and, even in the gloom, Moniah could see Clovis go pale while his Queen, Marina, grasped his hand, trying to smile confidently.

Young prince Darius was standing with his legs slightly spread as if ready to draw his little sword at the first hint of trouble. He eyed Moniah with humility but studied him carefully as if trying to discover his truth or falsity. Medean sighed. A dog howled in the distance.

"We have not lied, Elria, no harm has been caused to Diana," Moniah assured her tenderly.

"I believe you speak truth from the heart, lord Moniah," Elria said, as she searched the floating golden specks of his pupils, lantern light reflecting warmly in his large blue orbs. Medean gestured to Moniah and he moved a few feet away to confer with the mystic. Clovis and Darius hurried to join Elria.

"I am no longer certain what motivates this new Auran generation," Clovis said nervously, wringing his hands. He added, "We've lived with them long enough to know it's vain folly to attempt to defeat the Aurans if they intend us harm."

Elria smiled calmly at the boy who was angry because his mother was fearful. The boy could still recall infant memories of his father and mother struggling to stay alive during the days of Varrick. He was mature for his age, even for a child of a primitive culture where maturity must come quickly.

"Moniah once spoke of an evolution. I feel this growing in my heart of understanding. The old ways are truly dying—and the moons? Mayhaps they are but inert bodies in space. I could well be the last priestess of Diana. The knowledge of the people increases. They gaze at planets with telescopes and learn Auran teachings, they outgrow the cult of Diana and the uncivil past."

Clovis nodded solemnly, glancing at the ground then peering into the eyes of the priestess whose heart and intellect he prized as much as that of any member of his family or court.

"Wisdom comes from you, priestess Elria," Marina said, watching Moniah with his fellow Aurans.

"If what your beloved Moniah created be truly alive. Then I do not doubt a word spoken," Clovis said and Marina grasped Clovis and Elria by the hands.

"New wonders approach with these sky cities above. Remember, Clovis?" He kissed Marina's hand and then Elria.

"Let's pray this is true."

* * *

From a hundred miles above Earth, Arhahnis Talsaiyr had altered the history of Earth without having set foot on its soil. Shortly after dawn, as cool breezes gave way to summer heat over the sweeping broad lands outside Renthia-Acadia, the Arhahn arrived.

It was never a secret that the Arhahn would come to Earth. Moniah transcended had promised the event and Moniah incarnate pinpointed the time months before the actual date. Sailing ships filled the harbor from every part of the world to witness the spectacle.

Later, it would be estimated that the greater portion of the population of Amernius had gathered at Renthia-Acadia, swelling its coffers to untold wealth while the Aurans, using the resources of *Aurauii* saw to it that no mouth went unfed, further securing the ongoing benevolent reputation of the second dynasty.

THE MORNING OF DIANA DAY, APRIL 25 ,IN THE YEAR OF THE ANCIENTS, 835 AJ. *"After morning meal my good lord Moniah assembled our court in the palace of Maethus-Dia, which his transcended father had set up to receive his gracious sovereign. Therein before myself and my son, the prince Darius, Moniah Talsaiyr stood before my husband and set upon him a diadem proclaiming him before the people."*

—MARINA HUGHERNI, QUEEN OF RENTHIA-ACADIA

To save time, Moniah moved the court via Satarships to the broad meadows west of the city. The three silver craft settled onto ankle deep lavender and rich green grasses where thousands of people had already gathered for the historic event. Moniah bounded from the Satarship while steam still vented from its underside. It was nearly noon and the day was getting away from him but he had been compelled by an inner voice to reaffirm Clovis at his palace.

He lifted his robe hem and ran ahead of Medean and Kaylon toward a raised, canopied platform. The sun beat on his mantle so that he squinted. Behind him, Clovis, Marina and Darius disembarked from the second Satarship with Elria and Robert the Tall, Man-at-Arms to the king.

Vetaeos, Caras, Uletis and Rete hurried toward the platform to join the Oscileans, Prestant and Halfstep. The dragons were happily anticipating the arrival of the Arhahn because of the joy it generated in the Earth-dwelling Aurans. Prestant sang to Moniah, who paused long enough to kiss the beast on the jaw, while Halfstep lounged in the grass licking flowers, blissfully unconcerned, with bees cavorting around her head.

Moniah took cover under the canopy, where he found a large barrel filled with cold water. He scooped water from it with his hands and splashed his face. Kaylon arrived. The Seal Bearer immediately removed his mantle and then scanned a portable data link.

"How long?" Moniah said, just as Medean arrived, panting. Kaylon reached down and helped Medean up to the platform while Vetaeos and his Wizans created a perimeter with help from Robert the Tall and Clovis's guards.

"Anytime now, brother, although I cannot relay *Auruaii's*_spatial sensors to this link. I detect a large atmospheric anomaly," Kaylon said, peering closer into the data link device he held.

"It must be the fleet," Medean said, dipping a cup into the water barrel. Moniah smiled at Medean ruefully and tapped his mantle.

"Too much exercise for you today, brother?"

"I seem to recall advising small amounts daily, not mad dashes across fields in the glaring sun."

"And certainly not burdened with this garb," Kaylon said. He glanced up to scan the area and clicked his teeth. All around them the meadows were now literally teeming with multitudes.

Medean moved to the edge of the platform with Moniah, who was looking for Clovis and the others, but the human royals were lost in a confusion of dancers, food vendors and a million voices chattering to compete with singing birds and whining horses.

A cool shadow passed overhead and Moniah sighed, shielding his eyes from the sun.

"Thank gods, clouds."

"Not clouds," Kaylon said, and the three Aurans lifted their faces toward the sky. Around them Moniah was dimly aware that the noisy people had become utterly still. *Auruaii* had been at rest so long in the harbor that people had forgotten what it was like to see it fly, making the arrival of the *Maethuean* with her attendant vessels all the more spectacular. Sunlight glistened from the ships as they descended slowly; their miles-long hulls cast long, cool shadows over the meadows and all the way to the city and harbor.

"Kaylon, turn on the sonic amplifier," Moniah said, as Caras hurried through stunned onlookers. He bounded onto the platform.

"What do you make of it, Caras?" Moniah said, studying the graceful, silver, fish-shaped hull and its streamlined, clamshell bow. Kaylon handed Moniah a microphone.

"Very similar to *Auruaii* but more refined. You see those clouds forming at the aft molecular drive array? The ship is generating a powerful electro-magnetic field."

"A weather maker," Kaylon interjected.

Moniah keyed the microphone. His voice boomed from a speaker on the top of the canopy and all eyes turned toward him.

"Good people, for your safety remain where you are. The vessel is unifying itself to our air. There is nothing to fear," he turned off the amplifier. "Is that clear do you suppose?"

Kaylon shrugged while Caras nodded and Medean simply smiled at the sky. *Maethuean* descended to within a hundred yards in front of the platform where it hovered at station keeping less than two hundred feet above the ground. The ship would not land but it filled the air with seismic rumblings.

Lightning streaked from its lower hull to the ground as the flagship created an electrical ecosystem, generating an anti-gravity realm beneath her. People backed away instinctively. A few ran away in panic, pausing to glance over their shoulders and then run a few more yards, stop and repeat the process.

Birds careened away, singing in the breeze. The other vessels hovered over the forests to give *Maethuean* a wide berth. There was utter silence when a small fleet of shuttles emerged from the ships but then spontaneous applause and cheers rose up and the musicians began to play fanfares.

"Wind city…is a loud song," Prestant sang to Moniah, shaking his head and flapping his ears as seismic pulses from the ship thrummed the air with deep rhythmic tones.

* * *

"Look there!" Clovis cried, unable to restrain his joy. All eyes gazed at the *Maethuean.* A hangar door opened and twenty Oscileans flew out, all bearing Wizan riders. The flying dragons and those on the ground sang loudly to each other. Directly behind them, a splendid air barge, with graceful painted lines in bright red and gold, emerged.

The barge landed. Moniah, Kaylon and Medean emerged from under the canopy of the reviewing stand and paused. The dragons sang a beautiful melody and four Aurans emerged from the graceful shuttle. Moniah and his brothers went to bent knee, lowering their heads.

"Which one is Arhahnis? Elria, do you know?" Marina asked, fanning herself.

"The one with the broad shoulders, black robe and sash," Clovis said, looking about. From their remove, it was difficult to see faces and they could not hear what was being said for all the pressing of the crowds.

"No father, he is called the Grand Ambassador, Danis. I know this because of an image lord Medean showed me at the library," young Darius interjected, while Robert the Tall barked at a group of people to stand back from the royal party. A child wailed near them and Robert elbowed a path so they could move further from the crowd.

"He shan't be the one with the blue and green robe for that is the High Taen, Ammanmus," Marina said, craning her head to see.

"The slighter one in build is I believe, uh, Alaysi, the High Chamberlain," Darius said, pointing, Marina gently slapped his hand down.

"The one with the fire and midnight hair, whose skin is the color of autumn leaves and who wears the black robe with gold filigree. He is the Arhahn," Elria said, quietly, while the others strained to hear her.

Arhahnis held out his arms to Moniah and they embraced.

"I have a memory, my right arm is returned," Arhahnis said to Moniah, who smiled and dipped his head in return.

"I perceive this memory, brother," he said, indicating the reviewing platform. While Medean and the others came down to stand before the Arhahn, Moniah waved to Robert the Tall and, with the help of Vetaeos and Uletis, a way was quickly cleared for the human royal party to approach.

The sight of Arhahnis, whose green eyes and gold pupils were pools of wisdom, hypnotized a transfixed Elria. Breezes played in his waist length hair and she stood perfectly still as though made of stone when Moniah introduced her.

"I have a memory of thee, a priestess of my bruthers bruther." Elria heard. The Arhahn's accent was heavy and his voice melodious and soothing.

"Great one, long have I waited to meet thee," Elria said, with a trembling voice.

Overcome with emotion, Clovis knelt before Arhahnis, who instantly raised him to his feet. Clovis swallowed nervously, his expression transfixed by Arhahnis, who, to the amazement of all, removed the translator from his ear. In a single sentence from Elria, he had mastered the human language.

"There is no need to offer obsequious gestures to me, Sir, I am but a child in years compared to you," Arhahnis said, and then he turned to Marina, who wept tears of joy while Darius struggled to restrain his trembling body.

* * *

Corina and Mayron ignored the jostling around them. Unaccustomed to traveling in Renthia-Acadia, their caravan was lost in a sea of crowds and they could not find a guard who could assure them escort to Clovis and the Talsaiyr lord, Moniah.

Exhausted, they settled in a relatively open space on a gentle hill of scrub pines. For some time they simply watched in awestruck fascination as the Aurans disembarked from their traveling sky cities.

"Oh wonders, wonders and blessings upon us," Mayron kept muttering, glancing at Corina, who could not speak. She rubbed her eyes and stared at the sky vessels. Before sunset, four structures, that appeared to be buildings, emerged from the hangars of the escort ships and lowered to the ground. Corina helped Mayron to his feet and they pointed to the wondrous sight. All the while, Mayron muttered obscure and ancient incantations.

The spectacle of entire buildings, of gorgeous compelling architecture, settling into place in the outskirts to the south of Renthia-Acadia, stunned an already speechless population into awestruck wonder.

"By the gods," Corina said, finding her quavering voice.

"Come, come, my dear, we are invited to the palace and 'tis miles hence," Mayron urged, tugging her arm. He paused to hold her.

"Shush now, no need to weep and tremble,"

"The structures are as graceful as flowing silk. Behold that one! Its towers like the uplifted wings of birds," Corina said, shaking her head as though to convince herself she was not deluded.

A guard spotted Corina's colors. He nudged through smiling faces, angling his body sideways through the crowd to reach the Queen of Canelor.

"Your majesty, priestess Elria, in leaving for Maethus-Dia has left word that you are welcome to her abode in her absence."

Corina glanced at Mayron, who was breathing with difficulty due to the excitement, while chewing his lower lip, his eyes scanning, taking in all he could.

"Mayhaps we should?" Corina said, but the old shaman frowned. "I die soon anyway but not afore I behold regal Arhahnis," Mayron insisted, jutting out his chin.

Colonial Court

Elria roamed the Great Hall of Maethus-Dia, recalling her own brief but sweet memories of the palace. The place resounded with Aurans and nobles of the combined courts of Clovis and the newly arrived Arhahn, and everywhere Elria turned Aurans, men and women exchanged ideas and discussed immediate concerns. She took interest in a statue that appeared to be new, an intricate carving of a dragon the size of a small dog on top of the staircase ballister.

Elria leaned forward to study the miniature Oscilean. It blinked, warbled and took flight, careening up and away. Startled, Elria swallowed and caught her breath.

"Priestess, will you follow me?" a voice said, and she turned to see Medean in his green robe, smiling at her. In another time and incarnation, he would have addressed her by name. At the top of the curving stairs, Medean led Elria to the outer ramparts.

"The First Lord awaits you," Medean said, softly.

Elria whispered her thanks. She looked out at the rampart then turned to Medean to smile and tell him how moved she was by the miracle of the new generation appearing but he was already walking away. It struck her then that although the new incarnation of Medean remembered her, he was not connected to her in the same way his predecessor had been. Gathering her wits, she strode outside onto the rampart walk into warm sunshine. She looked to the right and saw an Auran standing with his back to her, facing a view of the Atlantic.

It was Moniah, *her* Moniah. He had to be, for his midnight locks were streaked in white just as she had last seen him. From somewhere nearby a trumpet sounded and she quickened her step to reach Moniah while hummingbirds hovered nearby in trestles of flowers.

But, as she closed the distance between them, it became clear that Moniah's hair was raven black, the illusion of white caused by sunlight reflected from its sheen.

Moniah sensed her presence and turned to face her.

Elria's expression was that of shattered fantasy. Gone was the

Moniah whose face had been that of a god. She recognized his son incarnate's softer features. Her love stood before her once again but irrevocably transformed. She hesitated, as if trying to form words, and Moniah could see tears welling in her soft eyes.

"Forgive me, lord Moniah, I have been foolish," Elria finally managed to mutter with dignity.

Moniah studied the woman he was getting to know and whose memory he held in hazy images of dream memory. She regarded him with a blush on her cheek, regal and alluring and with a friendly countenance.

"In what way, Elria?" He enquired, gently and Elria chuckled, nervously wiping a tear from one eye, regaining her demeanor although it was clear her laughter was self-conscious, a polite gesture to avoid embarrassing the First Lord.

"The affairs of my heart are not in order; I should not have come here today. I apologize for squandering your time," she said, candidly, meeting his eyes.

"There is nothing to apologize to me for, Serenity. I would not question brave motivations of a loving heart." Elria reached into a pocket of her silken gown and withdrew the lock of hair Moniah had given her in another lifetime.

"Your father gave this unto me when he left Renthia-Acadia to found the Wizan city." She handed it to Moniah incarnate.

The moment he touched the lock of hair, Moniah's memories of his father and Elria surged into his consciousness. Elria watched the sparkling lights within his eyes drift into dream memory. Birds twittered as they flew over the rampart. Moniah blinked and his eyes refocused on Elria.

"Moniah transcended lived for the future, a future you helped conceive," he said, so quietly that Elria had to lean toward him to hear what he said.

"Yes, he did, *we* did. I am sorry for the loss of Saeonar."

"I thank you. The great Wizan Saeonar was killed only moments before his Transmaking. We are deprived of his progeny. Will you remain here in new purpose? We need you, for the future," Moniah said, giving her back the lock of hair.

She took it and folded the long braid back into her gown pocket.

* * *

The little dragon, unnerved by the scrutiny of the Earth woman, soared up to the upper chambers of the palace in search of Arhahnis to escape the excitable and noisy Humans.

Humans yammered incessantly, clapping their hands and hurrying about to and fro until a small one had few places to escape their unceasing din. The giant Oscileans of Earth warned little one of the human 'condition', a diplomatic way of referring to the smell and noise these beings created.

Little one avoided collision with an Auran as he soared around a corner. The Auran, a Templar Wizan, scowled at him, muttering, "Learn your wings."

Little one flew inside the second floor throne hall just as the doors were being closed. He flapped to the throne dais base and landed quietly near the huge carved seat of the Arhahnis. Clovis discreetly pointed out the dragon to Corina and to Mayron, who chuckled delightedly, while Marina held Clovis by the arm, squeezing his hand.

"You look as wonderstruck as a wee thing, my queen," Mayron chuckled. The sound of hard boot steps drew everyone's gaze to see gleaming metal men enter the throne hall, stunning everyone into silence. The metal men shone of polished brass with intricate colorful designs engraved into their chests. The faces were friendly but curiously blank, like neutral, incomplete beginning studies from the clay of an artist. Two of the metal men took position at either side of the doors while others circulated among the group with trays of drinks and food.

Some of the bolder dignitaries reached out, tentatively, to touch the robots.

Alaysi entered through an oval door covered in fine metal tracery, near the throne dais. He was slight of build compared to his counterpart, the hulking Danis, and more aesthetic in manner. People were already aware that Alaysi was a genial soul for his smile came easily and his genuine laugh was unpracticed and spontaneous. He smiled at the assembly,

"Welcome, distinguished and honored guests. Receive my brother Arhahnis Talsaiyr, Emperor Awclotan." Arhahnis entered the room through the same door. Everyone bowed, some knelt.

"Please, my friends, I ask you to remain at your leisure and be comfortable," Arhahnis said and, hesitantly, the human leaders settled back into chairs arranged into rows before the dais. Only then did Arhahnis take his throne.

"Accept these libations from our Talldroids," he said, gesturing to the roving metal men.

"Alaysi, let's dispense with the gloom, shall we?" Arhahnis muttered to his brother, who activated a device. Two exquisitely carved panels of wood and gold behind the throne slid away to the sides, moved by unseen forces, revealing a large and beautiful amber-tinted window. Diffused sunlight streamed in, filling the throne hall with golden light, just as Elria hurried to a chair.

"I am told everyone looks better in this light," Arhahnis said and Elria laughed discreetly. Lining the room at either side, marble obelisks floated up in perfect synchronicity to hover a few feet above the floor.

"Even the stones themselves pay homage to the Arhahn," Mayron whispered in awe.

"Who is *this* splendid Auran?" Corina said, leaning toward Clovis and nodding in the direction of Danis, who escorted another Auran into the hall. The Auran was tall and lean, his hair silver-blond and his vibrant blue eyes fairly twinkled.

"Haolae Auran Tajaen, Deshale Arhahnis, resaie xi Maethuean. Sorrea vemussesie maenaevo loi inneasti Arhahnis Awclotan eartos sum. Inlarateom Aurocearia citol, earto, eartos primor. Vocai lii Ertim Lorra-Sers, Gosachaei Eartos," The Auran said while everyone but Arhahnis, Danis and Alaysi glanced, dumbfounded, at one another.

"In the language of the people, if you please, Ertim," Arhahnis interjected. The Auran blushed then he bowed and turned to face the people while fitting his ear with a translator.

"Hello Auran families, Infinite Arhahn, Salute to the mantles. Peace I extend to you and with your permission, according to the edict of Arhahnis Awclotan, Voice of the Sphereworlds, now at Earth, Earth prime, know I am Ertim Lorra-Sers, Governor to Earth." Everyone applauded, though some whispered the word "governor" with cautious suspicion.

Arhahnis smiled.

"People of Earth, we are before you in realization of a dream. With Moniah, Kaylon and Medean you have ratified the delicate nature of governing laws for the furthering of coexistence between us." While Arhahnis spoke, Corina studied the faces of those around her, the leaders of Amernius, Europa, Indra, and Omer—all of whom were smiling although, truth be told, some of them appeared overwhelmed. Mayron held his open mouth with a palsied hand, tilting his good ear toward the throne dais.

"The laws Moniah transcended affirmed with you to enable peaceful enterprise shall be treasured. Any attempt to enforce or subjugate human destiny to Auran purpose or any form of coercion for the purposes of corrupting the peace is forbidden. I can further assure you such a perversion of coexistence is anathema under the Angelus Codes, which are the most sacred laws of Aurocearia," Arhahnis said and Mayron's eyes brimmed with tears.

Not only was the Arhahn reinforcing what Moniah had created, he was making it clear that any hint of subjugation would be intolerable. Here, at last was reason. Clovis stood up and Arhahnis smiled, deferring to him.

"Infinite, our beloved Moniah transcended prepared a government. One he dreamed would join our ways, with a new order. He called it, the free citizen code."

"This is true," Mayron said, as loud as he could with his enfeebled voice.

"A voice for all was the plan of his thought," the chief of the Allegheny mountain tribes said, nodding to those around him.

"Now, 'tis time they heard your voice as queen of Canelor," Mayron said, nudging Corina, who stood up slowly. She paused to collect herself and bowed to the throne.

"Infinite, in Canelor we lived many turns 'neath the bondage of a tyrant. Under his rule, no man held voice in safe council. Even in times of peace, such as we rarely enjoyed…war and corruption could take hold in the blink of an eye, making riot of men's dreams," Men grunted agreement while others stared at her with new respect, including Clovis.

Arhahnis leaned slightly forward in his throne. In a millisecond, he took in this Corina of Canelor. She was a lovely creature, not exotic like the priestess, but her open heart-shaped face with its fine delicate bones and lovely pale color with pink blushed cheeks, framed her impassioned eyes in a noble setting.

"The nature of evil subverts good cause. Let us agree to convene council and formulate the accords of Moniah transcended and Renthia-Acadia to guarantee independent rights for each city and for each person, man, woman and child."

Ertim leaned to Danis and pressed a finger to his ear to make certain he was hearing the translation correctly. The Governor smiled at Danis, who was overseeing Alaysi as he recorded the words of the Arhahn.

"Well done, Corina, your father, Ciros, lives in you," Mayron said, buffing her cheek.

"Brother," Moniah's voice said, drawing everyone's attention to the back of the room. Elria smiled. Moniah was standing with arms folded over his chest, deferring to his sovereign but present and attentive to every word.

"My father dreamed that one day all citizens could advance by learning the disciplines of knowledge of the world and Aurocearia. Through this means, might coexistence be ultimately fulfilled."

Elria beamed at Moniah for she heard in his words the wisdom of her lost love.

"We shall study these concepts. Now, good people please let it be known I am Emperor only beyond the boundaries of Earth and have not come to rule your destiny but to share our purpose with yours," Arhahnis said very plainly, his marvelous eyes roaming the room.

Applause and cheerful debate spread about until everyone noticed that Mayron desired to be heard. The old shaman stood and bowed to Arhahnis.

"Infinite, we ask that you will receive the petitions of our goodly leaders on behalf of the people when'er a difficulty arises."

"I am overseer to your purposes," Arhahnis agreed.

Danis thumped his staff.

"This council is adjourned," he announced, and everyone began to circulate in lively debate while Mayron bravely pushed his way to the throne.

"Infinite, I be Mayron, elder of Canelor. Many things have I seen, great one, but this day I behold the wonder of heaven on Earth." Arhahnis listened, hands folded before him, leaning slightly forward toward Mayron's shrunken frame. Corina approached.

"I am honored by Mayron of Canelor and Queen Corina. Please remain at Maethus-Dia for the duration of the councils?" Arhahnis said. Mayron's lips quivered with emotion.

"We have been offered residence in the city Infinite," Corina said, but Arhahnis waved his hand gently before him.

"Take chambers here, at the palace. This residence is your home as much as mine."

Corina curtsied.

"We shall. Thank you, Infinite."

The little dragon sniffed at Mayron's ankle. Arhahnis reached down and lifted the miniature dragon into his lap.

"I call him Satimins, in my tongue it means, little blossom," Arhahnis explained, and Corina petted the dragon, which cooed in delight. Mayron's eyes opened wide. He hesitated. Arhahnis handed the dragon to Mayron, who held it like a child.

"I think you have a friend here, Mayron," the hulking but friendly

Danis said, and Arhahnis chuckled. Years fell away from Mayron's countenance, as the dragon licked his chin and the old man giggled.

* * *

That first long night after the second-longest day in human reckoning, Mayron lay awake in Maethus-Dia for several hours, studying the colorful murals interplaying with shadows over his bed. Too excited for repose, he threw off his coverlets and jumped up, giggling, child like, to whirl about in his nightshirt, his bare feet tapping out a gleeful dance against the marble floor.

"I bed in a palace built for gods, oh, what a miracle am I, " he sang, flailing his arms. A wall chronometer struck a gentle ping sound and Mayron clutched his side. He grimaced with a look of disappointment, laughed and fell dead to the floor with a satisfied smile.

* * *

Medean listened to the night birds on his terrace overlooking the forests of what was now known as Maethus-Dia province. The chronometer had just struck the hour, one AM, and the mystic sighed.

"Oh no!" He turned away from the night and entered his suite where Alaysi was still bent over a table laden with pulse discs, scrolls and books. A holoscreen database computer glowed reflections of lists onto the chamberlain's face. Alaysi rubbed his eyes and pushed himself back from the table, suddenly alert to the fact that something had disturbed Medean's reverie.

"Medean? What is it?"

"The shaman Mayron has died. Just now."

"Shall I awake the Queen, Corina?"

Medean considered this and paced toward the desk. He paused and frowned, staring at Alaysi, though his focus was elsewhere.

"No. There is no purpose served by spreading the gloom of night into the soul of the Queen. I will inform Himself at dawn," Medean decided, pouring water from a pitcher. He sipped it slowly.

"Himself? Oh, you mean Arhahnis." He added, "Is not Moniah the Himself, on Earth?" Alaysi said and Medean reached over to turn off the holoscreen, dimming the chamber to a more diffused light from the glow orb chandelier.

"There is only one such Auran," Medean said, and came round the table to take Alaysi by the hand. The chamberlain stood up and Medean led him to a set of divans near the terrace. A cool silent breeze lifted drapes and in the far distance a lone wolf howled in the forest. Alaysi lifted his hand and smiled.

"Did you hear that?"

But Medean simply gazed at Alaysi and the pupils of his eyes flashed light in time with his breath and heartbeat. Alaysi glanced at the floor then raised his eyes slowly to meet the enigmatic countenance of the mystic.

"What I hear, Alaysi, is the ardor of deceased voices from our past. It is the love we shared in another life."

Alaysi reached to his side and fingered a vase of flowers. He lifted one and smelled it. Medean opened a bottle of Oprasia wine and poured two glasses, offering one to Alaysi, who took it but set it down without tasting the rare contents imported from Auros Prime.

"It is not my intention to pressure you with subjects of discussion you may find troublesome," Medean said.

Alaysi held the flower in his lap. He met the tender, so knowing, eyes of the mystic without shrinking.

"I believe they call this a Rose. This one smells pleasing without the cloying sweetness I have experienced with some other nameless flower. During my first nights in sleep, before we departed from Auros, I beheld the dream memory of our past and felt the power of love therein. But here I am free, Medean. I have only the dreams of night to connect me with Alaysi transcended but I imagine that, as a Greenrobe, you have inherited more substantial abilities to connect to what was."

"My gifts are curses. In time, you will know this to be true as our transcended ancestors did. I have no desire to inflict this upon you."

"You cannot inflict anything on me, Medean. I walk on a new world and have much to accomplish. Initially, I thought Arhahnis acted out of hubris to bring us so soon to Earth. Yet, now I thank Arhahnis from the core of my being. Could it be I am so thankful because this adventure permits me a means to ignore the past? Perhaps, but I am forged anew, on Earth," Alaysi said, and he stood up and handed the flower to Medean.

"As it is said on Earth, good thee night Medean."

* * *

The Talldroid robots, assisted by floating servodroids, clanged and hummed around a large, intricate clock in the Great Hall of Maethus-Dia. Moniah and Clovis watched a Constructorbot hover over the staircase where it lasered a hole into the marble wall and rotated to drill in a very large hook..

"That is a splendid device indeed, Clovis."

"We are most pleased it pleases thee, lord Moniah. We had begun work on the clock some time ago. It is the effort born of many artisans,"

Clovis said. A group of Templars gathered to watch as Talldroids fixed a chain to the clockwork case. It was still early and the plan was to mount the clock before the palace awoke to the day's proceedings.

"Very well then, up with it," Moniah said, with delight and Caras rolled up his robe sleeves and keyed in a command to the Constructorbot on his portable comlink. The robot sphere rose up and the chain tightened its slack. Moniah hid a smile behind his hand; amused that he was watching two disparate technologies attempt to accomplish a simple task.

Antigravity plates on the Constructorbot glowed yellow as it increased force to lift the clock. Servodroids buzzed around the Constructorbot, helping it nudge the clock onto its hook. The chain was removed and there it hung.

"Excellent! A wonderful piece of work," Moniah enthused and Clovis nodded emphatically. They clasped arms and laughed. The clock was a success. It hung above the graceful curve of the stairs for all to see and Moniah moved closer to appreciate its design: a rectangular box of dark stained wood, carved with owls and other birds on the upper case with deer, horses and trees on the lower woodwork. In the center, a 12-hour time face held also two moons and the sun.

Behind the large minute and hour hands, one could see intricate gears through a thick piece of glass. Caras tapped his keypad and the Constructorbot flew out of the palace to the location in the courtyard where it remained when not actively working.

"Where in the world, one may ask, are my servodroids which are late in their tasks?" Alaysi said, bounding down the stairs. He paused, looked at Moniah, who pointed to the wall and then slowly descended, taking in the sight of the new fixture.

"The best comes soon," Clovis whispered to Moniah, who nodded, touching a finger to his lips while consulting a fob containing his chronometer. Alaysi reached the bottom of the stairs just as a set of doors opened over the numeral twelve on the clock. A mechanical dragon emerged from the doors and flapped its wings while a set of hidden chimes and bells rang nine times.

Alaysi clapped his hands and Moniah tossed back his head to laugh with abandon. The Templar Wizans crowded around Clovis, patting his back and toasting him with salutes, while Caras wiped away tears of amusement.

"I dub thee, Chimera," Clovis said. Alaysi marched up to the squad of hovering Servodroids, tapping in commands to each of them, at which they hummed off in separate directions to ready baths and prepare breakfasts. Moniah joined the Templars and accepted an Ol pipe from one of them. He puffed it and handed it to Clovis.

"Aren't you happy it runs by batteries, Clovis?"

"The Chimera? Oh indeed, my lord. Next to the glories of plumbing that makes one's morning a pleasure, batteraries, er batt-er-eyes 'tis the best thing in the world," Clovis said and the Templars laughed and took their leave.

Danis came striding forth, carrying a portable computer. Clovis bowed his head and Danis bowed his head lower still.

"Ah, is it good thee nigh—no, a moment. Yes, good morrow everyone," Danis said.

Clovis accepted a mug of Soffa from a passing Talldroid while Danis snatched up a handful of breaded fruit and two mugs of Soffa. Alaysi shook his head at Danis, who shrugged.

"One is hungry."

"I regret to stifle this joy; there is no easy way to report this. Mayron of Canelor died last night," Alaysi said and Moniah sighed. Danis reconsidered his appetite and hastily returned his food on a tray carried by the Talldroid, spilling Soffa cups as he did so.

"There's a rotten shame," he said and Clovis pressed a knuckle to his beard. Moniah gestured for everyone to follow him and led them into the Solarium to escape the first arrivals of food vendors and couriers from the city.

"I expected as much. He was tireless but older than most," Clovis said, holding his lower back and groaning as he sat down to a breakfast table. Elria entered, carrying a satchel and, seeing the puzzled expression of Moniah, she set down her brief, glancing first to Danis, then to Clovis.

The Governor, Ertim, arrived just then and Moniah spoke to him in Aurocearian. Elria lifted a stemmed glass absently, turning it over in her graceful fingers as she listened to the melodious language. She glanced at the lean figure of Ertim with skepticism and leaned toward Clovis.

"After all this time I am still a fuddle with Aurocearian," she said, while Clovis opened the lid of a Servodroid, which contained scrambled eggs and toast. Danis rubbed his hands and then laid them flat on the table.

"I would be happy to teach you our language, priestess Elria," he said, accidentally elbowing a Servodroid that spun away and returned to offer its contents of fruit, bread and the large vegetables the Aurans ate. Clovis grimaced at the selection Danis heaped onto his plate and raised his finger.

"My lord Danis, mighten you try these eggs and meats? They are tasty and filling I assure you." Danis hesitated then grabbed the other Servodroid while Moniah and Ertim sat down and continued to speak in low tones.

"I think I shall eat the eggs and well then, I'll try this. What do you call it?"

"'Tis a link made of meats."

"Interesting flavor; rather of spice, I should say."

"Ah, yes, the meat 'tis pressed within a clear skin of inner organs of the animal it…my lord? Have I disturbed you?" Clovis asked, noting that Danis had set his fork down and stopped chewing. Even Moniah and Ertim were glancing sideways at Clovis, who was suddenly embarrassed and coughed slightly. He seemed at a loss and Elria smiled at Danis.

"I should be grateful to learn more of the Aurocearian language, my lord. I have a few words but the sound moves so quickly it is difficult to capture the meanings and when the music sound is made for the Oscileans, I am lost," she said, her gentle eyes meeting Danis', who blinked and smiled while discreetly pushing the sausage links away.

"We shall have to remedy this travail," Danis said and Ertim spoke up. His voice was still heavy with the accent of Auros and by now the people were accustomed to the fact that, when Aurans first spoke in human languages, they often sounded like someone from the eastern regions of the old country.

"Maaay it please priestess Elreeea. The Musemaun language of the Oscileans is a muuusic in the minnnds of Aurans," Ertim said, and he bowed his head.

Elria frowned and tasted her fruit cup.

"Moniah transcended once confided to me that he dreamed mayhaps the day would come when I too could sing to Prestant," Elria said. Ertim straightened his back and chewed his lip, processing what he had heard.

Moniah caught a glance from Danis and Clovis squirmed in his chair. Moniah leaned to the side to address Ertim and Clovis nudged Elria with his knee.

"I wish Marina were hereabouts. What plagues you Elria?"

"This Ertim is beguiling with his eyes like stars on a winter's night, but what is a governor of Earth. Why does he deny my rights to learn?" Elria whispered. Her cheeks blushed with fire and her gorgeous eyes were hardening like stones. In fact, the banter of conversation at table receded like the hiss of waves drawn back by the tide from pebbles on a shore. Clovis sipped his coffee while one of his eyes caught a twitch.

"My ears heard a different tune," he said to Elria, with tightened lips, but she ignored him and merely stared at Moniah with a quiet, enigmatic expression while Moniah regarded her steadily through the steam rising from his mug of Soffa.

* * *

Corina dismissed her women, who were fussing to put her hair up in a headdress couplet and decided to let her soft brown tresses fall about her shoulders to save time. "The suit of armor awaits thee, majesty," her Lady of the Privy said and Corina turned to a mirror held by her lady of the chamber to examine her form in a summer gown of pale yellow silk.

The other women murmured quietly in the outer chamber, stealing glances at a Talldroid robot that stood motionless in the foyer of her receiving room, waiting to escort her to the Arhahn.

"I must be on with it," Corina said to her lady, who winked and opened the door for the Queen, who strode through it and approached the Talldroid. The metal man appeared inert, its polished body gleaming in the morning sunlight streaming through high, arched windows. Corina wrung her hands and stepped a pace closer to the robot, which extended its right arm toward her. The hand rotated at the wrist to face the palm up where a slit revealed a thin tickertape that read, "Please follow me."

The Talldroid escorted Corina along a familiar corridor and then, abruptly, the contraption turned to the right in mid-stride, using rotators on the soles of its feet and continued down another hallway, turning again. They passed a transept hall leading to the eastern ramparts and finally arrived at a set of golden doors that swung open by unseen forces to reveal a large chamber. Inside, heavy ornate cross beams supported a vaulted ceiling. A splendid stained glass window and beautiful padded chairs faced a large black desk trimmed in gold, where Arhahnis was seated, staring at a glowing holoscreen.

Corina turned around, but the metal man was gone and the doors were closed.

"My, how silent," she said, and then pushed the toe of her shoe into a soft carpet of dark burgundy, bordered with birds she had never seen before. Arhahnis appeared dwarfed by the bulk of the desk even after he stood to gesture to Corina.

"Haolae Corina, please come within," Arhahnis said.

The little dragon chortled and Corina glanced up to see it eyeing her from one of the ceiling beams. The dragon flapped its wings and flew down to land on the desk.

"I once saw a bird from the jungles whose colorful feathers remind me of little Satimins," Corina said, taking seat and nodding toward the miniature dragon. Arhahnis came round the desk and sat facing her. He opened a Servodroid, revealing a lovely breakfast and poured tea for her and Soffa for himself. They enjoyed the repast while Arhahnis enquired of her kingdom. What was it like? How far away? What was its history?

"Mayron can elucidate many things to you, Infinite, though it is not like him to sleep so late, or is it your pleasure to speak only to me?" Corina said, setting her cup down.

"I must tell you that the good Mayron sleeps eternally. He expired last night and was found on the floor of his chambers with a smile upon his countenance. We offer our regrets," Arhahnis said, his flashing pupils beating a slow pulse.

Corina gazed at his eyes set in the handsome features of a face that shone like the smooth color of clay pottery. She sat back, lowered her head, wept quietly, and then wiped tears from her eyes.

"How can I assist you Corina? Should I summon Medean or a Taen physician?"

"No, I pray thee. I expected this but the knowing and the dawn of its truth are separate pains. Mayron was a father to me. He served my blood father, King Ciros," she said.

Arhahnis lifted a pipe from a box and filled it with Ol leaves.

"Because of the man, Varrick?" Arhahnis asked. Corina patted the lap of her gown. Arhahnis lit the pipe.

"Yes. Though none could prove it, we know Varrick killed my father after a terrible winter that took many lives, including that of me mother but he daren't not kill me for the people would have risen 'gainst him. Mayron was shaman and councilor to Ciros and so Varrick kept us both safe from harm to mark his power firm. I was but an infant when my father died but I grew in hatred of Varrick. He thought one day to make me his Queen. I'd have plunged myself to Hades had he wed me. Canelor is a large, rich land, Infinite. Ee'n Varrick would tremble had the landlords risen against my death. It was a life in…"

"Stasis. You were a prisoner, as was Mayron. But you are free now, Corina, and the good Mayron has gone to eternity with his heart made free and his mind at rest," Arhahnis said, with smoke from his pipe curling around his face.

"This in thanks to Moniah transcended, and to you, Infinite."

"Let us be comfortable, if you shall call me Arhahnis, I will douse this pipe that I see offends you," Arhahnis said, holding the pipe over a vase of flowers. Corina looked at the pipe, then at Arhahnis, who arched one eyebrow. She smiled and nodded and Arhahnis dropped the pipe into the vase. The little dragon cooed what sounded like "uh-oh" and Corina laughed aloud, despite her somber mood.

* * *

A summer shower drenched the palace and surrounding forest the following morning but, by the time the Chimera chimed ten o'clock, the brunt of the storm had passed and Maethus-Dia bristled with activity. Moniah strode out of the north gate, oblivious to the last of the rain, while Alaysi hurried before him to the mall green where a Satarship hovered over a carpet of rich, green grass, sparkling wet under the sun.

A herald on the ramparts sounded a fanfare and Moniah turned around near the Satarship to glance at the high walls, where he saw the herald and Medean, who was joined by the shorter form of prince Darius. The mystic had taken to running the school begun by his father on the ramparts and he waved to Moniah, who paced with one arm on his hip, glancing at his timepiece fob. Danis emerged from the north gate with Clovis and, seeing Moniah's posture, they ran across the mall to join him at the ship.

"Hurry on, we're behind schedule," Moniah called. Another Satarship took off from the east mall as Danis and Clovis arrived, winded, from their exertions. Danis shielded his eyes, watching the ship bank over them and then angle toward the west.

"It is ferrying the body of Mayron to Canelor," Moniah said, indicating the ship. He signaled an Auran in the doorway, who disappeared back into the ship and presently the aft and wing molecular engines ignited and the ship began to hum with the vigor of preflight.

"Ammanmus has done good work in Canelor. He reports that the people are of good cheer, but he found a city in dire need of Taen ministrations," Danis said as they stepped into the Satarship.

"Take off, captain," Moniah said to the pilot and Clovis hurried into his seat, anxiously strapping himself in. Moniah and Danis sat near him and Moniah reached out and tapped Clovis on the knee.

"You've flown these ships before I was born Clovis, are you still worried?"

"My lord, the truth of it is I love it much but it doth challenge my courage." Moniah swiveled his seat to face the front as the ship lifted off. He locked the seat in place.

"Let's hope Ammanmus stays his course at Canelor. I've enough to attend to without undo meddling on his part," Moniah said in

Aurocearian, which caused Danis to swivel his chair to face the flight deck as well. He stared sideways at Moniah and sighed.

"Before we arrived, I heard a councilor to Ertim voice his concerns aboard *Maethuean.* He wondered of anomalies and I admit, Moniah, this gave me pause. You do not imagine Ammanmus would overstep his authority," Danis said, also in Aurocearian.

Moniah glanced discreetly at Clovis but the old King leaned his head slowly toward a viewing window and watched the landscape flow by. Moniah turned his attention back to Danis.

"Ammanmus has taken careful pains to avoid conferring with me on matters pertaining to coexistence. Almost as if—now that he is on Earth—he does not recognize my authority in overseeing issues here."

Danis leaned his head back into his headrest. He frowned and Moniah studied him for a response but the Grand Ambassador was suddenly lost in his concerns. Presently, he angled his face to meet the unrelenting eyes of Moniah.

"My immediate concern, Moniah, is that none of us enter into a competitive state. I humbly remind you, as is my duty that it was Moniah transcended who held sway with power over the mission but brother that has changed. You are the exemplar but Arhahnis reins," Danis said, quietly, and Moniah lifted his chin and grunted. The ship jumped over a pocket of turbulence and Moniah turned to smile reassuringly at Clovis, whose cheeks and lips quivered. Nonetheless, he waved his fingers as though to indicate that all was well.

"Your gift is true, Danis; we would be lost without you. Tell me why Arhahnis will not let me meet Admiral Sey or his commanders? This Auran was a trusted friend of Moniah transcended." Danis lowered his head and met Moniah's eyes with such a determined expression that Moniah was riveted. He had never seen the affable Danis look so grave and serious.

"Arhahnis desires to control all matters of the fleets. He placed me in charge of the colonial fleet on the eve of our arrival, during council. I was not consulted. It was shrewd to do so, for, without your presence, the supreme command would have fallen to Sey. Now, think on *this,* Arhahnis is the issue of the Angelus who, as you know, worked to ensure that all high mantles would be contained in our house."

Moniah pulled at his robe collar. Something in his blood raged as he relived the anger Moniah transcended had known with regard to policies he felt were blatant nepotism and which had fueled the Speherewar. Danis paused and Moniah had to look back at him, only then aware that he must appear agitated enough to extract what was painful but urgent information.

"Yes, I am with you," Moniah said, dryly.

Danis pointed into the air, his resolve and focus undeterred.

"Like it or not, the fact remains. When Arhahnis determined that we should follow the course of the desire of the Angelus Arhahn to come to Earth, he had to ensure that Tius would be left with considerable power to wield. I mean *considerable* power."

"Thus, he gave the fleets to Tius and made you the defacto sub commander of the colonial fleet, acting under his authority, of course."

"Of course."

"And, if I may continue to extrapolate, Arhahnis then desired to ensure his power and, being so far removed from Aurocearia, he elected to withhold ultimate command of the colonial fleet for himself," Moniah postulated.

Danis narrowed his eyes nodding all the while in agreement, murmuring, "Yes."

"More pith I have yet to hear from any here present," Danis said, with a wink, his eyes flashing mischievously.

Moniah paused to ruminate, rubbing his knuckle against his chin while staring at the bulkhead. He realized that the Arhahn was a good and noble soul but he was also set on his own path of priorities where the fate of Earth was concerned. He respected the Arhahn's scientific prowess but Moniah incarnate was not much of a scientist. His Wizan skills were diluted, as though being born on Earth had melded him with mankind and he was now only partially Auran, despite his outward appearance. Perhaps that was why he felt so resentful toward Ammanmus, whose ancestor foresaw that through living on Earth, the physiology of Aurans would be altered.

Moniah shook himself from his thoughts. Danis was appraising him quietly. The First Lord determined to steer the conversation elsewhere. Some things were his alone.

"I thank you, Danis. One thing more, we must do something about Ertim. His candor is brutal and the Governorship is not understood by the people. Arhahnis has been less than clear about this matter."

Danis blinked. He breathed deeply and snorted.

"Ah, that is another concern. Include Medean when you and I address it but…" The pilots' voice interrupted them.

"Landing now, my lord."

"We're in the heart of the city already. Praise it be look how clean and bright," Clovis piped while straining to peer down through the window over the central plaza. The ship settled down near the long levee docks Moniah had ordered to be enlarged and which the people enjoyed for their broad expanse and the view of the bay.

"Come then, let me show you what I think is our next concern," Moniah said, throwing the lever on the hatch door. They emerged to crisp salt air. White caps danced in the bay and gulls cavorted overhead. Nearby, a squad of Constructorbots was lined up on the levee, which Danis studied with interest. He waved to a fishmonger who proudly lifted a basket of crabs.

"We need a Council Hall, here, and soon," Moniah said, in the human language, while Clovis listened intently.

"You ask for so little," Danis chuckled. Moniah licked his lips and, frowning, titled his head. To Danis it was obvious he was having a dream memory while to Clovis it must seem Moniah were merely pondering.

"Someone else said that to me but I cannot place who or when," Moniah mused.

A Promise to Coexist

Blue skies hummed with the hypnotic drone of Constructorbots converging at the site chosen for the Aurocearian-style Council Hall. Even though people were accustomed to the spectacle and sound of the sphere-shaped Constructorbots, the sight of the gleaming metal orbs buzzing overhead like a stream of giant pearls was still odd enough to turn heads and bring a pause to daily life.

The Constructorbots settled in a perfect line on the stone levee, one by one displacing bemused and curious gulls, squawking in complaint that any other competition should encroach on their territory. A stirring breeze whipped Kaylon's robe into a flurry of blue around him and he cursed under his breath, yanking the distracting cover robe away and tossing it aside while he took stock of the Constructorbots. Clovis gathered the robe before it blew into the Bay and followed Kaylon along the stone levee.

"Too few yet, we're going to require another two hundred of the fifty footers and a plethora of twenty footers to begin the next phase," Kaylon said into his comlink, referring to the robots by their various diameters. He held out his comlink to one side so that Clovis could see the small image of Moniah, who seemed to chew his lip in thought.

"Very well, I'll have Admiral Sey send them down from on high. I take it no more constructors are in *Auruaii*?"

"Not a one. You took so many to the quarry and what about the Blermetal? We have used all we had on the foundation and lower buttress supports. Although these men are brave and willing to scaffold higher, I caution against it," Kaylon said, turning with Clovis to look at the construction site.

From their vantage on the broad stone levee, they looked directly west into the central plaza where young men collected thousands of implanted rods flashing red and green that demarcated plumb lines around the base of the structure.

The Council Hall was rising quickly amidst the hammers and chisels of men and the hot sizzling lasers and metal arms of hovering

Constructorbots. Satarships lowered quarried stones to dusty staging areas around the site from which Constructorbots then lifted them into place under supervision of Auran and human architects.

The massive base of the building consumed much of the precious, invulnerable Blermetal, which could not be forged on Earth. Although Moniah hoped his Council Hall would rival its inspiration on Auros Prime that was not to be. The Terran structure would rise five hundred feet.

Kaylon squinted at the site, watching men scurry around on metal and wooden scaffolds around the jagged edges of the nave and clerestories. Without more Blermetal, there was no way the main structure could ascend further.

Kaylon sighed impatiently while Moniah took time to consider his plan. At last, the First Lord smiled.

"Simple enough. I will disassemble the totem hall Arhahnis brought with him. It's an empty shell and has all the Blermetal we'll need for some time."

Kaylon cocked an eyebrow, glancing at Clovis, who scratched his chin. The so called "totem hall" named by people who saw in its shape something akin to similar wooden structures found in tribal lands of the great northwest was originally intended to be the residence of the Arhahn, who had transported the building from Auros and set it down on the day he arrived.

Since then, it had remained on the outskirts of the west meadows of the city, gathering dust, discarded by Arhahnis in lieu of Maethus-Dia.

"What if Himself objects to the destruction of his palace?" Kaylon said, with a twinkle. Moniah zoomed his imager. Clovis instinctively jumped back a pace despite the tiny size of the image.

"Leave that to me. I will be onsite shortly." The comlink transmission disconnected and Kaylon jammed the comlink into the top of his boot. A loud crash of lumber kicked up dust in the distance, near the west main portico and entrance.

"Oh, mighty be," Clovis yelped. Kaylon tugged his sleeve and they ran down the levee steps to where they could hear a confusion of voices, but the accident scene itself was still too far away and obscured by plumes of dust so they still couldn't see what had happened and if anyone was injured.

"Shall we ride?" Clovis said, corralling two horses. They mounted the steeds, trotting up the dirt floor of what would be the interior nave. With a mile to go to reach the main portico, Kaylon gently spurred his horse into a canter but Clovis leaned into a full gallop, his graying beard and hair bouncing in time with the stride of his horse.

At the portico, they found a heap of stones and shattered beams. The workers and Aurans who had been closest to the failure scene were coated in a fine amber-colored dust and sand.

"Is anyone hurt?" Kaylon called out, standing in his stirrups. A Taen approached, wiping grit from his face, while a hovering Constructorbot activated a high-speed fan to clear the accident scene of dust, effectively blowing it downwind toward what remained of the city square. The wind dispersed a crowd of gawkers.

"No, my lord, the men are above," the Taen priest said averting his face from the wind made by the fan, whose brief hurricane transformed him from a ghost of dust back to his former, if still soiled self. Kaylon backed away from the building and gazed up to see a team of men and an Auran looking down on them. The men waved reassuringly and the Auran turned away to inspect something. Visibly relieved, Clovis dismounted and poured a bucket of water over his head. The whir of a Satarship engine assailed them as the wind shifted and the craft descended from the west.

"Lord Kaylon, I've a good stew for the men. Will you ev' any?" a happy crone said, startling Kaylon as she touched his leg. He looked down from the saddle and smiled. Her eyes were a merry green twinkle set in lines hard-earned from life and there was little remaining of her teeth but there was nothing to show complaint about her.

"Perhaps Moniah will put me in your concoction, dear lady," he said, indicating the Satarship while dismounting and patting the horse. The crone's head danced and wobbled with genuine amusement. She pointed to the heap of ruined scaffolding, then coughed and tried to check herself but Kaylon chuckled and she convulsed with warm and infectious glee. Though he seldom ate food prepared by humans, Kaylon followed her to the lunch tables where the women and children readied meals for the workers. The crone smoothed her hands on her apron and carefully ladled steaming contents into a bowl for him.

"I promise, lord, it ain't witchity grub," she said with a wink.

Everyone chattered about the excitement of the morning, including the Aurans. While Kaylon tasted the stew, the Satarship settled onto the levee, scattering gulls but attracting children and fishermen. The crone bit her lower lip and lifted her fingers to tickle the air, her eyes fixed upon Kaylon, who tasted the food again and then dug in. He wiped his mouth with a soft clean rag she had given him.

"Good woman, your food is a wonder. I thank you," he said and she muttered something with a tender tone and blushed while she tilted her chin to her left shoulder and dipped her body in a comical but coquettish curtsey.

By now, Moniah, Danis and young Darius were hurrying along the causeway. Kaylon finished his alfresco stew and waited until Moniah was in earshot. The First Lord strode toward him, his hair pulled into a ponytail, wearing a tunic, belt and peasant shirt. Ladies at the lunch table ignored the rough, loutish dining of their men folk to eye Moniah and whisper among themselves.

Moniah cut a fine figure. Work suited him and days in the sun and wind had burnished his skin. He was a more dynamic being than the pleasant but reserved Auran of his first days and his passionate energy for the Council Hall project was clearly evident as he scanned the ruined heap, craning his head back to study the scene of the mishap.

"I see we need the Blermetal desperately," Moniah said to Kaylon, while Clovis pointed out different aspects of the site to Danis and the young prince Darius, who was fascinated by all aspects of the endeavor.

"I suppose we should delay until Arhahnis approves your request for it," Kaylon said, but Moniah waved his words into the gusting wind and strode into the nave.

"The wind raises more concern today. Take everyone save the robots off the building. I'll soon have our metal," Moniah said, shielding his face from the glaring sun. He inspected the skeleton of the structure.

"We should have Talldroids here to lend hands to the men for detailed work. Do you think Arhahnis will part with any of his precious, metal slaves?" Before Kaylon could respond, Moniah chucked him on the shoulder and scrambled over a block of marble to join the others outside the portico. Kaylon followed and twirled his hand over his head signaling the various foremen that work was done for the day.

"It will be a gradual increment of stairs leading to the doors. See, upon this paper, the steps rise as graceful as an open fan," Clovis was saying to Darius who pursed his lips and ran his hands over a tilted drafting table. The eager boy leaned close to the drawing and pointed to the diagrams of the entrance.

"The doors will be big, poppa," he said, and Clovis nodded, "Sixty feet tall, my son." Danis joined Moniah and Kaylon for Ol pipes in a cooling breeze. It was past noon and the wind from the Bay was picking up. In the distance, purpling storm clouds pushing cold air over the Atlantic rolled toward shore.

"Darius grows by the day. It is a fascination to observe," Kaylon noted, while Danis maneuvered his bulk to block the wind so that Moniah could light his pipe.

"I took him from Medean today. He excels in the school," Moniah said. Danis rolled his huge shoulders and cracked his neck. He expelled a cloud of smoke and pointed his pipe at the building.

"During the flight here he spoke of nothing else. When will it be finished? Could he help? No wonder Alaysi runs when he sees the prince," Danis said as the air buzzed with the familiar drone of flying Constructorbots.

"Ah, metal rain from heaven. Kaylon, your help arrives," Moniah said, pointing up through the approaching clouds to where a squadron of Constructorbots came down like silver pearls. The formation descended rapidly to land in perfect rows in the nave.

"Lord Moniah!" Darius called out, running toward the Aurans. Moniah turned to the young prince, who was thrilled by the sight of so many robot spheres. Danis lifted his face to the sky and held out a palm as the first cool spit of summer rain fell. Men gathered tools and masons threw oilcloths over their most delicate work, while women and children gathered the vestiges of the meal from the tables.

"Tell me how they work, please lord," Darius asked, leading Moniah by the hand to the drafting tables. The sun shone again and Moniah looked at Clovis, who smiled with such pride that the First Lord lifted Darius to a box so the child could easily see the complex diagrams. A phalanx of twenty-footer Constructorbots descended down toward the ground nearby and lined up outside the length of the long nave.

"What if they break, lord Moniah?" Darius asked, squinting up. Moniah looked to Danis, who shrugged, and to Kaylon, who wiped sweat from his face with a damp rag. Clovis nodded and placed his hands on his hips and then scratched his beard.

"I've a wonder of the same," Clovis said, glancing at Danis and Kaylon, who regarded Moniah with a twinkle and a hesitant stare, respectively. Moniah leaned over and grasped the drafting table. He smiled at Darius. They had given him a place to begin and now Moniah would enlighten, just as his father had.

"Sometimes our engineers repair the machines but most of the time they do so themselves. You see, these Constructorbots are really machines *within* machines," Moniah explained. At that, Clovis made a face and the young prince scratched his armpit. Danis twitched his nose and turned away but Kaylon sipped water from a jug, eyes fixed on

Moniah.

"The size of insects or smaller," Kaylon said, but Darius and Clovis merely stared at him. A few men gathered nearby and Moniah motioned for them to step closer.

"There are nano machines inside the spheres. Let me explain it a different way," Moniah said, drawing a circle on the upper edge of a plan. Faces crowded around the table, peering at it as though into the Well of an oracle.

"There are tiny machines inside the robot spheres,"

"The Con, eh, construtiutor botos," Darius said.

Moniah smiled, "Constructorbots. Yes", he said, "The tiny machines inside move very rapidly. Some of them are visible to the eye, about the size of an insect, but most are even smaller than a grain of sand. Most of these nanobots—another word for these tiny machines—move very rapidly, quicker than the eye can catch, and these tiny machines are also factories."

Blank stares. Moniah pressed on.

"Imagine everyone at this building site, the workers, those quarrying the stones, the artists and the masons, even the architects, all in one room. A complete factory, able to design, replicate, repair or cast metal and build," Moniah said, looking around. One of the younger men tapped the blueprint diagram where Moniah's notes were fast becoming smears of lines.

"And the foreman, the overseer be in there, too?"

"Yes, yes indeed. Nothing is wasted so there is always material. There are structures of machines that *oversee* everything and often it is these machines that repair something before it breaks. Just like here, well, with the exception of today, of course."

Laughter. He had them now and Kaylon smiled, leaning onto the table to watch Moniah excel. He spread his arms wide.

"Now, with something this big it takes more time to build and to move around and through, because of its dimension and girth."

"Like, er, ah , when I builds me house it took a month at best but this great lug a stone en metal tasks us a month and nigh has raised er the trees yonder," a wiry man interjected and Moniah beamed with a smile. He pointed to the man excitedly. The man jerked back a bit like a bird caught at feeding.

"Exactly! Excuse me, sir. I did not intend to startle you. Anyway, where was I?"

"'Tis easier when small, but why?" Darius said and Moniah clicked his fingers and turned to the boy.

"Small things move fast, yes? Flap your arms; go ahead, yes, like a bird, that's it. You sir, will you oblige, thank you. Now look, the man's arms are longer than yours, so he cannot flap them as quickly. See? I can tap my fingers on this table more quickly than *either* of you can flap your arms. A fly makes a buzz sound because its wings move so fast but a bird's wings do not buzz, do they?"

Darius tried to flap his arms as fast as Moniah tapped his fingers. The wiry man, having grasped the concept more quickly, stopped and chuckled, elbowing an elderly man, who stared at Moniah as though he were the sun and stars combined.

Kaylon surreptitiously keyed in a command to his comlink and one of the smaller so-called "finisher" Constructorbots, four feet in diameter, flew to the table and landed on a stack of stone.

"Perfect," said Moniah as Danis—intrigued by the captivated audience—moved closer.

"There are assemblers in this robot and these machines have quality control systems like you, sir. Yes, you. The assemblers can study and identify unwanted variations or like when you find rough stone that does not fit," Moniah said, pausing to look at Darius, who was all ears.

"Mistakes?" The boy said and Moniah snapped his fingers.

"Yes, mistakes. When one of the assemblers or repair machines finds a mistake, it discards the atomic-sized particles, nevermind, eh, the smaller mistakes, and removes them. Very quickly." The wind picked up and, while Moniah paused again to down water so fast that he spilled most of it on his shirt, Kaylon piped in.

"The assemblers and replicators are like you stone masons, bonding the right atoms or smaller pieces together. When there is a large structure, such as the *Auruaii* ship, the machines move faster because they have that many more smaller machines to work with."

A rumble of thunder preceded a cold wind, rich with the scent of salt spray and dampened dust.

Danis wrestled a laser tool from one of the larger robots and, keying it into his comlink, powered up the torch long enough to cut a hole in the surface of the finisher Constructorbot. Then, he hefted a Blermetal mallet. Everyone jumped aside as he swung the mallet down with a terrible crash onto the finisher robot.

"There now, quickly, look inside," Danis said and everyone crowded around to peer into the guts of the machine. Moniah lifted Darius to the top of the table so that he could peer down into the machine where an army of flea-sized robots transported metal plating from a plasma conduit.

"Crackety, looke here, like swarm'in ants," the wiry man said.

In less than a minute, the hole created by Danis was sealed and the robot sphere appeared as good as new.

"I see, me lord, they are indeed like ants shoring up their warrens," Clovis said, squeezing Darius's shoulder. Moniah smiled and set Darius to his feet.

"Thank you for the illustration, 'twas worth much description," Moniah said to Danis, while the men thanked him and began to disperse to their homes as the day darkened into what promised to be a summer night of wind and rain. Despite the onset of foul weather, a few of the inspired crouched around the inert Constructorbots, examining the Aurocearian machines with new interest.

Clovis led Darius to the Satarship with Moniah, Kaylon and Danis quick on their heels. The boy could be seen excitedly pointing to the site, then to the partially submerged *Auruaii*. Around the construction site, Constructorbots settled into inert modes to ride out the storm, waiting to work more of their magic for humankind.

"I have encountered a sufficient number of children to realize that Darius is highly mature for one of his age," Danis said, kicking a broken stone from his path. Moniah scooped up a handful of dirt from a block of masonry, allowing it to scatter to the wind.

"You opened the doors today," Kaylon said to Moniah, bobbing his head over his shoulder in the direction of the construction site.

"It was a bit tricky when my mind saw carbonic anhydrase, conveyor mechanisms, mass per unit and acceleration motions, but I somehow found the words," Moniah agreed while, ahead of them, Darius and Clovis bounded up the levee steps and hurried into the Satarship as the first whips of rain came down.

"You found more than words, Moniah, much more," Danis said. The Auran brothers hurried up the steps in pelts of rain. Danis ducked his head to scurry into the ship hatch. The craft was firing its molecular wing and aft engines and Moniah could see water droplets sizzling as they struck the glowing thrusters.

He paused at the hatch door and turned to survey the construction site. The day that had begun with such a banal edge had transformed into one of his finest moments and he felt his heart, that greater part of his father, beating in pride. In his mind, the building rose to kiss soft clouds and it would surely succeed because of the sweat of men and of his Auran brothers and the dreams of a boy coming into his own, a dream that would now inspire older men.

For a brief moment, Moniah Incarnate experienced a dream memory in which Moniah transcended infused his Wizan powers into a man, woman and child. He sensed the consternation of the deceased Saeonar and the scrutiny of Vetaeos, Medean, and the other transcended Auran generation but, for Moniah incarnate, it was more than a memory. It was the beginning of a legacy. A cold wind snapped at the ship and Moniah turned and entered the hatch door.

* * *

Moniah lifted his father's Coracle-diant from the dusty niche and held it up into the dim light. Outside, rain pounded Maethus-Dia palace in torrents and rolling thunder held sway over the evening. Glow orb chandeliers and torchieres activated automatically, lending a warmth to the gloom-soaked chambers as well as to Moniah, who studied the fine engravings of the Wizan wand of Moniah Incarnate. Toward the base of the handle, he could make out an engraved legend, worn smooth by the grip of titans, etched in the platinum and gold stem. It read, *Erfros beloved of the Wizan and chosen of Moniah.*

"Saeonar," he muttered, and gently placed the wand back into its special niche beside his shoulder mantle.

"He was a good friend to Moniah transcended, as much a brother as any of us," Medean said from behind him, near the fireplace where he extended his hands toward the welcome glow of a crackling hearth. Moniah turned slowly and stared at Medean, who was at least fifteen feet away with his back to the First Lord. Moniah flipped a book closed and buttoned the top of his robe, annoyed with Medean's intrusion on his privacy.

"One is hard pressed for a private moment when you're around," Moniah said, pouring a glass of wine.

Medean turned sideways and angled his face toward Moniah, his eyes glinting.

"You invited me."

"I do not understand the songs of Oscileans. That part of him is less than a memory to me," Moniah blurted out in confession. He sipped the wine then threw the rest of it down his throat, before immediately pouring another glass.

"Perhaps the Wizan spirit is not meant for your life, Moniah," Medean said, gently, but Moniah's eyes flashed in time with the storm. He checked his wrist chronometer.

"Are you ready yet?" he said, stuffing pages and pulse disks into a folder.

* * *

CODEX ENTRY: SECURE:

ABOVE ALL THINGS, A GREENROBE MUST HAVE TIMING AND I FEAR MY OWN SENSE WAS LACKING LAST NIGHT. MONIAH RETURNED TO THE PALACE IN HIGH SPIRITS BUT, WHEN HE EXPERIENCED A MOMENT OF TENDER CONTEMPLATION, I WAS TOO BRUTAL IN MY EFFORT TO COMFORT HIM. THERE IS A PLACE HE MUST GO WHERE NO ONE IN OUR TAJAEN FAMILY CAN JOIN HIM, A PLACE WHERE HE IS A STRANGER. TO AIDE HIM, I MUST ENDEAVOR TO CURTAIL THE IMPETUOUS NATURE OF MY VOICE AND FIND MY INNER PEARL OF WISDOM.

-MEDEAN TALSAIYR

It was a stunning morning, clear and temperate, following the storms of the night. The air smelled of summer flowers, pine and fresh salt air from the Atlantic where, beyond the cliffs and mall greens of the palace, breakers rolled to shore in a steady rhythm that was both muted and comforting. The palace buzzed with activity. Its denizens awoke to a fresh start after debates among the court and newly-formed councils, whose members labored until all hours to effect the political aspirations of Clovis and Moniah, as well as the promises of Arhahnis.

Elria emerged from the east gate. She smiled at a Templar guard and bent toward a planter of flowers. The quick snap of heels turned her attention to the gate where she saw Arhahnis, just as he stepped out of the archway shadow into daylight.

"Good morning."

"Haolae, Elria, so much of our time was devoured last night. Will you walk with me?" Arhahnis said, smiling as he approached. They moved down the terrace stairs onto the rich, verdant grass of the east mall green.

"Thank you, Infinite. Matters were a bit heated. It is good to be out of doors where nature rules," Elria said, while they walked at a relaxed pace toward the cliffs.

"So many things are dying whilst new things come into being," Elria added, pausing to look at a dead bird by a tree. Arhahnis touched her back, gently prodding her to continue walking. He stared at the ground and rolled back the cuffs of his richly-embroidered sleeves.

"What else do you feel is dying, Elria?"

"Everything from our past, so much of which needed to die. Now, we learn, explore new fascinations. Our path is set upon discovery," Elria said, halting under the swaying tendrils of a weeping–willow tree.

"And do *you* feel that you are somehow a remnant of the past?"

Arhahnis asked, stooping to pick a flower and enjoy its scent. He turned to meet her eyes. She was tired, her own lovely orbs red due to lack of sleep and the tension of debate.

"When I saw the beams of light, the Saen beams, strike Diana before your vessel landed, I was terrified. I knew then that the gods we worshipped are but things in the dark beyond Earth. Just as I had seen with Moniah transcended."

Arhahnis regarded her in silence, observing the epiphany Elria was experiencing. He was aware of her deep love for Moniah transcended and it was an unspoken truth at court that the love she nurtured for Moniah incarnate was in a delicate state of denial. Arhahnis was not aware, nor was anyone else, that her desire to resurrect the lost love drove her strongly enough to attempt a form of crude sorcery upon Moniah.

There was little doubt that all this angst was reaching its apex in her soul.

"Perhaps I held onto the religion of Diana partly for the power it rendered me and partly for…I cannot guess," Elria confessed.

Arhahnis took hold of her hand gently. She looked into his magnificent eyes, the ancestors of which had conceived life on other worlds, possibly even hers.

"A remnant of love cannot transform what has passed, nor renew itself for our designs about what love should be," Arhahnis said. Elria blushed. Arhahnis let go of her hand, adding, "Moniah has not confided his feelings for you to me. He is too private a soul to share such intimacies but I sensed your need and…his emotions."

"I am lost," Elria whispered, as much to herself as declaring it.

Arhahnis smiled.

"Lost only in what was, Elria. You are conceiving a future and soon you will no longer linger in past realms. As to your religion, you *believed* Elria and you had faith. This is not fault or delusion but rather manifestations of spiritual strength." Arhahnis pointed to the sky where a pale moon, Treehoomena, could be seen high above.

"When you saw the moon move by force of Saen beams, the revelations you were already privy to blossomed. This was disturbing because it shed light into shadows concerning your worship of the twin moons."

Elria rubbed her hands together.

"We were wrong," she whispered. Arhahnis met her eyes and held them in a firm stare, his golden pupils twinkling with the promise of eternity.

"In Aurocearian faiths, we acknowledge inherent divinity in all things created. Planets contain their own divinity. So, it follows that you could not have been, as you say, wrong."

"You make plain sense of chaos, Infinite. What are people's minds, compared to an Auran's?"

"Are we so different? You have a name, as do I. We breathe and yearn together in the Gods' firmament. Once, we were separated by a bridge of stars and now we tread the same soil."

Elria's features softened. He could see her eyes reflect a new peace. She gazed up at the pale visible moon and chuckled.

"Mirth! A beginning to an end of all travail," Arhahnis said.

"Our second moon."

"Ah yes, Trehoomena."

"In my old way, I believed he was the incarnation of dreams but you are that incarnation, Arhahnis," Elria said, turning to smile at him. Arhahnis smiled reassuringly but stepped back from her, apparently disturbed.

"It is my name translated. Centuries ago, the proponents of a cult decreed the worship of Arhahnis transcended and this caused great suffering in Aurocearia," he said and, even though Arhahnis had done everything possible to dispense with belief in these dangerous concepts, the way Elria continued to look at him, indicated the failure of his precautions and suggested that she, and other humans, idolized him.

"I see," she said. A shadow passed overhead, caused by an Oscilean and Wizan rider that soared above them, flying sentry duty. The wing beats faded and the green and brown-scaled dragon arced over the sea, and banked in a slow turn to return over the west gate.

"It is fitting that your arrival here drove away the false gods," she said. Certainly, the old ways of Earth were changing and, as an intelligent woman, Elria expressed this undeniable reality.

"You prepare to end an epoch while I strive to oversee a new evolution for Auran and mankind. Gods be with us both," Arhahnis said.

* * *

The dragon sang to the day and Wizan Rete petted its neck.

"It is beautiful, eh, my friend?" he sang back to the Oscilean and looked down to see the Arhahn and the priestess strolling through waves of green grass.

* * *

Elria cast her eyes down and turned a corner, entering an alcove. She saw a set of doors and tried the knobs. The doors were unlocked and she quickly entered.

"Just a few moments alone," she muttered, and closed the doors behind her and leaned against them, looking about to find herself in a room in the palace she had never visited. It was a Solarium with wooden walls of finely-detailed paneling, covered in gold, and a floor of blue, sea green, ochre, teal, white and sienna-red tiles forming lotus flowers, leaves, stems and delicate palsies set into intricate marble patterns. One huge brass chandelier hung above the center, its glow orbs darkened.

Afternoon light poured in through tall arched windows. She moved, hesitantly, deeper into the room, turning once to hear the muted sounds of arguing voices beyond the doors, but the voices soon faded away. A shaft of bright sunlight filtered through the windows, its passing rays illuminating a mural painting. Elria stepped closer to examine the painting. Her lips trembled and she raised her hands to her mouth.

She walked to the portrait and stared at it. There, life-size, rendered in oils, was her lost love, Moniah transcended. He was depicted surveying a landscape from a moss-encrusted rock. Elria reached out tenderly, touching the frame.

"My love, if you but knew how many people claim that spot as their land, it would amuse you," she said, laughing.

In the painting, Clovis and Marina were clearly recognizable, sitting at Moniah's feet. Elria touched the canvas, longing to be in that distant time, frozen in the embrace of Moniah. She stepped back to gain a full perspective. Moniah seemed about to move, so lifelike was the rendition. The artist had painted a soft nimbus halo of light around his handsome head. His raven hair gleamed jet black and cascaded over the ample sculpture of shoulders. His round biceps conveyed his power and his strong, large, beautiful hands were positioned one behind to his side with two fingers extended suggesting caution, yet summons, while the other was lifted just above his waist, moving forward, pointing to the horizon. His deep, blue eyes were weirdly lifelike, the color deepening but more azure in tone where the false sunlight of the painting caught his expression. His face was tilted at a slight angle as he gazed into the distance.

The pupils were but infinitesimal pinpricks of gold but softly executed. His skin smooth and tanned. Even the attitude of his pose captured his confident yet casual stride. The full sensual lips were imperceptibly parted, as though he would speak, and the powerful thigh of his right leg pushed at the flowing fabric of his robe. There was a slight curve in the powerful neck as though he was about to turn his face and his stride suggested that he might turn at any minute to encourage everyone to follow.

"Oh my love," Elria whimpered, as tears streamed down her cheeks. At sunset, she was still in the solarium, seated on a chair, eyes fixed on the portrait.

The Reach of Mankind

On the gas giant planet of Exciluea, two floating cities merged into one mammoth tetrahedral structure composed of a light metal alloy, similar to Aurocearian Blermetal but without the heavy density and weight of its counterpart.

The Exciluea factories, miles below, were busy transforming hyper heated gas and plasma in a planet-wide effort to create more spacecraft.

Recent strikes by meteoric bodies had penetrated more deeply into the upper atmosphere than previous encounters with celestial debris had done—raised alarms with the hovering Excilue Beings, who suffered the loss of several thousand casualties at the point of the meteors' impacts due to resulting explosions. Compelled by their own scientific progress and the first real threat from outer space bodies, the Excilue united their efforts to create substantive defenses, which because of their efficient nature, were combined with the expansion of the space-faring fleet.

The Excilue ambassador moved through a corridor tunnel, using its undulating topsail and the expulsion of helium and nitrogen from its gill vents to propel the orb-shaped body at sufficient velocity to effect speedy travel though the floating cities.

The ambassador glowed red and pink, issuing a high pitched sonic pulse to alert the other denizens that he was not inclined to slow his speed and they should move aside with all haste. He emerged into a cavernous chamber, four miles high, where thousands of Excilue waited patiently, hovering in groups. Their round gas bodies projected a rainbow of colors around a chamber, which soared up to an apex of gradually receding hexagons outlined with tubular webbing that glowed with a dull illumination.

Below the hexagonal "ceiling", triangular-shaped windows composed of water-fused sand looked out on a vista of gray, red and purple gases and cumulus clouds rising thousands of feet to where the tops of the super cells were stretched into thin bands by the hurricane level winds of the upper reaches.

Ambassador *Reforming Mind* paused to study the view and then hovered to a water globule where it extended its drinking trunk to suck the cool liquid in. The water bubble shrank as the ambassador's hot pink color morphed into a calm blue and the inner organs pulsed more slowly. Apparently satiated, *Reforming Mind* drifted toward a select group of his fellow creatures, who hovered over a large oval pool of gas and water.

"The divine Arhahn succeeded in dividing his government and has, himself, ventured to a planet known as, Eros," The Excilue *Wise in Words* stated into a liquiform amplifier.

"News travels slowly to us. I have heard this world is called Earth," *Reforming Mind* hurried to add, flashing a self-amused flurry of gold to green back to gold then blue again within its circumference. Others of the inner circle bleated a soft chorus of bell tones of laughter for it had been some considerable time since the Arhahn's fleet was tracked trough space on route to Earth. *Wise in Word*s ejected gas from gills under its topsail, which quivered in annoyance.

"I endeavor as best as I can to achieve. I remind you that had it not been for the fact that the divine Arhahn was magnanimous enough to share his secrets for real time communication—we would suffer greater silence in the void than now," *Wise in Words* sang and a silence prevailed while the others pulsed colors. Never one to be easily corrected, *Reforming Mind* expanded his body to force methane up to his gills and thereby released a small explosion of flatulence as comment.

Excilue possessed extremely good sight and their radius of eyes encircled the mid circumference but did not blink or possess any visible lenses. These eyes were also hard to discern as such by Aurans and appeared to be a simple string of crab-like unblinking dots or skeletal structures, which was one reason why the Angelus Arhahn had been so unnerved during his encounter with *Bold in Love* centuries earlier--for the Auran could not tell how he was being perceived.

Wise in Words, what study does the Arhahn offer as to the readings we have detected in the system of the giant orange star?" *Reforming Mind* demanded to know, resorting to a formal voice as its body shone blue, red, followed by rapid pulses of green, yellow and gold.

"The Auran emperor is otherwise focused on the world, Earth. We glean from communications to the Sphereworlds that important progress ensues in this endeavor. I propose patience. The Wizan must be aware of what transpires around the orange star and shall, if need be, respond in due course," *Wise in Words'* melodious voice responded. *Reforming Mind* flashed a series of red, silver, yellow and even black pulses, "I am concerned that Wizan attention will be too late? The angelus Arhahn's directive must proceed for the sake of all concerned. Human progress must not be contaminated. The path Auros takes leaves no room for failure. Biometric signatures on the primary planet of the orange star are disharmonic and excessively forceful."

"It is our belief that all anomalies observed from the Sphereworlds were destroyed subsequent to the conflict within the Sphereworlds. We must be patient," *Wise in Words* replied.

"Let's to the observatory; I wish to behold the Sphereworlds," *Reforming Mind* sang out, and the group took flight, ascending to a hydra of tunnel junctures branching off in all directions. They angled into a gentle rise within a tunnel and then accelerated into a vertical shaft where gas jets positioned every hundred feet created a veritable wind tunnel, adding to their buoyancy and speed.

The Excilue inner circle emerged into an oval chamber half a mile in radius in which a vortex pool of silvery liquid congealed within a gyroscope of photon accelerators.

While *Wise in Words* adjusted the photon lens of the apparatus, the others took positions around the radius of the aperture.

Excilue beings had gained much from the visit of *Bold In Love* when the alien had arrived unexpectedly at the Sphereworlds during the reign of the Angelus Arhahn. *Bold In Love* had brought back samples of the atmosphere of Auros Prime within special airtight bladders he could seal into his orb body. Once returned to Exciluea, the samples were studied for analysis to make it easier for succeeding generations to visit the Aurocearians and, in doing so, be fully immersed and acclimated without need for portable atmosphere chambers.

The reason for this was obvious simply for the ease of travel and to facilitate one-to-one encounter and it was possible due to the Excilue physical nature, which, because of its complex mixture of oxygen, nitrogen and helium, permitted the Excilue to exist in various densities of atmosphere. Evolution on the gas giant of Exciluea had necessitated that all Excilue adjust their respiratory systems as they traveled from the low depths to the high reaches.

The unspoken reason for adapting their respiratory functions was best expressed by the deceased Ambassador, *Bold In Love* who had said, "Any creatures as delicate as we must learn all that we can from the bipeds who are dense of form and structure and live in a more impervious reality." Paranoid by nature, in part due to their physical selves, the Excilue were actually more resilient than even they were aware. The translucent jellyfish-like membrane comprising their basic form was elastic and substantial. The brain was centered in the orb body, around which the eye stems radiated to the outer surface. The most delicate organs surrounded the brain and were protected by a large series of lung and lift chambers that were in turn encased in a thick muscular placenta with a powerful stem, rising to the "top" of the creature, from which the fluke sail sprouted.

The sail was used primarily for movement and propulsion in tandem with vents located around the outer circumference as well as under the fluke that expelled pressurized gas. Under the fluke sail were gills. The edges of the sail contained hundreds of prehensile fingers and tendrils capable of the most delicate handling of materials. Four larger trunks could be extended as much as ten feet from the body for drinking and eating.

Bold In Love had no way of knowing that, when he made the first visit to the Sphereworlds, he encountered Arhahnis at the moment of supreme agony due to the Spherewar and the subsequent metamorphoses resulting in the loss of the Auries. For the remainder of his life, Arhahnis transcended never delved into the unique capacity of the Excilue, but the fact remained that the Excilue were descended from the residual energy of creation Arhahnis had radiated when he became a catalyst of the Gods on the Mountain of Beginnings.

Part of that creation energy had diffused from Auros Prime into the void, traveled through space and rained down into the atmosphere of what became Exciluea.

By this process, the energy transmitted sentient life to the planet in the form of a God spark consisting of the mind and Birthfire of Aurocearians that in turn evolved into the Excilue. The result was that each Excilue was born from its clutch with an innate awareness of the Aurocearians, whom they revered and whom they sought to emulate.

But, the Excilue were also endowed with the Aurocearian desire for striving toward the Godsrealm. Their paranoid nature transmuted this desire into a cautious appraisal of history, particularly due to recent events, and because it was known that the Aurocearians, by directive of the Arhahn himself, had sent an important expedition to the remote planet of Earth, a world the Excilue were certain held the key to the next evolutionary stage of their destiny. They had even unconsciously copied the Aurocearian government structure of ambassadors and governors, which they found suitable due to the massive size of Exciluea.

Reforming Mind touched the rim of the lens, drumming its liquiform base with hundreds of its "fingers". Exciluea was now in periapsis with the Sphereworlds and, even better, the star of Exciluea was in periastron with the Suum Nebula in a rare conjunction of cosmic objects.

Wise In Words ran his fluke across a series of globular controls and the gyroscopes began to whirl quickly, attaining a speed that in turn accelerated the photon field. A mile above them, in the roof of the chamber, a series of guns fired Saen light beams around the radius of a thick convex lens that was now free to scrutinize space as the Saen beams cleaved through the planet's thick and ever-present clouds.

The Excilue converged more closely around the circumference of the lens rim. An unobstructed view of space formed in the liguiform radius of the viewing circle. The Excilues' colorful bodies flashed patinas of excitement in pastel hues while the image deepened through black riches of the void into the pink gases of the Suum Nebula and, at its core, the Sphereworlds.

"I have never beheld the Sphere in such clarity. Well done." *Reforming Mind* crowed, at which *Wise In Words* quivered its fluke sail and blinked in a continuous cycle like lights timed in a sequence that traveled around the radial eyes.

"My gratitude. You will note in the archive, images projected from our beloved *Bold In Love*, captured at the time of his journey to Aurocearia, that depict the delicate mechanism of the inner sphere planets in relation to each other. There is ample room for these worlds within the sphere and there is even night—despite the enclosed stars—as the distance between the planets permits diffusion of the small stars' radiance," *Wise In Words* explained.

One of the Excilue expanded its fluke to point to an image from the Archive.

"There appears to be superb temperature regulation? The stars…"

"Triune."

"What?"

"The inner sphere stars are called Triune stars because there are three and they are artificially created."

"Yes, I understand. The residual heat from the stars is then somehow accreted to the outer sphere shell?"

"Precisely; examine the sphere itself."

"It is magnificent."

"In fact it is."

"Silver in tone."

"If we can restrain our emotional response-"

"As I was articulating, note in this magnification the outer surface of the Sphere. Do you see? It is porous at close range."

"Ah! And these porous structures act as the ejecta vents."

"Just so."

Reforming Mind hovered dangerously close to the lens rim, his orb body hovering only scant feet away from the lacerating, whirling rings of the gyroscope.

"I have wondered, how is the accreted heat formed into such massive coronas? There must be mechanisms within the sphere shell constituting some form of accelerant."

"I concur. Think, if the accreted heat were to be simply allowed to drift out of the pores of the sphere it would take eons to effect significant cooling. However, to super heat these gases and project them dissipates the heat most industriously."

"And creates the perfect defensive weapon. If the Aurans never achieve anything else, they are the supreme builders. We have seen enough today. Let us not invade the privacy of the Aurans further at this time. We study their worlds in admiration and for the purpose of fostering understanding but let us limit ourselves to this purpose," *Reforming Mind* sang and *Wise In Words* deactivated the lens.

As the gyroscopes slowed and the Saen beams ceased their glaring thunder into the clouds, the image faded.

For some time, the Excilue remained hovering around the lens rim, silently paying homage to their gods.

* * *

Seated in his Elevan Chamber study, Arhahnis glared at the image of Tius Talsaiyr on a floatscreen, transmitted from the Sphereworlds. He glanced at Moniah, who paced at the other side of the large black desk, oblivious to the muted whimpers of the miniature Oscilean, Satimins, who begged for his attention.

"Thank you for this concern, Tius. We shall see to the matter," Arhahnis said, clearing his throat and glancing at Moniah, whose eyes erupted with sparks of subdued fury.

"Haolae, brothers," Tius said, and his image on the screen faded as it folded back into its concealed location in the ceiling beams.

Arhahnis leaned back in his seat, watching Moniah pace back and forth in front of it. Finally, Moniah stopped pacing and petted the whimpering Satimins, but the steely flashes of his eyes were not abated. He was afraid he should never have surrendered his authority as system governor of Earth. Had he not, Moniah reasoned, he might have thwarted the duplicity of Ammanmus. He could excuse it all away by telling himself that Arhahnis had made the decision to revamp the government processes before coming to Earth but the hard fact was that Moniah could have taken a more proactive stance in those first days.

At least, it seemed that Arhahnis was similarly disgusted.

"I cannot accept that Ammanmus has done such a stupid thing. Without a wink to us, he creates this needless concern," Moniah said, turning away to clench his fist. Arhahnis sighed and depressed a control on the desk, "Alaysi, bring the Wizan into the Elevan chamber and inform Ammanmus he is to attend me here."

Moniah fumbled for his Ol pouch. Only a few days ago, he had enjoyed a rare state of elation at the construction site of the Council Hall, and now? Now, before he was prepared for it, he would be face to face with his Wizan comrades. Comrades? But they were strangers to him and he had spent almost no time in their company. He had been planning to visit Myzinos-Wur to see the results of the effort of his father, but his own destiny had just found its song, and before he could embark on his journey to Wizankind on his own terms he had found himself with stones hurled at his feet to make his way impassable, obstructions thrown before him by his *own brother*.

Arhahnis petted the miniature dragon nestling at his feet, which, sensing the emotional temperament of the room, had flown there to lean against his leg and tremble.

"I am partly to blame. I sent Ammanmus to Canelor with the body of Mayron some time ago and directed him to render all assistance. I wanted him to ease the path for Corina, to encourage her to remain at court," Arhahnis said, lifting Satimins to his lap.

"And Ammanmus interpreted his task at Canelor as an assignment of governorship," Moniah said, angling his body to level a firm gaze upon Arhahnis. He added, "Tius is wise to communicate this nonsense to you."

The Zymbelstern chimes above the golden doors rang and Arhahnis let Satimins touch the speaker plate on his desk.

"Enter," Arhahnis said, and the doors swung open, allowing the Wizans Rete and Vetaeos to enter. They sank to one knee with arms outstretched and bowed their heads. Moniah took in a long draught of Ol, his gaze fixed on the waist of Rete, whose high flight cloak was thrown back over his shoulders, revealing his waist sash and holster and the sheath of his Coracle wand.

"Rise, and be comfortable, Wizan brothers. There is Soffa and other refreshments on that sideboard," Arhahnis said. The Wizans bowed to

Moniah, who nodded in return, and, as they passed him, he closed his eyes and took in the scent of wind, saddle and dragon that they exuded. They were his legacy but he was not yet fully part of them.

Moniah and Arhahnis huddled over the black "Daid" desk, clouding the air with their pipe smoke, and considered the situation. Venturing to Earth and transferring some of the highest mantles of authority outside of the Sphereworlds, necessitated a division of authority. The Angelus Arhahn had dealt with this effectively by creating the mantle of "Camera Arhahn" in the person of Tius but the Camera was more than a mirror voice of Arhahnis. There was no getting around the fact that Tius' authority and influence was extraordinarily powerful. Fortunately, this was in itself not a problem for Tius Incarnate was a practitioner of the Greenrobe mystics and, therefore, a pacifist who was not swayed by Taen or Wizan interests.

"One of us must return to Auros," Arhahnis said.

Moniah shook his head with sad disgust and moved toward the stained glass window.

"Where is Kaylon?" Arhahnis asked and Moniah glanced at Rete and Vetaeos, who whispered banalities about the coffee and then stood awkwardly looking first to Moniah then Arhahnis.

"Here, at the palace."

"Summon him," Arhahnis said, and a chronometer chimed away uneasy moments. A Talldroid opened one of the brass doors to the Elevan chamber and Kaylon strode in.

"What goes on? I have just spent an hour riding a horse and my legs ache," Kaylon announced, massaging his thighs, and then noticing the grim faces of the others.

"What is it?" he asked, with a crooked smile at Moniah.

"Ammanmus seeks to limit Wizan relations with the people. Can you imagine! We are the founders here, not him or his…influences," Moniah said, his voice rising. Rete looked on silently but Vetaeos nodded, his eyes smiling at Moniah, who was too engrossed with Kaylon to note that he was inadvertently winning his way with his Wizan brethren without setting foot outside Maethus-Dia.

Arhahnis simply petted Satimins and smiled weakly, looking down at the cooing dragon in his lap.

Ammanmus entered, just in time to hear Moniah lambaste him.

"*We* did not come to Earth, brother," Ammanmus said, while Rete and Vetaeos bowed lowering their heads, and then glanced at each other with electric expressions of discomfort before rising again to enjoy the spectacle. It was a guilty pleasure for Rete and clearly fascinating for Vetaeos.

"Agh! You mingle truths but I suspect you seek to limit human study of the Wizan while, no doubt, encouraging, even *fostering* recruitment into Taen doctrines," Moniah said, loudly enough to make Arhahnis cringe and Satimins bury his face in the Arhahn's robe. Danis and Medean arrived and Arhahnis privately thanked Alaysi for his foresight in realizing they would be needed.

"Someone open a window," Danis muttered, and a Talldroid, who had arrived in response to the noise, instantly did so.

"What is the disturbance?" asked Medean, whose gentle gaze roamed over the faces of the Wizans.

"Ask him," Moniah thundered, pointing to Ammanmus, who lifted his arms and shrugged.

"Moniah's passion clouds his judgment," Ammanus said.

"His passion does not explain why you found it necessary to communicate concerns to my Camera authority without first consulting me," Arhahnis interjected, and the room fell into an instant and complete silence. Danis poured Soffa and yawned as though he were at any daily conference.

"All these arguments are the same," Danis muttered, cringing in case someone would overhear him unconsciously voice his mind.

"With all respect, Arhahnis, I addressed my concerns regarding human participation in Auran temple beliefs. I thought—apparently mistakenly so—that addressing this matter to your Camera authority might emphasize the weight of my concerns to you," Ammanmus said.

At this, Moniah turned his back and folded his arms over his chest to gaze at the cliffs and ocean.

"I see no need to create a policy or pronouncement in this matter," Medean said, and, unseen to any, Moniah smiled. Ammanmus turned to Medean.

"It is relevant to the angelus directives, which firmly command that no Auran creed be imposed on the people." Medean took a seat, accepting a cup of Soffa from Danis.

"No such imposition has occurred. Mankind is eager to delve within the tenets of our faith. I see no reason to dissuade their interest, nor hinder their efforts to understand us."

"I agree completely," Danis said, his easy smile hardening as Ammanmus glanced at him with the silent but clear suggestion that he should remove himself from the debate. Feeling his error wrapping itself tightly around him, Ammanmus spun to face Arhahnis.

"Infinite, this is oversimplification of my concerns."

"Is it? Why should we restrict the very actions that cause coexistence to prosper?" Moniah said, vehemently, turning around and stepping into the center of the room as he did so.

"In Canelor, the people walk around with swords strapped to their legs," Ammanmus shot back, over his shoulder.

"As they do here at Renthia. Thousands of Aurocearians perished during the Spherewar by more ferocious weapons than I have seen used in human warfare. Is this your reasoning to subvert our purpose?"

"Coexistence is a *process* of evolution and must be guided toward cautious advancement. Wizan is a rite of mystery. A rite most Aurans do not grasp. Must I remind *you* that the ability to manipulate elemental powers is fraught with danger? Think of the ramifications if people should become Wizan before they can fully conceive of the terrible consequences of misusing such power," Ammanmus said, passing his gaze over Rete and Vetaeos, who regarded him keenly, offering slight bows of their heads but never lowering their eyes.

"Nonsense," Danis said, chuckling. He downed his Soffa and leaned against the sideboard, pointing at Ammanmus with his cup.

"You're delaying a natural progress, leave it."

Ammanmus folded his arms in his robe sleeves and looked to Medean, who sighed with boredom.

"This counsel from our competent admiral, who vacillates between duty and entertainment." Danis crashed his cup to the sideboard and stepped to within inches of Ammanmus.

"You pompous toad," he bellowed, making the little dragon screech, Medean avert his gaze, Moniah smile, Rete cringe openly and Vetaeos cover his ears.

"Danis!" Arhahnis said, demanding silence. The Grand Ambassador and Admiral pro tem swallowed his rage and cleared his throat. He made a face as if he had just eaten something most displeasing and met the calm expression of Arhahnis, who simply whispered,

"Enough."

"I propose we institute the Observatore mantles to monitor all Auran and human interaction. That way, we proceed with coexistence without stumbling into efforts at cross-purposes to each other," Medean suggested.

Arhahnis weighed this idea. He stood and walked from behind the desk while his dragon flapped onto the desk surface and crept along as the emperor paced, afraid to be too far away from his tranquil master.

"Here is my word. For the time being, the Wizan will withdraw from public participation," Arhahnis said, moving toward Moniah, Rete and Vetaeos.

"I regret that Ammanmus is correct in his assessment of matters Wizan. Humanity is not prepared to participate in the Mysterium. Therefore, I direct that until such time as might be deemed safe—all Wizan functions will remain secure in the city of Myzinos-Wur."

"As the people say, that's a pity," Alaysi said from the doorway where he had arrived in time to gain the pith of the discussion. It was unusual for the Palace Chamberlain to align himself in open debates.

"However, Wizan Templars will always be welcome at Maethus-Dia and will remain my honor guard," Arhahnis added, pointedly, looking at Rete, who nodded, while Vetaeos winked at the stricken Moniah, who in turn glared at Ammanmus in such a way as to make the priest avert his face. Everyone waited.

Arhahnis paused to indulge in a moment of silence as he lit an Ol pipe.

"Brothers, you have succeeded in tiring me. Danis?" Arhahnis said, waving a hand.

"This council is adjourned," Danis said, indicating the doors as an invitation that everyone depart. As the Aurans took leave, Arhahnis raised his pipe.

"A moment, Ammanmus."

Moniah restrained a smile until he was well out of the Elevan Chamber and the doors closed behind him. Inside, Ammanmus turned to face Arhahnis, who slowly crossed the distance between them.

"I have allowed concession to your concerns, Ammanmus. However, two matters; first, if we are to thrive in coexistence, we must become selfless in our leadership. I direct you to meditate on this and secondly…" Arhahnis paused, moving very close to Ammanmus, his golden pupils firing like engines within the deepest liquid pools of his blue-purple eyes. Ammanmus leaned back, his head tilting further away so that his posture was made uncomfortable, but still the face of the Arhahn pushed closer to his own.

"Do not ever make the mistake of attempting to subvert my authority again," Arhahnis said, very quietly, though his words crashed and resounded into the soul of Ammanmus as if he were being subjected to Mesmer.

Ammanmus could not respond and, when Arhahnis at last turned away, the priest rubbed at the gooseflesh on his forearms and wiped away a patina of sweat from his brow. As he exited the Elevan Chamber, he was unsteady on his feet.

* * *

Moniah strolled down the staircase under the rotunda of Maethus-Dia, oblivious to the sounds of courtiers, staff and Talldroids as they filled the Great Hall and transepts with the buzz of regular afternoon activity. Several persons smiled at him and he did his best to meet their happy faces with something resembling joy, but he could not conceal his detached air of resignation.

Ammanmus had served him coldly and Moniah had fully expected Arhahnis to deal with Ammanmus harshly but the crafty prelate had emerged from the revelation of his duplicity in triumph. The Chimera clock struck three times when Moniah reached the first landing and he did chuckle while looking at the clock, which had been augmented to include organ pipes, another set of chimes, and bells, as well as several articulated figures of Oscileans.

As he descended into the Great Hall, Moniah caught sight of Vetaeos and Rete, who had just taken their leave of Alaysi. Normally, the Wizans would have found an encounter with Moniah to be somewhat uncomfortable because of the distance he maintained from his Wizan heritage but today they dipped their heads to him and smiled with respect, touching their fingers to their chests in the ancient sign of admiration.

Moniah glanced at Alaysi, who in the brief moment saw that the First Lord did not want to make small talk. The Chamberlain distracted himself with someone requesting his attention, leaving Moniah to approach the Wizans.

"We shall build another Dome temple," Moniah said, matter of factly to Rete and Vetaeos, and the two Aurans studied him with keen interest, ignoring the sounds of music and the voices around them. Rete found his voice first.

"Forgive me, Wisdom, but I do not understand?"

"My brother Ammanmus seeks to curtail our influence with the people. Well, time alone reveals the will of the people but one thing is clear, we have no restrictions against founding a *second* temple," Moniah said, with a twinkle in his famous eyes.

Vetaeos stepped close to Moniah to clasp his arm.

"True spoken, yes indeed, true spoken."

Moniah led them out of the east portico into the courtyard where he paused to regard two Oscileans being fitted with their saddle seats by

Talldroids which gleamed brightly in the summer sun.

"For three years, I've sought fulfillment of projects that I know my father would want me to see realized. I assure you, I will visit Myzinos-Wur soon. It is a place Moniah transcended loved and where his heart truly rests. Be patient with me awhile longer, brothers, and when the time comes please help me make my way. Here, give Prestant my ring to wear about his neck. It is all that I have that will help him know my heart," Moniah said, handing the ring to Vetaeos, who accepted it as though Moniah had handed him Saeonar itself.

He carefully stowed the ring in a pouch worn on his waist sash.

"I will see Prestant this night and give him your gift."

"And convey to Caras and Uletis my words. Tell them what has transpired today but, for the rest, discretion is the watchword."

"As you command, Wisdom," Vetaeos said, smiling broadly. He saluted Moniah by bowing his head, tapping his chest and stepping back two paces. Moniah watched the Wizans mount the saddles of the Oscileans and wave to him before the beasts took wing into clear, blue skies, then he turned abruptly and went back into the palace.

* * *

Kaylon waved to the people then turned to Moniah and Arhahnis. "Tius will be very pleased to have such an able assistant, Kaylon," Arhahnis said, raising his voice over the band of musicians who were playing on the dock nearby.

"Haolae, brother."

Kaylon faced Moniah and they clasped arms. Gulls screeched overhead and Kaylon squinted into the sky and then paused to examine the containers being loaded into *Auruaii*.

"Part of me leaves with you," Moniah said to Kaylon, then nodded to Alaysi, who stepped out from under a sun umbrella held by a Talldroid. The gleaming brass and platinum body of the Talldroid reflected blinding flashes of sunlight onto the scene. Alaysi handed Kaylon a small box.

"Plant a seed from Earth on Auros Prime," Moniah said, as Kaylon opened the box to find seeds in small glass containers, each labeled with words: Wild Rose, Lotus, Hibiscus, Fern, Sunflower, Oak, Willow and Pine.

Despite himself, Kaylon had to purse his lips for a moment to restrain a slight quiver of his jaw. He met the eyes of Elria, Corina, Clovis, Marina and prince Darius with his own handsome smile. His cold blue eyes glistened with moisture and that made his pupil lights flare like fireworks seen through fog.

"Now I understand what it means when you say, absence stirs the heart. I am honored you came to bid me farewell," Kaylon said. Momentarily overcome, Elria threw her arms around his neck and kissed his cheek. She drew away, blushing, and Kaylon turned to take a last look at the city and the unfinished Council Hall, looming like the carved peeks of an artificial mountain over the new central plaza. Despite the crowds, a silence prevailed while Kaylon surveyed the horse guards of Clovis. The workers and their families waved tentatively to him, while Taen priests, Greenrobes and architects watched from a distance, near the quay. Even at some remove, they could feel the emotional connection of the Seal Bearer to the people.

Although there were no Wizan present, they all having been directed by Moniah to prepare for his arrival at the mountain Keep of Myzinos-Wur, the First Lord wore his father's mantle and the Coracle diant, Saeonar, in honor of his departing aide.

The people cheered. Arhahnis stepped forward, embraced Kaylon and held him by the shoulders.

"Ertim departed without notice to anyone. But, as you see, your leave-taking is another matter."

"My heart rejoices to know I will soon behold Auros, but it is a bittersweet moment, Arhahnis." Kaylon turned quickly away and strode toward the ship. He paused, once, looked back from the forward gangway of *Auruaii* and then entered the vessel. Marina rested her head on Clovis' shoulder.

Water around the hull of the mighty vessel churned with subsonic humming. A few horses neighed and stomped their hooves in agitation at the noise. The huge ship lifted slowly at first and then its long streamlined hull pulled out of the water's suction. A moment later, and the *Auruaii* lifted several feet from the surface. Moss, barnacles and seaweed clung to its underside but, as the ship rose higher, its outer hull appeared to sizzle and all the harbor growth suddenly fell away, along with cascades of water, as electrical and sonic forces activated to free its smooth features of detritus.

The growth fell in to the water in gobs and splashes, to the delight of the gulls and terns, and the hull of the ship was now as pristine as it had been on the day of its construction. Someone further along the levee dock shouted, pointing to one of the observation blisters under the bridge domes and there, barely detectable behind the thick Blerglass, stood Kaylon, waving, his blond hair ashine, visible through the glass before filters darkened the surface of the blister.

Auruaii turned due west, its prow casting a long shadow over the plaza. From the ship's bridge, some people could be seen to crouch down instinctively. But most of the onlookers simply waved and lifted their arms as the mighty ship, which had sat for years in the waters off Renthia-Acadia, rose higher into the air.

As *Auruaii* passed over land, water continued to fall from its hull, landing upon the crowds of dignitaries and common folk, to their delight, raining cool respite from the heat of the day. The ship engines emitted a low, hypnotic pulse of humming tones that escalated into higher tone cycles as it floated over the city.

Auruaii ascended higher still and made a long slow turn to the south to pass over Maethus-Dia. The vast ship resembled a gigantic flying whale as it continued over the cliffs and the Atlantic. Then, the green whisker lights under its forward prow activated and the air sang with higher pitches, tickling the ear with subsonic resonance.

Finally, very quickly, *Auruaii* achieved its trajectory and the large engine bays of the aft section could be seen to light up in white heat. In seconds, all that remained was a long trail of white vapor rising into clear, blue skies.

* * *

Auruaii accelerated, rising quickly into blue sky. Within the ship that had transported his ancestor to Earth, Kaylon placed his hands against a blister dome, taking in the sights of Renthia-Acadia. Everyone he knew shrank into tiny dots scattered across the six-mile long port harbor docks of white marble, which gleamed in the sunlight.

At the south end of the harbor, a three hundred foot lighthouse, capped by fifty foot bronze dragons holding a lantern, beckoned explorers to a majestic capital. In the central plaza, the Council Hall he had labored on looked like a ruin from on high. The sweeping structures of the new Quasim Observatore seemed nearly complete, while an airborne fleet of Constructorbots flew in and around the Stratosin Academa, the emerging learning center placed where once the humble library and school of Medean had stood.

Kaylon chuckled at the sight of the Totem Hall, very much a ruin, since Moniah had pillaged it for Blermetal. *Auruaii* turned west; Kaylon shielded his eyes and glimpsed reflected sunlight from the dome temple at Myzinos-Wur. A smile touched the corners of his mouth.

"And your seed has taken firm root, Moniah." He ordered the ship to slow down as it traversed Maethus-Dia and then as *Auruaii* proceeded over the sea he took seat and sealed the auto doors.

"Computer, present manifest," he said, and settled back as the stratosphere of Earth evaporated into the endless night of the void. The floatscreen before him listed a sum of reports, coded pulse discs from Medean to his fellow mystics, databases, some gifts from Clovis for the museum on Auros-Prime. Aside from the artifacts, there were seventy Aurans returning besides the Captain and his crew and, Kaylon himself.

AURUAII: DATE: 022.5014.32 TERRAN YEAR: 838 AJ:

"THE CREW AND PASSENGERS WILL SOON BE GATHERING IN THE MAIN SALON FOR OL AND SOFFA, AND, NO DOUBT, TO PRESS ME FOR CONVERSATION I AM NOT OBLIGED TO OFFER. IN TWO DAYS, I WILL ORDER EVERYONE INTO HYPER-SLEEP. THIS WILL PROVIDE ME PRIVACY AND SHORTEN THE APPARENT DURATION OF THE VOYAGE. A GLANCE OUT OF THE PORTAL SHOWS ME THAT WE HAVE JUST PASSED OUT OF THE INNER SOLAR SYSTEM, TWENTY MINUTES AFTER BREAKING EARTH ORBIT. THE CAPTAIN IS ACCELERATING TO SUPRA-LIGHT SPEED AND I FEEL VERY MUCH BETWEEN WORLDS IN MORE WAYS THAN I AM PREPARED TO ARTICULATE. I HOPE TO EXPERIENCE DREAM MEMORY WHILE IN STASIS AS WELL AS TO SAVOR MY OWN BRIEF ENCOUNTER WITH MANKIND."

—KAYLON TALSAIYR, COMMANDING

* * *

"When do you suppose it will be completed?" Arhahnis asked, gazing at the Council Hall, as the shuttle soared home to Maethus-Dia.

"Probably when Tius realizes he has our ears and eyes at his side," Moniah said. Arhahnis turned away from the view to smile at Moniah, who grinned mischievously. Arhahnis signaled to Alaysi, who closed a curtain partition, sealing the forward salon from the main cabin.

Moniah rubbed his brow and whispered thanks to Arhahnis, who took a seat and quietly filled an Ol pipe.

Beyond the curtain, they could hear the muted voices of Danis, Medean, Clovis, Marina and the others, but the Arhahn and First Lord were not in the mood for company. The day had been trying, with Ammanmus refusing to attend the departure of Moniah's Seal Bearer, which in itself was simply a petty show of power but, coupled to the complex emotional situation, had added just enough of a cutting edge to what was already a sharp sword.

"Are you sure you would not care to have Elria join us?" Arhahnis teased, at which Moniah lifted his face and smiled ruefully.

"If you will attend Corina, by all means." Moniah said.

"The future holds all our keys," Arhahnis said, pouring Soffa.

"And the past, locked doors," Moniah said.

* * *

Ammanmus had not slept well, his mind troubled by a disturbing dream memory. The palace was already awake when he made his way to the ground floor state chambers. Turning a corner he stumbled into the Arhahn's little dragon and nearly lost his footing. The Oscilean screeched, then warbled nervously, backing toward a statue.

"Smoky lanterns lurking about," Ammanmus muttered and little Satimins eyed the High Taen, who was fussing with his robe. The creature saw a fire in the eyes of the priest and, having heard his comment, Satimins promptly ejected a puff of smoke in comment. Taken aback, Ammanmus retreated, waving away the smoke.

* * *

In the temple courtyard near the north gate of the palace, Arhahnis watched the wind flutter in the trees; spring showers were on the way. He gazed at the swaying treetops, watching the wind caress branches and leaves. A guard coughed discreetly and Arhahnis swung around to see Corina approaching him with her retinue.

"I have bid my farewell to Clovis, Infinite," she said, while a Satar shuttle landed nearby. Arhahnis took her hand in his, walking slowly with her onto the grass. He paused, searching her face with his own unfathomable orbs.

"Are you certain you will not remain with us a while longer? Your visit has been brief."

She regarded Arhahnis with a gentle ease, though her soft features were troubled by a hint of weariness. Her lips parted…

"Attention!" A Wizan Templar cried to the guards, startling Corina. Talldroids were already loading her baggage into the shuttle. Corina paused to take a last look at the line of petitioners waiting their turn to address Arhahnis. Three times a week, while Clovis held council within, the Auran emperor patiently made himself available to the people, personally receiving their concerns. Corina returned her attention to Arhahnis, who regarded her with a bemused expression.

"I confess my heart longs to remain, Infinite. However, I would be remiss to ignore my duties at Canelor. I must return," she said, quietly, her eyes watering.

Arhahnis' strong hands took hers into their warm grip.

"I am always Arhahnis to you, my lady, please, no titles between us."

"Yes, thank you."

"Come, let me walk you to the ship; you're not afraid." He insisted gently.

A cool breeze heavy with the scent of rain blew a strand of hair from her diadem into her face and she brushed it aside.

"You have removed fear from my heart, remember?" They laughed.

Arhahnis glanced at the ship and purposefully addressed the Auran pilot who stood in the hatchway.

"You will see to it that Queen Corina is safely home." The Auran bowed his head immediately.

"Of course, Infinite."

"This is not the first time I have taken my leave of you…of Maethus-Dia," Corina said to Arhahnis. She studied the palace as though it was a good friend. She added, "I could not find his grace, Ammanmus. Pray thee kindly thank him for me, for all Canelor."

Arhahnis steadied her hand while she stepped into the shuttle.

"Return to me, Corina, and let us not allow years to pass between visits, though I have many in which to await you."

Corina glanced inside the shuttle, her body quivered.

"Mayron was a practical mind, he said never to mourn the dead for they live," she said. Arhahnis kissed her hand, which stunned her women, who hurried into the ship. The shuttle engines hummed to life.

"You are a lifetime from death, Corina, and you will return, *to_me*."

Corina pursed her lips and waved one trembling hand, and then she was gone. The shuttle lifted from the grass and gently arced to the west. Arhahnis watched the sleek silver form of the Satarship until it veered safely out of reach of purpling cumulus clouds. Then he approached his outdoor throne, a simple but substantial device. Before he could take seat on it, though, a man groped his way through the crowd. He was middle-aged but world weary, with deep-set eyes, his frame pitifully thin.

"Infi…" the beggar croaked, nearly collapsing. Arhahnis caught the man in his arms.

"I hail from from Valce, famine is set upon us, great one," the beggar muttered between gasps for air.

"Guard. Take this man inside. See he wants for nothing," Arhahnis commanded, helping the man into the powerful arms of a Templar Wizan.

"I-in-there?" the beggar coughed, his eyes blinking in wonder while he was helped to the palace where a Taen hurried to meet both he and the Templar. Arhahnis took seat on his throne. A sea of smiling faces craned to make eye contact with him and subdued phrases drifted to Arhahnis from the throng.

"Such kindness."

"A heart of gold has he."

Arhahnis waved the first petitioner forward; there was still a great deal to accomplish in the day.

* * *

While the spring storm held off, raising thunderheads over the mountains, Moniah and Elria emerged from the south gate.

"Poor Arhahnis, finally he can enjoy some part of the day," Elria observed, indicating the emperor, who was ambling alone on the mall green, amidst buzzing bees and dragonflies. The little dragon, Satimins, flapped around him, warbling for attention.

"Three hours of petitioners is enough for any day," Moniah agreed and they both turned to watch a Satarship arrive, and settle down just outside the forest edge.

"How long shall you be in Valce?" Elria asked, swallowing nervous tension that she attempted to conceal by placing her fingers on the lower cheeks of her face, though the gesture only served to draw attention to her discomfort.

Moniah glanced into the distance then smiled at her.

"I cannot be certain. Caras and Vetaeos assure me that the Constructorbots are making good time in building our new dome temple. But I know nothing of the King there. Time is needed to make proper acquaintance of him."

"King Indulth is not a fellow at ease with the world. I met him many years ago but only for a short time."

Moniah studied her. Grey streaks threaded her long braids and small lines the people called "crow's feet" heralded her undisclosed but well-advanced age. She wore the Green robe well. A simple collar of Ol leaf was her unique and elegant touch.

"My work here is nearly done," Elria said.

"Medean has a great mind in his ranks with you, Elria," Moniah observed, casually, but she hesitated, still uncomfortable in discussing her new life style as a Greenrobe. Moniah was proud of her. She and the resourceful Medean had truly thrown a gauntlet into the face of Ammanmus with her conversion into the Mystic Council.

Moniah realized that some small part of her had converted in support of him, or at least of Moniah transcended.

"Has the synod ratified the clock meetings?"

Elria's face lit up, her back straightened.

"They *insisted* upon it! The right of representatives to come before the court is unprecedented. We never enjoyed such freedoms, in the old ways." Her mood darkened and Elria glanced at Maethus-Dia, as though it were the embodiment of treasured memories.

"There is no need to leave the palace, Elria," Moniah said, quietly.

She studied him, heart fighting against hope.

"I am a partial memory to you, painful at that, for I realize how much you loved Moniah trans—I mean, my father. We are friends, Elria. I want you to make Maethus-Dia your home."

"My lord, you are kind to me," Elria said, her eyes brimming with tears. She added, "There is nothing for me at Renthia. The temple of Diana is a dusty relic now. The end of the worship of Diana comes more quickly than anyone expected."

"I am sorry to hear that," Moniah said, his cheeks flexing and his silver pupils flashing like stars in blue seas, but he tried to lighten the moment.

"I suspect much of the dust lavished on your temple is due to construction of the Council Hall."

"Mayhaps, but the heart of the temple is empty as well."

"Even more troubling."

"Why?"

"An end of tradition in this form disturbs me," Moniah replied, cryptically.

She knew him well enough not to press the matter.

"Forgive my inquisitiveness; it is more than enough you express such tender concern."

Moniah looked at her deeply. Did he see in her a hope of love, and a promise far greater in personal terms than for coexistence?

"Sometimes I feel as though I am but a sleepwalker," Elria confessed.

Moniah smiled taking her hands in his as he had seen Arhahnis do with Corina.

"Then, sleep walk with me," he said.

* * *

On the ramparts, Medean had just adjourned his daily class. He watched Moniah and the Wizans board a shuttle. Elria waved to him.

"A day for farewells, I wonder…" Medean said as young prince Darius approached his teacher.

"Lord Medean?"

"Hmm?" The Auran purred, his focus still upon Elria, who was watching Moniah's shuttle depart.

"Why did Aurocearians come to Earth?" the prince asked.

Medean turned to look at the young man, who was biting his lip. The prince dropped a book, bent to pick it up and waited, brow furrowed, his attention centered upon Medean with the singular concentration only human children can achieve. Medean glanced at Elria and, as he watched, she turned to the palace and strode toward it. Even from the height of the rampart, Medean could see her radiant smile.

"For love," he answered Darius.

* * *

Moniah entered the dome temple of Myzinos-Wur which his father had built; this time with bags in hand. He had visited the mountain temple only briefly on a previous occasion, and had been glad to leave when the pressure it induced on his lack of Wizan skills became too great to endure. Now, he would linger, to feel the presence of Moniah transcended, to gain through osmosis that part of his Wizan self which he felt within his heart but had, until now, never had the time to explore.

He stood in the grand gallery under the dome itself, his nostrils flaring at the scent of the incense Caras created by mixing Ol and Jasmine. Moniah took in the ambiance: a curving flight of stairs hugged one side of the dome, hugging a wall and rising to the gallery that encircled the inner dome. At the center of which, a portcullis revealed the sky from which dusty beams of sun shone into the gray stone and marble interior.

Bird song echoed down from the galleries that connected to the outer dome and a tender breeze carried a few leaves to flitter down and bring in a hint of wildflower scent that commingled with the incense.

The central fire pit was cold and appeared to have been used sparingly. Moniah felt the hand of Vetaeos brush against his own as the Wizan took his bags. As he continued to scrutinize the temple, taking in the large circular room and the ancillary corridors branching from it, Moniah realized that the temple seemed too large for the four Wizans who waited patiently on his pleasure.

A welling of emotion seized Moniah and, before he could control it, his eyes brimmed with tears and he gasped a sob that could not be denied. A deafening silence followed while Moniah wiped his eyes with the back of one hand and his other clenched into a fist. Somewhere above, a bird sang sweetly. Uletis stepped forward with a glass of tea.

"The birds are wont to take to the galleries while the Oscileans are in the Keep," he said. Moniah sipped the tea and smiled at the Wizan while Caras and Rete busied themselves with polite chatter, discussing what to eat and similar banalities.

Vetaeos took up Moniah's bags and nodded toward one of the corridors.

"Wisdom, will you see the master suite now?"

"Yes, my friend."

They proceeded down a corridor and into a covered crosswalk, open to the sky that bridged the temple to the Keep and the living quarters. Moniah paused to refresh his tear-stained face and take in the vista overlooking mountains. He gazed serenely upon a verdant valley and beyond that, to the northeast, a breathtaking view of the lowlands where tiny streams of smoke from a thousand hearths marked the city of Renthia-Acadia.

A cold wind was picking up and the mountains were alternately bathed in bright light and dulled by passing shadows from thunderheads gathering overhead.

In the Keep structure, they proceeded directly to a set of doors at the top of the building adjoining the crosswalk. Vetaeos opened the doors and stepped inside. Moniah followed him into a long room of the same gray marble and smooth stone that he saw everywhere. There was a large fireplace on the north wall and windows facing east and west. A huge table with a dust-laden Blermetal box, pulse discs and papers, occupied the center of the chamber. Thick carpets covered most of the stone floor and there were a large glow orb chandelier and wall sconces decorated to look like Ol leaves and flowers. A skylight over the desk table let the room be soaked with light on clearer days.

Adjoining the larger chamber through the south wall was a large bedroom, which contained a splendid sunken tub filled by a waterfall-like spout, situated high enough to act as a shower as well. Moniah glanced around for signs of any personal effects of his father's, but the room was relatively bare, save for candles on a bedside table and a dusty chair. Evidently, Moniah transcended had scarcely had the time to leave his mark.

Moniah sighed and walked back into the large chamber with Vetaeos at his heels. Thunder rumbled over the mountain.

"Vetaeos, I will take the night alone."

But the night did not take to Moniah. He tossed fitfully in sleep where his dream memory presented a frightful nightmare of an Auran face leering in triumphant madness. The Auran lifted a magnificent glowing blue orb. Moniah could hear it sing, see its pulsing energy reflecting blue light into the face of the mad Auran with ivory hair and black eyes.

A terrible noise ensued, like the scream of heaven. Suddenly, the mad Auran punched frantically at a control belt he wore. A kind of black translucent field began to surround the Auran, whose hair was blowing in wind generated from the orb. Nanobots, appearing as a maelstrom of glittering snow, careened out of the control belt, solidifying into the translucent field, which quickly became midnight black.

An echoing roar of defiance…

Moniah sat bolt upright in his bed. He swallowed and fumbled for a pitcher of water, spilling it as he drank, gasping, "Enough, enough, but a dream. Just a dream." He stood and moved to a window, part of his mind still trapped and depressed in the terrible images of the nightmare. Outside, heavy clouds darkened the morning and pine, maple and oak tree branches swayed in a strong wind accompanied by spitting rain.

* * *

The giant orange star the Selosians called "Efu", settled into a horizon of dunes and dwarf trees that were twisted into severe angles from prolonged exposure to the winds of planet Selos. High above, clouds in the silver-tinted firmament glowed in a deep umbra of red and orange that raked across the stratosphere and kissed the boundary of the outer darkness of space.

Night was falling on Selos. Efu sank lower beyond scrub hills and dunes, casting a phosphorescent sheen upon the sands, transforming the swamp grasses outside the city into orange-tipped spears swaying with the coming sirocco.

The prism of Annevnos hovered over sands vibrating from the sonic pulses it emanated. The prism itself was entirely black in its normal state of impenetrable sheen, which appeared, on closer inspection, to be an oily film. The longer one examined it, the more unfathomable the prism surface became, as though to stare at it was to seek entry into a terrible abyss.

No one ventured too close to the prism, or the god it contained, for it was known that the dweller within did not suffer intrusion while it contemplated the star and communed with the outer realms.

Inside his traveling lair, entity Annevnos was completely still. The tentacles of its lower body where once had been legs and feet, were in repose, cushioning the distorted trunk of its body, which heaved in slow rhythms of wheezing breath. One scale-encrusted hand massaged the central neck while the other clenched and unclenched in a fist.

The central head of the hydras, larger than the rest, stared directly ahead through an opaque window of the prism, which revealed a view of the setting star, Efu. Another of the heads, the manifestation of Lust, lay asleep, its hydra neck curled like a snake ready to strike while its fearsome unconscious face quivered, revealing sharp teeth, and the weary, sunken eyelids twitched.

The head of Anger reposed directly atop the central mind, its mouth agape, mumbling almost silently through raspy teeth, its bloodshot eyes with their red pupils flashing repeatedly but the central head remained with its gaze fixed on the spectacular sunset. Still retaining the long white hair and features of the mortal Annevnos, the core intellect of the central head stared longingly at the sunset that, for an instant, as it dipped below the horizon, appeared as a fine sphere.

Acid tears fell from the black eyes, awash in silver pupils, and the lips muttered…

"Auros."

With a flick of his finger, Annevnos turned the side of the prism facing the sunset into a magnified and unobstructed view. Now, rich orange light flooded the interior and Anger lifted its head from atop the core intellect of Annevnos and, using its snake-like neck, slithered toward one ear of Annevnos, where it whispered incessantly.

Lust awoke and blinked in the orange glare; it averted its face, coiled its neck to cover the head, and snored. Fury darted about like a reptile seeking escape, its head struck a side of the prism and its mouth spit curses until the right arm snapped out and slapped it into stunned silence. Greed simply stared at the light, drooling, while Lust joined Anger to whisper horrible nothings into the opposite ear of the Annevnos head.

Envy sulked, its head lying across the twisted lap, eyes darting from one manifestation to the next.

The central Annevnos head hissed, driving Anger and Lust from its earshot. The two manifestations perked up like horned antenna and waited while Annevnos absorbed more of the energy of Efu.

Annevnos had been born of the Gods' energy that radiated in every star. He had lived to become the master of the greatest star in the universe, the sphere of Aurocearia. Though the Gods had tried to call him back to the Godsrealm, he had fought their summons, refusing judgment in his battle to transform into their equal. Now, he was a divided creature, forged into his prism formed with irony, from the boundless power of heaven, into a realm of captivity.

All stars sing their energy into the void as engines of the Gods and, through that power and union with space, faint though it was as it traveled on solar winds, Annevnos could trace a delicate path to the world where his polar opposite dwelt, where the signature of Arhahnis resided.

Efu bathed the outer prism with its solar power while, within, Annevnos unified his mind to the special ability he never let go of, which permitted him to feel, to see and to hear the exquisite articulation of the energy inherent in space. His mind fashioned spores that erupted on the outer surface of the prism, like blisters.

The spores, resembling oval seedpods, burst into being on the prism exterior resembling oval seedpods. Fed by solar power, the spores grew steadily and quickly. Annevnos held them fast to the prism, to husband their power, coating them with electro-magnetic energy. While the central mind concentrated in this endeavor of creation, its eyes closed and its lips tightened into a craggy line. Only the hands gave hint to its mental machinations as they moved slowly about like a conductor directing a Largo, functioning as unconscious extensions of the creating mind at work.

Greed closed its eyes and lowered its face toward the lips of the central mind. It listened and the lips began to mutter. The greenish orbs and red pupil lights of Greed's face flickered and the ruined lines around the small ugly mouth began to chuckle with a ferocious interpretation of joy.

Suddenly, Greed laughed with a staccato cackle, attracting the attention of the other heads, which slithered and undulated toward it. Greed spoke to them quietly for the central mind was still locked in creation.

While Greed explained the plan of the master, the outer surface of the prism continued to break out in a rash of spore bumps and, as the star Efu set, the wind came on carrying the gasping, careening laughter of the other manifestations across the night.

When dawn came and the silver-coated sand storms of the night abated, the planet of Selos entered its brief season of spring. The Selosians seized the opportunity to emerge from their fortress structures. The prism god called them to the swamp mire and dunes outside the city with a constant humming tone that swelled and lowered in volume, alternating between major and minor tones.

The prism soared in the lower atmosphere, descending rapidly while revolving periodically to allow each face of the outer surface sections to bathe in the glow of Efu. Within it, Annevnos studied the landscape below, where the tall silver-skinned humanoid Selosians were gathering to his call.

The pitiful giants, whose adults stood seven to eight measures, were certain to invest devoted and committed loyalty to any power they conceived greater than their own limited experience, making them perfect candidates for subjugation to Annevnos' purposes.

Toward this end, Annevnos conceived the idea of presenting himself as an incarnation of their warrior god, to appeal to their vainglory and compel their barbaric minds to worship him. However, actually realizing this plan, as well as fueling his other concepts, required that the prism regularly ascend to orbit the planet, to collect unfettered solar radiation so that Annevnos could store visible spectrums of light to project images.

Other than during an eclipse of its one large moon and lit by its vast star, the planet Selos rarely knew total darkness except during the seasons of sirocco in the spring that brought howling winds and storms that dulled the day and, when raging into the night, obliterated even the stars.

But now it was the season of the midnight sun, and the tall beings, their skins permanently stained by silver pigment blown by unceasing winds—emerged from their city, called Kalladrios, to commune with the golden god who had returned from ancient myth to sing to them within its sacred prism…

The Selosians waited for the appearance of the prism. Its voice grew louder while men and women huddled in groups all wearing chain-mail face guards, or sat upon boulders. The chief warlord removed his face chain to scan a crimson horizon for any sign of the glowing, tapered column of the prism. He wiped sand from his thick black eyebrows and rubbed one enormous knuckle against his lantern jaw while nearby oblivious children chased beetles the size of melons.

The beetles flew about in soaring leaps, their wings buzzing, before landing to burrow into the sand, attempting escape.

"Vaaraogee!" A profundo voice bellowed and the warlord turned to follow the cloaked figure nearby, who pointed to the east. The Selosians squinted their black eyes to peer into the horizon. Emerging from storm clouds, absorbing lightning strikes as it descended, came the prism, its song echoing from the city walls and the very boulders and stones around the Selosians.

The prism approached rapidly. Around the perimeter of its unfathomable black surface, a hot yellow glare outlined its form while it settled down to hover over sand pulsing from the prism's sonic energy.

The prism became translucent, revealing an image of a tall, muscular Selosian whose golden skin and armor glowed so brightly that the Selosians had to shield their eyes from the apparition.

"Beautiful ones, my children, come unto me," the voice of Annevnos boomed. The Selosians were athletic and powerful by nature, forged by their extreme environment, and Annevnos saw in them a trusting innocence, despite the brutal reality of their world.

He would win them politically by answering the base needs of their struggles, thereby bending their social will. He would win them spiritually by captivating them with demonstrations of power they could not imagine and what few resisted this hypnosis would be converted to blind obedience via the nanospores he emitted.

While children crept closer and adults stared longingly at the prism god, the giant orange star bathed planet Selos with its strange light.

Later, in the city of Kalaadrios, warriors of the Chaffra council assembled to receive the prism god, who deigned to enter the city temple.

Ancient stone statues lined the oval circumference of the interior, surrounded by walls covered in beaten silver, decorated with images depicting a collection of battle scenes. Dirty Selosian children, wearing animal pelts and silver jewelry—played at the rear of the hall on a grimy stone floor, staging their fantasies.

At the front of the temple, a single black pit, like the maw of hell's mouth, emitted a constant moan of wind. Behind this, statues of "Res" and "Ser", the twin Selosian gods of fertility, loomed over the pit, surveying the temple with dull ecstatic silver eyes, their stone and silver-plated limbs locked in conjugal fervor.

Warriors approached the pit carrying dead animals. They turned to face the other Chaffra warlords, lifting the animals into the air. Three Selosian women stepped out of the crowd, chanting, "Nakshl! Nakshl!" and suddenly the warriors and women tore at the dead animals, rending them into pieces with their bare hands.

The women tore their garments and spread the blood of the animals onto the arms and chests of the warriors and, while everyone knelt before the pit, the warriors set the mutilated animal carcasses near its edge, while the crowd chanted, "Annevnos, Annevnos."

Vile yellow light pulsed up from the pit's howling abyss, from which the prism arose to hover, pulsing sound and light. The midnight surfaces of the prism faded into translucence, revealing the golden-lit false image of Annevnos as the Selosian warrior god.

"My children, through me, you are become great and ever powerful. Only I will lead you to untold realms in glory. Have I not proven my love for you? Have I not shown you how to increase your crops by lighting the caves?" the echoing melodious voice said, washing the Selosians with Mesmer.

"We love you, we serve you," The crowd chanted.

"Secrets of the universe shall be made to serve you and wonders you have not conceived will manifest through my will," Annevnos said, each word pulsing yellow Mesmer light and sonic waves upon the crowd.

"Beyond the dome of my realm in the stars, lives a race, hateful to me, of false gods who are vengeful and full of deceit. They are devoid of my light. In time they shall fall to their knees under thy yoke." The Selosians swayed in Annevnos' power. Gradually the Mesmer plasma abated.

"Bring the chosen unto me," Annevnos commanded, and two terrified young lovers, one male and the other female, were dragged toward the pit. Annevnos raised his arms and a web of yellow light shot forth from the prism. The web light seized the youths, lifting them into the air. Too horrified to scream, they held each other tightly.

"Receive these supplicants, mighty Annevnos, for thy lust," the chief warrior said, with a quavering voice, and the once star-crossed youths screamed in terror while the web light issued from the master of cosmic nightmares, lowered them into the pit. Their voices fell away until only dull screams echoed distantly.

Inside the prism, Lust preened and drove its face against the prism. It licked its lips and chuckled, drooling acid spittle.

"This pleases me, my children. Now, receive my will," Annevnos said, and a rain of spores flew off the prism, showering upon the Selosians.

The machine bacilli spores sank into the flesh of the Selosians, who fell to the floor in ecstasy as the spores triggered pleasure centers in their brains, simultaneously implanting instructions for a later time.

* * *

"It is going splendidly," Moniah said, and he patted Vetaeos on the shoulder. Vetaeos smiled warmly. The two had become close friends during the difficult first days at Myzinos-Wur. Moniah paced the courtyard of the new Dome Temple. The site of the new temple was on a rise atop a wide valley of the Allegheny mountain chain, two hundred miles north and three hundred miles due east of the more remote Myzinos-Wur. The view afforded an unobstructed view of the lowlands and the basin of Renthia-Acadia.

"Not as inaccessible as Myzinos-Wur," Vetaeos agreed, shielding his eyes from the sun to observe a group of Wizans planting seedlings in terraced gardens below the outer forecourt.

"What are they about now, more plantings?" Moniah asked, pulling his hair into a ponytail.

"Caras is seeding corn, and, look there. Can you believe that is Rete putting in wheat?"

Moniah chuckled and squinted into the distance. Vetaeos handed him binoculars and, peering through them, Moniah could see Uletis further down the slope near the river delta, cursing at a Constructorbot.

"Poor Uletis," he said, handing the binoculars back to Vetaeos, who studied the scene.

"Yes, he appears to be making a hash of putting in a hybrid of rice we've determined can thrive here. The locals have a hard going of it in winter and, of course, their farming techniques are wasteful. This should help," Vetaeos explained.

"I had not realized how adept the Wizan are as farmers and tenders of nature, though it doesn't surprise me. My knowledge increases, thanks to you, my friend," Moniah said. He turned fully around once, slowly, taking in the scene. Sunlight shone from the mosaic-covered dome and reflected from a squad of airborne Constructorbots which resembled giant pearls floating about the site, their green and red laser torches sealing mortar, welding and lasering into the marble intricate designs.

Moniah and his new friends had conceived.

"I feel the name. We will call this temple, Oazerum," Moniah said, raising an eyebrow to Vetaeos, who nodded and smiled.

"The second canticle; a fitting name, Moniah."

"Lord Moniah! Look to the eastern slope." A Templar cried out from the ground floor forecourt. Moniah and Vetaeos moved closer to the oval railing. A few miles below, they could see a steady stream of men on horseback were winding their way up a trail that would lead them directly to the temple.

"King Indulth?" Vetaeos said.

"Time to meet the neighbors," Moniah said, nonchalantly.

While Moniah, Vetaeos and a guard of Templars strode down the path to meet King Indulth, the First Lord experienced a profound sense of Deja-Vu, for, in fact, he was following very closely in the path of Moniah transcended, in founding a Dome Temple and braving encounters with primitive strangers to establish mutual accord.

On the roof, Prestant was taking the sun atop the new Keep, lying still, and resembling an enormous gargoyle. From his vantage point, he could see Moniah and the others walking toward the horde of men, whose horses were sniffing and chortling. Prestant lifted his head to shake the insects away from his long gray whiskers.

The giant Oscilean angled his massive head to the right, where Wholestep sat with her wings extended to her sides, snoring.

"Moniah is brave…and sings as his father. Send our son down to him…time to help," Prestant sang to Wholestep, who lifted her head and blinked lazily in the sun.

"Viola-Sorda…too young," she sang back.

"His wings…fly true…send him," the Oscilean grumbled.

"What? Aye the sounds?" Wholestep sang, impatiently.

"Horses…smell us," Prestant sighed and Wholestep lifted her head to sing into the air.

The horse column stopped. Moniah smiled and waved broadly. He was far from an impressive sight. His tunic marked by sweat, and his boots, still muddy from the morning.

"Haolae, in our language this is a greeting," he announced cheerfully, electing not to confuse the caravan by telling them it could also mean "farewell". A huge man dismounted and swaggered toward Moniah. He was a great brute in appearance, with a large head and beard and his hands looked as though they could seize a tree trunk. Behind him, men pointed to the Dome Temple.

"There, my leige, the metal balls are aflight on unseen wings." one of them called out. Vetaeos turned around casually, seeing two Constructorbots lasering stone on the dome itself.

"Robot shock," Vetaeos whispered to Moniah, who nodded, keeping his eyes fixed on the huge man, obviously King Indulth himself, who was now only a few feet away.

At that moment, Viola-Sorda arced down to the trail road. There was a heart-stopping moment as several men cried out in fear. A few dismounted and ran for the tree line. The young Oscilean landed near Moniah with a thump that lifted dust into the air.

"I come…upon Prestant's command. How to help?" it sang to Vetaeos but, before he could answer, Moniah whispered a command for silence and sang gently, "When the time is right, let the human meet you."

Vetaeos grinned at Moniah and the First Lord smiled. King Indulth leaned forward, hesitantly, his beady, alert eyes studying the Aurans and Viola-Sorda.

"You can understand the Oscilean song most clearly, lord." Vetaeos muttered with glee.

"I can. No need to translate for me," Moniah said, and a tear glimmered in his eyes. He leaned close to Vetaeos, whispering thanks.

"We hear tell you are a great ruler, Mo-neye-ah, wonders of Acadia are told the land over," King Indulth said, and Moniah put a finger to his ear to press his translator device.

"Your majesty, my brother, the great Arhahn, is ruler of my people. We have come to your lands, to share knowledge and to make peaceful accord with all peoples," Moniah replied.

King Indulth absorbed the words of the Auran prince, while his eyes remained fixed on Viola-Sorda.

"You could lay me low as you did Varrick," Indulth suggested, angling his head, testing Moniah's truth.

"Varrick died at the hands of his general, but, know this, we have not come to make war, only to live together, in peace. You shall be welcome here for trade and in hardship—all your people," Moniah said, stepping closer. Of course, Indulth suddenly leaned very far forward, his mouth fell agape as he studied the eyes of Moniah with utter fascination.

"What of the dragons?" Indulth asked, clearing his throat, his tone sheepish.

"The dragons are not the demons of your myth but beloved intelligent creatures. In time, you will see this is true. Let me prove it. Come forward and meet this dragon, who is called, Viola-Sorda," Moniah said, inviting Indulth and gesturing to the Oscilean.

King Indulth stepped forward to within a few inches of the dragon, which gently sniffed at the King's beard. The air tickled Indulth's nose and he chuckled but, still on his guard, held his ground, though he swayed backward, eyeing Moniah for reassurance. The First Lord smiled.

The King swallowed, twitched his heroic mustache and reached out to pet the dragon's head. Viola-Sorda took in the scent of the king. Fear, sweat, the horse smell and red wine created a patina around the most singular aura—confusion.

Patiently Viola-Sorda waited while the smelly human examined him. There was a marvelous clump of the honeysuckle flowers not thirty yards away and Viola-Sorda longed to end this diplomatic ordeal so that he might rub his nose in the wonderful Earthian flowers, to lick out the subtle sweetness they contained.

The Aurans and humans seemed poised in indecision, so Viola-Sorda decided to charm the human. Impulsively, he licked Indulth's face, and refrained from grumbling despite the sour and unwashed aftertaste that was his reward for licking a human.

Indulth laughed as the sandy tongue rubbed his face and neck. He turned to his men and, with an air of bravado, stroked the dragon's neck. The men cheered and moved closer while Indulth achieved a posture he imagined would be historically significant, one hand on his hip, chest puffed out.

* * *

By nightfall, Indulth's men were encamped near the Dome Temple and, when he was certain all was well, Moniah visited Prestant in the watch Keep. The old dragon lazily chewed alfalfa and hay.

"Is that to your liking, my friend?" Moniah sang to the dragon.

"Could be…with berries," Prestant sang. Moniah sat on a barrel.

"I will see to it that you have berries."

Prestant lifted his head.

"Good enough for horses…good enough for one as old as I. All foods…the same in the end," he sang. Moniah chuckled and lit an Ol pipe.

"You sing…as Wizan now," Prestant purred.

"Yes, thanks to you, old one, and my teacher, Vetaeos."

Prestant grumbled. His immense torso lifted to a half-seated posture, the dragon's long neck slowly extended toward Moniah, who fixed his attention into the eyes of his father's familiar.

"Heed a hurting song…away in the void," Prestant sang in a death like-rattle, in a tone that shook through Moniah's core.

* * *

Though his remorse was dulled by the grapes of the gods, bottled by his father, in Moniah's heart beat a steely resolve as he ruminated at his desk in his quarters at Oazerum, waiting for the floatscreen to connect him with Maethus-Dia. However, the wine succeeded in mellowing his body and Moniah kicked off his boots and pushed himself further away to set his feet on the corner of the desk.

He sipped from a glass King Indulth insisted that he drink, the hulk of a human guffawing as he slapped Moniah on the neck. The steady pulse of the twinkle in Moniah's eyes exploded in quiet but flashing rage at the hard crush of Indulth's heavy hand. Moniah whirled around, withering rays of his glare scorching Indulth, who grunted in pain, covering his face with an elbow while moaning.

In an instant he would never forget, Indulth saw the power of dawn light in the face of the First Lord.

Moniah stood and patted Indulth on the back and saw that he was calmed down before Vetaeos had him escorted from the private chambers. Moniah smiled from ear to ear, not in a leering stupor but with the warm hum of his loving heart, at peace in hard fought triumph.

The First Lord was at last at ease, empowered and *free.* Moniah returned to his desk and plopped his feet upon it awaiting the bowshot signal to engage.

What had been the prison of Wizan, the singular inheritance of his past, was now transforming within him to reveal a new threshold of sounds and senses, of language and perceptions, as though he stood on the brink of the rest of his days and could perceive what path to take and how to articulate his life.

"Connection established. Codex secure," the floatscreen announced, and its blue screen transformed into the face of Arhahnis, who cocked his head, for the image transmitted to him was of the soles of Moniah's feet!

"We trust you are in health, brother?" Arhahnis said. Moniah chuckled and moved his feet to the floor, his smile turning to an expression of longing and curiosity while he studied the face of Arhahnis.

He leaned closer to the screen, suddenly aware that he genuinely missed the company of his strange and all-powerful brother.

"Matters here at Oazerum are at peace between Wizan and King Indulth."

Arhahnis smiled and the image of his face shifted to reveal a wider angle of vision. Now, Moniah could see Medean and Danis standing next to the Daid desk with Arhahnis seated behind it. Danis waved and Medean bowed his head with more than a courtesy dip…did he know?

"Moniah transcended won the king of the south and Moniah incarnate has done the same in the north. Each of you have made for Wizan a foothold and I see in you an image of my dream memory, of the powerful Moniah transcended who created Wizan," Medean said.

He knew.

"You are a changed Auran, Moniah. Your skin is kissed by the sun and the power of wind and trees is in your frame," Danis said, running a finger over the Wizan Skren he wore, in honor of the Mysterium, on his shoulder mantle. It was a silent but potent sign of respect for Moniah.

Moniah lifted his face so the up glow of the screen light outlined his expression in dramatic shadow.

"Then I can challenge you to three falls," Moniah teased. Danis flexed his right arm, ripping his robe sleeve.

"That will be welcome, as none can stand with me here."

"This is not a Templar arena," Arhahnis interjected, raising one hand with his palm facing out.

Moniah hiccupped, doing his best to conceal it while blurting, "Templars? I will send a cadre to the palace, Arhahnis. We have no need of them here."

Arhahnis demurred.

"Keep *half* the cadre."

"Renthia is calm but you have few Maetie guard. I am, on the other hand, safe on unassailable crags, but you are in sight of preying brigands.

You should have more protection."

"Are you in the wine, Moniah?" Arhahnis said, with one orange and red-haired eyebrow cocked like a feather over his purple gem-like eyes, which glistened with amusement.

"He means we are vulnerable," Danis said.

"Danis, sometimes your pith is sad for such a mind," Alaysi sang out, but shut his yap at signal from Arhahnis, whose miniature dragon even hissed at the Chamberlain.

"I mean, I see Renthia spread out like a carpet. Yes, Danis, thank you. That is precisely what I meant and yes, Arhahnis, I am in the wine," Moniah said.

"As you wish."

"When do you return? There is a lady you know well who pines for you as do we, though with less the fervor." Arhahnis said with, was it a begging tone?

Moniah scrutinized Medean, who simply folded his arms, while Danis consulted a sheaf of papers, then set them down and smiled at Moniah. Arhahnis revealed a slight trace of anxiety by the movement of his hands, one of which tapped the desk surface. They needed him.

"How goes my Council Hall? I see floatscreen images and progress seems to continue but I wonder if the Architect is ambitious enough," said Moniah, folding his arms on his desk.

Arhahnis looked to Medean and the mystic shrugged.

"It is such a large endeavor that it is difficult for us to discern daily progress. But, on the whole, the building is magnificent and will stand the test of time when it is realized."

"I'll soon see it done," Moniah said.

Danis clicked his fingers and tapped his forehead.

"I almost forgot, expect a shuttle with the supplies you requested."

There was a knock at Moniah's door.

"Shall we send Elria as well?" Arhahnis asked. Moniah paused.

"With the baggage? No. I am of my mind in other pursuits here as you are aware. Leave her to me and impart my concern and best wishes to her and my hope of seeing her soon." Arhahnis smiled, with a twinkle in his eye and the interlink terminated.

"Enter Vetaeos," Moniah said and turned slowly in his chair to face the large oval room. The doors opened and Vetaeos entered. He paused and clapped slowly, purposefully.

"Well done, Wisdom, you know my footfall."

"It is the canticle of awareness and the sense of your presence. Come in, friend, I've just spoken with Himself and my brothers; you are not intruding. Where is Indulth?"

"The king has fallen into slumber," Vetaeos said, while crossing the room to reach a set of doors opening to a balcony overlooking the mountains. A storm was brewing and the cold wind of the oncoming rain already swirled on the balcony and caused a billowing of the heavy curtains. Vetaeos reached to close the doors.

"Leave it, we've no fear of the weather," Moniah said, lighting his Ol pipe. Vetaeos smiled. He took a seat near Moniah and accepted the pipe. There came another knock.

"That will be Uletis. Shall I…?" Vetaeos said, and Moniah cut the air with one hand. He closed his eyes and extended his hand then grunted while slicing his hand downward and, twenty feet away, the door latch jerked, but did not open. Eyes closed to slits, Moniah sucked air in through his nostrils and the door latch shot up and the door swung open, banging the outer corridor wall, where Uletis jumped back into the rain soaked rampart bridge he had just crossed.

Uletis smiled and hurried inside. Moniah's shoulders slumped; he opened his eyes and serenely smiled at Uletis.

"Forgive my presence," Uletis said but Vetaeos shushed him and gestured impatiently for him to enter. Uletis handed Vetaeos a scabbard and retreated as quickly as he had come, though he had a time closing the door since Moniah had unsettled it from its hinges by the force of his will.

Moniah looked up, sniffed and wiped his upper lip. He took a draught of smoke from the pipe and rubbed a drop of blood from his nose as thunder grumbled around the mountain.

"What have you there? I seem to have lost a moment."

"Remember, Wisdom, it was only Uletis. He brought this," Vetaeos said and handed Moniah the scabbard. The First Lord opened the holster carefully and withdrew Saeonar, the Coracle-Diant wand of his father, tarnished, its inscriptions hard to decipher and the Saenstone tip dulled by the film of dust and disuse.

"Prestant sang to me a command last night, instructing me to fetch the Coracle of Moniah transcended from Myzinos," Vetaeos said. Moniah gently placed it on his lap.

"Shall we begin?" said Vetaeos, with an arched brow and Moniah merely nodded.

The two Wizans closed their eyes and breathed steadily. Their bodies were motionless as they sat facing one another and, finally, only the sound of rain falling onto the balcony and blowing inside could be heard in the silence.

Moniah felt his mind connect with that of Vetaeos in trance. Images came to him from the past, carried by the dream memory of his cortex. His heart soared in love for Elria, and he laughed with Saeonar on the bridge of the *Auruaii*, and then ached while Saeonar's body disappeared into the ether while held in the loving hands of his father as he lay dying in a street of Renthia. His progeny cheated from life by mere moments.

The image shifted to that of Erfros, the once Tetra-Lachaen of Wizankind and Moniah felt the power Erfros transmitted in surrendering his life as the electricity of that surrender coursed through him, transmitting to Moniah the blood electric.

Oblivious to their surroundings, neither Moniah nor Vetaeos noticed or heard the sparks of lighting that flittered from the balcony into the chamber or saw it strike the walls, leaving ashen veins in the stone. Nor did Moniah feel the sparks jump across the air to light on his head and hands, because a dream trance with Earth communed in him, uniting the god spark of ancient creation to the evolving currents within him; activating his higher mind to control elements and joining the world with his purpose.

Moniah jumped to his feet, gasped, and opened his eyes at the same instant as Vetaeos, who leapt up, blinked, and looked at a table holding candelabra of unlit candles. The candles lit and immediately exploded in a rain of melted wax.

Made in the USA
Lexington, KY
24 August 2012